Shannin
16th Birthday

P9-DEG-267

TREAD UPON THE LION

BOOKS BY GILBERT MORRIS

THE HOUSE OF WINSLOW SERIES

1. *The Honorable Imposter*
2. *The Captive Bride*
3. *The Indentured Heart*
4. *The Gentle Rebel*
5. *The Saintly Buccaneer*
6. *The Holy Warrior*
7. *The Reluctant Bridegroom*
8. *The Last Confederate*
9. *The Dixie Widow*
10. *The Wounded Yankee*
11. *The Union Belle*
12. *The Final Adversary*
13. *The Crossed Sabres*
14. *The Valiant Gunman*
15. *The Gallant Outlaw*
16. *The Jeweled Spur*
17. *The Yukon Queen*
18. *The Rough Rider*
19. *The Iron Lady*
20. *The Silver Star*

THE LIBERTY BELL

1. *Sound the Trumpet*
2. *Song in a Strange Land*
3. *Tread Upon the Lion*

CHENEY DUVALL, M.D.
(with Lynn Morris)

1. *The Stars for a Light*
2. *Shadow of the Mountains*
3. *A City Not Forsaken*
4. *Toward the Sunrising*
5. *Secret Place of Thunder*

SPIRIT OF APPALACHIA
(with Aaron McCarver)

Over the Misty Mountains

TIME NAVIGATORS
(For Young Teens)

1. *Dangerous Voyage*
2. *Vanishing Clues*

9608

TREAD UPON THE LION

GILBERT MORRIS

BETHANY HOUSE PUBLISHERS
MINNEAPOLIS, MINNESOTA 55438

Tread Upon the Lion
Copyright © 1996
Gilbert Morris

Cover illustration by Chris Ellison
Cartography by Phillip Schwartzberg, Meridian Mapping, Minneapolis

All rights reserved. No part of this publication may be reproduced, stored in a retrieval system, or transmitted in any form or by any means electronic, mechanical, photocopying, recording, or otherwise without the prior written permission of the publisher and copyright owners.

Published by Bethany House Publishers
A Ministry of Bethany Fellowship, Inc.
11300 Hampshire Avenue South
Minneapolis, Minnesota 55438

Printed in the United States of America.

Library of Congress Cataloging-in-Publication Data

Morris, Gilbert.
    Tread upon the lion / Gilbert Morris.
        p.   cm. — (The liberty bell ; Book 3)
    I. Title. II. Series: Morris, Gilbert. Liberty Bell ; bk. 3.
ISBN 1-55661-567-1
813'.54—dc20   96-25296
                                             CIP

To Mickey and Sondra Williams—

There's an old song entitled "Precious Memories." That describes very well how I think of you two. Time erases many things, but I keep the memories of our days together locked up safely. Often I take them out and am reminded of how much I treasure both of you!

GILBERT MORRIS spent ten years as a pastor before becoming Professor of English at Ouachita Baptist University in Arkansas and earning a Ph.D. at the University of Arkansas. During the summers of 1984 and 1985, he did postgraduate work at the University of London. A prolific writer, he has had over 25 scholarly articles and 200 poems published in various periodicals, and over the past years has had more than 70 novels published. His family includes three grown children, and he and his wife live in Colorado.

CONTENTS

PART FOUR
The Fall of Fort Washington
October—November 1776

THE LIBERTY BELL

🔔 🔔 🔔

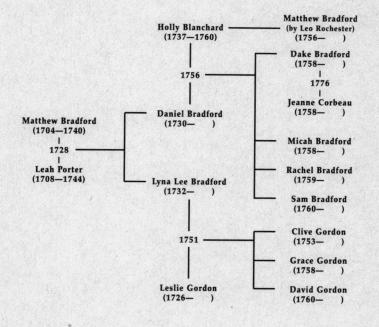

Matthew Bradford
(1704—1740)
|
1728
|
Leah Porter
(1708—1744)

Holly Blanchard
(1737—1760)

Matthew Bradford
(by Leo Rochester)
(1756—   )

1756

Daniel Bradford
(1730—   )

Dake Bradford
(1758—   )
|
1776
|
Jeanne Corbeau
(1758—   )

Micah Bradford
(1758—   )

Rachel Bradford
(1759—   )

Sam Bradford
(1760—   )

Lyna Lee Bradford
(1732—   )

1751

Clive Gordon
(1753—   )

Grace Gordon
(1758—   )

David Gordon
(1760—   )

Leslie Gordon
(1726—   )

PART ONE

—

EXODUS FROM BOSTON

March—May 1776

1

WEDDING DAY IN BOSTON

KATHERINE YANCY HAD HATED the ugly brown sofa from the day her parents had picked it out—and now as Malcolm sat down on it and gave a startled grunt, she wished for the old Windsor chairs the sofa had replaced.

I don't see why they couldn't have bought that pretty little sofa I liked so much, she thought ruefully. She had picked out one with a pleasant green color that was well padded and gracefully shaped. It would have fit perfectly in the corner across from the fireplace, but her choice had been disregarded, and her father had chosen the monstrosity that now dominated the best parlor.

Sitting down carefully, Katherine felt an intense disliking for the sofa—a miserable, nasty, narrow thing with wood jutting out at every corner on which to break your elbows. To Katherine it was, as she had told her father, "unimpressionable as flint," and she hated the unyielding, slippery seats and the bolsters that were as hard as hickory logs! Aside from the discomfort of sitting on it, the piece was covered with a horsehair fabric of a leprous brown color and cast a pall over the entire room.

"I say, this sofa is a bit hard, isn't it now?"

Malcolm Smythe lifted his eyebrow in mock anguish and thumbed the bolster with his knuckles for emphasis. He smiled then and moved closer to Katherine, adding, "But at least it's better than standing up." Smythe was a rather handsome young man of twenty-three. He had pale blond hair, light blue eyes, and a pleasant set of features. In one sense he liked sitting down better, for he was long waisted with rather abbreviated legs. This meant that he was slightly taller than the young woman sitting down. They were both, he knew, exactly five feet ten inches in height, but he liked to be taller than the woman he was courting.

Smythe was quite a dandy in dress, and for his call that early afternoon he wore a brightly colored green waistcoat, a pair of charcoal knee britches, and his neck was adorned with a pure white neckcloth and a ruffle that spun out below his chin. Even in the heat he wore a frock coat with buttons down to the edge just below his knees, and the cuffs, which were dotted with silver buttons, were turned back almost to his elbow. He appeared to have dressed for this occasion with a special care. This was not the case, however, for Smythe loved fine clothes and had a room full of the latest fashions at his home.

Katherine Yancy allowed him to take her hand as a smile creased her lips. She had a wide mouth, far too wide for beauty, but which somehow held a sensual cast. A tiny dimple appeared on the right side of her cheek, and her light gray-green eyes seemed to reflect the humor that lay just beneath the surface of a rather sober exterior. She had a wealth of rich brown hair with just a few tints of red or gold that caught the sun as it shone in through the mullioned windows. Her face was square, her eyes were wide spaced and very large, and, as always, they crinkled when she grinned or laughed, so that they became almost invisible. She was an attractive young woman—not beautiful, for she had features too bold for that. It was an age that valued petite prettiness rather than strong features—and Katherine Yancy was strong if nothing else!

Looking down at Malcolm's hands, she laughed suddenly. She had a deep voice for a woman, and when she sang it filled the rooms of the largest buildings with a rich contralto. "This is a *miserable* sofa!" she announced firmly. "Even the dog won't sleep on it, will you, Pluto?"

The large, shaggy dog with a massive head blinked and thumped the carpet with his tail but did not lift his head.

"It shows he's got better sense than we do. Come on, I can't *stand* this sofa!"

Rising quickly to her feet, Katherine drew the young man after her. Since she knew he was sensitive about his height, she had learned to wear low slippers and had been amused to discover that Malcolm always wore the highest heels he could find when he came to call on her. This gave him an advantage of two inches, and now she said, "That's a new suit, isn't it?"

"Yes, I picked it up in Philadelphia. Do you like it?" Malcolm asked as he straightened out his frock coat.

"Very colorful, and it fits you so well."

"Well, a man must have a good tailor, or what's he good for?"

Katherine almost replied, *A man is more than his clothes, isn't he?* But she had learned that Malcolm did not take teasing easily, so she said, "Come along, let's taste these tea cakes that I made this morning." She led him to a drop-side Hepplewhite table against the wall, between the two windows, and poured two cups of steaming tea from a silver teapot into beautifully executed china cups. She watched as Malcolm tasted the tiny cakes and nodded his approval. She sipped her tea then, and the two moved before the window.

Spring had come early in March of 1776, and the warm rays of the sun had coaxed the sharp blades of emerald grass up through the dull clods of earth, making the tiny yard in front of the Yancy house look as though it were sprouting fine green hair. "The flowers will be up soon," Katherine murmured. "We'll have a lot of them this year, I think."

The two stood by the window talking for some time, speaking of unimportant things, then finally Smythe set his teacup down and turned to face Katherine. "Katherine, I've got to talk to you," he said, his brow wrinkled with effort of serious thought.

Katherine inwardly grew tense, for she sensed what was coming. "What is it, Malcolm?"

"It's about this awful rebellion. We've talked about it before and we don't agree." Smythe took her hand and put his arm around her, drawing her close. He pressed her closely against him, and his hands moved across her back in a caressing gesture. "You know how I feel about you, Katherine," he whispered, and then he moved forward to kiss her.

Katherine knew that she was going to be kissed, and for one moment she almost drew back. She sensed that Malcolm, for all his ardent declarations of love, was not doing this out of passion. Nevertheless, she remained still as his lips fell on hers. He held her tightly, and she neither resisted nor encouraged him. Finally he drew back, an annoyed expression on his face. "You've got as much passion in you as a . . . as a dead woman!" he exclaimed.

"I don't think you're interested in kissing right now," Katherine said. She stood before him very straight, and the bright yellow sunlight that streamed through the window highlighted her, bringing out the color of her dress. It was a simple dress made of patterned fabric, light blue on darker blue. She wore a small lace apron, and the bosom of her dress was adorned with light yellow taffeta bows. A tiny white cap perched on her abundant auburn curls that fell freely down her back rather than being put up in the popular styles. She made an attractive picture as she stood there, but she was not aware of it. She felt that she was too tall for true beauty, and her features were not dainty enough.

Her eyes were fixed on Malcolm and she said, "I can't change my mind. How could I, Malcolm? This is my country."

Smythe shook his head violently. "No!" he exclaimed. "*England* is your country. I'm an Englishman and you're an Englishwoman. This rabble in arms—why, it's doomed. They haven't got a chance!"

Anger quickly flashed in Katherine's eyes, and her lips drew firm in a tight line. She held herself tautly upright and said, "And what about my father and my uncle? Were they fools for fighting for their freedom—and for your freedom?"

"We *have* freedom, and your uncle and your father were simply caught up in a riot. It came to little more than that."

Malcolm felt uncomfortable speaking of Katherine's father, Amos Yancy, and his brother Noah. The two of them had fought with the patriot forces at Breed's Hill during the first full-scale battle of the rebellion but had been captured during the retreat. They had both been held in the hulks, as they were called—old rotting ships where prisoners of war were kept. Smythe was aware that squalid conditions were every bit as bad on those vessels as rumor had it, and he could not meet Katherine's eyes.

"If you'd listen to reason, Katherine, I have an idea that might do something to get your father and your uncle released. My family does have some influence with the Crown, you know."

The Smythes were an old New York family, well-off and loyal Tories to the very bone. The thought of challenging the Crown and the British empire was a horror to them. Malcolm's courtship of Katherine had begun a year before the revolution broke out at Lexington and Concord. He was genuinely fond of Katherine, but the course of true love had not run smoothly between them.

Katherine turned away from Malcolm, anger coloring her cheeks. Most of the time she possessed a placid and calm temper, but at times anger would come almost in a blinding flash. She had learned to control it for the most part by simply waiting until it passed. Now she looked outside and forced herself to watch a robin that had snared one end of an enormous angleworm. The robin had braced his claws against the earth and was pulling with all of his might. Katherine fancied she could almost hear the bird grunt as it tugged at its next meal. Finally, he succeeded in yanking the worm out, mounted to the air with a flutter of wings, and flew directly to an apple tree, where he completed his meal with relish.

Turning back to Malcolm, Katherine said quietly, "I'm sorry, Malcolm, but I can't agree. The Colonies have tried everything to get justice from England. Neither the Crown nor Parliament understands what we are all about over here. We are not just a little branch of the British empire. The Colonies are the beginning of a great nation, a whole new continent. It can't be run from a Parliament thousands of miles across the sea."

Malcolm began to speak rapidly, but he soon saw that it was useless to argue with her. "I'm sorry," he said stiffly, "I hope that you'll think this over, Katherine." He started to say something else, then shook his head slightly as if denying the thought. "I must be going now. I have an appointment with my tailor."

Katherine walked with him to the door and handed him his tricorn hat. She watched as he pulled it firmly over his head, and for one moment she thought that he would try to kiss her again.

Opening the door, he stopped and turned toward her. "I'll see you soon, I hope," he said.

"I'm going to a wedding this afternoon. Dake Bradford is getting married."

"Yes, well, perhaps I'll call tomorrow then."

"Goodbye, Malcolm." Katherine watched as he turned and walked down the brick pathway to where his horse was tied to an iron hitching post fashioned in the shape of a horse head. He took the reins, swung into the saddle rather awkwardly, touched his hat, then rode off down the street. Katherine listened as the horse's hooves rang on the cobblestones, then she slowly turned and went back inside.

She was still disturbed over their disagreement twenty minutes later when her mother came in, carrying a basket under her arm. Katherine spoke to her shortly, and her mother demanded at once, "What's the matter, Katherine?"

Susan Yancy, at forty-five, still had the dark-haired beauty that she had possessed as a girl. She had beautiful mild brown eyes and attractive features, but she was thin, and her face had the worn lines of a chronic invalid. Setting the basket down on a table in the hall, she moved over to Katherine and looked into the girl's face. "Malcolm didn't stay?"

"No, he didn't."

From the very brevity of Katherine's tone, Susan Yancy knew something was troubling her daughter. "You two quarreled, didn't you?"

"Yes, over the war, of course. Malcolm just can't understand how I feel about it."

"Well," Susan said as cheerfully as she could, "you'll make it up. Come now, you must put on your best dress for the wedding."

"All right, Mother." Katherine turned and moved away to her room, but even as she entered and began to prepare for the wedding, her

17

thoughts were on Malcolm and the impassable gulf that seemed to be widening between them. She stared at herself in the mirror for a moment, and the thought came to her, *I don't see how we can ever marry—not until this question about England is settled once and for all....*

⚜   ⚜   ⚜

Daniel Bradford stood at the front of the large auditorium, observing the crowd that had come to celebrate his son's wedding. Every seat and every pew was filled, and a number of latecomers stood lined along the back of the wall. Moving his head slightly, he glanced to his right where his son Dake stood, his eyes fixed on the front doors of the church. *He's only eighteen. Too young to be married, especially with a war facing us,* Daniel thought. He took in the strong form of this son of his, fully six feet tall and one hundred eighty pounds. Dake's straw-colored hair was drawn back, tied with a black ribbon. His hazel eyes were clear, and a happy expression drew his lips upward into a slight smile as he waited for his bride to appear. He was wearing a simple suit of brown with white stockings and black shoes with silver buckles. *A fine-looking bridegroom— but too young.*

Dake and Jeanne had planned to wait until the war with England was over before marrying, but then they had decided to take advantage of any time they could have together, as no one knew what the future held.

Just then a brief whisper swept the crowded room, and both Daniel Bradford and his son looked to see the bride entering.

As Jeanne Corbeau came down the aisle, Daniel thought of the strange fashion in which this beautiful young woman had come into the Bradford family. She was a lovely girl of eighteen. Her black hair was too curly for many of the popular hairstyles of the day, so she arranged it loosely around her face. She had blue-violet eyes, the most unusual Daniel had ever seen, high cheekbones, and beautifully formed lips. *She's beautiful, all right, but it's a wonder she didn't wear buckskins,* Daniel thought wryly as she reached the front of the church.

Dake's bride was from the woods of the North. She had encountered Clive Gordon, Daniel's nephew, on his return trip from Fort Ticonderoga to Boston. Stranded in the forest, sick with fever, Jeanne had saved Clive's life. With her father gone, Clive could not leave her alone in the wilderness, so he had brought her to Boston and courted her—but it had been Dake who won her heart.

Poor Clive, he lost a beauty, and it hit him hard, Daniel thought. He thought of his sister, Lyna Lee Bradford Gordon, Clive's mother. He, himself, had come to America as an indentured servant. Lyna Lee had

18

married Leslie Gordon, an officer in the king's army. They had been re-united only recently, and sorrow came to Daniel Bradford as he thought of the Gordons, who served King George III, and the Bradfords, who were patriots and determined to follow General Washington and fight for their freedom. *It must be hard on Lyna Lee*, Daniel thought soberly. *Truth is, it's hard on all of us.*

The bride came to stand facing the minister, who wore his black robe and held a large worn Bible in his hands. Dake took his position beside her, and the ceremony began. As the minister led them through their vows, Daniel found himself unable to concentrate on the words. Looking out over the congregation, he noted his own family in the front pew on the right. This included Matthew, his oldest son, and Micah, at eighteen, the identical twin to Dake. Next to them sat Rachel, his only daughter at seventeen, who looked to him more beautiful with her red hair and green eyes than even the bride. She had a heart-shaped face like her mother, and Daniel loved her very much. Finally, beside Rachel, sat his youngest son, Samuel, already quite a handful at sixteen.

Shifting his eyes he looked on the other side, halfway back where Leo Rochester sat with his wife, Marian. A sharp anger touched Daniel as Leo stared back. He was actually *Sir* Leo Rochester, and had been Daniel's master in England. Because of Leo's lies, Daniel had ended up in a cold prison accused of attempted murder. In the end, Leo had offered him his freedom if Daniel would agree to come to the Colonies as a bound servant. As Leo Rochester smiled, Daniel felt a sense of satisfaction in noticing one tooth that did not match. His sister, Lyna, had knocked that tooth out years ago when Leo had attacked her one night in a drunken stupor. Leo, he noted, was overweight, and his face was lined with dissipation.

Beside him sat Marian Frazier Rochester—at forty-one still the most beautiful woman that Daniel Bradford had ever known. She had dark auburn hair, green eyes, and a heart-shaped face. She looked at him suddenly, her eyes catching his, and Daniel quickly turned away. He had fallen in love with her, and she with him years ago on her first visit to Fairhope, Leo's estate in Virginia, but Daniel had been an indentured servant and Marian was a wealthy young lady. Daniel had finally married Holly Blanchard, who was carrying Sir Leo Rochester's child. By the time his wife, Holly, had died, Marian had married Sir Leo Rochester. Though Daniel had moved his family to Boston to work in John Frazier's foundry, he still could not forget his love for Marian—and knew that he must never speak of it to anyone.

He shook himself as the silence was broken by the clear voice of the minister, rising up to the high arches of the ceiling. The gray stones that formed the sides seemed to capture and soak the words into themselves as they had many other ceremonies of this nature. Through the stained-glass windows the light filtered in and bathed everything in beautiful reds, yellows, greens, and amethyst. As the minister's voice spoke clearly, a holy silence settled in the room.

Finally, the minister said, "... and I now pronounce you man and wife."

Daniel grinned as Dake reached forward, without reservation, kissed his bride thoroughly, and noted that Jeanne Corbeau Bradford held to him with all her strength. He moved forward and said, "Have you got a kiss for an old man, Jeanne?"

Jeanne turned from Dake and threw her arms around Daniel and kissed him soundly on the cheek. "Now, you have another daughter," she smiled, "and I promise to be much more trouble than Rachel."

"I don't doubt it," Daniel grinned. He liked this girl and suddenly was glad that she and Dake had found each other. It always had seemed like a miracle to him when a man and woman found each other out of the millions on earth—and were happy. This brought a touch of sadness to Daniel Bradford, for he knew that he'd had such a chance with Marian—but had lost it years ago. Now he was happy that his son had found the one God meant for him.

Stepping back, he made his way to the side of the church while the newlyweds were swarmed by those who came forward to congratulate them and wish them well. His eyes were drawn irresistibly across the room where, once again, he encountered the gaze of Marian Rochester. He tried to turn away, but was almost powerless to do so. It was, indeed, a power that Marian held over him—one which he would not deny, although he never spoke of it to a living soul.

☙ ☙ ☙

The reception was held in the pastor's home—a large parsonage with an enormous parlor designed, no doubt, for exactly such festive occasions.

Leo Rochester stood beside the table, sipping from the goblet in his hand. He looked down at Marian and muttered, "You'd think they'd serve some real whiskey at an event like this, wouldn't you?"

Marian looked up without comment. She had been surprised when Leo had informed her that he was attending Dake Bradford's wedding. When she had allowed the surprise to show in her eyes, he had grinned and said, "That takes you off guard, doesn't it, my dear? Well, at least I'll have a chance to see one of Bradford's whelps out of the way. Besides," he had added, and a grim look had settled in his face, "I want to talk to Matthew."

Now Marian studied his expression and found something that had troubled her before. "Don't you feel well, Leo?" she asked quietly.

Leo blinked his eyes, and his lips twisted into a scowl. "Why this sudden wifely interest in my health?" he snapped. "You haven't cared for me in years."

This was not exactly true, but close enough. Leo Rochester had been disappointed in his marriage. He had wanted a son to carry on the family name, and Marian had produced no children. This failure, as he saw it, drove him from her. He had proved to be a womanizer, and their marriage, for all practical purposes, had ended years before. Now he studied her face and said, "You'd like that, wouldn't you? If I got ill and died you'd end up with Fairhope and all my money—then nothing could stop you from marrying your lover, Daniel Bradford."

"That's not true, Leo," Marian protested.

"Of course it's true. Do you think I don't know? Didn't I catch you two in each other's arms in my own home?"

"It was . . . just a mistake, Leo. Nothing had happened before. I'm not his lover."

Leo grinned sarcastically. "So you tell me, but every time he looks at you he's like an infatuated schoolboy." It was his custom to taunt her with this, but Rochester privately was convinced that nothing scandalous had ever taken place between his wife and Daniel Bradford. Nevertheless, he hated the man, and had ever since he was a boy back at Milford Manor in England. He had used Daniel—with his fine sense with horses—to build up his plantation, Fairhope in Virginia, and now Leo's obsession to have an heir gave him even a greater reason to use the man he despised.

"I'll have Matthew one way or another!" he spoke abruptly.

"You can't have him, Leo, can't you understand that?"

"He's my son!" Leo kept his voice low, but there was a fierce determination that glittered in his light blue eyes. He ground his teeth together, then said fiercely, "He's my son, Marian! Can't you understand that—what it *means* to me?"

"You forfeited all right to Matthew. You abandoned his mother, and Daniel married her just to give her son a name. There's no proof that he's your son anyway, and no court of law would ever admit it. Daniel was married to Matthew's mother when he was born."

"There's proof all right," Leo said. "Look at him! He's the mirror image of what I looked like when I was his age."

Marian looked over toward Matthew Bradford and could not help but agree, although she said nothing. This son was not like the other Bradfords, who were all strong, husky men. Matthew was slender with none of the rugged features of the Bradfords. He had brown hair and blue eyes. He looked, in fact, exactly like the picture of Leo Rochester that hung in her own parlor, one that had been painted when Leo was twenty.

Still, she was aware of how fiercely Leo hungered for a son—a man to carry on the Rochester name. She was also aware that he had gone to Matthew and told him the truth—that he was his father. He had offered him his name and all that wealth could bring. So far Matthew had resisted, but Marian wondered how long the young man would hold out. She knew he wanted to return to England to continue his study of art, and that Leo had offered to introduce him to many of the famous artists he knew.

To change the subject she said, "Look, I must go speak to Abigail."

"The Howland girl?" Leo's interest was caught. "I'll go with you," he said. "She's a toothsome wench. Alluring eyes if I ever saw them."

"Hush, Leo, she'll hear you!"

Leo grinned but said no more. They came to stand before Abigail Howland and Douglas Martin, who had once been one of her suitors. Seeing the two approach, Douglas said, "I'll see you later, Abigail. I'll come to call."

"That would be nice, Douglas."

Abigail Howland, at the age of nineteen, was as beautiful a woman as Massachusetts could boast. She had an oval face, hazel eyes, and brown hair. She was very full-figured with an exquisitely tiny waist, and always wore exactly the right thing. She wore an amber dress with deep pleats and, unlike most of the women, a wide pannier. It emphasized the smallness of her waist, and her figure swelled against the bodice, which was made of pleated taffeta. She was one of those women who would look good in anything. There was an air of sensuality about her, even as Leo had stated, but she looked somehow troubled as she said, "How are you, Sir Leo—Lady Rochester?"

"Very well," Leo said, "and how is it with you and your mother?"

For one moment Abigail Howland hesitated. She was usually a rather outspoken young woman, but there seemed to be a reticence in her that neither Leo nor Marian had ever noticed before. "Not as well as I might like."

Instantly Leo said, "Since Washington drove the British out, it's been a little hard on us Tories."

"Not on you, Sir Leo, but on my family." Her father had been a staunch Tory before his death, and now only her mother was left, and she was not well. The two of them had been driven out of their fine home by the patriots and were staying in a small cottage, which belonged to an old friend of Saul Howland's.

As they stood there speaking, Matthew approached. He nodded toward Leo, calling his name, spoke to Marian, then turned and said, "Abigail, it's good to see you again."

Abigail's face lit up at once. The presence of a young man seemed to bring new life into her. Leo did not miss the sudden change. He watched intensely as the two spoke, his eyes going from the face of this son who would not claim him to the young woman he so eagerly spoke with.

Why, I think the pup is in love with her! At least he wants her—which is about the same thing, Rochester thought. *I don't blame him. She could bring a statue to life—but she's in poor shape—as all the Tories are here in Boston.*

Marian said, "I'll be coming over to see you and your mother. I'm sorry I haven't called earlier."

"Mother's not too well," Abigail said. She turned her eyes toward Matthew and said, "I've missed you."

"I've been busy painting. I want to show you some of the things I've done."

"I'd like to see them. I don't know much about painting, though, as you well know, but I love the portrait you did of me."

"Well, I'll do better ones later." Matthew smiled and had apparently forgotten Rochester. He was not a typical colonist, having spent the last few years in England and on the Continent studying painting. He was not in sympathy with the revolution, and having been confronted with the secret of his birth, he felt out of place with the Bradford family. Now he suddenly turned and looked at Leo, saying, "I received the paints and the brushes you sent me, sir. Thanks very much."

"An artist must have the best," Leo nodded. He started to say more, but a sudden, odd feeling had come to him. It had happened like this a month before. He stood there unable to speak a word, for it was suddenly as if his heart and everything within him were composed of very fine, fragile glass. He felt that if he moved or spoke all would be shattered! He had never experienced anything like it before—until three weeks earlier. Then he had been so stricken he had gone straightway to bed. It had passed away—or so he thought—but now the same disturbing sensations were coming on again. He stood there listening as the others talked, aware that Marian was watching him strangely, but he did not dare to move. His breath came shallowly, and he stood absolutely still.

Finally, the moment passed. He took out his handkerchief, mopped his forehead, and turned away without a word. As he left the house, he was aware that Marian had followed him.

"Are you ill, Leo?"

Again the question angered him. He'd never had a sick day in his life, and the thought of sickness was something he had never considered. He had been, as a matter of fact, rather contemptuous of those who were ill, and now he looked at her with anger in his eyes. "Stop pestering me! I'm all right!"

Marian knew Leo very well, and she had never seen him look like this. His face had turned almost gray. She knew that he was not well despite his protestations. "Perhaps we'd better go home," she said quietly.

"I'll go home by myself. Go on in. You and Daniel can get together— maybe plan what to do with all of my money after you've buried me. How long would you wait if I died?" he said, turning toward her. "A week? A month? Maybe even a year to make things look respectable."

Marian shook her head but said nothing. Finally she said, "I'd rather come home with you."

"No, I want to be alone. Go on back inside." Rochester turned and moved toward the carriage. He got into it, moving carefully, saying, "Take me home, Rogers."

"Yes, sir." The cabbie spoke to the horses, and they moved out smartly. He threaded the carriage down the streets until the church was out of sight. A short ugly dog with clipped ears came out to bark at the horses' heels. Rogers leaned over and struck at him with his whip. With satisfaction, he caught the animal across the rump and laughed when the hound yelled and tucked his tail between his legs.

"That'll teach you to snap at my horses' heels," he said, then chuckled in his chest. "Come on, boys, home now. . . !"

2

A MAN'S WORD

THE STREETS OF BOSTON were almost deserted as Leo Rochester made his way down the main thoroughfare. Before the British army had departed, driven off by General Washington and the guns of Henry Knox, the British soldiers had done their best to destroy and deface as much of the city as they could. Some of the shops that Rochester passed were boarded over, having had their windows broken and the interiors raided by the furious troops of King George III.

Rochester passed by a small shop, then halted as a thought came to him. Turning, he entered, ducking his head as he passed through the doorway. He was greeted by a small, wizened shopkeeper who bowed mechanically three times as if he were wound up. His name was Phineas Johnson, and his tiny, dark eyes glowed as he fairly bubbled over to greet his customer. "Ah," he said, exposing a mouth full of obviously artificial teeth carved out of hippo ivory, "Sir Leo, a pleasure, sir, to see you, sir!" He came across the shop wringing his hands, stood before Leo, and bowed three times again quickly, then said at once, "How can I serve you this afternoon, Sir Leo?"

"This filthy wig—it doesn't fit properly. It won't stay on," Leo growled. Removing his tricorn hat, he jerked the powdered wig from his head and practically threw it at the shopkeeper.

"Oh, to be sure! Let me take care of that." Quickly Johnson moved over to a table where several wig stands had their station, fastened the wig to one, and began working with it at once. As he snipped and poked at the artificial hairpiece, Leo stood impatiently waiting. *This wig business, it's idiotic! If I had any sense, I'd stuff it down this miserable shopkeeper's throat and never put one on again!*

He knew he would never do so, however, for the wig craze, which had begun in England years before, had become *de rigeur*. No self-respecting aristocrat would be seen without one! *This craze has,* Roch-

25

ester thought, *become more bizarre*. Some women wore towering mounds of false hair, filled with puffs, feathers, and any number of fancy ornaments. Young girls cut off their own hair or shaved their heads sometimes so they could be fitted for a wig. Poor girls who needed money sold their hair to wigmakers. Rochester had heard that one Virginia father, William Freeman, paid nine pounds for a wig for his seven-year-old son. With the average worker making twenty-five to thirty pounds a year, it's obvious that the wig craze was in full sway.

Phineas Johnson worked like a squirrel, chirping and turning his hippo teeth in a broad smile from time to time as he moved around the wig stand making adjustments to the hairpiece. Finally, he pulled the wig off and came forward, bowed three times, and said, "Now, Sir Leo, let's try this. . . ." Leo bent his head, and the wigmaker put the wig on, settled it, and stepped back. Smirking with satisfaction, he rubbed his hands together, bowed three times, and in his mechanical ritual said, "There, sir."

"Very well," Leo said. "Oh, my servant has lost his wig pick."

"Oh yes. Here. This is a very fine one made of silver."

Rochester took the instrument, gave it a caustic glance, then stuck it in his overcoat pocket. Wigs were so hot and heavy they made the head sweat—and sweat attracted lice. The pick was for removing those tiny visitors. Since wigs were washed very seldom, the invaders made themselves happy homes and had to be picked out by the servants with wig picks.

"Well, sir, the army is gone—a sad day for loyal subjects of King George," Phineas Johnson said, pocketing the coin that Rochester handed him. He looked around furtively, then whispered, "The patriots have threatened to raid my store. There's no one to hold them back now that the blasted rebels are in charge."

"Well, we had our good days, now we'll have to take the bad," Leo said callously. He left the shop, well aware that the wigmaker's plight was not uncommon. The Tories had ridden high as long as the British army held the city, but now many of them had been tarred and feathered. Some had been thrown out of their homes, and their property seized by the Continental government. Leo, himself, had not been affected, for his own plantation in Virginia seemed safe and secure, and he owned no property in Boston.

Bright April sunlight illuminated the streets as he moved along, dodging refuse that piled up on the sidewalk. There was little attempt at street cleaning, especially in the middle of a war. Some shopkeepers simply threw their trash out, and passersby had to walk around it or wade through it.

Arriving at a two-story red-brick structure, of which the first floor was occupied by a shipping agent, Leo turned to the stairs that led up one side and slowly ascended them. He passed under a sign that read *Henry Settling—Surgeon.*

Opening the door, he stepped inside and shut it behind him. For a moment he stood there, taking in the long narrow room that served as a reception area. It contained only seven cane-bottomed chairs, a desk, and a cabinet at one end. At the other end, a small window looked out on the street below.

"Settling!" Rochester called out. He waited for only a moment, and the single door leading to the interior opened.

Dr. Henry Settling stepped into the reception area and peered over his glasses. "Oh, Sir Leo. I didn't hear you come in." Settling was a gaunt man of fifty with a set of light blue eyes and a Vandyke beard. He wore a powdered wig, knee britches, and a white shirt, over which he had on an apron that was stained with a few splatters of brown, dried blood. "Will you step inside, Sir Leo?"

Leo stepped into the inner office, which was rather crowded with a large rosewood desk, a skeleton on a rack in the corner, and a collection of various instruments and paraphernalia in glass-fronted cases flanking the walls. An acrid smell of chemicals filled the room—distinctly unpleasant—and Leo wrinkled his nose with distaste. "It stinks in here, Settling."

"The penalty of my profession, I'm afraid." Settling's steady gaze rested on Leo and he asked, "Is this a social call or a professional one?"

Leo hesitated for one moment. He took off his hat, tossed it onto a chair beside the wall, then turned to face the physician squarely. "Something's wrong with me, Settling. I don't know what it is, but I've got to find out."

"What are your symptoms, Sir Leo? Will you sit down while we talk?"

Reluctantly and nervously Rochester sat down. "I've been healthy all my life. Never had a surgeon put his blasted knife on me. Stayed as far away from you fellows as I could."

"I'm glad to hear it." Settling smiled slightly. "But all of us have our physical problems. How old a man are you, Sir Leo?"

"Forty-seven." Rochester shifted uncomfortably on the chair, then looked up at the doctor. There was a trace of fear or deep anxiety in his eyes. He ran his hands over his wig, straightened it, then shook his head sadly. "It's in here," he said, tapping his chest. "And here . . ." He held up his left hand.

Doctor Settling listened as Rochester described the pain in his chest and the numbness in his left hand. When Leo finished he said, "Remove your coat and shirt, and we'll have a look." He waited until Leo pulled off his shirt, and he noted that the man was not in good physical condition. He was overweight and his face was marked with the signs of heavy drinking. He said nothing, however, but kept up a cheerful line of patter as he leaned his head over and listened to Leo's heart, took his pulse, and thumped him front and back. Next he looked down his throat, pulled the pouches of his eyes down and stared in his eyes, then smelled his breath. Finally, he leaned back and gave his patient a thoughtful glance. "You do seem to have some problem."

"Well, I know *that*, blast it!" Leo growled. "What's the matter with me?" He took a deep breath and felt again the light fluttering, the sense of intense fragility, and expelled it carefully. "What is it—this ache in my chest?"

"Impossible to say for sure. Have you ever had a sharp pain, somewhat recently, here in your chest?"

Leo thought for a moment. "Yes," he nodded finally. "About three weeks ago. I woke up in the night and felt almost stifled. It was like my chest was full, and I could hardly get a breath." He thought hard then nodded. "This arm"—he held up his left hand—"was tingling. I remember that too. I had trouble flexing the fingers the next day." He fell silent then, studying the face of the surgeon, trying to read his fate there. Sir Leo was not a man given to fears, but this physical weakness had hit him hard. He asked almost timidly, "What is it, Settling? You've got to know *something*."

"You do have a bit of a problem. That's obvious. As to the exact nature of it, that's difficult to say."

"Is it a stroke?" Leo asked abruptly. This had been what he had come to ask the doctor, and now he waited as a felon waits at the bar of justice for the judge's sentence.

Settling saw the fear in Rochester's eyes. He was a good doctor, and one of his policies was to always speak the truth to his patients. "I think you may well have had either a stroke or perhaps a heart attack." He held up his hand quickly as the fear filled Leo's eyes and said, "Both are apparently quite minor at this point."

"What can you do for me? Is there medicine for a thing like this?"

"The best medicine is a reasonable diet, no alcohol, and regular exercise."

Rochester scowled. "You mean turn from my sins and lead a clean life?"

"I'm afraid that's it, Sir Leo. There's no substitute for the things I've mentioned."

Leo sat there. He was pasty-faced from indoor living, and his long hours spent in the taverns of the city consuming large amounts of alcohol had blunted his features. He flexed the fingers of his left hand, then said, "What if I don't follow your advice?"

"I think you already know the answer to that," Settling said flatly.

Settling knew well the disreputable reputation of Leo Rochester. He had treated Leo's wife, Marian, and was impressed with the woman's quiet demeanor and modest behavior—as well as with her beauty. Settling was an inveterate collector of gossip, but he kept to himself what he had learned about his patients' personal lives. He knew that Sir Leo Rochester had shown no moral restraint and spent many nights away from home rather than with his wife. Settling could not understand this, but then he had given up trying to understand human nature some years earlier.

Now he spoke, convinced that he was wasting his breath. "I'll make out a diet, things that you should eat and those you should avoid. Of course, your drinking will have to be moderated. Maybe a glass of whiskey at night. One, perhaps, in the midday—but if you continue to drink as heavily as you have, I guarantee you'll be signing your own death warrant before long. You're not getting any younger," he said quickly, seeing the stubbornness start to gather on Rochester's features. "You should have several years ahead of you if you'll listen to sound advice and take care of yourself."

Rochester stared angrily at the physician as if it were somehow his fault. Leo was a spoiled man, having been given everything the world values at much too early an age. For years he had sought his pleasures in every form without a thought to the consequences that might catch up to him someday. Now a cloud of ominous thoughts seemed to gather over him, and he shook his head. "Not much to live for. I might as well become a Quaker."

"Something to be said for their clean living," Settling shrugged. "Now—while you get dressed I'll make out a diet and also a tonic. Maybe something to help you sleep at night."

Leo dressed, took the paper the doctor gave him, paid the fee, then left in a somber mood. As he made his way down the steps, he was filled with a sudden apprehension about his future. He shook it off as he got into a carriage and rode out to the edge of town where Marian's father, John Frazier, had built a fine home many years ago.

When he arrived, he stepped out of the carriage, gave the driver a coin, and entered the house. He was met at the door by Cato, the butler, a black man of some forty-five years, who took his coat and hat at once, murmuring, "Good day, Sir Leo."

"Is your mistress at home, Cato?"

"Yes, sir! She's in the small parlor."

Leo walked down the hall, which was floored with cypress, and turned into the small parlor that occupied part of the lower floor of the large house. The room into which he stepped was bright and colorful, though no larger than twelve by sixteen. On one wall hung a painting made of French wallpaper, a rather graphic scenario that had been designed by Joseph Dufore. It portrayed an exotic scene, a blue-green river flowing in a serpentine path through a dense forest. On the fore bank, two Indians, copper-skinned natives, were in the process of killing a spotted leopard that had climbed up in a tree. One stood over the leopard's head, chopping at him with an ax. The other on the ground had pulled a hunting bow to full draw and was about to send an arrow into the beast. To the right of the picture a series of craggy rocks was capped by two Indians wearing turbans and puffy white britches. One of them was sounding an alarm on a curling ram's horn. Far off to the left rose a strange-looking tower—some sort of Maya Indian structure—and at the base of it a turbaned man clothed in a white robe and red sash sat astride a powerful steed that was rearing up in the air.

Leo had chosen this picture, although he knew that Marian had never liked it. Now he turned his eyes and swept the room that he had furnished and had become his favorite room in the house. Several side chairs flanked the wall, backed against the chair rail. Two padded Windsor chairs were at one end of the room, but there was a comfortable sofa with Griffin feet and a gaily colored covering of wine and yellow. Two large windows in the room let in the yellow sunlight, and in the center of the room a large walnut table rested under an ornate glass chandelier. The surface of the table was covered with a silver tea service and some fine china imported from Holland.

"Have you eaten, Leo?"

Rochester looked to where Marian had risen from her chair, laying her sewing to one side. She stood to face him, and he studied her as if he had not seen her for some time. He was struck with her beauty and her choice of dress. Rochester knew a little something of women's fashions, having spent some time with those who were interested. His wife wore a modified empire gown with a low neckline edged with a narrow, sheer collar. The sleeves were puffed and flared, and the skirt of the dress, though full, was made of a soft fabric that fell straight to her feet. It was a simple dress, white with vertical pale blue stripes, and it set off her figure admirably. *She always was beautiful*, Leo thought, and regret came to him as he considered the years he had spent chasing other women. However, he said only, "Yes." Going over to one of the horsehair-covered stuffed chairs, he slumped into it and looked up at her, waiting for her to speak.

"Father's better today. I think he can come down. Will you be at home for dinner?"

"I suppose so."

Marian was puzzled by his behavior. He had been acting strangely, as a matter of fact, for several weeks now, and she could not fathom it. For one thing, he was staying home more. It was not uncommon for him to leave for weeks at a time, and even when he stayed in Boston, he spent every night in the taverns and with other women. She had long since resigned herself to the failure of her marriage and to the fact that Leo's actions were something over which she had no control. Long ago, she had determined to keep her own manner as gracious as possible. That was all she could do.

"Leo, do you think we'll go back to Virginia soon?"

"Do you want to?"

"I miss the horses," Marian said simply, "and the quiet there. It's been a trying time here in the middle of this war."

"Yes it has." Leo looked up at her suddenly. "Would you leave your father?"

"I thought I might persuade him to go with us."

"I doubt it," Leo said morosely. He sat there for some time, and the two spoke of the possibility of returning to Fairhope in Virginia. After his meeting with Settling, he now had no desire, really, to go there, and finally he said, "No, I'll stay here."

He rose abruptly and went to his study, leaving her alone. When he closed the door, he went at once to his desk and began going through his papers and books. There was an intensity in his manner that was unusual, for he did not like bookwork. Later that afternoon he left the study and headed for the front door.

"I'll be back for dinner," he said and left the house abruptly.

Marian watched him go, puzzled by his behavior. His face was puffy and his color was bad. She had a way of noticing things, and had caught the fact that his left hand was giving him problems. Once she had even seen him reach over with his right hand and pull the limp arm into position. "Something is wrong with him, but he'll never tell me," she said. Then she turned and went upstairs to see to her father, wondering what all this would mean for their lives.

T   T   T

"Katherine, this letter came!" Susan Yancy had met her daughter as she came back from the market. Her face was troubled, and she thrust the one-page letter at Katherine, saying, "I'm afraid it's not good news."

Placing her market basket on a table, Katherine quickly scanned the few lines written on the piece of rough paper. The writing was almost illegible, but clearly it was her father's. She did not like the wavering looks of the handwriting and squinted at it as she read aloud:

My dear wife and precious daughter—

I take this occasion to send word that Noah and I have endured our imprisonment as well as could be hoped. The conditions here are not good. The food is poor, and the prison itself is uncomfortable. I regret to say that Noah has contracted some sort of disease, for such things are rampant here. I myself, at this point, praise God, am not affected. I know that you must be concerned about us, and I encourage you to pray to our Heavenly Father that we will be strengthened and kept in this place. I pray for you daily, and, indeed, there is little else to do. The Scripture says, "Whom the Lord loveth, he chasteneth," and we must look upon this as part of the discipline of a loving father. Try not to worry any more than you can help about us.

With all my love and affection,
Amos Yancy

Despair overwhelmed Katherine, filling her like a black cloud as she thought of her father and uncle locked in the cold and squalid skull of a ship. "This is awful!" she exclaimed. She read the letter again, then she and her mother talked about the poor quality of the handwriting.

"Father always was such a careful penman," Katherine said.

"Yes, look how the lines waver. I'll be bound he has fever himself and didn't want us to know it."

Biting her lip, Katherine shook her head. "And poor Uncle Noah! He wasn't a well man when he was taken prisoner." Noah Yancy was fifty-five and had already endured some severe health problems before he had been captured and taken away as a prisoner.

"From what I hear of those awful hulks, even if a person was well he'd be sick soon enough down *there*," Katherine said, clamping her lips together.

"Where did the British take their prisoners?" Susan asked.

"Halifax. That's in Nova Scotia," Katherine said sullenly.

"It seems so far away," Susan sighed as she folded the letter and stuck it in the pocket of her apron. She moved over to the window and stared out. Hot tears spilled from her eyes, and there was a catch in her throat as she said, "My . . . poor husband! Would God he had never gone into the army!"

"He felt he had to do it, Mother," Katherine said. "He was doing what he thought was right." The two women comforted each other as well as they could, but both felt the despair of being so far away and helpless to ease their suffering in any way.

For the next two days Susan grew more and more morbid. She was not well herself, and it was all Katherine could do to keep her mother's spirits up. Finally, on Wednesday afternoon when her mother had lain down to take a nap, Katherine was surprised to hear a knock at the door. She went at once to open it and blinked with surprise. "Why, Malcolm," she said, "I didn't expect you."

Malcolm Smythe stood there awkwardly and pulled his hat off. He was dressed rather formally, but this was common enough for him. "I have to talk with you, Katherine," he said quickly.

Alarmed by his manner, Katherine said, "Of course—come inside." She led him into the parlor and turned to him at once. "What is it? Is something wrong?"

"Nothing new," Malcolm said carefully. He bit his lip, chewing on it nervously, a mannerism of his when he was disturbed. Clearing his throat he said, "I've been . . . thinking of our situation, Katherine."

"Our situation?"

"Yes, I mean, we've been seeing each other for two years now, and I'm very fond of you."

Katherine suddenly knew what was coming next. The very choice of words, "Very fond of you . . ." was not the language of love. Malcolm had said much more passionate things in the past when he was pressing his suit with her. Now Katherine stared at him and said quietly, "What have you come to say, Malcolm?"

"I . . . I don't know how to put this," Smythe said carefully. He cleared his throat nervously, stared out the window, and fumbled with the tricorn hat that he held in both hands. He turned it around several times, as if trying to find the best way to hold it, a ploy to give him time while he sought for the proper words. "I consider myself a man of honor," Malcolm said finally, and managed to meet her eyes. "And I intend to be. But I think we need to . . . reconsider our relationship."

Like a signal given in the night that suddenly mounts up and explodes, Katherine understood immediately his meaning. She was a perceptive young woman, far more than most her age. Now looking at the young man in front of her, she knew exactly what he was stumbling to say. "Are you trying to tell me that you want to break our engagement, Malcolm?" she asked flatly.

Malcolm turned the hat over several times rapidly and crushed it in his hands. "Well," he said, "I wouldn't want to put it that way. . . ."

"What other way could it be said?" Katherine demanded. "I want to look at this thing straight on, Malcolm. Tell me what you're thinking."

"Well, I'm concerned about our future. We're so . . . well, *different*, Katherine. For some time now, I've been afraid that our political differences might be too . . . well, too great for us to bridge."

At that moment Katherine knew that she would never marry this man. Standing there, she watched him continue to twist his hat around nervously. A sudden flash of anger came to her as it sometimes did. She forced herself, however, to remain still and wait until the worst of it passed, then finally said calmly, "I think you're right. We would never be able to overcome this part of our lives." She saw relief leap into Malcolm Smythe's eyes and knew that she had been correct. It was a hopeless match between them.

"Perhaps after things settle down, we can begin to see each other again?"

"Goodbye, Malcolm," she said. "You don't want to see me again. Go find a nice Tory girl with lots of money. Marry her and have lots of Tory children."

Smythe flinched at the bluntness of her words. He saw the anger and resentment in her face and swallowed hard. "I . . . I'm sorry it's come to this, Katherine." He sought to say something to ease the tense moment, but was intelligent enough to realize that there was nothing more to say. "I think it might be best if you announce that you've broken our engagement."

"Yes, that would be best."

The words were stark and bare and even. This was a side of Katherine Yancy that Malcolm had seen before. Truthfully, he was somewhat overwhelmed by the almost fierce independence of this young woman. His parents had been apprehensive as well, not only of her political convictions, but that she was not appreciative enough of their family position and status. Relief came again, and Malcolm Smythe gave her a compassionate look—at least for him it was compassionate.

"You're a strong-willed girl, Katherine. I wish you well, but we would never have been happy together."

"No, we would not. Goodbye, Malcolm."

Katherine led him to the door, opened it, and felt a sudden impulse to give him a shove as he passed through it. Restraining herself, she shut the door and leaned heavily against it. Despite herself she began to tremble as tears filled her eyes. She had fancied herself in love with this man. It was true enough that she had wondered at times if their love was strong enough to build a marriage on, but a woman must marry, and Malcolm had been witty, amusing, had come from a good family—and if he had not been as romantic and challenging to her intellectually as she might have liked, still he had been a stabilizing factor in her life for the last two years.

Abruptly she dashed the tears from her eyes. "Now, what'll I do, trying to explain to everyone what's happened?" she muttered. She knew all too well the wagging tongues of Boston and was aware that the next few days would be a tiresome, difficult time explaining such a thing—even to her own mother. Slowly she moved away from the door, knowing that her mother would not understand. With her father and uncle gone, her mother would have considered a marriage to Malcolm some welcome stability to their plight.

T   T   T

Katherine had been exactly right. Explaining the broken engagement had proved difficult—very difficult. She had spoken about it to her mother first, of course, and Susan had stared at her with an air of incomprehension in her mild brown eyes. She had protested, "But, Katherine, it's all settled. He's so well connected, and you two get on so well. I don't understand it."

Katherine had wearily explained the situation to her mother, but it had been hard. It had been almost as hopeless when she had announced the broken engagement to her friends and to her pastor. All of them were mildly shocked, and they all equally disapproved of what they considered an ill-advised and hasty course of action. However, she had weathered the worst of the storm and for almost a week had endured.

During this time she had spent a great deal of the days alone, either in her room or walking the streets of Boston. There was a park not far from her house that she often retired to in the heat of the day and watched the children who played there. She enjoyed watching the squirrels as they eagerly scampered around her feet for the scraps of food that she tossed to them. She fed them absentmindedly, laughing at their playful antics at times—but it was a sobering time for Katherine Yancy.

She was a young woman who needed activity, and now there was little enough to do. With Malcolm no longer calling on her, she mostly took care of her mother, who was unable to do the housework. Katherine saw to the meals and cleaned the house, but all of this occupied little of her time. She was concerned, deeply concerned, about her father and uncle, and spoke once to her pastor. All he could do was recommend prayer, which she, of course, was already engaged in daily.

The thought that finally came to her was startling at first, and she put it aside. It came back, however, very strongly, and one night she stayed awake practically the entire night, thinking of how the idea that had forced itself on her might come to pass. It seemed difficult and impossible, but slowly she thought and worked out the details.

The next morning she met her mother at the breakfast table, and after she had asked a simple blessing said, "Mother, I'm going to Halifax."

"To Halifax!" Susan stared at her daughter wide-eyed, sure that her broken engagement with Malcolm had sorely affected her senses.

"Yes, I must go," she said. "Father is not well and Uncle Noah needs care."

"But it's so far away!"

"I could get a ship. It'll not be a long voyage. I'll take food and warm clothing and blankets for Father and Uncle Noah."

"But will the officers let you see them?"

A stubborn look swept across the face of Katherine Yancy. "They'll be so sick of me, I think they will," she said, nodding firmly. She thought ahead then of the trip, the voyage, the trouble she would have with the officers in charge of the prison, but her courage rose and she said, "I'll stay until Father and Uncle Noah are well. I must do this, Mother!"

3

THE HULKS

BANKS OF LOW CLOUDS hung heavily over the harbor at Halifax. They seemed to be drenched with their own weight and had the texture of heavy dough, though they were much darker. Katherine moved down the gangplank of the merchant ship *Dominion*, glad to be finally free from the foul smells and unruly pitchings of the ancient vessel. For all her fine name, the *Dominion* was afloat only by the herculean efforts of a doughty captain who drove his men like galley slaves. They had left the port of Boston six days earlier and had hit rough weather almost at once. The ship had bobbed like a cork and leaked at the seams so severely that Katherine became frightened, fearing that they would never make port.

Now reaching the land, she took a deep breath, savoring the freshness of the air and the firmness of earth. A drizzle was beginning to fall, but the inclement weather did not bother her. *At last I'm off of that awful ship*, she thought. *I didn't know anything could stink so bad!* The small cabin she had been assigned to she had shared with three other women. As soon as the ship began to pitch on the white-capped waves, two of them got sick immediately. They remained sick all the way, throwing up continuously. The only escape from the clammy foul air was to go topside, where one ran the risk of being washed overboard by the heavy swells that came crashing down across the deck. Katherine had tried to take walks a few times to escape the confines of the cabin, but the deck was filled with gear, and more than once, leering sailors had grabbed at her when the officers were not looking. *Not that the officers cared a great deal*, Katherine thought with distaste as she made her way across the wharf toward a series of low, weather-beaten wooden buildings that leaned against each other for support.

Finally she reached a narrow cobblestone street and stopped an elderly man who was pulling a small cart with large wheels. "Can you tell me the way to the British camp?" she asked.

The old man stopped and straightened up and peered at her out of a face that was as wrinkled as a prune. Deep lines marked his face and eyes, and he had no teeth, so that his nose and stubbled chin attempted to meet. He suddenly looked like an ancient nutcracker to Katherine, and when he spoke she could barely understand his mumbled words. "That way—down toward the church on your left. Aye, that's where the soldiers be."

"Thank you." Katherine smiled, then turned and made her way down the street. It was a poor enough city, not at all as nice as the wharves and docks at Boston. Moving along at a rapid pace, she began to see the red coats of soldiers and wanted to ask one of them for directions. She waited until she saw a tall, erect officer in a spotless crimson jacket with crossbelts across his chest and a saber at his side. He wore the tricorn hat of the British officer, and his shirt was white enough to have put the clouds to shame. "Pardon me, sir. Can you tell me where your headquarters is located?"

"Why, I'm headed that way now, miss. If you would permit me to accompany you. . . ?" He gave her a careful examination out of a pair of watchful gray eyes and said, "I'm Lieutenant Steerbraugh."

"Thank you, Lieutenant. That would be most kind."

Lieutenant Steerbraugh positioned himself to Katherine's right and shortened his long steps to accommodate her pace. "Did you just come in on the *Dominion*?"

"Yes." She hesitated, then added, "My name is Katherine Yancy, Lieutenant. I would like to see the officer in charge of the prisoners."

"Indeed?" Steerbraugh was interested and tried not to appear too curious. "I'm not sure exactly who that would be. There aren't very many of them, though, Miss Yancy."

"Who would you suggest I see? My father was taken prisoner in Boston, and I think all the prisoners were brought here, were they not?"

"Yes, I believe so." Steerbraugh took several more strides, thinking deeply. He had a long face with a prominent mustache that covered his upper lip. "I think, perhaps, you may as well see General Howe."

"Oh, that would be wonderful!" Katherine exclaimed. "Do you think he will see me?"

"Not to be familiar," Steerbraugh grinned behind his dark mustache, "but I don't think General Howe ever refused a chance to meet an attractive woman. No offense, Miss Yancy."

"None taken."

Steerbraugh led her through a labyrinthine path, passing through ranks of soldiers that were roaming the mean streets of Halifax to a camp just outside the town itself. Tents had been set up in neat, orderly rows, and a squad was presently drilling, directed by the raspy voice of a sergeant. A troop of cavalry passed by, their hooves kicking up spongy turf from the wet earth. Finally they arrived at a house centered in the middle of the camp, and Steerbraugh said, "This is General Howe's headquarters. Let me accompany you, Miss Yancy."

"That would be very kind, Lieutenant Steerbraugh," Katherine said, grateful for his help. She had not missed the stares from the soldiers as they had made their way through the streets.

Steerbraugh led her up the steps to the house, which was old and covered with peeling white paint. Stepping inside, she saw that the foyer had been made into an outer office. A sergeant sat behind a small desk, but he rose at once and saluted the lieutenant.

"Is General Howe in, Sergeant?"

"Yes, sir, he is. Shall I see if he's busy?"

"Yes, tell him that I have a young lady here who would like to speak with him."

The sergeant gave Katherine a thorough examination, but nodded and turned to disappear through the door at his back.

Steerbraugh turned to face Katherine and made polite conversation, asking how her voyage had been. The sergeant came back, however, almost at once. A grin tugged at the corners of his lips, for the general had asked, "What sort of a looking wench is she?" Upon being told that she was a peach—in the sergeant's words—Howe had straightened his wig and said, "Have her come in then, Sergeant."

Steerbraugh moved forward and opened the door for Katherine. She entered and found herself in a room filled with worn furniture, including a couch, chairs, and a large rosewood desk, beside which General Howe was standing.

"Sir, I have a guest who's just come off the *Dominion*. May I present Miss Katherine Yancy from Boston. Miss Yancy, General William Howe."

"Good morning, Miss Yancy," Howe said, stepping forward. He was a fine-looking man, very tall, yet rumpled in his dress. His dark hair curled in unruly knots and escaped the ribbon that fastened it behind his neck. His eyes were large and fun loving, and his full-lipped mouth made him look generous.

Lieutenant Steerbraugh said, "Miss Yancy has come to visit her father and uncle."

"Oh," Howe said with some surprise, "and how is that, Miss Yancy?"

"My father's name is Amos Yancy, General. He and his brother,

Noah, were taken as prisoners at the Battle of Breed's Hill."

At the mention of Breed's Hill, Howe's features clouded. Neither he, nor Gage, nor any who took part in that battle remembered with pleasure the sight of so many slain Redcoats that had covered the green hill. It had been a senseless slaughter. Howe's generous mouth tightened somewhat, and he said, "I see, and what is your purpose in coming, Miss Yancy, may I ask?"

"I'm afraid he's not well, General. I would like to visit him and provide him with warm clothes, blankets, food, and medicine that I brought, if possible."

"I'm afraid that is not possible," General Howe said. "It wouldn't do—a young lady like you out on the hulks."

Katherine was not wearing ornate clothing. She was, however, looking very pretty in her simple gray dress. The bonnet framed her squarish face, and her cheeks were rosy from the walk from the harbor. "Please, sir," she pleaded. "I know it's an unusual request, but it's very important to me that I see my father and my uncle. In the last letter we got, my father said my uncle was very ill. I would so much appreciate it if you would let me visit them."

"I'd be happy to accompany Miss Yancy to the *St. George* to see that she's safe," Lieutenant Steerbraugh said quickly.

Howe's features grew less stern, and he almost winked at the lieutenant. "I'm sure you would, Lieutenant, but we have no precedent for this kind of request."

"Not to put too great a point on it, General," Steerbraugh said, "but I can't see what harm it would do—just one visitor. We're not likely to have many all the way from Boston out here in Halifax." He nodded at the young woman who was waiting, almost holding her breath. "I know she's shown great courage in coming this far alone."

Howe was of the same opinion. If he had not had Mrs. Loring with him—the wife of a civilian supplier of goods to the army—he might have pressed his own case. But for the time being, Mrs. Loring's charms were sufficient. Waving his well cared for hand, he said airily, "Well, I suppose it can do no real harm."

"Oh, thank you, General." A flush tinged Katherine's cheeks, and she looked very attractive as she stood before him. Impulsively she put out her hand, and he squeezed it at once. "I'm so grateful to you. Will I need a pass for my visits?" She took the chance of making a way for a series of visits instead of one.

Howe recognized the ploy immediately. He smiled, however, and winked at the tall lieutenant. "Have my sergeant make out a pass and I'll sign it."

"Yes, sir," Steerbraugh said with alacrity. He stepped outside the office, and Howe inquired more closely into the situation of the Yancys. Soon, however, Steerbraugh returned with the slip of paper. "Here you are, sir." The two waited as Howe moved to his desk, pulled a quill from a holder, dipped it in a bottle of ink, and scribbled something on it. He poured fine sand over it to serve as a blotter, cleared it with a puff of his breath, then folded it and handed it to Katherine. "There you are, Miss Yancy. Let me know if I can be of further assistance. I know this is a difficult time for you."

"You've made it much easier, General. Thank you very much."

Steerbraugh led Katherine out of the building and said, "Do you have a place to stay, Miss Yancy?"

"Why, no, I don't."

"I think that might be somewhat of a problem. With all the troops that we brought in, and many of those faithful to the Crown who have accompanied us, it's very hard to find accommodations."

"I'll find something," Katherine said.

"Let me recommend the Dolphin Inn. I have friends who are staying there, civilians from New York. I'm sure you could work out some arrangement with the innkeeper. I know you're tired, so perhaps we ought to see to that first."

"Thank you, Lieutenant. That's very thoughtful of you." Katherine was very tired, and she surrendered to Lieutenant Steerbraugh's kindness. It did not take long to walk to the Dolphin Inn, and she stood waiting as Steerbraugh practically forced the innkeeper to make room for her. She finally was placed in a tiny room in the attic, barely eight feet square. The room had a single bed, a small chest that served as a washstand, a small window of diamond-shaped glass that let in a few feeble rays of sun, and a worn green carpet.

"This isn't much," Steerbraugh said cautiously.

He then accompanied her to the *Dominion* and commandeered an army wagon to carry her small chest full of supplies that she had brought with her. When they returned to the inn, he carried the chest to her room. Now he shook his head doubtfully, "Not much in the way of luxuries, I'm afraid."

"This is fine, Lieutenant. I'm very grateful to you for your help. I don't know what I would have done without you."

Steerbraugh flushed at the compliment. He found himself attracted to this pretty, young American, and said, "Perhaps you'd like to freshen up. Later on this afternoon I'll take you to the prison ship."

"Oh, really, Lieutenant. I'd rather go now. I'm so anxious about my father—and I can rest later."

"Very well. What would you like to take to your father?"

At once Katherine began pulling items out of the chest and placed them in a small canvas bag. She had randomly thrown in some food and warm clothing before she had hastily left Boston.

When she had gathered it all together she said, "I think this will do for a start."

Steerbraugh insisted on carrying the bag, and Katherine carried the blanket folded beneath her arm. They left the Dolphin Inn, and he led her back to the wharf. When they arrived at the docks, a misty haze had fallen over the harbor so that it was almost impossible to see. The sun filtered through it, making iridescent reflections on the water. He pointed and said, "There's the hulk out there. There's only one now, an old ship called the *St. George*."

"How do you get out there?"

"I'll hire a small boat. There are always men around the docks wanting to pick up a few coins."

"You're very efficient, Lieutenant," Katherine complimented him. She followed him down to the shoreline where the water lapped at the pilings of the dock. Soon he found a small dory and a fisherman who offered to row them out to the *St. George* for half a crown.

Steerbraugh helped Katherine into the boat, then stepped in, placing the bag on the floorboards of the dory. They sat in the bow, facing the stern of the boat, and watched as the fisherman jumped in, shoved off from the dock, and began rowing with strong sweeps of his oars. The tiny craft bobbed up and down, but this was nothing to Katherine, who had endured much worse during the voyage. Overhead, gulls wheeled and swept down making raucous cries. "They're not very pretty birds, are they? And they sound awful," Steerbraugh said with a grimace. "I don't know what they're good for."

"I suppose all of God's creatures are good for something."

Her words caught at Steerbraugh. He turned toward her and studied her more carefully. The wind tugged at her bonnet, and strands of her dark brown hair had escaped. When she turned to smile at him, he noted that her eyes were the most unusual color. *Green like the sea sometimes*, he thought. *But gray too. Most unusual. A deucedly pretty girl*. He chatted with her on the way, and when they pulled up beside the *St. George*, the oarsman shipped his oars and held on to the cleats of the ladder that was nailed to the side. "Ahoy," Steerbraugh called out, "Lieutenant James Steerbraugh. Visitor by order of General Howe."

"Come aboard, Lieutenant," a voice hailed at once.

"Perhaps you'd better go first, Miss Yancy. If you fall, I'll be there to catch you."

She was a strong, athletic girl, and climbing the ladder was no problem. However, it was a little awkward for Katherine. She was aware that the oarsman and Steerbraugh himself were staring at her as she climbed up the wooden ladder. When she reached the top she saw a tall man in a blue coat with a strange-looking hat staring at her. He stepped forward at once and thrust out his hand. When she took it, it had the texture of hard tree bark. His eyes were half-lidded after many years of sun on the sea, and he said, "Watch your step, miss." Then he turned to Steerbraugh and said, "Do you have authority from General Howe?"

"I have it," Katherine said. She reached into the small reticule that she carried by a string around her wrist and fished out the pass.

The officer read it and looked at her. "Somewhat unusual," he muttered. He pulled at his muttonchop whiskers, then turned his light blue eyes on the Lieutenant. "You vouch for this young lady?"

"Yes I do, Captain."

"And this is General Howe's signature?"

"It is, sir."

"Well, I suppose it will be all right." Still he hesitated. "You can't go down in the hulks. It wouldn't do for a woman to be down there."

"Perhaps you have a room somewhere where Miss Yancy could meet her father."

"He's a prisoner, is he?"

"Yes," Katherine said at once. "His name is Amos Yancy. His brother, Noah Yancy, is also a prisoner aboard this ship."

The captain clawed at his muttonchop whiskers for a moment, then shrugged. "If you'll step this way, I have a room that might serve for a visit."

The two followed the captain, whose name was Simms, down the deck. The *St. George* was an old vessel that had seen its share of use. It smelled of tar and rotten wood. She had once been a fighting ship, but that had been years ago. Now she was barely afloat, and the trip from Boston to Halifax proved likely to be her last. Another foul and unclean smell filled the air. It rose, Katherine realized, from the prisoners' quarters below deck.

The captain opened a door and stepped inside what appeared to be a general meeting room. A man was sitting at one of the two tables eating something out of a dish. He rose at once and Captain Simms said, "May I introduce Miss Yancy. Miss Yancy, Major Saul Banks. He is one of the surgeons of our army. He is in charge of all the prisoners confined to this ship."

"Happy to meet you, Miss Yancy." Major Banks was short, fat, and red faced. He had blue eyes and strangely colored cinnamon hair that he kept slicked back with some sort of grease or oil. He had a froggish expression almost, with bulging eyes and an extremely wide mouth. When he spoke, it was as if his tongue was too large for his mouth and he mumbled his words. "Pleasure to meet you, ma'am."

"Miss Yancy has traveled all the way from Boston to visit her father, Amos Yancy. Do you know him?"

"No, not by name, Captain. Too many for that, you understand."

"Well, I'll have one of my lieutenants fetch him." Turning then to Katherine, he said, "You can meet with your father in this room."

The captain turned and left the room, and Major Banks stared at the two. "Most unusual. You have permission for this, Miss Yancy?"

"General Howe has given her a pass to see her father," Steerbraugh said.

"Most unusual."

There was an awkward silence in the room. Katherine was aware that the surgeon was looking at her slyly. An attractive woman, she had learned to interpret this sort of expression, and in Banks' case it was not difficult. He licked his lips intermittently and turned his head to one side, studying her with his pale blue eyes. He asked several questions, which she answered as briefly as possible.

Finally, the door opened and a heavyset marine sailor stood there, saying, "I'll have to remain on guard outside. Let me know when your visit is up."

As soon as the door closed, Katherine turned to the prisoner standing there. "Father!" she cried out. She moved forward at once, grief in her tone and in the agonized expression on her face.

Amos Yancy looked like a thin scarecrow, not the strong, tall man she remembered. His hair, which he had always taken such pride in keeping clean, was now lank and hung in filthy strands. His clothes were nothing more than tattered rags, and his frail body showed through rips in the pitiful excuse for a shirt that he wore. He smelled as foul as any human Katherine had ever encountered. Nevertheless, she moved toward him and put her arms around him and buried her face against his chest, murmuring, "Father, I'm so glad to see you."

"Katherine!" Amos Yancy's face was gaunt, but a gleam of hope had sprung into his brown eyes, and he reached awkwardly to stroke her back as she clung to him. "I never expected to see you here, daughter."

"I've come to take care of you, Father. Now, how are you? Tell me about yourself and about Uncle Noah—" She turned suddenly and found Major Banks watching her and said, "Would you excuse me, Major, and you too, Lieutenant? I'd like to have some time alone with my father."

"Certainly," Steerbraugh said at once. "Naturally you'll want to see your father alone." He stared at the surgeon and said, "Major Banks, perhaps you'll show me the ship."

Banks' face reddened. He did not approve of leaving them alone. He put the best face on it, however, and said, "All right, Lieutenant." But he stopped at the door and said, "You'll be needing to talk to me about your father's physical condition. After you finish your visit, I'll be happy to do so."

"Thank you, Major," Katherine said shortly. She waited until the door slammed, then turned and hugged her father again. "I'm so glad to see you," she said, then she moved back and looked at him, shaking her head. "You're ill."

"I'm fine," Amos Yancy said. He still could not believe what he was seeing. He passed his hand before his eyes in an unbelieving gesture and whispered, "I can't believe that you're actually here, Katherine. How did you manage it?"

"Oh, we'll have time to talk about that, but let's get some good clothes on you. Here." She opened the canvas bag and fished out a pair of trousers, a clean shirt, and some socks that she had knitted herself. "I'll turn my back, and you change into these. Throw those rags away."

"Well, I don't know—"

"Father—now do as I say." Anger was running deep in Katherine Yancy. Ever since she and her mother had received the letter from her father, she knew the conditions had been bad. Even before she had made her decision to come to Halifax to help them, the stories of what Tory prisoner ships were like were the concern of many families whose menfolk had been captured. She had prepared herself as best she could, but the gaunt expression of illness that lined her father's face frightened her. At the same time, knowing the suffering he and Uncle Noah had endured made her furious. "Get into those clothes. If anyone gives us a problem, I'll go straight back to General Howe."

"All right, daughter," Amos said, taking the clothes she handed to him. When she had turned around, he slowly removed the rags that covered his frail body. Silently he thanked God, for the mere sight of his daughter standing there overwhelmed him with emotion. When he was finished, his voiced choked as he said, "It's . . . it's so good to see you, daughter."

Katherine came to him at once, saying, "What you need is a hot bath."

"There's not much of that on this ship. I haven't had a bath since I was captured."

Amos had been a prisoner aboard the *St. George* for many months. It seemed, indeed, like a lifetime. Belowdecks in the dreaded prison was a population of prisoners condemned to a dismal existence—all sick and starving. They were crammed in a space too low to stand up in, and too small to stretch out without ramming their feet into another prisoner. As the weeks passed, their number continued to dwindle as death claimed another life.

The prisoners' quarters were secured by an iron hatchway, and the only ventilation came through the tiny round portholes in the sides of the ship. As the days of captivity moved into an awful rhythm, every morning the prisoners heard the cry, "Throw out your dead." Amos had been one who had climbed the rope ladder with the wretched corpse of one who had died that very morning. It mattered not whether by starvation, disease, or their own hands. The names of the dead were taken whenever possible, and the bodies were slipped over the gunnels to a watery grave. Those who clung to life were thrown their pitiful rations for the day. They took turns boiling the poor scraps of meat and the peas in a huge brass cauldron of salt water that was set into a bricked-up furnace at the ship's bow. Some were so starved they ate their food raw, and those who were not quick enough to grab what they could were condemned to fast for another twenty-four hours.

Amos stared at this lovely, clean daughter of his and thought of the loathsome food. The bread was moldy and unfit to eat, the bits of meat alive with worms. There was an occasional gill of rum and hardly ever any fresh water. The only possible variance in the routine was when a prisoner disobeyed an order and was whipped—sometimes to death. Other times men were hung upside down from the bowsprit to strangle on their own blood. Each punishment served as a solemn warning against agitation or disobedience of any sort. He said nothing about this, but he thought of those turncoats who had enlisted in the British service. Always there were a few who did that. There were always those who buckled and traded loyalties to end their suffering. Now he stood there, his face haggard, his unkempt hair hanging down over the new shirt, his beard matted and foul, and whispered, "I'm glad you've come. Tell me about everything."

"First you will eat, or you can eat while I talk."

Katherine began to pull food from the bag. She pulled out a dried fish, cut a slice of hard bread, and said, "Eat this, and tomorrow I'll get some fresh vegetables and bring them to you." She watched as her father tried to keep from gobbling the food up. She opened one of the bottles of rum that she had brought and saw how his eyes lightened at once.

Finally he shook his head and said, "I'd better not eat too much."

He thought for a moment, then said, "I wish I could give some of this to every prisoner down below, but they wouldn't let me take it with me."

Katherine held her father's hand. "We'll get you out of here someday. You'll be free."

"It's not myself. It's Noah I'm worried about." Amos shook his head. "He's very sick."

"Take some of the food to him," Katherine urged.

"Right, I'll do that. I know that'll help."

"I brought enough clothes for him, too. Can you take those to him?"

"Yes, it'd be good for him."

The two talked for some time, and then a knock sounded on the door. It opened at once and the surgeon stepped inside. "I'm afraid that's all the time permissible, Miss Yancy. Bosun, take the prisoner back down below."

Banks watched as the girl kissed her father. He eyed the new clothes and saw the pockets bulging with food. When the door shut behind them, he moved closer, saying, "Now, my dear, let's talk about your father's case."

"His case, Major, is that he's starving and he's sick. It doesn't take a physician to see that."

Banks blinked with surprise at the fearlessness in the girl's face. It only made him grin, however, and he said, "I like to see a woman with spirit. Now then"—he moved close enough to put his hand on her arm—"I think something, perhaps, might be done. We might make a— shall we say a *special* case for your father."

Something in the tone of his words alerted Katherine, and she pulled her arm away instantly. "I will appreciate anything you can do for my father. He needs care, and my uncle is even worse."

"As I say," Banks said, "I would be happy to see to it that they get a little something extra. In the meanwhile I would be delighted if I could show you Halifax—not much to see, but we do have a little society here of respectable people."

"Thank you, Major, but I didn't come for a social outing. I'll be most grateful for anything you can do for my father."

Banks saw her resistance. "Well," he said, "we will see about that. Will you be coming tomorrow?"

"I intend to come every day, Major. That's the way the pass reads."

"Is it, now? Well, we shall see about that." There was a threat in his words, and his pale eyes glittered. He had fat, pudgy hands, and as she passed by toward the door he put his hand on her back in a familiar pat.

She stepped away instantly and pulled the door open. Steerbraugh was there, and she said with some relief, "Lieutenant, I'm ready to go now."

Steerbraugh glanced at her, seeing the agitation in the girl's face. "Of course, Miss Yancy." He gave the surgeon a cold look but said nothing. "If you come this way I'll see you back to your inn."

The two left and Major Saul Banks stood in the center of the room, his face flushed with anger. Muttering, he said, "Thinks she's too good for me, does she? Well, we'll see about that. . . !"

⚑   ⚑   ⚑

For three days Katherine made the trip to the *St. George*. She purchased some green vegetables from a farmer and was glad to see her father's face take on fresh color.

"Noah's enjoying the food and the drink, and the warm clothes, too," he had said to her. "If we could just get him to some fresh air, I think he would be much better off."

"I'll ask the captain."

"No, it's the surgeon you'll have to ask—Major Banks." Amos did not notice the troubled look that crossed his daughter's face. "He's a hard man. Banks does practically nothing for the men. He's drunk half the time. When he does come, he doesn't do anything, but he's really in control of the prisoners, not the captain."

Her father's words sent a chill over Katherine. Nevertheless, the next time she saw Banks she said, "Would it be possible to get my father and uncle transferred to some sort of jail in town out of the hulks?"

Banks moved forward. "Anything is possible with the proper *friends*." He moved closer again and managed to put his hand on her arm. He was always touching her, and Katherine was furious but could not afford to show it. He put his arm around her and pulled her toward him. Katherine could not move for a moment. She managed to turn her head aside so that his lips planted a kiss on her cheek. She struggled, but he had strength in his stubby arms. "Now, don't be like that, my dear Katherine! After all, you want something, and I want something. What could be more natural than that we help each other. Eh?"

"Let me go!" Katherine struggled furiously. She ripped herself from his embrace and glared at him. "You're no gentleman, sir!"

Banks had risen out of the gutters of Glasgow, gotten the rudiments of medical training, and enlisted through the help of a friend as an officer, a surgeon in the British army. He had little skill as a surgeon and was shunned by most of the officers who were of the upper class. All his life Banks had longed to be a gentleman, and now Katherine Yancy had thrown it in his face that he was not. He stared at her, his froglike features twisted with anger. "Not a gentleman? Well, we shall see about that! The one thing I am is surgeon in charge—and I am declaring as of this day that your visits will cease until further notice."

"You can't do that! I have a pass signed by General Howe."

"General Howe is a busy man, and even if he questions me I will see to it that you do not set foot on this ship to see your father. You can depend on that."

His words were prophetic. Katherine, on the following day, was not permitted to visit her father. She had gone, at once, to General Howe's headquarters and found the General amiable but strict. "I cannot go against the advice of the surgeon. He tells me it's dangerous for you to be there. There's sickness on board."

Katherine begged and pleaded, but the general, in this case, would not be moved. She left the headquarters sick at heart and walked the streets searching for a way out. To give in to Banks was unthinkable— yet still she knew Banks was capable of making life more miserable for her father and her uncle. Finally she returned, dejected, to the Dolphin Inn, and as dark fell over Halifax it seemed to close around her own heart like a fist.

4

A Desperate Case

ON APRIL 13, 1776, George Washington arrived at Manhattan Island. He had sent Benedict Arnold off on a futile mission to Canada in December, and General Charles Lee, the most experienced officer in the Continental Army, had left the main force to take command of the segment of the Continental Army in the South.

When Washington arrived in New York, he found the city swelling with a population of nearly twenty-five thousand, much different from siege-worn Boston. Everywhere there was a bustle and elegance on the streets, which were wider and more regular than those of Boston. Broadway, its main thoroughfare, which ran northward a mile from the ancient stone fort at the Battery, was shaded by rows of trees and lined with fine residences, churches, and public buildings. Beyond the limits of the city, country roads meandered through the wooded hills, marshes, and farmlands that stretched some twelve miles to the little wooden Kings Bridge that crossed to the mainland. All of this began to change at once when Washington arrived with his troops. Without delay he put his men to work completing the fortifications that Lee had started to build in Manhattan. All kinds of ambitious barricades and obstructions had been thrown across streets, and some were sunk into the riverbed to defend what was truly indefensible—a long, thin island surrounded by waterways easily navigable by enemy warships.

One immediate effect of the arrival of Washington's army was the plight of the loyalists of New York. Fearing reprisal, many of them fled the city in terror. The streets were full of shouting men and women, stunned or sobbing children, as they scurried back and forth from their homes to the docks, trundling carts, trucks, wheelbarrows, and handcarts all loaded to overflowing with all sorts of baggage and personal belongings.

Those who did not flee were subjected to indignities on the part of the triumphant patriots—some of whom got completely out of hand. Dake Bradford, who had left his bride after a brief honeymoon to return to his unit, witnessed one nightmarish scene. He was walking down Broadway on his way to the camp when suddenly a man emerged from an alley dressed up like a grotesque, nightmarish bird. Out of this strange-looking creature, whose mouth was red and gap-toothed, came horrible screams of pain.

Dake realized at once that the poor man was probably a loyalist and had been tarred and feathered. A rowdy mob followed him, yelling and laughing at their victim. They finally seized him after poking him with pointed sticks and put him on a rail, holding him high enough so that he could not reach the ground with his feet. The more the man writhed and twitched, the more feathers flew into the air, and the louder his tormentors shrieked and laughed.

Dake was disgusted by the sight and shook his head. "We don't need that kind on our side," he muttered grimly. But the crazed mob was completely out of control and he could do nothing. When he arrived at the barracks that had been assigned to his unit, he took a great deal of ribbing from his friends about his new status as a married man. He managed to field the many jokes with a smile, knowing that the more he protested the more ribald they would become. Finally he spoke to his sergeant, a tall, lanky Virginian who had been at Bunker Hill with him. His name was Silas Tooms. He was thirty-five but looked older, worn down from a lifetime of hard work on a farm. He was, however, a good soldier and a fine sergeant, and Dake had taken a liking to him. "What do you think, Silas?" Dake asked when they had a moment alone. They had procured some cider and were sipping it gratefully, for it was an unusually warm spring day.

Tooms took several swallows, his Adam's apple bobbing up and down, before he answered. Finally he wiped his mouth with the back of his sleeve and shook his head dolefully. "Mighty poor place to try to make a stand," he rasped. His voice was high-pitched and filled with gloom.

"What do you mean?" Dake asked instantly. "General Lee's thrown up a lot of fortifications."

"Maybe he has, but we can't defend this whole island. Look over there." He pointed toward the East River, which ran by on their right, then swung around. "You can't see it, but the Hudson's over there. If the British come back with their navy, which they're bound to do, what'll we do then?"

"Well, they've got to get at us," Dake said.

"You gonna fight off a ship of the line with that musket of yours?"

Tooms demanded. "We'll be caught like rats in a trap if we're not careful."

"General Washington knows all that, Silas. We'll be all right. You wait and see."

Silas looked around at the troops who were drilling and considered the thing. "What we got here is mostly militia," he said. "They're not trained to stand and fight."

"They fought at Bunker Hill."

"Yes, they did, but then we were up on top of a hill, and the British had to come up. We could hide behind the walls and shoot them as they advanced. Here, they can anchor their warships all around us and pick us off with their guns. I wish we'd leave here."

"Leave? What about the city?"

"Let the lobsterbacks have it! It ain't nothing but a pest hole of Tories anyway," Tooms growled. "I say burn it to the ground!"

Although Tooms did not know it, several of Washington's officers felt the same way. They met in a council of war, and several of them almost came to blows over the question of whether to defend New York or not.

Washington, however, had put the matter at rest. He had stood before them, a tall man with a long face and deep-set gray eyes. "The Congress has expressed their desire for our army to hold New York. It would be giving too much away to the British for us to let them have it without a fight."

Lee had scoffed. "Burn it to the ground!" he had shouted. Others had disagreed.

"We will hold New York for as long as we can," Washington had said in the end.

Not all went smoothly for the general, for one plot emerged that almost took his life. The general's cook was a faithful black man who had traveled from Mount Vernon with Martha Washington. One Thursday afternoon he brought in a special dish of green peas, and one of Washington's aides, for some reason, became suspicious.

"Where did you get them?" he asked the cook.

"Why, someone's serving maid brought them to the kitchen."

Washington was about to begin the meal when the aide said, "General, there are those who would like to see you dead. Do not eat those peas."

Washington looked surprised but shrugged. "Very well, if you say so, Lieutenant." He pushed the dish aside, and later, when the cook cast the peas to the chickens he kept outside the kitchen door, the entire flock died.

The story of the dish of poisoned peas spread rapidly. A conspiracy was uncovered, and rumor had it that the Tory conspirators had planned to poison both Washington and General Putman, then stab them when they were unconscious. Other reports circulated widely, arrests were made, and many Tories took to the woods, although about twenty of them were caught before they could escape. The most active participants were captured, and some of them saved their necks from the gallows by telling all they knew.

One of them, Sergeant Thomas Hickey, refused to talk and was charged with treason, having been implicated by some of the other conspirators.

A general court-martial was convened by a warrant from General Washington. Samuel Parsons presided over the trial in which Hickey was accused of mutiny and treason. Washington, himself, made little of the matter, but the trial went on.

Hickey pleaded not guilty but was found guilty by the court-martial. He was sentenced to be hanged. A gallows was erected in a field near Bowery Lane, and the last day of Thomas Hickey's life was a fine one. The sun shown brightly and the breeze was cool. Eighty men with loaded muskets, twenty from each brigade, were ordered to guard Hickey. He was marched onto the field to the beat of drums, and the fifes struck up a tune called "Poor Old Tory."

Hickey was brought to the place of execution. All the buttons had been cut off his uniform coat, and the red insignia of a sergeant had been ripped from his shoulder. He looked scornfully at the crowd that had gathered by the hundreds and held his head up high. When he reached the foot of the gallows, he was met by a chaplain. For just a moment, Hickey's reserve broke down and he gave in to tears, but then quickly wiped them away with his hand. The blindfold was adjusted over his face, he mounted the steps of the platform, and the rope was placed around his neck. As the snare drums rolled dramatically, the platform was yanked away. Hickey's body swung, writhing for a moment, then finally went limp.

A yell went up from the crowd, but Dake, who was not far from the gallows, shook his head. "The death of one Tory won't help us much when the British get here," he murmured to Sergeant Tooms. He looked out over the water as if he expected to see the British battle fleet arrive, but there was nothing except the blank expanse of empty horizon shadowed by white clouds that wandered around the blue heavens like fleecy white sheep.

♜   ♜   ♜

After the departure of the British, followed by the exodus of Washington's forces, Boston seemed much like a ghost town. Things went badly for those who had been loyal to the Crown. Abigail Howland and her mother had reached the end of their meager resources, and now they faced utter destitution.

Abigail had taken the last of their money and had gone searching for food. There was little enough to be had, for the siege had driven the prices of everything up. Many of the shops were boarded up, and the whole city seemed wrapped in gloom. Finally she managed to procure two loaves of bread, a small basket full of wilted carrots and onions, and a portion of lamb that had a rather rank smell about it. Carrying her provisions, Abigail passed through the streets of the city, a cloud over her spirit. When she arrived at the small house where she and her mother had taken refuge after being put out of the family home, she was met by her mother.

"Abigail," Mrs. Howland said, coming to greet her, "we have a letter from my sister-in-law, Esther."

At once Abigail put the basket down and came to take the single sheet of paper that her mother held out to her. She scanned it quickly, and a glimmer of hope came to her. The letter was a brief invitation stating simply:

> I cannot say how things will be in New York now that it seems to have been chosen for the next site for battle, but if you and Abigail would like to come and share my home, Carrie, I would be most happy to have you. At the present time there seems to be plenty of provisions, and I know things are difficult for you there in Boston.

Abigail instantly said, "Let's go, Mother!"

"Well . . . we don't know how it will be there. The loyalists have been treated rather badly, I understand."

"It can't be any worse than here," Abigail said firmly. She looked at her mother, noting the feebleness that had become much worse lately, and knew that she, herself, would have to make the decision. Firmly she said, "We have enough money to get to Aunt Esther's house. You can rest there, and there are fine doctors in New York. I'm worried about you, Mother."

Carrie Howland was too tired and sick to argue.

"Very well," she said. "It can't be any worse for us there than here."

Abigail nodded. "I'll pack our things, and we'll leave tomorrow by coach. It'll be a hard trip, but when we get there Aunt Esther will take care of us."

5

"ARE YOU IN LOVE WITH MY PA?"

"SAM . . ."

Rachel Bradford paused and placed her hands on her hips before calling out again. "Sam Bradford, you come out of that workshop this instant!" She turned her head to one side, and the breeze caught her red hair, making golden gleams in the heavy tresses. There was an alertness in her green eyes, and she called out again in a stentorian voice, "Sam Bradford, I'll have Pa take a strap to you if you don't come here this instant!"

The backyard of the Bradford house contained a small vegetable garden. Flowers occupied small plots, and on the property line in the back stood a neat rectangular shed with a low-pitched roof. Just then the door opened and Sam Bradford stepped outside. At the age of sixteen he was already five ten and strongly built like his father, Daniel. His uncombed hair caught the sun and glinted with the same trace of red his sister's had. He trudged toward the house, carrying some sort of object in his hands, and when he got to the porch he said, "Aw, you didn't have to bust my eardrums. I heard you the first time." He was a cheerful young man and had a great affection for his only sister. Now, however, he was put out, and when he came up to her he bumped her with his hip, sending her backward. "You want all the neighbors to hear you screaming like a wounded panther?" he complained.

Catching her balance, Rachel flew back at him. Reaching out, she grabbed a huge handful of his hair and yanked his head back and forth. "Don't you push me around," she cried, then tugged him into the kitchen after ignoring his cries of protest. When they were inside, she turned to him and pointed to a huge bowl of potatoes sitting on the

55

table. "I told you to peel those potatoes two hours ago," she snapped, "and you haven't done one of them. You sit right down there and peel them right now or I'll take a strap to you myself!"

Sam set the machine in his hands down on the table, reached for her, and pinioned her arms. She was one year older but was no match for his powerful grip. "I think I'll just squeeze you in two, sister," he said. "Then I wouldn't have to put up with your nagging anymore." He picked her up and swung her around, laughing at her futile protests. Finally he put her down and said, "Now, you mind how you speak to a gentleman from now on."

Rachel beat on his shoulder with her fist, but laughter danced in her eyes. She was very fond of this youngest brother of hers. Her twin brothers, Micah and Dake, were only eighteen, but it was she and Samuel who had grown up together fishing, exploring the woods that surrounded Boston, and now she could not but feel a surge of admiration for him. "You sit down there and peel those potatoes right now! The men will be in soon, and I want to have supper ready."

"No problem." Sam gestured in a grandiose fashion to the object on the table. "There you have Professor Samuel Bradford's patented, dyed-in-the-wool, world's champion potato peeler." He laughed at the disbelieving expression on Rachel's face and added, "It'll peel apples, too. Let me show you."

"I've seen enough of your crazy inventions, Sam. They never seem to get anything done," Rachel said. However, she was fascinated and moved closer. The contraption that Sam had placed on the table was simple enough. It had a metal arm that rose out of a base made of walnut, with another arm extended at right angles over which Sam jabbed a potato. Then he moved another upright arm forward, which had a blade of some sort attached. Grasping a small wheel attached to the second arm, he winked at her and said with excitement, "Now, you just watch this! It'll peel that potato in three seconds. No more sittin' there with a knife picking the eyes out and all that stuff," he crowed. "Watch this, Rachel!"

Sam advanced the second upright arm until the blade was touching the potato. As he began to turn the wheel, the blade performed a circle around the potato, which was held tightly. "Look at that!" he said proudly and pulled the peeled potato off its mount.

Rachel took it and shook her head in disgust. "Why, this won't work!" she exclaimed. Reaching down, she picked up the peeling. "Look at this. You've got peelings over half an inch thick." She held the potato in one hand, and the peeling in the other and shook her head. "We'd have to cook the peelings! All you have left here is half a potato."

Sam was disgruntled, for he had put great stock in this invention. "Well, that's just a technical problem," he mumbled. "I'll just have to set the blade a little bit farther back." He had already begun making adjustments to the invention in his head, for he loved to make things, but Rachel gave him no help.

"Get that thing out of the way," she said. Reaching over to the table she picked up a short knife and said, "Here, you peel those potatoes right now. I've got to tend to the rest of the supper."

"All right, but one of these days when I'm rich and famous from my potato peeler, see if I give *you* any of the money," Sam called out as she turned and busied herself at the stove.

🛡️   🛡️   🛡️

Daniel Bradford entered the dining room after washing his hands and paused to look at the supper that Rachel had prepared. "Why, this looks good enough for a king!" Turning, he reached out and put his arm around Rachel and squeezed her, careful of his strength. He was forty-six years old and in perfect physical condition. One inch over six feet, he weighed one hundred eighty-five pounds, and there was not a spare ounce of fat on his body. His upper body was heavy and strong from the years he had spent at the forge, and there was an air of power about all that he did. He released her and said, "If that's as good as it looks—and smells—I'm probably going to commit gluttony."

He moved to the head of the oak table, took his seat, then waited until Micah, Rachel, and Sam had seated themselves. He bowed his head and said a simple prayer, then looked up and smiled at them. "I hate to say it, but I wouldn't regret it too much if Mrs. White stayed sick another few days. Your cooking is better than hers, Rachel." Mrs. White was the housekeeper and cook in the Bradford household since he'd come to Boston from Virginia with his family, and Daniel Bradford did not really mean what he said. He always liked to praise Rachel whenever he could, for he was fiercely proud of her, as he was of his other children.

"You eat so fast you never taste anything, Pa," Rachel said, but flushed with his compliment.

"Hurry and cut that meat up, Pa," Micah Bradford said. At eighteen he was within an inch of his father's height and weighed almost exactly the same. He also had the same straw-colored hair and hazel eyes of Daniel Bradford, and when he smiled his eyes crinkled the same way his father's did. His twin brother, Dake, had the same hair and eye color, of course, as did Samuel. There was a strong family resemblance between these three, and more than once Daniel had said to Rachel, "I'm glad you took after your mother and not after me, daughter."

The four ate heartily of the meal that Rachel had prepared. She had roasted a leg of lamb and baked some fish caught early that morning in the sea. They were expertly cooked, and the meat was tender, almost falling apart. She also had prepared potatoes, beans cooked with her own special recipe, and carrots. Sam ate so fast he hardly spoke for a while. "This is sure good bread," he said, breaking off a piece of the fresh baked loaf and stuffing it into his mouth. "Did you tell Pa about my new invention?"

"What invention's that?" Micah inquired. "A perpetual motion machine?"

"No, nothing like that yet," Sam said, swallowing a huge bite and shuddering as it went down. He cut a piece of lamb off, approximately half the size of his fist, lifted it on his knife, and bit off half of it. Chewing with great enjoyment he said, "It's a potato peeler, and it peels apples too."

"The only thing is, the peeling was so thick there was no potato left," Rachel laughed, her eyes gleaming in the lamplight. They all teased Sam for a time about his invention, and finally Rachel said, "How did it go at the foundry today, Pa?"

"It's going to be more trouble than I thought, Rachel," Daniel said.

He had fair skin by nature, but stayed outdoors as much as he could, which gave him a ruddy complexion. He had a rather thin face with high cheekbones, a broad forehead, and a cleft chin. A scar ran across the bridge of his nose, and with his wheat-colored hair and eyebrows he looked, Rachel thought, like the old Vikings might have looked on their sea-going ships. "What's the matter?" she asked.

"Just that we've never tried to make muskets before," Bradford said, "but General Washington wants me to try it."

"We'll get it, Pa," Micah said. He was a soft-spoken young man who talked with slow speech, unlike his brother Dake, who rattled off like a preacher. Micah chewed thoughtfully on a bit of the lamb and then nodded. "It'll just take a little longer than we thought."

Sam listened as they talked about the problems of turning the foundry into a musket factory. Finally he broke in impatiently. "Pa, I want to join the army."

"I believe you've mentioned that before," Daniel said dryly, "about a thousand times at the last count."

"Well, Dake's there, and he's only two years older than I am."

"Sam, we're not going to discuss this anymore—not at the table."

"But, Pa, James Seely signed up yesterday, and I'm two months older than he is."

"That is between him and his parents. This is between you and me."

"The war might be over before I get a chance at it."

A cloud crossed Daniel Bradford's face, and he said, "I doubt that, son. I very much doubt that." He put his fork down, leaned back in his chair, and stared at this younger son of his. His thoughts went back to the time in England when he had served in the cavalry of King George. He remembered the blood and agony and death . . . and he knew that this young son of his had no idea of what being a soldier really meant. He also understood the yearnings of youth for excitement and color and now said, "I know life's dull for you, Sam, but your first job is to get an education."

"You can't fight the lobsterbacks with a Latin book, Pa," Sam protested.

Micah listened quietly as Sam argued sturdily, knowing that his father would never give in. Micah, himself, had been under pressure to join the army. Many young men of his age had already signed up, and a few had already taunted him for being a coward. Yet something in him refused to join in the clamor to shake off the shackles of England. Dake, his identical twin, was like a brand fully ablaze. Already he was serving with Washington in the Continental Army, but Micah was a young man who thought slowly and somewhat more profoundly than his brother Dake. He finally said, "There's lots to do around here, Sam. You can help the army more by making muskets. Anybody can carry one, but the Colonies have to buy guns made in Europe."

"You don't care about the war, Micah," Sam said almost angrily.

"That's enough, Sam!" Daniel Bradford's voice clamped a silence on the room. When he spoke in that tone, everyone knew that it was not wise to push the thing any further. Daniel stared at Sam, daring him to speak, then when Sam tactfully kept the silence, he said, "We'll speak no more about this. You understand?"

"Yes, Pa." Rebellion ran through every line of Sam's body, but he understood his father well enough to keep his peace—at least for now.

"Oh, I forgot to tell you," Rachel said. "A note came from Marian Rochester today." As soon as she spoke she saw her father's head suddenly lift and knew that the others had not missed the attention that the name had for their father. "I'll get it." She got up, left the room, and came back with a small slip of paper. They all watched as he unfolded it, and all three of them had their own ideas about their father's relationship with Marian Rochester, though he had never spoken a word to them about it.

None of them actually knew how Mrs. Rochester and their father felt about each other. Outwardly they were polite, but there were rumors around and they had heard them. Rachel thought suddenly of her father's early life back in England. She knew the story well. He and his sister, Lyna Lee, were orphaned at an early age and had become indentured servants of the Rochester family. Leo Rochester, the oldest son, had developed a lust for Lyna Lee Bradford and a hatred for Daniel, who had stood against him, even as a servant. Rachel also had heard fragments of the story from her father—and some from her aunt, Lyna Lee Gordon. The two had been deceived, and Daniel had been driven away from the Rochester household and cast into prison. Lyna had been forced to run away to avoid Leo's attentions. Daniel and Lyna had been separated for years, and through the cruel lies of Leo Rochester each had believed the other dead. To escape dying in prison Daniel had accepted Rochester's offer and followed Leo to Virginia as an indentured servant for seven years. Only recently had the two had a spectacular reunion. Lyna Lee Bradford was now Lyna Lee Gordon, the wife of Colonel Leslie Gordon of King George's troops that had come to force the Colonies into submission.

But more than this Rachel thought of how Leo had become determined to marry the daughter of a wealthy Bostonian, John Frazier. Her name was Marian, and when she had come to visit Leo's plantation, Daniel had fallen in love with her—or so Rachel guessed. Her father never spoke of such a thing, but there was something in his manner toward Marian Rochester that had caught the quick-eyed girl's attention. Now, whenever the two met, Rachel always studied them closely. Her mother had died at the birth of Sam, and her father had never remarried. Rachel had decided it was because he was in love with Marian Rochester and, loving her, he could never marry another woman.

Unaware of his daughter's scrutiny, Daniel looked up from the note and put his eyes on Sam. "Marian says the plumbing you fixed for her won't work. You'll have to go tomorrow to fix it."

"All right, Pa." Sam was always ready to get out of school and said, "I thought of a few new ways to improve it. It may take all day."

A sudden smile turned the corners of Daniel Bradford's lips upward. "I was sure you'd find some way to get out of that Latin lesson," he said.

After the meal was over, Sam helped Rachel clean up while Micah and Daniel retired to the study to work on drawings and to talk about the problems of manufacturing the muskets. Sam complained loudly about the injustice of life, primarily because he was not allowed to join the army as he wanted to.

"I hope you never have to go in the army," Rachel said. Sadness came to her eyes then and she said, "I feel so sorry for Jeanne. Here she and Dake get married, and the first thing he does is run off to fight."

"Why, a man's got to stand for what he believes," Sam protested.

The two argued for some time, and finally Sam said, "Rachel—?" He hesitated for a moment, then reached up and clawed at his hair, leaving it to fall over his face. Brushing it back he said, "Do you notice how Pa always looks kind of—well, funny, every time anybody mentions Marian Rochester?"

Quickly Rachel shot a glance at her younger brother. He seemed totally caught up with hunting, fishing, and inventing things, but now she saw a worried expression on his smooth countenance. "Why, he's just interested in people, I guess."

"It's more than that, isn't it?" Sam turned a dish around in his hand, dried it thoroughly, then put it on the shelf. Turning to her he said, "I had a fight last week. Tim Denton said something about them."

"About Pa and Marian?"

"Yes, and I busted him for it. He won't say that again, at least when I'm around." He turned to her and chewed on his lower lip nervously. "It makes me feel kind of funny."

"Well, you don't have to worry about Pa or Marian. They're both fine Christians. And besides, she's married. But people have wagging tongues. That Mrs. Denton's got a tongue long enough to sit in the living room and lick the skillet in the kitchen!" she exclaimed vehemently. "I'd like to pull it out!" Anger flashed in her green eyes, then she turned to Sam and calmed herself. "Don't worry about it, Sam."

"Well, *I'll* never get into a mess like that!"

"You don't know what you'll get into," Rachel remarked, and suddenly her shoulders seemed to slump.

"Well, I won't!"

"Let him that thinketh he standeth take heed lest he fall," Rachel quoted. "That's what the Bible says." Then she reached out and mussed his hair again fondly. "How about another piece of pie?" She took his mind off the problem, but she, herself, was troubled by what Sam had said, and as the two sat there eating the remnants of the apple pie she wondered what would come of it.

      🌞   🌞   🌞

The morning sun filtered through the tall window composed of small triangles of glass. The triangles broke up the yellow light into fragments as it fell on the silver and gold vessels that adorned the white tablecloth of the table where two men and a woman sat. A black servant moved around them, attending to their needs, his dark eyes watchful to anticipate their needs before they asked.

Marian Rochester ate sparingly of the eggs and fruit on the china plate before her and noticed that her husband, Leo, ate even less. *He doesn't look well*, she thought, noting his features were somehow gaunt yet puffy at the same time. Leo was a big man who until recently had been overweight. He was still somewhat fatter than usual, but the white shirt he wore was not as tight around his neck, and she knew that he had lost weight. She had asked him several times if he was ill, but he had always snapped at her, and now she dare not say more.

Matthew Bradford sat at the table too. He was the oldest son of Daniel Bradford, and at the age of twenty bore little resemblance to either his father or his twin brothers or Sam, for that matter. He was slender with brown hair and blue eyes, and he had none of the heavy muscular strength of the Bradfords. Looking across at Leo he said, "This might not be a good day for a visit, sir. Are you sure you feel up to it? You don't look well."

Rochester blinked and cast a warning glance at his wife, but he managed a smile and shook his head. "Just a little under the weather. I've been looking forward to it, Matthew. I've got some new prints in my study I'll show you after breakfast. I think you'll be interested in them. They came earlier this week on the *Argosy*.

Marian sipped her tea, listening quietly as the two men talked of art, and thought of the strangeness of the situation. She had married Leo Rochester in a romantic moment and had lived to regret it. She had learned quickly that he was a brutal man, for he treated her little better, if as well, as his fine horses. She knew also that she should have married Daniel Bradford, even though he was only an indentured servant at the time. This thought she could not bear, and even as it arose she thrust it away and tried to concentrate on the talk of drawing and painting and famous artists.

Studying the two, she saw the resemblance between the two men. She thought again of the painting of her husband when he was Matthew Bradford's age, and at that age he had looked exactly as did the young man sitting across from her. The tragic irony, of course, was that Leo was the father of Matthew Bradford. She had learned the story from Leo himself, told from his point of view, and then Daniel had told her the rest. After Leo had come to America, he had been attracted to a young woman, a servant in the house named Holly Blanchard. He had forced his attentions on her, and then when Holly became pregnant he cast her off without a thought. Daniel had married Holly out of pity and had given her child his name. He had never told Matthew, and it had been only recently that Leo had discovered that he actually had a son.

Marian sat there looking at the two as they spoke about art, and finally when she arose they stood with her. "Shall I bring coffee to the drawing room, Leo?"

"Not now," Leo said brusquely. "We have a lot of talking to do. Maybe later." He turned and left the dining room.

Matthew, however, paused long enough to smile and say, "Thank you for the fine breakfast, Mrs. Rochester."

Something about his smile touched Marian, for there was a gentleness in this young man that Leo lacked. "Since I didn't cook it, I can hardly take credit, but thank you, Matthew."

The two men went to Leo's study, a rectangular-shaped room sheathed in glowing walnut, furnished with a rosewood desk, Windsor chairs, and several fine pictures on the wall.

"Here we are. You sit here, and we'll put them on this easel," Leo said. He pulled a print from the large leather case on his desk, set it on the easel, and said, "Now, look at the lines of that. That's what I call real drawing! What do you think?"

The two men talked for a long time about the drawings that Leo produced slowly. Leo wanted to make the moment last, for he was a cunning man. He knew he had to convince Matthew that taking the name of Rochester was his one chance at a life filled with fame, success, and money.

As Matthew looked at the prints, he thought of the strangeness of his situation. How few young men had the chance to become rich without lifting a hand! After his brief visit to Fairhope, he now understood well how his mother had been forsaken. When he had confronted Leo, he had not denied it. Leo had pleaded that he did not know there was a child to come and was relieved to see that Matthew did not seem to harbor ill will.

Ever since his youth, Leo Rochester had been a man to seize things for himself. Through his trickery and skills of manipulation, he had honed his selfishness almost into a fine art. He had taken what he wanted without thought and, being wealthy, had indulged his every whim. But now the one thing he wanted the most he could not have. Marian had produced no children, no heir to carry on his name, and now this young man sitting there, so much like himself at an earlier age and even now, Leo desperately wanted to claim.

Finally, he hesitated, then said, "I've been feeling a little ill these days. You probably have noticed?"

"Why, yes I have, Leo. Have you seen a doctor?"

"Oh yes, but what do they know? I know what I need." Leo put his full attention on Matthew and said intently, "Sunny Italy—that's what I need. Have you ever been there?"

"No, but I've heard about it all my life, though."

"That's where all the great masters painted. With so many museums there, you could go for years and not see them all." Leo went on describing the glories of art that abounded in Italy, then finally took a deep breath. "Come with me, Matthew," he said quietly but with a steady force. When he saw the surprise wash across the young man's face he pressed him, "I need you. We could leave next week. There's a ship leaving Boston for the Continent."

"Why, I can't do that, Leo."

"Why not? What's holding you here?"

For one moment Matthew could not answer. The truth of the matter was that he longed to leave Boston. He was tired of the place, and the thought of going back to the Continent was enticing. Still, there was something that rebelled against the thought of giving up his name, and he knew this was on Leo's mind. He hesitated for one moment, then shook his head. "Well, I need a little time, Leo. Actually," he said tentatively, "I'm going to New York."

"New York? Whatever for!" Leo exclaimed. "That'll be the scene of the next battle, don't you know that?"

"Yes . . . I expect you're right about that." Matthew knew, as did everyone, that General Washington had turned New York into an armed camp. He also knew that the British who had fled to Halifax would return soon with a powerful force. New York would be fought over as two dogs fight over a bone.

"I have a friend, a man I met in England. He's a Dutchman," Matthew said slowly. "His name is Jan Vandermeer. We became great friends in England, although he's older than I, about fifty. He's a great painter, Leo, although he's never been recognized, and he's living in New York now with some relatives." Matthew's face lit up and he said, "I received a letter from him recently, and he asked me to come and visit with him. He said he'd like to teach me a few things. It's a great opportunity."

Disappointment rose in Leo, but he kept his voice even. "Well, of course, that would be fine, but there are so many fine artists in Italy that could teach you even more." Then he saw Matthew's face grow stubborn and said at once, "But, of course, I understand young men must have their way. Tell me more about this fellow Vandermeer. . . ."

🔔　　🔔　　🔔

Hearing the sound of banging outside her window, Marian drew back the curtains. Seeing Sam outside doing something to the plumbing, she opened the window and called out, "When you get through,

Sam, come inside. If you're hungry I've got something you might like."

"Won't be long, Mrs. Rochester," he said cheerfully, then turned again to bang on the hot water tank that he had invented and installed. It was a simple enough device—a steel tank with a wood fire box underneath where servants could build a fire. The water was heated in the tank, then ran through pipes that Sam had brought into the house. He was proud of this invention—a duplicate of the one that he had installed in his own house. Finally satisfied that he had solved the problem, he went to the back door and knocked. When Marian answered he said, "My hands are all greasy."

"Come on in—you can wash at the sink."

Sam marched over to the sink and pumped water out. Using the soap Marian furnished, he said, "You know, you ought to have hot water in the kitchen, too."

"Do you think that could be possible?" Marian asked. "It would be lovely."

"I don't see why not. If I can put it in a bathtub, I can put it in the kitchen sink. I'll work on it."

He dried his hands and said, "Are those donkers I smell?"

"Yes, they are. I made them just for you, Sam. I know how much you love donkers." Marian had saved meat leftovers during the last week. Earlier that morning she had chopped them together with bread and apples and raisins and savory spices, then fried them. As Sam sat down, she served it up with boiled pudding, and he ate as if he had not had a bite for days.

"Don't eat so fast, you'll choke yourself," Marian admonished him. She sat there looking at the boy fondly, then said, "I miss my hot bath, Sam. That's the greatest invention in the world, I think. Every house in Boston ought to have one."

"Well, that'll never happen," Sam shrugged. "It costs too much. Only rich people can have their own bathtubs, especially with hot water piped in from the outside."

"I'm glad I'm rich then—at least rich enough to have one of your nice bathtubs." She leaned forward and watched him eat, smiling at his eagerness. "Tell me about things at home. How's Rachel?"

Sam waved his spoon around, gesturing dramatically, as he described his new invention and how Rachel was going to love the potato peeler when he got it perfected. When he finished, she gave him a mug of hot coffee, which he loved, and as he drank it she sat back and listened to his youthful exuberance. When he told her about how his father had refused to let him join the army, she shook her head sympathetically, but inside was thinking, *Good, I hope the awful war's over before Sam joins up.*

For a long time Sam sat there talking with Marian, and finally without warning, in the way of youth, he asked bluntly, "Mrs. Rochester, are you in love with my pa?"

Taken completely aback, Marian's face suddenly grew scarlet. "Why—Sam, what a thing to ask!"

"Well, are you?"

"Why do you bring this up, Sam?" Marian tried to gain control of herself. She could not give him the simple truth, for if she said, "Yes, I am in love with your father," she knew what he would make of that. To gain time she replied, "It's rather impertinent of you to ask such a thing."

Sam stared at her and admired her as he always did. She looked much younger than her forty-one years, with her rich auburn hair, green eyes, and heart-shaped face. He was aware she loved horses, could play the piano, and do all sorts of things. He knew also that she was very unhappy in her marriage, for Leo's reputation was common knowledge to anyone who knew the Rochesters. Now he said lamely, "Well, I just wondered, that's all."

"Have you heard talk?" Marian asked, trying to hide the caution that threatened to make her voice waver.

Sam hesitated, then shook his head. Finally he said, "I've heard some. And you two act funny around each other. I mean, every time you come into a room Pa just kind of—well, he kind of lights up. Why does he do that, do you think, if he's not in love with you?"

Marian knew she had to say something. She breathed a quick prayer for wisdom, then leaned forward and put her hand over Sam's hand, noticing how strong and thick they were—like his father's. "Sam, I'm a married woman, and if you'll think about it, knowing your father's values, you'll understand that your father is the last man on the face of the earth to pursue any interest with a married woman—or anyone else. Isn't that true?"

Sam blinked with surprise, then swallowed hard. "Why, sure it is," he said. He stared down at her hands, so well kept and soft, yet strong on his, and it gave him a feeling of pleasure that she would touch him like this. "I guess I'm just an old blabbermouth like I sure don't want to be." Though he felt embarrassed, he looked up then and said, "You do like him, don't you?"

"Your father and I have admired each other for many years. It all began with my love for horses. He taught me how to ride—or thinks he did." She smiled and then began to tell stories of the time when she had first come to visit the Rochester household in Virginia and Daniel Bradford had been the one who had helped her with her riding. Finally she said quietly, "You were very worried about this, weren't you, Sam?"

"Well, kind of."

"I understand that. Your father is a very attractive man, and he's never married again. He must've loved your mother very much."

Sam glowed with pleasure and said, "I'm glad I asked you. I feel a whole lot better now."

"Well, why don't you talk to me like this more, Sam." Marian squeezed his hand, then folded her own together and said, "You know, I've never had any children. I've always wanted to have a family, of course, as every woman does. Do you suppose I could be a sort of mother to you? Kind of a combination friend and mother? I don't have any practice with sons, especially big ones like you, but I'd like to have you to practice on."

"I . . . I guess that'd be all right," Sam mumbled. The thought pleased him immensely and he said, "I think that would be just fine."

Seeing the pleasure in his face, Marian suddenly rose, leaned over, and kissed him. "There! Now, come along. I'll show you my new filly. She can beat anything in Boston, I think. . . !"

𝔗   𝔗   𝔗

Leo Rochester went about depressed for several days after the day he spent with Matthew. He did not feel well, and the depression over Matthew's refusal to go to Italy made him feel worse. He began to drink, in spite of the doctor's strict orders, and knew that he was making a fool of himself again in the taverns.

"There's got to be a way," he muttered one evening, going down to dinner. He had put the bottle away and felt somewhat better as he entered the dining room. It gave him a sense of security, and he thought, *Maybe this sickness, whatever it is, is leaving. I could live a long time yet.*

Marian was surprised at Leo's attitude. Her father, John Frazier, was so ill he could not leave his bedroom. He was an invalid now, practically confined to his bed, and Leo asked about him, which surprised her. "Why, he's not much better I'm afraid, Leo."

"Too bad." Leo had never given much thought to Frazier's illness, but now it was very real to him. "You think it would help to see another doctor?"

"Why, I doubt it," Marian said. "Dr. Bates knows his case better than any." She longed to ask about Leo's illness, but knew that he would not like it. Encouraged by his manner, she began to speak of small things, and finally she said quite by chance, "Have you heard about the How-lands?"

"Howlands? You mean Abigail Howland and her mother?"

"Yes, I feel so sorry for them. They've lost everything, I think."

"Too bad . . . the Tories haven't fared too well since the patriots took over." He made a grimace and said, "They'd have probably tarred and feathered me if I weren't here in this house. What about the How-lands?"

"Why, they're going to New York."

"Whatever for?" He thought instantly of Matthew and said, "Matthew wants to go there too, he tells me. What's the big advantage in going to New York? The whole place could be blown off by Wash-ington's cannons, or when the British come back they'll probably take it away again."

"Mrs. Howland has a sister-in-law there. She's invited them—a Mrs. Esther Denham."

Leo listened as Marian described the situation, and finally said, "Well, the girl's a beauty—a little bit shop worn. Everyone knows she had an affair with Paul Winslow and maybe with his cousin Nathan, but she's pretty enough. Men will be willing to forget that."

He left the table and moved to the study for a time, finally coming back to ask Marian, who was in the sewing room, "Did you hear when they were leaving, the Howlands, I mean?"

"Right away, I think. Why?"

"Oh, just curious. Matthew was quite taken with her at one time. I thought they might see something of each other when they're both there." He turned and left the room, and a thought that had come to him began to grow. He nourished it for a while, letting it take shape, then finally he said under his breath, "It might work—it just might work. . . !"

6

A Tempting Offer

A SONG SPARROW PERCHED on a branch of a blossoming apple tree just outside of Abigail Howland's bedroom window. She was sitting there stroking her long brown hair listlessly with a brush, and the song caught her attention. Turning her eyes outside she saw among the white, puffy blossoms a bird with his head tilted up throwing his song onto the morning air of May. Something about the joyful song of the bird caught at her, and she thought, *There was a time when I felt like you do and could sing a song. I wonder where it all went?*

Restlessly she turned from the window, tossed her brush down, and rose to head for the door. She stepped outside into the hall of the small house, intending to go to the kitchen, when a knock sounded on the front door. Abigail was in a bad mood, having had a difficult night. She had lain awake tossing restlessly, reaching out with her mind, trying to think of some other way to go with her life. She had come up with no answers, and finally tears of frustration had risen in her eyes and she had buried her face in her pillow, trying to blot out the bleakness of her future.

Moving toward the door when her mother did not appear, she opened it and stood stock still. "Paul!" she gasped with surprise. She was instantly aware that her face was puffy, and that she was wearing a drab brown dress that did nothing for her. At the same time a streak of anger touched her nerves. She held on to the door with one hand, preparing to shut it. "What do you want, Paul?" she demanded in a hard-edged voice.

Paul Winslow stood before her, dressed as if he were on his way to an evening ball. He wore a gray frock coat with a sloping shoulder line, a green double-breasted waistcoat, a pair of fitted dark brown britches, and striped stockings with figures in the form of embroidered clocks. He swept his hat off his head, a felt narrow-brimmed affair, and smiled at her with one eyebrow cocked in a quizzical expression. "Why, Abigail," he said. "Is that any way to talk to your friend and former lover?"

Abigail stared at him almost with hatred and slammed the door—or tried to. Paul Winslow reached out and caught it easily and stood there looking at her. Even as she watched him she was impressed with him. He was one of those men who had a neatness about him, both in feature and in figure. He was of no more than average height, but there was a natural grace in his body—a depth to his chest that hinted at strength. He had a handsome face, and his dark hair lay smoothly in place like a cap. His large brown eyes studied her carefully, well set in the plains of a face smoothly joined to form a pleasing picture. Smiling easily he said, "I thought we might have tea together. We haven't seen each other in a while."

Abigail wanted to strike out at him, but there was something in the man that drew her. They had been lovers for over a year, and yet during that time she had not come to know him at all despite her efforts. She finally stepped back and said, "Well, you can't stand there in the doorway; all the neighbors will be talking."

Paul stepped inside the door, spun his hat in his hand, and tilted his head to one side. "I think they probably said all that could be said about us. We're no longer an item for the gossips, Abby. Now, how about that tea, and if you have any breakfast I'd be glad to share it with you."

Abigail shrugged her shoulders and said, "I'll see what there is. Come along."

Paul Winslow followed Abigail to the kitchen, and the swaying of her body, which he traced with his quick brown eyes, brought back memories of their torrid affair. It had ended when she had forsaken him for Nathan Winslow. This had occurred as a result of Abigail's strongly developed sense of self-preservation. When she had seen that the patriot forces were going to retake Boston from the British, she had immediately switched her allegiance to Nathan, whose family were prominent patriots. Paul had revealed the truth to Nathan, who had been shocked by Abigail's perfidy. Since that time, Abigail had not spoken to Paul, and now as he followed her to the kitchen he regretted it.

"I'll fix tea and some eggs if you like. We have a few left, not many."

Paul nodded agreeably. "Food has been scarce in the city. I thought it was scarce while the rebels were surrounding us, but it seems like all the food supplies have dried up. Boston's not the same as it once was."

Abigail shrugged. "No, it's not." She busied herself gathering the things together for a breakfast of sorts. As she prepared the meal, she listened closely to Paul, who related several humorous incidents of how he had managed to scrape by, even though he was regarded as a Tory.

He had always had the gift of charming her, and she found his conversation amusing after the dreary days she had endured.

Finally the two sat down and ate, and Paul smiled across the table at her. "It's good to see you again, Abigail. I've missed you."

"Have you?"

Ignoring her cold tone, Paul nodded. "Why, of course I have. After all, I've always been very fond of you." Paul took a bite of the scrambled egg, chewed it thoroughly, then swallowed it.

"You have an odd way of showing it."

"Because I revealed your little scheme to Nathan? You would never have been happy with Nathan. He's a holy man, you know, and you're not—"

Abigail's cheeks were suddenly flushed with red, and she said, "That's none of your business anymore, and I'm as holy as you are!"

"Exactly right!" Paul nodded. "Neither of us are good people, Abigail. Perhaps we ought to marry just to spare two other innocent victims from a life of tragedy if they marry us." Paul Winslow was a realist and knew himself to be worldly to the bone. He also knew Abby was no different. "What about it?" he said.

Abigail sat sipping her tea. She put it down, and then stared at him, asking him frigidly, "What about *what*?"

"Why, about us." Reaching across the table, he captured her hand. She tried to withdraw it, but he held it tightly. "Don't fight against me, Abby," he murmured. "As I say, I'm very fond of you. You're one of the loveliest women I know. There's still a great deal of fun to be had in Boston. Or, if you like, we could go to Philadelphia."

"And live on what?" Abigail asked. She jerked her hand back, picked up a piece of bread, and nibbled at it thoughtfully. Her lips curved upward in a bitter smile and she said, "We can't live on love, if that's what it was we had."

"Oh, there are ways. I might have a good day betting. And my family's always good for a touch."

"No thank you, Paul."

Paul leaned back in his chair and studied the girl carefully. Even dressed in a dowdy dress with her hair not fixed, there was a beauty in her that shone forth. Her skin was almost translucent, and there was an attractiveness in the set of her lips and in the shape of her eyes. She had the longest eyelashes he had ever seen, and she knew well how to use them. "What do you intend to do, then?" he demanded finally. "You and your mother aren't doing too well, I take it? I thought I might be able to help a little bit with the finances."

Abigail blinked with surprise. "Well . . . that's kind of you, Paul," she said, "but we're leaving Boston."

"Leaving? Where are you going?"

"New York."

"New York? You'll be caught right in the middle of another battle."

"I know. That's what everyone says, but that's where we're going."

"Why would you want to go to New York?"

"My aunt lives there. My father's sister. She's quite well-off—Mrs. Esther Denham. She's invited us to come and stay with her at her house."

"Quite well-off?" Paul sipped his tea and chewed on that information. "Perhaps elderly and quite infirm—not long for this world? Perhaps a little inheritance might be coming down the way to you and your mother?"

Abigail stared at him with distaste. "You always think of things like that, don't you?"

"Oh, you're just going because you love the dear old lady."

Abigail suddenly grew angry. Her eyes flashed and her lips drew tight. "You haven't a decent bone in your body, Paul Winslow. Not one!"

Winslow suddenly felt ashamed of himself—a rare occurrence for him. "You're right," he said, "the scum of the earth, and you're looking at him. Well, I wish you well, Abigail, you and your mother. Do you need help, money to make the trip to New York?"

Abigail hesitated. "Well . . . I . . . I really do, Paul. We're almost destitute."

"I have a little here. Had a good night at the tables last night." Paul Winslow reached into his inner pocket and pulled out a few coins. He divided them in half and gave some to her. "Partners in this at least." He stood up and said, "Thanks for the breakfast." And when she stood he took her hand and kissed it. "I do wish you well, Abigail. I'm a rotter and always will be, but you know I always thought there was something in you that I'd like to see come out."

Abigail stared at him in bewilderment. "What do you mean by that, Paul?"

"I mean, outwardly you're a diamond—beautiful and all that, and I see you have a hard streak in you—but beneath that I've always thought there was another Abigail." He thought for a moment, his brown eyes considering her carefully. He shrugged finally and smiled. "I guess I'm trying to say there's a sweetness in you somewhere that you've been hiding all these years. You've always been the hard, bright, beautiful Abigail Howland, and that's been enough for me, but anyway, I'd like to see some of that other Abigail."

Abigail followed him to the door and opened it. He took his hat from the peg, settled it firmly on his head, and smiled. "As my cousin Nathan would say, God bless you, Abigail."

He turned and walked briskly away, leaving Abigail to stare after him. She looked at the coins in her hand and wondered for a moment if she was making a mistake. Turning back inside, she shut the door and moved slowly back toward the kitchen, where she sat down and poured herself another cup of tea. For a long time she sat there staring at the wall, then took a deep breath.

"I've got to go, but I'd give anything if I had something more to look forward to than just being a long-term guest at Aunt Esther's house." She had a streak of pride in her, and it galled her to have to accept charity. Finally she rose and began to fix breakfast for her mother.

🜋 🜋 🜋

Abigail's second guest's visit came as even more of a shock than that of Paul Winslow. She had gone to the market and had come back with a few parcels of food. Her mother was sitting in the parlor embroidering when she came in, and called out to Abigail as she passed by. "Abigail, come here a moment, daughter, after you put the groceries down."

Abigail was somewhat surprised but did as she was bidden. When she returned to the small parlor she stopped abruptly, for she found her mother was not alone.

"Why, Mr. Rochester," she said, turning to meet the man who had risen as she entered. "I didn't know you were here."

Leo Rochester was wearing a fancy suit as usual. It was well tailored, but he had lost weight, so it seemed to hang on him, making him look gaunt. When he smiled she saw the hollows in his cheeks and that his eyes were not as bright as she remembered them.

"I took the liberty of coming to call on you, Miss Howland. Your mother and I have been having a very nice talk."

Abigail Howland knew that Leo Rochester was not the kind of man who made calls on uninfluential widows who were having financial problems. Quickly she understood that Leo had come to see her, but she made no mention of it. Instead she sat down, and for some time the three of them sat there as Leo spoke of various things.

Finally Mrs. Howland rose and said, "I'm sorry to be such a poor hostess, but I'm not too well, Sir Leo. If you don't mind, I think I shall leave my daughter to entertain you while I lie down for a time."

Leo rose at once, and a look of compassion came into his gaunt features. "I'm sorry to hear it, Mrs. Howland." He hesitated, then shrugged self-consciously. "I have not been too well myself lately, so I can have some sympathy. Odd how when we have health we don't appreciate it, and when we get sick, immediately we see what a blessing it was."

"That's very true, Sir Leo. Well, you will entertain our guest, daughter?"

"Of course, Mother. Try to get some rest. We'll be leaving tomorrow at ten. It'll be a difficult trip."

After Mrs. Howland left, Leo said, "You're going to New York, I understand."

"Yes, to stay for a time with my aunt."

"So I understand. As a matter of fact, that's why I've come to see you." They were still standing and he turned to say, "Could you sit on this sofa? I have something rather strange to say to you, Abigail—if I may call you by your first name."

"Of course." Abigail took her seat beside Leo on the sofa and turned to face him. She was struck again by the unhealthy pallor of his cheeks and wondered about the nature of his illness. She only knew him slightly, so she asked, "How is your wife, Mr. Rochester?"

"Marian? She's very well; she always is."

The very brevity of his reply strengthened Abigail's understanding of what she already had heard—the two had no marriage at all. Leo Rochester was a well-known rake, and everyone who gave ear to the wagging tongues about the city knew he not only visited the brothels in Boston but throughout the Colonies. She could not understand it, for Marian Rochester was a beautiful woman—however, Abigail had long since given up trying to understand such things. "And how is Matthew Bradford?" she asked.

"Ah, it's about Matthew I've come." Leo leaned forward, an intent look in his eyes. "I don't know how much you know, but you must understand that Matthew is more than an acquaintance." He quickly told her how he had discovered that Matthew was the son of his own blood—the son of a servant in his house. He spoke straightforwardly with some regret in his voice, to be sure, but the regret was that he was unable to convince Matthew to take his name and become his son legally. Finally, Rochester put his hands apart in an eloquent gesture of helplessness. "I've done all that I can to convince the boy to see that he can have a wonderful life if he'll do as I ask."

"But he refuses to leave his family, I take it?"

"Exactly!" Leo grasped his hands together, squeezed them, then shook his head. "It's a fine thing—loyalty to one's family—but he's not like the other Bradfords."

"Not like them in what way?"

"Well, he doesn't *look* like them for one thing, but that's not important. The fact is, the Bradfords are skilled tradesmen. They are blacksmiths and know how to run a foundry. Good people, I dare say. I've had my difficult times with Daniel, of course, but that's neither here nor there." He leaned forward and his eyes became more intent as he spoke almost passionately. "I could do so much for Matthew! He has real talent as an artist. If he would come with me to England and to Italy he could have the best teachers. Why, he could have his works hanging in the National Art Gallery in London."

"Portraits by Matthew Rochester—is that what you're thinking?" Abigail suddenly demanded.

"Exactly! I'll never have another son. He's the only hope I have and . . . and I want my name to go on. He'd be Sir Matthew Rochester, Lord of the estates in England, or he could live in Virginia at Fairhope, my plantation there."

Abigail listened as Rochester spoke on, and she was quite puzzled. Finally she asked, "Why are you telling me all this?"

"Because I think you might help me, and I certainly would be grateful for your help—not just emotionally, but in a financial way."

Immediately Abigail's attention grew sharper. "What could I possibly do for you?"

"I think Matthew's half in love with you, Abigail."

"I'm not so sure about that."

"Well . . . I've watched him pretty closely. That time he was painting your portrait, you were all he could talk about. Not just as a subject, but the times you spent together." Leo tapped his chin thoughtfully with a forefinger and nodded slowly. "I think I know men and women pretty well, and I think I recognize infatuation, at least, when I see it. I'm convinced you've caught his attention."

Abigail thought about those times she had spent with Matthew. She had liked him a great deal, but as far as she was concerned he was not the sort of man she would be permanently interested in. There was not enough money in the Bradford family—but with Sir Leo that was different. She knew he was immensely wealthy, and suddenly a door seemed to open and she said, "What would you want me to do?"

"Make him fall in love with you," Leo said at once. "He's already halfway there. You're a woman who knows how to use men."

Abigail stared at him. "What do you mean by that?"

Leo shook his head. "Well, let's not get upset, shall we? I think most of Boston knows you had an affair with Paul Winslow, and perhaps with his cousin Nathan. You're not a Puritan. I don't mean to be insulting by that, for I'm not the one to point the finger at anyone, but it's true enough, isn't it?"

Abigail flushed and said, "Yes, it's true enough."

"Well, I'm glad to see you are able to listen to reason. Now, here's what I want you to do. You're going to New York and so is Matthew. It would be natural enough for you to see him there. Draw him on, Abigail. You shouldn't have any trouble fanning that spark of interest he has for you. Make him fall in love with you; then you could be of some help to me."

"If you think I can make him do what you can't, that's impossible."

"I don't think so. A man in love doesn't think straight. Why, he may even want to marry you."

"And what would you think about having me for a daughter-in-law?"

"I wouldn't mind in the least," Leo said, smiling cheerfully. "As long as I have a son, I think it would be wonderful for him to have a wife. I'd want grandchildren. You look like a good bearer to me. You and Matthew would have a beautiful son. Think of that. You would be Lady Abigail Rochester one day."

Abigail sat there, her fists clenched tightly together, listening as he painted an enticing future. Finally she looked at him directly in the eye. There was no need to think further about this. She thought briefly about what Paul had said about her having a gentle side to her nature very far down, but she knew that it was very deep indeed.

"What about it, Abigail?"

She knew what her answer would be, but she said, "I'll have to think about it." Her mind was already made up, but she was seeking for better terms.

"Of course." Leo rose and said, "It's a big step. I'll pay your expenses to New York, and if you convince him to do what I ask, you'll never have to want for money again. And, of course, if you marry him you'll be getting a good man."

"When will you have to have an answer?"

"You're leaving for New York tomorrow. I could help with your expenses if I knew by then."

Suddenly Abigail said, her voice tight, "I can't put on an act with you. You know I'm going to do it, don't you?"

A sudden streak of regret filled Leo Rochester's eyes. He stepped closer to her and put his hand on her hand gently. "I don't want to force you to do this. I've done enough to be sorry for in my life. I think you might do me some good, and I think you'd be doing Matthew a great favor—and of course, I think you would be helped too. You've had to fight and struggle for money and position. If you had that, perhaps you might have time to find out what's really inside of you."

Instantly Abigail was shocked, since this was almost the same thing that Paul Winslow had said. Trying not to show her feelings, she said, "It's just a business proposition, Mr. Rochester."

Leo Rochester was not a man of sentiment. He looked down at this girl with the beauty that most women would have given most anything for and saw that she had steeled herself. "Very well," he said quietly. He reached into his pocket and brought out an envelope. "I came prepared to offer you this. There'll be more if you need it. Write me when you get to New York and let me know how things are going."

After Rochester had left, Abigail Howland stood in the hall holding the envelope. It was thick with bills, and she opened it and counted the money. Slowly she put it back, then walked down the hall. She thought about Matthew, his innocence, and a thought came to her. *He'll be easy. He is in love with me, or almost so.* Somehow the thought disturbed her, and she tried to shake it off, but it came again and again. She knew there was no other way out, and finally she shook her head and said angrily, "God, forgive me, what else can I do? We've got to live, Mother and I, and after all, it is the best thing for Matthew. He'd be a fool to choose a life of poverty and obscurity when he could have a title and the money and power that goes with it."

Such thinking did not assure her, however, and there was discomfort and almost pain in her eyes as she slowly made her way to her room and sat down to stare out the window. The bird with its joyful song was gone—only empty branches now—and she sat there staring at them for a long time.

PART TWO

SUMMER OF INDEPENDENCE

June—July 1776

7

DAMSEL IN DISTRESS

THE SEA HAD ALWAYS FASCINATED Katherine, but on the morning of June 8, she paid no heed to the beauty that lay before her as she approached the harbor. A flight of screaming gulls wheeled around overhead, descending and opening their mouths wide as they clustered around her, hoping for a morsel of food. Several times she had brought bread crusts and scraps with her, for it had delighted her to watch the aerial acrobats swoop down to snatch fragments from her hand. One small boy had shown her a trick that had fascinated her. He had put a piece of bread on his head, and the gulls had simply scooped it off neatly. Grinning at her with a gap-toothed smile, he had said, "You want to try it, lady?"

Now as Katherine walked slowly toward the piers, she glanced out over the harbor, noting the stately naval vessels anchored there. A magnificent ship of the line had drawn in closely, the cannons run out and gleaming dully in the late afternoon sunlight. The water lapping at the shoreline as she approached was as clear as wine. Twenty feet out it turned into a pale green, and out farther still, into a dark blue. The horizon lay before her, sharp and level as the blade of a knife, and the light blue sky was dotted with high-flying, fluffy clouds that covered the sun from time to time, then let the bright rays pierce the earth as it rolled beneath them. Katherine breathed deeply, inhaling the salt tang of the sea unconsciously, for her thoughts were on her father and her uncle.

For over a week she had come every day to the *St. George*, but each time she had been turned away by the officers. Nevertheless, she had stubbornly made her way to the headquarters to see General Howe, but with the same result. A steady diet of failure to convince him to change Banks' orders had dampened her spirits. She knew now only a dull, glowing anger at the system that would allow helpless men to perish for lack of simple care that was readily available.

81

"Good morning, miss." A thin fisherman with a black stocking cap on his head and a striped jersey greeted her cheerfully. "Be you going back to the *St. George* again?"

"Yes, please."

The fisherman nodded his head, reached out, and helped the young woman into the bobbing dory. When she was seated, he sat down and grasped the oars. Shoving off with one of them, he aimed the small craft at the hulk anchored a hundred yards offshore. As he rowed with the skill of a lifetime of practice, he studied the young woman surreptitiously. Through half-hooded eyes he took in the simple blue dress, the bonnet that half shaded her eyes, and the white lace at her throat. *A good-looking wench, I'll say that for her*, he thought, taking regular strokes with the oars. *Too bad about her pa and her uncle—but that's the way it is in a war. Don't see that it'd do the British any harm to let her take a little food in to her folks* .... Aloud he said, "I hope your pa and your uncle be doing better today. Too bad they had to get caught."

Katherine gave him a slight smile. "Why ... thank you. I don't suppose I'll be able to see them, but I've got to try." She sat there trying to think of new ways to convince the authorities to allow her to see her father, but nothing came to her. This was not a new thought, for day after day and night after night she had struggled with her hatred for Banks. She had seen him three times since he had closed the door to her visits, and each time she had to struggle to keep the white hot anger that rose within her concealed as much as possible. Even now as the dory skimmed across the sprightly white caps, she thought of his grinning red face, and her fist clenched tightly on the handle of the basket she carried. Almost with a physical effort she forced the thought of the surgeon out of her mind and tried her best to think more positively.

The dory arrived at the side of the ship near the wooden ladder, and, as usual, a lieutenant was waiting at the top to help her in. The fisherman said, "I'll just wait here, miss."

"Very well," Katherine said. She allowed the lieutenant to hand her aboard. His name was Smith, and glancing at his face she saw regret there and knew what he was going to say. He was a tall, thin officer with black hair and dark brown eyes. He was homely enough, but he had always been polite to her each time she had come aboard.

"I'm sorry, Miss Yancy, but you made your trip for nothing again, I'm afraid."

"Couldn't I see the captain?" Katherine pleaded.

"Miss, I'll have to tell you. The captain asked me not to bring you to him. There's really nothing he can do, Miss Yancy," Smith said regretfully. "In the service the surgeon has total control over the sick prisoners, and Major Banks has given strict orders that your father and his brother are not to be allowed any visitors. I'm sorry, but that's the way it is."

A huge bird flew over suddenly, and Katherine glanced up startled. "What's that bird?" she inquired.

Looking up, Smith took it in with a casual eye. "That? Why, that's an albatross, miss."

"Albatross? I never saw one of those."

"Supposed to be bad luck for sailors sometimes," Smith remarked. "Sailors are a superstitious lot, you know." He moved his feet uncertainly and said, "I could offer you a cup of tea, Miss Yancy, but there's no hope of seeing your father."

"Will you at least see that he gets this food?"

Katherine looked up and there was such anxiety in her gray-green eyes that Smith could not find it in his heart to say no. Banks had left strict orders that no food was to be given to the prisoners, but Smith was an independent sort for a lowly lieutenant. Leaning forward he took the basket and whispered, "I'm not supposed to do it, Miss Yancy—but I'll do the best I can. It'll be the worst for me if I get caught, but I'm sorry for your trouble."

Katherine's eyes glistened with sudden tears at the man's unexpected kindness. "Thank you, Lieutenant Smith," she whispered and dashed the tears away quickly. She gave him a tremulous smile and said, "May the Lord bless you for your kindness to my poor father and my uncle."

"Well . . . it's little enough to do," Smith mumbled. He was stricken with the girl's beauty, but having a wife and two children at home, he quickly put any romantic thoughts out of his mind. Glancing around he saw that several of the deckhands were watching and wondered how he would explain the basket of food to them.

Katherine said quickly, "I'll be going back then, but I'll be here tomorrow to try again."

Smith helped her down the ladder and watched as the oarsman pulled the dory away and made for the land. Turning around with the basket in his hand he caught one husky sailor staring at him with a broad grin on his face. With a voice that roared he said, "You don't have enough to do, Jenkins? I'll see if I can find a few more extra jobs for you." He watched with some regret as Jenkins hurried away, thinking, *He's a good man, and I shouldn't be ragging him like that.* He carried the basket at once to his quarters and concealed it, his mind humming with schemes on how he might get the food belowdecks to the Yancys.

As the dory reached shore, Katherine stepped out and handed the fisherman a few coins and thanked him. He touched his forelock quickly and said, "I suppose I'll be seeing you tomorrow, miss?"

"Probably so," Katherine nodded. She turned and made her way from the harbor, walking quickly through the town. The thought that her father and her uncle might get some of the food cheered her, and she thought, *Well, there are some good men among the British, at least. They're not all like Major Banks.*

When she reached headquarters she marched into the commander's office. The lieutenant who greeted her said at once, "Now, Miss Yancy, do we have to go through this again?"

"I would like to see General Howe."

Lieutenant Redman shook his head. "I've explained that eight days in a row, I think. The general cannot see you, miss. He's a very busy man, and even if he did see you he would give you the same answer. He cannot countermand the standing orders of the surgeon."

Katherine stood there helplessly, knowing that Lieutenant Redman was right. She turned and walked out of the room frustrated and angry as usual.

After she left, Redman heard the voice of the general calling him, and he entered the office immediately. Before the general could speak he said, "That young woman was here again, General—Miss Yancy."

Howe looked up and ran his hand through his thick brown hair. He was not wearing his wig, and he looked much younger. "She doesn't give up easily, does she, Redman?"

"No, sir." Redman hesitated then said, "I really can't see what harm it would do to let her see her father."

"I know. I feel the same, but we have a chain of command. Once I start making exceptions, there'd be no order left in the ranks." But Howe's tone was regretful, and for one moment he was tempted to break his rule. He was, however, basically a military man tied into a rigid system, and he would not break that system except with great provocation. The picture of the young woman's face swam before his eyes, but he said with resolve, "I just can't. We must keep order, Lieutenant."

Outside the headquarters building Katherine walked slowly. There was nothing now to do except go back to her room at the inn or spend the rest of the day walking aimlessly through the town. She had no friends, and loneliness bore upon her constantly. Halifax was no more than a small fishing village, but now had been stuffed to capacity by the influx of sailors, soldiers, and civilians who had fled from Boston.

For half an hour she walked along the main street, looking without interest into the shop windows. She was accosted more than once by soldiers attracted by her fresh beauty, but she ignored them as if they were invisible. Finally she straightened her shoulders, and a steely light came into her eyes. Her lips grew tight and she said, "I won't be treated this way!"

With resolution, she turned and headed back toward the headquarters. She found the building used for a hospital easily enough by simply asking a passing private, then marched up the steps to the plain, square brick building that had once been a barn of some kind. When she stepped inside, she found herself in a gloomy room whose darkness was broken only by some light coming from a few narrow dirty windows high up. The floor was made of stone, however, and echoed hollowly as she walked across it toward a desk where a youthful corporal sat watching her.

"Yes, miss, can I help you?"

"I need to see Major Banks."

"Why, yes, ma'am. If you'll come this way. His office is right over here."

Katherine followed the corporal to a room that had evidently been added. It was made of rough lumber, and when the corporal knocked on the door she heard Banks call, "What is it?"

"A visitor, sir. A young lady."

Katherine stood there, and when the door opened she saw satisfaction fill the pale blue eyes of Banks. "Ah, Miss Yancy. Please step inside my office. That'll be all, Corporal."

Apprehension filled Katherine at once, but without a word she stepped into the office. It contained a desk, a cot, a rough bookcase containing several worn volumes, and a washstand. Somehow the major had obtained a bright green rug that added a touch of color, and a window had been made—apparently as an afterthought—to let in the red beams of afternoon sunlight.

"Major, I've come to plead with you again," Katherine said.

"Well, now, sit down. Here, take this chair, and I'll sit on the bed. But first we'll have a little refreshment."

"Oh no, I couldn't really!"

"Nonsense!" Banks said jovially. "I just had some flip made. I think you'll like it." He took a glass decanter from the table, found two stoneware cups, and poured a liberal amount into each. "There," he said, handing her one of them. "Now, you'll find that the best flip this side of England!"

"Really, I couldn't!" Katherine said and saw his eyes grow tight with anger. "I'm not used to such things." She set the glass down and said, "Major, I've come to plead with you about my father. I haven't seen him in over a week. Please let me see him."

Banks drank the contents of his cup, belched slightly, and gasped as the fiery liquor bit at his throat. He blinked his eyes and came up off the bed. Moving over, he picked up her cup and said, "Well, if you're not going to drink this we can't have it go to waste. Aye?" He drank it down, then said, "All the sweeter for the touch of your fingers on it, Miss Yancy. Or may I call you Katherine?"

Katherine was aware that Banks was already drunk. He had the veins of a drinker in his face, and his movements were uncertain. He pronounced his words carefully, as drunks do, thinking that they are disguising their condition. Knowing that he might deny her request again, she determined to keep trying. "If you won't let me see him, would you at least allow my father and my uncle to receive the things I've brought?"

"Well, we will have to talk about that, won't we?" Banks was standing beside her, and he put the glass down, then turned to face her fully. His uniform was dirty and stained with food, and there was a carelessness about him not seen in most British officers. "Well now, my dear." Suddenly Banks reached down, took her hand, and pulled her to her feet. He held her hand as she struggled to free herself. Then without warning he threw his arms around her and kissed her.

Katherine twisted her head furiously. His lips, however, pressed against her own, and she was thoroughly disgusted. As he started to run his hands over her body she shoved him away with a desperate burst of strength. Banks staggered backward, but his drunken eyes were filled with lust, and he came back at her again. At once she stepped to the door and opened it. Banks stopped abruptly, for she said calmly, "I'll scream if you come any closer, Major Banks!" He stopped where he was and looked at her, befuddled. "I'll come back tomorrow when you're feeling better. I must warn you I intend to take this as far as to General Howe."

"That won't do you any good. You've already tried it," Banks muttered. "Now, why don't you be reasonable, my dear. You want something and I want something. We can make a bargain, you and me."

Disgust filled Katherine, and she turned at once without a word and left the hospital.

Banks stared after her, noting that the corporal was watching as well. "Keep your mind on your business, Corporal!" he snarled and moved back inside, slamming the door. He poured himself another drink, gulped it down, then nodded as he muttered, "She'll come around. Yes, she will, or I'll see that her father and uncle rot!"

🐯　　　🐯　　　🐯

Clive Gordon had no official standing in the British army, but since he had performed in a semiofficial way at Fort Ticonderoga under his father's orders, he had been accepted as a welcome civilian volunteer in the regiment. He entered the officers' mess and noted that the general was not there. Taking his seat beside Lieutenant James Steerbraugh, he asked, "Where's General Howe today?"

"High strategy, Clive, my boy." Steerbraugh nodded wisely and winked at him. "I expect he's having a meeting with Mrs. Loring to plan how to take New York away from the rebels."

Clive glanced around and saw grins on the faces of several of the other young officers. It was amazing to him how a man of General Howe's stature could lower himself to an affair with the wife of a subordinate. Everyone knew about Mrs. Loring. The patriots even wrote crude songs about them.

The two young men sat there speaking about the strategy that had brought them this far, and Steerbraugh said finally, "I just don't see how we've been beaten. We've got a well-trained army, and Washington's got nothing but a rabble in arms, mostly untrained militia. How did they beat us out of Boston? Why didn't General Gates lead us out?"

"You may have forgotten how far it is to England, James," Clive said. "It takes a great deal of money to get one British soldier here to the Colonies. If we lose him, another one has to be sent. That's double the money. Furthermore, he's got to be fed, clothed, and given ammunition. All that is straining the empire pretty thin to keep this stupid revolution fought back. If Gates had marched us out and we had lost our army, what would have happened then? Why, England would have lost her share in the New World."

Steerbraugh argued vehemently that the ragged troops of Washington should not beat the trained soldiers of England.

"They did pretty well at Breed's Hill and on the way back from Concord, in Lexington."

"Nothing to the purpose," Steerbraugh argued, waving his hand with disdain. "The cowards shot at our men from behind fences at Concord and Lexington. And we had to fight our way up that hill to get them when they were entrenched behind embattlements at Breed's Hill."

"Then we never should have gone after them," Clive said. That was his firm judgment, as it was many of the officers. He knew that General Gates, who had led the attack had been badly shaken at the terrible losses. "I think it will be a long time before any British officer leads troops against the Americans behind embattled positions."

The two were interrupted by two officers who came in and took their places. Steerbraugh said, "I see that the surgeon is drunk again."

"That's pretty well a chronic condition, isn't it, James?"

The surgeon sat down, and it was obvious to every officer at the table that he had been tipping the bottle again heavily. He was always an obnoxious sort of man, and when he was in his cups his temperament got even worse. Soon he began talking about a young lady who he was trying to force his attentions on.

"Who's he talking about, James?" Clive asked.

"A young woman named Katherine Yancy. She's come all the way from Boston to help her father and her uncle, I believe. They're prisoners on the *St. George*." He glanced with disgust at the surgeon and said scathingly, "Banks can't keep his eyes off the young woman, and word has it that he won't let her see her people until she gives him what he wants."

"That's pretty foul!" Clive said sharply. "Why does the general put up with the man's debauchery?"

"You know Howe—he's a stickler for organization. He won't go over his surgeon's head." Clive sat there and toyed with his food, listening to the surgeon as he boasted about his coming conquest. The man's ribald manner ignited an anger in Clive, and he left so as to avoid listening to the rest of the surgeon's crass boastings.

Leaving the headquarters, Clive walked along the streets that were now growing dark, making his way to the small house that his father, Colonel Leslie Gordon, had managed to rent for his family while they waited for the British troops to move into New York as was previously planned. When he stepped inside he was greeted by his mother, Lyna Lee, who came to him at once and kissed him.

"Why, you should've come back earlier, Clive. We waited supper for you." Lyna Lee Gordon, at forty-four, was a beautiful woman. She had hair the color of dark honey and large gray-green eyes set in her oval face. She had clean, wide-edged lips, a firm chin, and a fair, smooth skin. She was wearing a pale plum-colored dress that set off her figure admirably and laughed as she said, "You didn't miss much at dinner, though. You probably had better food at the officers' mess."

"I doubt that, Mother," Clive smiled. He was, at six three, much taller than she was and looked down at her with fondness.

She studied him as they moved into the kitchen where the family was sitting at a round wooden table. He was lean with long arms and legs, and he had reddish hair and cornflower blue eyes in his tapered face. Lyna noted as she sat down that there was still a sadness or a regret that his open features revealed. *He's still sad over Jeanne Corbeau*, Lyna thought and felt a touch of regret that her son had lost what he considered the love of his life to her nephew Dake Bradford.

"Sit down and tell us how we're going to win this war, Clive," said David Gordon, the sixteen-year-old son of Leslie and Lyna. He had dark brown hair that was crisply curled, and brown eyes, alert and set in a square face. He was not tall, not over five ten, and was very lean and quick in all that he did. Now he threw questions at Clive constantly.

"Leave your brother alone!" Colonel Gordon said. He smiled at his younger son, shook his head, then added, "You talk like a magpie." At fifty, Leslie Gordon looked no more than thirty-five. He was tall, well-formed, with reddish hair and blue eyes. He glanced over now at Clive and winked. "This one's been pestering me to let him join the army."

"Let him do it, Father," Clive said. "I'd like to have him under my thumb for a while."

"Are you going to join the army, too, Clive?" Grace asked. The only daughter of the family, at the age of eighteen, had the same dark honey blond hair and attractive eyes as her mother. She spoke of Clive's plan— whether to make the army his career, even though he had studied to become a doctor. "I wish you wouldn't," she said. "You can be a fancy society doctor in London."

"Then I could have lots of money to buy you pretty dresses, Grace," Clive grinned. He sat down, and the family talked for some time about affairs.

Finally, David demanded, "When is General Howe going to take New York?"

"It might not be quite that easy, son," Leslie Gordon said mildly.

"Why, everybody knows we're going to have enough soldiers to wipe the rebels off the face of the earth," David said impulsively. His eyes shone with excitement as he said, "I wish I could be in the army. Why don't you let me sign up, Father?"

Leslie Gordon ignored his question as Clive shook his head, saying, "I'm just not sure yet about what to do." He sat there for a while, enjoying the pleasure of being with his family, then his thoughts ran back to the surgeon and he frowned unconsciously.

"What's the matter, Clive?" Lyna Lee had caught the expression on Clive's face, and being sensitive to his moods she asked, "Is something wrong?"

He glanced over toward Grace and David, who were arguing loudly over some insignificant matter, and lowered his voice as he spoke to his parents. "Something happened that angered me—a matter about surgeon Banks." He saw his father frown and said, "He's not much of an officer, is he?"

"Well, surgeons are a little bit different. They don't have to keep the rules quite as rigidly as the rest of us—but he's really not much of a surgeon."

"Apparently not." Clive had worked with the army some, although he had little contact with Banks himself. Banks was a newcomer to the regiment, having arrived just before the troops were evacuated from Boston. Since they had been at Halifax, Clive had offered to help with the sick men several times, but Banks, jealous of his position, had simply shuffled him off.

"What's he done, Clive?" Lyna asked.

"There's a young woman come from Boston. Her father and her uncle are prisoners on the *St. George*," Clive replied. He drummed his fingers on the table, studying them for a moment, then looked up, a heated anger in his eyes. "She's an attractive young woman from what I hear, and Banks won't let her see her people—unless she—"

Seeing her son's embarrassment Lyna said bluntly, "Unless she gives in to his desires?"

"That's exactly it! A rotten thing—but then he's a rotten man, I think," Clive said. He sat there for some time and the three spoke of the situation. Then Clive rose and said, "I'm going to study for a while. Good night." He leaned over, kissed his mother, nodded with a smile to his father, then left the room.

As soon as he was gone, Lyna helped the other children clean up the kitchen, then she and Leslie retired to their small bedroom. She undressed for bed, put on a cotton nightgown, got into the featherbed, and waited as he hung up his uniform carefully, then got into bed beside her. They lay there for a while speaking quietly, then he picked up her hand and stroked it, kissed it fondly, and she moved closer to him. "I'm worried about Clive," she whispered. The walls were thin in the house, and she could still hear David and Grace talking about something." I don't think he's ever gotten over his love for Jeanne Corbeau."

"He ought to go back to England and get away from here. Maybe he could forget her." Leslie turned to her then and pulled her close. "You ought to go back with him. You and David and Grace."

Lyna put her arms around him, pulled his head closer, and kissed him. "No, I won't leave you," she said. "If I do, one of these attractive American girls will grab you. Leave a good-looking thing like you loose over here in the wilds of America? Not likely!"

Leslie laughed quietly, ran his hand down the smoothness of her back, savored the touch of his lovely wife, then he said, "You really ought to do it. We'll win New York well enough."

"Will we?" she asked anxiously.

"Yes, England's sending the biggest expeditionary force in history over to win this revolution. I'm afraid Daniel and his friends are a lost cause." He held her for a moment tightly, then said, "I'm sorry about that. I think a lot of Daniel."

Lyna was grieved, but there was nothing she could do about that. She whispered, "God will take care of them." And then she drew his head forward and kissed him, moving against him.

8

"LOVE WON'T BE PUT INTO A LITTLE BOX?"

AFTER A RESTLESS NIGHT, Clive Gordon rose and found himself still thinking of the young woman that Major Banks had boasted of. Ordinarily he might have ignored such a thing, disgusted as he was, but in truth he was still suffering over the disappointing loss of Jeanne Corbeau. At the age of twenty-three Clive Gordon had never suffered a casualty to his emotional life, and as he set out his toilette to shave, he let his mind run over those days not very long in the past. Working up a rich lather he applied it to his cheeks. Then he picked up a razor and, yanking a hair out of his head, tested the sharpness of the blade. Grunting with satisfaction, he carefully drew the blade down his cheek, wiped the lather on a towel, then gave his left cheek the same treatment. As he worked carefully around his throat, he muttered, "He's a bully boy, Banks is. A disgrace to the uniform he wears!" He continued thinking moodily of the situation, and by the time he had finished shaving and brushing his rather long reddish hair back with a pair of military brushes, Clive found himself growing more and more dissatisfied with the girl's plight.

"What was her name?—Katherine something, I think. I'll have a word with Banks." The decision made him feel better, and he donned his suit carefully. Since he had not formally joined the army he had no uniform. Instead, he put on a seal gray pair of tight-fitting trousers, a frilly white linen shirt, and topped it off with a simple waistcoat. Then after donning his black leather shoes, he shrugged into a fawn-colored frock coat. Plucking his tricorn hat off of a peg, he settled it firmly on his head and studied himself in the mirror. "All right," he spoke aloud to his reflection, "let's go see what kind of stuff Major Saul Banks is made of!"

Clive left the attic room that he occupied at his parents' rented house, went downstairs, and said to Grace, who was cooking breakfast, "I'll get something at the officers' mess, Grace."

He left the house and with long strides made his way across town. It was a fine morning, with the red sky in the east still glowing freshly. A slight breeze stirred against his face, and he inhaled deeply, enjoying the smell of the sea. It was a smell that he delighted in, and he thought, *I should have been a sailor—but that's a hard life. I'm not sure I'd want to do it for a lifetime.*

He passed by many uniformed soldiers, some of them in his father's regiment. Reaching headquarters, he went at once into the officers' mess, where he sat again with Steerbraugh, and the two enjoyed a hearty meal of eggs, bacon, and fresh bread.

"What are you up to, Clive?" Steerbraugh asked idly. "I wish I had some of your leisure time. King George's lieutenants don't have much of that."

"I'm going to have a word with Banks about that young woman."

Steerbraugh looked at him astonished. "Well . . . by George!" he stammered. "Are you, now?"

"I think it's a disgrace the way the man's treating her."

Steerbraugh grinned broadly, his white teeth gleaming. "Good for you, Clive! You can get by with it. If I did it, I'd probably get court-martialed for assaulting a superior officer. I'll wish you the best with the scoundrel."

While the two ate Clive kept looking for the surgeon, but Banks did not appear. "Well," he said finally, "I can see him later. I'm going to meet the young woman. What's her name?"

"Katherine Yancy," Steerbraugh answered promptly. His eyes brightened and he said, "She's a pippin, Clive. I think I was the first one to greet her. By George, you'll be a knight in shining armor!"

"I don't know about that, but I'm going to do whatever I can to help her. I've asked around, and it seems Banks doesn't want any interference with his patients—but they're not patients. They're just poor devils trapped in that stinking hulk—most of them sick, and some of them are dying. I don't see why we have to treat prisoners like that!"

"They're probably treating our men just as badly," Steerbraugh shrugged philosophically. He had the typical soldier's callousness toward prisoners taken in a war and never stopped to think how it might be if he himself were suffering as a prisoner. "If you'd care to see the young lady, she's staying at the Dolphin Inn, not far from the harbor.

Small town like this, anyone can point you to it."

"Thanks, James."

As Clive Gordon rose and prepared to leave, Steerbraugh grinned again broadly. "Give the young lady my best," he said. "I'd step in myself, but I'd lose my commission if I punched the monster in the nose as I'd like to."

Clive nodded his assent and left the mess hall. He made his way down the street, and after a few inquiries found the Dolphin Inn without difficulty. It was a small inn with an overhanging second story, squeezed in between two larger buildings. When he entered, the barkeep, noting his well-cut suit, came at once from behind the bar.

"Yes, sir! May I be of assistance?"

"I'm looking for a young woman named Katherine Yancy. Is she staying here?"

"Why, yes, sir, she is. I'm not sure if she's up yet. First room at the top of the stairs if you'd care to go knock."

"Thank you."

Clive climbed the narrow stairs, and when he got to the second floor he peered down the murky hallway, illuminated only by small diamond-shaped windows at each end. He went to the first door, where Katherine had moved to from the attic, and knocked uncertainly. For a brief moment he thought no one was there, and had just raised his fist to knock again when the door suddenly opened. He stood there rather foolishly, fist in the air, staring at the young woman.

"Yes, what is it?" she asked rather abruptly.

"Miss Yancy?"

Katherine stared up at the tall young man standing before her, which she did not have to do with most men. She noticed that he seemed to be well-dressed and rather personable. Still she was wary, being a stranger with no family in town. "I'm Katherine Yancy," she answered curtly. "What do you want with me?"

"My name is Clive Gordon, Miss Yancy. I'm a physician. I'd like to speak with you if I could."

"You can't come in my room. If you'll go downstairs I'll meet you. What is it you want?"

"Well, I've heard your story from a friend of mine, Lieutenant Steerbraugh. I believe you have met him."

"Oh yes! He was very kind to me when I first arrived." Katherine peered more closely at the young man and said, "I haven't sent for a doctor. I'm not sick."

"No, but I understand your father is. I have access to the prison ship, the *St. George*. I believe I could arrange for you to visit your father again.

I understand you've had some difficulty along those lines."

Katherine's eyes lighted up, and her lips parted as she exclaimed, "You can? How wonderful—just let me get my cloak! And I have some food I'd like to take." She turned back into the room and came out almost at once, fastening a bonnet over her curls, and walked with him to the stairs. He stepped aside and let her go down first, then followed.

As they passed down the stairway and out of the inn, Clive noticed the innkeeper watching them closely. He saw Katherine look up and Clive thought, *She must feel uncomfortable. Still, this is too good an opportunity to miss.*

"Could you really get me in to see my father?" Katherine asked as they walked along.

"My father is Colonel Leslie Gordon. His regiment was stationed in Boston, but he's here now with the rest of His Majesty's forces. I'm not officially in the army, but I have been of some help to the doctors at Boston."

"Are you acquainted with Major Banks?"

There was a curtness in the girl's voice. She lifted her head high and turned to look at him. She had unusual eyes, he thought. At first he thought they were gray, but then he saw they had a greenish tinge to them. They were very large eyes with dark, heavy eyelashes that set them off well. She had a beautifully textured complexion, smooth as ivory, but a few freckles almost invisibly splattered across her nose. He thought of how Steerbraugh had described her as a pippin and found himself agreeing with the man's estimate. "Yes, I'm acquainted with him. I understand he's forbidden you to see your father."

"Yes, he has! I've been to General Howe several times, but he insists he can do nothing."

"Well, I hope I can be of some help—although I can't promise anything," Clive said. He had very long legs and slowed his pace to allow her to keep up. "You came all the way from Boston to see your father?"

"Yes, and my uncle. They were both taken prisoner earlier in the war—at Breed's Hill. I'm very concerned about them—especially my uncle. I haven't seen him, but my father says he's very ill."

"The hulks are a terrible place! I'm opposed to using them as prisons, but, of course, I have no say in such things."

His remark brought an approving look from Katherine. "That's very kind of you, Mr. Gordon." They walked several paces and she said, "I've been so discouraged lately. I've brought food and medicine to my father, but since the major forbids me to see him, I'm not ever sure if he gets them or not."

"Suppose we stop off at one of the shops and pick up some fresh fruit? I'm sure we could find something, and I'll stop by the apothecaries and replenish my supply. I didn't bring my bag, but I know pretty well what men in that condition might need."

"Oh, that would be so kind!" Katherine said, her cheeks glowing with pleasure. The two of them visited the two shops, and when they came out Katherine said, "These will help Father and Uncle Noah, I'm sure!"

"Well, come along and we'll see what we can do."

When they reached the docks, the same fisherman was waiting in his dory. He gave Clive a sharp look, then spoke to the young woman cheerfully. "Well . . . I see you have company this morning, miss. Same price for two." He watched as the tall young man helped the girl down, then sat beside her in the stern. Facing them, he shoved off and rowed expertly over the waves. He was a talkative fellow and did his best to discover the relationship between the two. The young woman merely answered noncommittally, so when he reached the *St. George* and let them up the side of the ship's ladder, he knew little more than he did before. "Shall I wait, miss?"

Clive tossed a coin down to the fellow and said, "Yes, wait. We shouldn't be too long. I'll make it worth your while."

"Thankee, sir!"

The lieutenant who had greeted Katherine each morning stepped forward. "Miss Yancy," he said, "I'm sorry but—"

"My name is Clive Gordon," Clive said crisply. "My father is Colonel Leslie Gordon, Colonel of the Seventeenth Regiment. I'm here in his name to give this young woman's father and uncle a visit."

Lieutenant Smith looked at him confused. "Well, sir. I'm . . . I'm afraid I can't permit that."

"You're going to violate Colonel Gordon's orders? I don't think that would be too wise, Lieutenant."

Smith flushed, then said hastily, "Well, I'll have to see the captain."

"We'll wait," Clive said firmly, "but not long! Hurry up, lieutenant!"

As Lieutenant Smith scurried off, Katherine giggled. "I'm so glad you did that. He's been nice enough, but I'm tired of his constant refusals. Do you think the captain will listen?"

"I have no idea. If he doesn't, we'll have to try something else."

Gordon's assurance pleased the young woman and she said, "I'm so thankful that you took the time to come. Why did you do it?"

"Well—" Clive Gordon was rather embarrassed—"I heard about your difficulties, and it bothered me. I'm not sure I can help, but I thought I'd have a try."

"That was very nice of you!" Katherine said. "At least some of you British are gentlemen."

Clive suddenly laughed aloud. "I thank you for your compliment and hope to be deserving of it. Tell me about yourself while we're waiting."

"Oh, there's little enough to tell. I have a mother back in Boston who's not too well. It's been rather hard with father being in prison like this."

She went on to tell how her father and uncle had been captured, and how she had been so concerned that she had made the trip with no assurance of success. As she spoke, Gordon admired her smooth features, her well-shaped lips, and the erect manner in which she carried herself. She had a trim figure, a very tiny waist, he noticed, and her hair caught glints from the sun as they stood on the deck of the *St. George*.

Lieutenant Smith came hurrying back, a smile on his face. "The captain says the navy can't be getting into the differences between officers. Since your father's a colonel, and the surgeon is only a major, he says to allow you to see anyone you want to, Mr. Gordon. If you'll come this way you can wait in here."

He led them to the usual room where Katherine had waited before and then left at once. The two stood there speaking quietly, and five minutes later the door opened and Katherine moved forward quickly. "Father!" she said. "It's so good to see you again."

Amos Yancy was blinking in the bright sunlight that streamed in through the single small window. The hold of the ship was dark and murky, and he held her hands for a minute until his eyes adjusted. His voice was husky as he said, "It's good to see you, daughter!"

He coughed, and the rasping sound of it caught Clive's attention. *That's not good*, he thought. *It could go into pneumonia.*

"Father, this is Mr. Gordon. He's been kind enough to help me to see you. He's a doctor, too. I want him to examine you and then Uncle Noah."

"Noah's not able to get up the stairs, I'm afraid." Amos Yancy coughed again, and he put his hand out to the younger man. "I thank you for your kindness to my daughter, sir."

"I'm only sorry to find you in such poor condition, Mr. Yancy. Sit down here, please, and let me listen to your chest. You know how we doctors are."

As Clive began to examine Yancy, Katherine asked, "Have you been getting the food that I've been sending?"

"The lieutenant brought something just yesterday. That's the first we've gotten. I suppose you've left more, but none of it ever got to us."

"That was Banks' doing!" Katherine said, then bit her lip. She did not want to complain during the time she had with her father. She stood to one side watching how the young man carefully examined the prisoner.

Finally after thumping and listening and asking several questions Clive said, "You shouldn't be in this damp place!"

"I suppose not, but it looks like I will be for a time."

Clive thought carefully and then said, "There is a smaller prison in town. At least it's dry, and there's some sunlight. I don't know if I can do it, but I'll see if I can get you and your brother transferred."

The father and daughter stared at the tall young man, and Katherine whispered, "Oh, that would be wonderful! Could you really do it?"

"I have no idea," Clive said honestly, "but I'll do my best. Now, suppose you visit with your daughter while I go below and see how your brother is doing. His name is Noah, you say?"

"Yes, the guard will take you down."

As soon as the tall young man left the room, Katherine said, "Isn't it wonderful, Father! He just appeared at the door this morning and said he wanted to help. I'd given up on finding any Englishmen with any manners or courtesy—but I was wrong."

"Yes you were, lass," Amos said. He managed a smile and coughed again. "It would be good to get to a dry place. I don't mean to be complaining, but it's Noah I'm worried about."

"Maybe Mr. Gordon can do it," Katherine said.

The two sat there talking. She gave him some of the food that she had bought and watched him eat, but he had little appetite. He had a fever too, she could tell, and when Gordon came back she saw at once there was a serious look on his face.

"I'm afraid your brother is in poor condition."

"Yes, he's not the only one," Amos Yancy said.

"Could you do anything for him?" Katherine asked.

"I think if we move him to a dry place he'll be much better off. Let me see what I can do. The only influence I have is through my father, and he would have to convince General Howe to make an exception, but General Howe's very fond of my father. In any case," Clive said, "I'll do what I can."

Suddenly the door swung open with a bang. The three turned at once to face Major Saul Banks. Banks had come on one of his periodical visits, and when Lieutenant Smith had informed him of the colonel's son who had insisted on Miss Yancy seeing her father, Banks had exploded with rage. His face now was glowing and his smallish eyes burned as he half shouted at Katherine, "What are you doing here? I gave strict orders that no one was to see my patients!"

Clive stepped forward at once. He towered over the short officer, which made Banks even more angry. "I'm responsible, Major Banks! I met Miss Yancy, and she told me of her father's illness—"

"I don't care what she told you! You have no authority on this ship! Now, get off! Don't let me see you back here again, Gordon!"

"I'm afraid I can't take that, sir!"

"This is a military ship. As a civilian, you have no authority here!"

"I hate to use my father's name, but I believe Colonel Leslie Gordon has some authority," Clive said coolly. He had no idea whether his father would back him up, but he rather suspected he would. In any case, it was the only defense he had. Now he said, "And furthermore, I'm not sure but what I should bring this matter to General Howe's attention!"

"Say what you please. The general will back me up," Banks said. "Now, get off this ship!"

Clive suddenly knew a moment of fury. He was ordinarily an even-tempered young man, but the injustice of it all suddenly infuriated him. "You, sir, are not worthy of the uniform you wear! You're no gentleman, and you should be ashamed of the treatment you've given a helpless woman! And, furthermore, I warn you, I'll do everything within my power to help Miss Yancy see her father and uncle off this hulk!"

Banks began to curse and rave, and in the same breath called Clive a vile name.

Angrily Clive said, "That's a term no gentleman would endure. I'll have my friend call on you, Major Banks."

Instantly Banks' mouth dropped open, for he had not expected Gordon to challenge him to a duel. He knew instantly that Clive Gordon would do exactly what he said, and he rather suspected the tall young man was a better shot and had a steadier hand than he did. He began to bluster, saying, "I would not dirty my hands on you, Gordon!"

Clive pressed his point. "If I hear one more word from you about this matter, I'll slap your face in the officers' mess! You'll have to accept my challenge then, and I promise you I'll shoot you right in the heart the next morning at dawn! It would give me great pleasure to do so, Banks!"

Banks stuttered and tried to find a way out, but the hard light in the young man's eyes convinced him he was in over his head. He gasped a few unintelligible words, then turned and stalked out.

As the door slammed, Katherine suddenly reached out and took Clive's arm. "Good for you! I wish you would shoot him in the heart! He deserves it!"

"Now, Katherine," Amos Yancy protested. "That's no way for a young girl to talk!"

"I know it. I'm sorry, Father—but he's been so mean, and he's done everything he could to keep you from getting well! You don't know what he's done!"

"I think this may make things much easier," Clive said quickly. "Let's go ashore, Miss Yancy. I'll go see my father at once. I hardly think the major is going to push this thing. He's a coward as well as a brute to women."

Katherine was so excited she could hardly speak. She kissed her father, saying, "It's going to be all right, Father. I know it is. Mr. Gordon's going to see to it."

The two left the ship, and when they were set ashore Clive said, "I'll take you back to your inn, Miss Yancy." The two walked briskly along, Katherine speaking brightly, her face suffused with excitement. When he left her at the inn he took his hat off, and she looked up at him with a grateful expression on her features.

"I . . . I can't tell you what this means to me, Mr. Gordon."

"I'm glad I could be of some help. May I come back as soon as I make the arrangements? I'm sure you'll want to hear."

"Please do," she said softly, and when he bowed and walked away, she stood watching his tall figure as he moved down the street. She had given up hope, and now Clive Gordon had brought it back into her life. She turned slowly and moved toward her room, thinking, *It's going to be all right! Thank you, God, for sending someone to help. . . !*

🔔   🔔   🔔

"Why, you look beautiful, Katherine!"

Grace Gordon had been helping her guest into a dress that had once belonged to her, but had been carefully tailored to fit Katherine.

Katherine looked in the mirror and smiled, saying, "It is beautiful— the dress, I mean, not me!" She was very pleased with the way the dress had turned out. For the past week she had spent considerable time with the Gordon family and had learned to admire them greatly. Grace, at the age of eighteen, was only two years younger, and she and the young woman had quickly become fast friends. Katherine admired the dress, which was a close-fitting Basque jacket with a striped blue-and-yellow pattern. The sleeves were frilled just below the shoulders, and the full skirt was a patterned satin, a peach color that gracefully reached the floor. "I shouldn't let you do this, Grace!" Katherine protested, all the while admiring herself.

"Nonsense! It's been fun, and you needed a new dress to wear to our celebration tonight!"

Looking in the mirror, Katherine liked the cut of the dress. She reached up and touched her hair. "I like the way you've done my hair," she said. Turning to the young girl she reached out her hands, and when Grace took them she said warmly, "You've been so kind to me—as kind as anyone could ever be. Things look so different now than they did a week ago."

Katherine found it hard to believe that only one week ago Clive Gordon had appeared at her door. Then, like a whirlwind, he had brought so many wonderful changes to her life. She remembered suddenly how he had made all the arrangements to have her father and uncle transferred to the prison, and how he had made it possible for her to visit them every day. He had also brought her to meet his family, and they had accepted her without question. Now she said, "If the English were as nice to Americans as you and your family have been to me, I don't think there would have been any revolution."

Grace smiled quickly. "I hope we get all of our misunderstandings ironed out soon. It's a shame for our men to have to go to war when it could be settled if they'd let the women take care of it!" She laughed at her own remark and said, "Now, tell me some more about that young Quaker who's been courting you."

"Oh, that's nothing! He just wants someone to keep house for him, I think. I couldn't be a Quaker anyway."

"Why not?" Grace asked curiously.

"They're too quiet and silent—and I like colorful dresses—like this one," Katherine said, smoothing her skirt. "Nothing will come of him."

The two girls talked for a while, and just before they left to go to dinner Katherine said, "I wonder why Clive hasn't married."

The innocent question, or so it seemed, brought a smile to Grace's lips. "Well, he almost did. Just recently in fact," she said. "He fell in love with a young French girl named Jeanne Corbeau."

"Jeanne Corbeau? Didn't she just recently marry Dake Bradford?"

"Yes. Dake is my cousin. He and his family are from Boston—do you know them? His father's name is Daniel Bradford."

"Why, yes, I know of them, of course. I attended Dake and Jeanne's wedding. They're a fine family. Dake must have been quite aggressive to beat out a handsome fellow like your brother."

"Well, Jeanne was raised all her life in the woods, and Dake is a woodsman to the bone. I don't think Jeanne and Clive would ever have been happy together. He'll be a physician, I suppose, in London someday."

"You don't think he'll join the army?"

"Sometimes he talks about it," Grace shrugged, "but I just don't know. I don't think he knows himself." She hesitated, then shook her head. "He's been very downhearted lately. Can you tell that?"

"Well, the few times I've been with him he seemed cheerful enough, but I suppose he wouldn't go around complaining."

"No, he's not much of a one to wear his heart on his sleeve, but it hurt him dreadfully, I'm afraid. He's never been interested in a young woman before, not seriously."

Katherine said only, "I'm sure he'll find happiness with someone."

"I'm sure he will. He's such a fine fellow. Now, let's go eat that supper mother's worked so hard to prepare!"

The two young women left the bedroom and found the entire family gathering together in the cramped dining room. With their guest, there was barely enough room for the family around the table, and Katherine flushed with pleasure at the attention that Mr. and Mrs. Gordon paid to her. After the meal they sat in the parlor and enjoyed a fine time of singing a variety of hymns. Katherine discovered that they were a very devoted Christian family, and she also found that she knew most of the hymns.

"Why, you've got a beautiful voice!" Clive said with approval. "Do you play the harpsichord?"

"Yes, I do, and my father plays the violin very well! We used to play duets sometimes." A sudden sadness flooded her and she said no more. Thoughts of her broken home came to her with a rush, and for a time she withdrew herself, only speaking when someone asked her a question, and not a great deal.

Finally, the evening ended, and Lyna Lee Gordon came over and kissed the young woman on the cheek. "You must come back as often as you can. We get lonely here, don't we, Leslie?"

"Yes we do. Good to have young people around." Colonel Gordon smiled. He took Katherine's hand, bowed low, and kissed it. "Bring her back, Clive, every chance you get."

The two left, and Clive escorted Katherine back to the Dolphin Inn. They walked along the streets that were now darkened except for the occasional lanterns that cast golden beams into the night. It was a fine evening in June. The stars overhead glittered brightly against a velvet sky, and the full moon poured its silvery streams upon them. They moved slowly, and finally Clive said, "Let's go have a look at the sea. I always like to see the ocean at night, especially on a night like this."

"All right."

They made their way down to the docks and stood together admiring the white caps illuminated by the silvery beams of the moon. "You see that track, the reflection of the moon?" Clive said suddenly, pointing to the V-shaped, bright reflection on the water. "The old Norsemen used to call that the whales' way. I don't know if there are any whales there, but it certainly is beautiful."

Katherine was feeling especially happy at how things had changed. Her father had seemed much improved that day when she visited him. Thinking of her good fortune, she now looked up at the stars and murmured, "I wish I knew all their names. Do you know the stars, Clive?"

"Just a few." He looked up, named several of them for her, and said, "I think that's Venus over there."

"Where?"

"Right there." He moved behind her and held his arm up, holding her left arm loosely and indicating the bright star. "I think that's Venus."

Katherine was very aware of his closeness. "I'd like to see a sunset on Venus."

He laughed suddenly and turned her around, holding her shoulders. "You wouldn't see much of one," he said. "Venus rotates so slowly it only has two sunsets in an entire year."

"Is that all—only two?"

"It's what I've heard. I don't know if it's true or not. That wouldn't be many sunsets to enjoy, would it?" He suddenly was very conscious of her loveliness. The warm summer breeze was fragrant with the smells of the sea, tangy and sharp. The waves were licking the dock at their feet in a sibilant manner, but more than this Clive was conscious of the sweet fragrance that she had on and of the contours of her lips. Her face was touched with the soft light of the moon, giving her features an argent cast. He thought he had never seen anything more lovely. For that one moment he forgot Jeanne Corbeau—or perhaps he remembered her. He never knew which it was, for the spell of the girl's beauty drew him. Strong emotions stirred in him, and almost recklessly, with a touch of desperation as the loss in him seemed to rise, he drew her close and bent his head.

Katherine knew he was going to kiss her and knew she should turn away—but she did not. Her heart was filled with gratitude to this tall young man who had showed such kindness to her. When his lips met hers she meant it as a sign of gratitude—no more than that. Katherine had been kissed before a few times, but something about this kiss was different. Gordon's strong arms wrapped about her, and he was so tall and powerful that she felt almost like a child in his grasp. His lips were firm, and to her surprise she found herself returning the caress. For one moment she stood there feeling more like a woman than she had ever felt in her life. Something in her urged her forward so that she held her own lips firmly against his—and then she drew away.

"I'm . . . I'm sorry," Clive said quickly. "I shouldn't have done that!"

Katherine struggled for a moment to regain her composure. She then smiled up at him and said, "I suppose one kiss isn't so terrible, is it?"

Clive had been shaken by the embrace. Somehow he felt confused. *How can I kiss this young woman, as pretty as she is, when I fancy myself in love with Jeanne?* He was disturbed and pulled his hat off, running his hand through his crisp hair. "I don't go around kissing women as a habit," he mumbled.

"I'm sure you don't." Not wanting to prolong the moment, Katherine said, "We'd better go back now. Will I see you tomorrow?"

"We'll go back to our house."

"That would be too soon for a visit."

"Oh, what does it matter if it's too soon or not soon enough!" Clive said. He was anxious to see whether she had been offended by the kiss, and by the time they reached the inn, he was sure that she was not. "Good night," he said, taking off his hat again.

"It was a lovely evening! Good night, Clive."

All that night and during the days that followed Katherine was reminded often of that single caress under the starry sky. She found herself spending more and more time with Clive, telling herself that it was because her father and her uncle tied them together. However, one evening when she was spending the night with Grace, the younger girl said, "You look like a woman who's falling in love."

Katherine gave her a startled glance, then shook her head. "You mean with Clive?"

"You're not seeing any other men, are you?"

Katherine shook her head. "No, that can't be! We're on different sides of a war. You're wrong, Grace!"

Grace Gordon was a thoughtful young woman, and one who had deep insight into people. She considered the face of her friend and said, "Be careful. I know you think it's impossible—but love won't be put into a little box, Katherine!"

9

AN OLD LOVE

CLIVE HAD NO SOONER ENTERED the door than his mother stepped outside the small parlor and called him down the short hallway. "Clive, come here, please!"

Sweeping off his hat and hanging it on a peg, Clive moved at once to meet her. One look at her troubled face and he demanded, "What's wrong, Mother!"

Lyna Lee held a single sheet of paper out to him. "It's a letter from Daniel," she said. "You'd better read it!"

Taking the sheet of paper, Clive quickly scanned the few lines:

Dear Lyna,

I trust that you and yours are well, but I am afraid that I do not have good news here. Some sort of epidemic has gripped Boston by the throat. In almost every household there's someone down, usually more than one. As usual, the doctors refuse to say exactly what it is, but I don't mind admitting I am terribly concerned about my family. Micah and I have not been touched by it, but Sam, Rachel, and Jeanne are all in poor condition. The doctors here are running themselves distracted, and every day there are scores of funerals. I hate to ask, but do you suppose Clive could come and help take care of my family? If this is impossible, do not worry about it. We are trusting God to bring us through this. I trust again my prayers are for you and all of my nephews and my niece.

Your loving brother,
Daniel.

Looking up, Clive frowned and shook his head. "It sounds very serious, doesn't it?"

"I'm afraid it is. Daniel is not one to ask for help unless there's no

105

other way." For a moment Lyna looked up into his face, then asked, "Do you think you might be able to go, Clive?"

With an expression of surprise Clive said, "Why, of course! It's a good thing I'm not in the army. I couldn't go then, but I'll leave at once and try to find out about transportation."

"Your father's already taken care of that," Lyna said quickly. "I'm afraid there's no time to waste. He has booked passage for you on the *Lone Star*, which is sailing in less than an hour."

"Well, that doesn't give me much time, does it?"

Lyna patted his arm. "I'll help you get your things packed."

Clive smiled at her. "You were pretty sure I'd go, weren't you, Mother?"

"Yes, I knew you would!" Fondness was in her tone, but a touch of worry clouded her fine eyes for a moment. "Just be sure you don't get sick yourself. I couldn't bear that! I'd have to come down there to nurse you and all of Daniel's brood, too!"

"Well, it's a risk we doctors have to take. I'm not sure about medical supplies there in Boston. They were getting pretty scanty when we left. I think I'll go to headquarters and see if I can scrounge up a few things there to take with me."

"And I suppose you'll stop to say goodbye to Katherine?"

"Well—of course I feel I must do that! I'll stop in and have one last look at her father and uncle."

"How are they doing, Clive?"

"Her father is much better—her uncle . . . well, I'm not sure. He can't seem to shake off this sickness in his throat and chest. He wasn't a healthy man, Amos tells me, when they were captured. They had no business being at that battle in the first place, but those Yancys are evidently a pretty stubborn lot."

"Tell Katherine to come by and see us while you're gone. You don't have to be here for that."

"I'll tell her, Mother." Clive quickly packed his clothes into a small trunk, and then kissed his mother goodbye at the door. "I'll write you as soon as I get to Boston. I'm sure Uncle Daniel will be writing to you all the time."

"Take care, son," Lyna said, holding to him for a moment. "God be with you!"

Clive left, carrying the small case down the street until he found a carriage. Tossing the chest inside, he got in and said, "Drive me to army headquarters."

"Yes, sir!" the driver responded and slapped the horses with the lines. "Get up there, Bess—Charlie!" The horses responded by breaking into a smart pace, and within ten minutes Clive was getting out at head-quarters.

"Wait here for me. I have another ride to make. I'll make it worth your while."

"Yes, sir, I'll be right here!"

Clive moved quickly into the hospital, where he found the quartermaster spinning a tall yarn with a corporal. He explained his predicament about his relatives in Boston. "I'll be glad to pay you for the supplies. I don't think there's any place else I could buy them."

The quartermaster, a short, stubby man with a pair of lead-colored eyes, gave him a caustic look. "I can't release supplies, especially for treating rebels," he said. "You'll have to get General Howe's permission."

Clive argued his case but the quartermaster refused to give him any medical supplies. He went at once to find General Howe, only to find the general was in a staff meeting with his officers. Glancing at the clock on the wall of the outer office, Clive saw he had no time to wait and turned and left the office. He knew of a small apothecary shop that sold a few drugs, so he rode there in the carriage, bought what supplies were available, then returned to say, "Take me to the Dolphin Inn." As the carriage moved through the narrow streets, he went over the things in his mind that he might do, but could think of nothing else.

When the driver finally pulled up at the inn, Clive said again, "Wait for me! As soon as I finish here I need to go to the dock right away! I have to catch a ship ready to sail within the hour." He went inside and ran up the narrow flight of stairs. Knocking on the door of Katherine's room he waited eagerly, but there was no answer. He knocked again, but was certain that Katherine was not there. Running back down the stairs he said to the innkeeper, "I'm looking for Miss Yancy."

"She went out some time ago, sir," the man said. "Probably be back soon."

"Well, I can't wait. Please tell her Mr. Gordon called." Clive thought for a moment, and asked, "Do you have pen and paper? I'd better leave her a note."

"Yes, sir! Right here."

Clive quickly took the scrap of paper and the pen and, dipping it in the bottle of ink the innkeeper provided, wrote a brief note:

Katherine,
    I'm called to Boston on business. My uncle Daniel's family needs medical care. I hope to be back soon. I will also pray for your father and your uncle.

He hesitated over the closing and finally wrote, "Your devoted friend, Clive Gordon."

Waving the paper in the air until the ink was dry, he then folded it and said, "Please see that Miss Yancy gets this." He handed a coin to the innkeeper, then hurried outside. Jumping into the carriage he said, "Make it fast. My ship leaves in fifteen minutes."

"Probably won't," the driver said matter-of-factly. "Them ships never leave when they're supposed to—and they never arrive in port when they're supposed to, but I'll get you there, sir. Hang on!"

Clive reached the ship in plenty of time, got aboard, and discovered that his father had already paid for his passage.

"You got here just in time," the captain said. "We're just weighing anchor. Ten minutes later and you'd have missed us."

Clive thanked him and, after stowing his gear in the small cabin that was assigned to him, went topside. Moving to the stern to keep out of the way of the sailors who were rapidly setting the sail, he listened to the clanking of the anchor chain. The *Lone Star* swung at once, catching the tide, and as the sails billowed out, surged forward. As she cleared the harbor Clive stood in the stern looking back at Halifax, which grew smaller and smaller. His mind was on Katherine Yancy, and he was surprised at the keen disappointment that touched him at the thought of not seeing her for a time. When the land became a thin, knife-edge along the horizon, he turned and walked slowly along the deck. His thoughts tempered by the whistling wind that shook the billowing sails with a clapping sound from time to time, Clive finally moved to the bow and looked forward, wondering what awaited him in Boston.

🛡 🛡 🛡

Matthew Bradford found New York a whirlwind of activity after the dormant quality of life in Boston. As he walked down the street with a large flat case of his paintings, looking for Jan Vandermeer's house, he was almost stunned by the furious activity all around him. Everywhere he looked men were busy digging, throwing up defenses against the British army that everyone knew would arrive soon. There was a colorful group that he saw on the streets—men in brown coats with green or yellow or red facings, with brown, black, or gray hunting shirts. He saw some of John Haslet's Delaware Continentals, and William Smallwood's Marylanders. These recruits interested him, for he knew all of them came from wealthy families from Annapolis and Baltimore. As he walked along he also caught a glimpse of John Glover's Marbleheaders.

Up and down Manhattan, picks and shovels made the dirt fly all the way down to the Battery, as men sweated and cursed as they dug like moles. Matthew took it all in. He even saw General Israel Putnam flying about bellowing commands everywhere. Not far behind Putnam was Henry Knox, now promoted to a full colonel of artillery. Knox and his men came by with guns and wagons clattering along the streets. Matthew stopped from time to time to listen to the talk of the soldiers and was impressed at how confident they were. He picked up the fact that they had an army of twenty thousand men and that they held a strong position. He was glad to learn they had powder in ample quantities, which he knew the Continental Army had lacked before during the siege of Boston.

Finally, Matthew sought directions, and a kind elderly shopkeeper pointed the way out for him. After walking another half hour through the busy streets, he arrived at the corner of Greenwich and Dey Streets, which contained several fashionable houses. One stately home had solid shutters on the ground floor, and venetian shutters above. All of the houses had shutters and blinds, apparently to keep out the worst of the sunlight. He finally came to a three-story house built of bricks, sitting almost on the street. The windows were all closed with green venetian shutters, and when Matthew knocked on the door he was admitted into a foyer, which surprisingly was cool and semidark despite the blistering sunlight that baked the streets outside. "I'm looking for Mr. Jan Vandermeer," he said, pulling off his hat as he faced the tall angular woman who wore a white apron and a white cap over her dark hair.

"He's up in the attic room. Take those stairs."

"Thank you, ma'am."

Matthew climbed to the third floor, then took the final steps, a twisting, winding, narrow way that led to a small landing. When he knocked on the single door, he heard a voice shouting something loudly from the inside. The door opened then, and Matthew was blinded by the bright light that flooded through the gable windows across the end of the large room. He was grabbed around the waist at once, and a thick guttural voice with a Dutch accent said, "Yah, here is my friend, Matthew! Come in, come in!"

Matthew was practically dragged into the room. He saw that it had a high ceiling and was terribly cluttered. He paid no attention for the moment, for he was grinning broadly at the short man who was pumping his hand and beating his shoulder at the same time.

"Gut! You haf come! Come, we have a drink together to celebrate your arrival!"

"How are you, Jan?" Matthew asked as Vandermeer towed him to a table that contained a tall wine cooler, various sorts of glasses and cups, and what seemed to be the remains of several meals.

"I am fine! Here, we drink!" Vandermeer poured a dark reddish liquid into two pewter tankards, shoved one into Matthew's hand, and said, "To the second-best artist alive today, my friend, Matthew Bradford!"

Matthew took a healthy pull at his tankard, then gasped for breath. It bit like fire and he wheezed, "What is this stuff?"

"You are spoiled, just a baby!" Vandermeer exclaimed. He stood there grinning, a short, round man with blond hair. Round he was, in form, with large round eyes set in a round head. His eyes, almost piercing blue, were excitable, and whenever he spoke he pumped and waved his hands in a wild fashion. Matthew grinned, for he remembered that Jan Vandermeer only spoke in the manner of an exclamation—even if it was just a simple sentence such as, "It's a nice day." Whenever Vandermeer said anything, it was half shouted, and so filled with emotion that if it were written it would have to be followed by an exclamation point.

"I've invited myself to stay with you at your invitation, Jan," Matthew said. He was still holding his suitcase and looking around the room. "If you have room for me, that is."

"Room? Of course, but what does an artist need mit room?" Vandermeer boomed. His voice seemed to fill the room, and he slapped Matthew on the back heartily. "Come, I show you!" Striding across the cluttered floor Jan kicked a stool out of the way, sending it flying until it hit the wall with a crash. "Here, this is all you need! A bed, a vashstand—" Grabbing Matthew's suitcase he threw it inside on the bed and slammed the door. "Come now, I vill show you what I haf been doing!"

Matthew could not help smiling at his friend, as he often did. During his time in England the two artists had become very close, but he had forgotten the wild excitement with which the Dutchman attacked everything. He had also forgotten the tremendous ego of the man. It had never occurred to Vandermeer to give Matthew a chance to get settled. Instead he was walking excitedly around the room, grabbing up canvases, some half finished, some barely started, others completed. Yelling and jabbing a round forefinger at them, he demanded an opinion from Matthew.

Finally Vandermeer put down a painting of a landscape that seemed to jump off the canvas with its bright, brilliant colors and demanded, "There, what do you think of this?"

Matthew stepped backward, for Vandermeer held the canvas approximately twelve inches from his nose. When he had gotten a good perspective he cleared his throat uncertainly, then said, "Well, Jan, to tell the truth it's a little—well, a little overdone, isn't it? I mean—the colors are all primary."

Vandermeer roared with laughter and whipped the canvas away. "Just an experiment, my friend, nothing more! An artist must try all forms! Now, let me see what you haf brought!"

Matthew hesitated, for Jan Vandermeer was prone to be excessive in his criticisms as he was in everything else. However, Matthew had come to New York for the express purpose of learning, and he knew that underneath the rather ridiculous facade of the small Dutchman lay a keen, analytical brain and a genius that allowed Vandermeer to grasp at once the failings and the virtues of any painting.

"Well, I only brought a few," Matthew said tentatively. Moving across the room he picked up the flat case, found a place on a table by moving several objects, then opened it up. Picking up one of the canvases, he held it up, saying, "This is a still life I did just last month." He eagerly watched the round eyes of his friend take in the painting. Suddenly he realized how much he wanted Vandermeer's approval. He, himself, was not certain whether he had genius, or talent, or nothing. Yet somehow Matthew felt that it lay in him to be a great painter, but he had not yet reached the stage that he had seen in others of absolute certainty of his gift.

"Let me see! Ve haf here a plate mit a loaf of bread, a fish, and a glass of wine!" Vandermeer cocked his round head to one side, closed one eye, and stuck his chubby hands behind his back.

As Jan stared at the painting, seeming to pull it into his own head, Matthew could almost hear the wheels grinding. Matthew watched his friend, but he got no hint at all of what Vandermeer was thinking.

Finally Jan said explosively, "It is a perfect painting!"

"Do you really think so, Jan?" Matthew asked eagerly.

"Yah, and that makes it a *bad* painting!" Vandermeer laughed loudly at Matthew's astonished expression. "You do not want a perfect painting, one that captures every detail exactly!"

Matthew was dumbfounded. He had worked for weeks on this painting, doing exactly what Jan had suggested. He had tried to capture every detail and to make the still life as much as possible like it really was. It had been his best effort, he thought, and now he said rather stiffly, "I am sure I don't know what you're talking about. A painter is supposed to paint what he sees."

"No!" Jan practically jumped up and down and moved over to shake Matthew almost fiercely. "He must paint vot he *feels*! You do not understand? Have you ever heard of Andrea del Sarto?"

"I . . . I don't think so."

111

"His real name was Andrea d'Agnolo di Francesco! He was a painter who lived in the fifteenth century! He was called 'del Sarto' because he was the son of a tailor, which is sarto, and he painted perfect pictures! As a matter of fact," Jan said, pacing the floor and waving his stubby arms around, "the perfection of his frescoes in the Church of the Annunziata in Florence won him the title of 'The Thoughtless Painter,' and he was *nothing*!"

"What do you mean nothing? How can a faultless painter be nothing?" Matthew exclaimed with exasperation running through his tone. "I have spent years trying to paint what I see as well as I can—as much like the original as possible—but now you're telling me that's not what I need to do?"

"That's exactly vat I'm telling you to do! Look, my friend! Come and look out the window!" Jan grabbed Matthew's arm, dragged him to the window, and gestured down at the busy street below. "If you were to paint a picture of that street, what would you paint? You see there the soldiers, some old ladies, and a young woman who's carrying what seems to be a baby. There are horses. Could you paint every one of them exactly? No!" he yelled and jumped up and down in excitement. "You would paint the *impression* of that street—the colors, the movement, the *sense* of the street, not as if you were drawing a scientific illustration for a class of physicians! You must decide vat it is about that street which is important, and then you must render it in your own fashion!" He pounded Matthew on the chest, driving the young man backward. "You must take what is in your heart and mix it with your paints—then you vill have part of yourself on the canvas! What you haf here," he shook the painting of the still life before Matthew's eyes, "is paint on canvas. But it is *not* Matthew Bradford!"

Matthew stared at the painting that he had labored on so assiduously and shook his head in despair. "It sounds to me, Jan, like you're telling me I haven't begun to be an artist yet."

"That is right! That is right!" Jan practically shouted. "You haf learned certain tricks of the craft of painting, but now that you haf mastered that, what must come out of you is this!" Reaching forward, Vandermeer grabbed Matthew's shirt in the vicinity of his heart. He twisted and pulled and beat at Matthew, crying, "We must haf your heart on the canvas, not just smears of paint, and ve will do it!" He suddenly stopped and saw the shock etched on his friend's face. "Ah, Matthew. . ." He shrugged his shoulders and released Matthew's shirt. "I haf gone too fast, but I tell you this. You are a better painter than you know, Matthew Bradford! But I vill have it out of you. I vill have it out of your heart onto this canvas!"

Matthew stared into the electric blue eyes of the small, rotund figure standing before him, and his heart seemed to sink. "It's all been for nothing, all my study?"

"Not at all! Not at all! It is your apprenticeship! Now," Jan Vandermeer said, reaching forward to hug his friend with genuine affection, "now, we go to work and I teach you to paint, not only with the hands— but with the heart. . . !"

𝕿   𝕿   𝕿

After two days of submitting to Jan Vandermeer's teaching, which was frenetic, to say the least, Matthew had just about endured all he could stand. It was with great relief that he received an invitation from Mrs. Esther Denham to have dinner with her that evening.

Matthew had been surprised, but he had written a note to Abigail, and obviously Abigail had prevailed upon her hostess to invite him. The note also included an invitation for Jan Vandermeer, whom Matthew had mentioned to Abigail.

When sunset came, Matthew put on the new clothing that he had purchased earlier in the morning. His britches were bone white and stuffed into jockey-type black leather boots. His shirt was made of cotton and linen, and the neck cloth made of pure silk, which he wound carefully around his neck, forming a bow. He put on his square-cut waistcoat, which was tan with stripes of darker brown, then slipped on the chestnut-colored frock coat. The tails ended at the back of his knees. He was interrupted as Jan Vandermeer entered and stared at him.

"Vell, there you are in all your glory." He walked around Matthew, studying him carefully, then punched him with a stubby forefinger. "You look vonderful," he said. "Now, if you drop dead vee won't have to do a thing except put a lily in your hand!"

Matthew laughed out loud, for he was now accustomed to the excesses of his friend. "Come along and get dressed. We've got to go."

Vandermeer stared at him. "Get dressed? You think I'm naked? I *am* dressed!" He was wearing a baggy pair of knee britches with a short waistcoat that buttoned up the front, only half the buttons were missing. Across his head, cocked at an odd angle, sat an old wig that had seen better days. The coat he wore was a glaring yellow with green-and-red stripes and a scarlet collar. Jan was obviously very proud of it, for he said, "This coat belonged to my father! I hope you like it!"

As a matter of fact, Matthew thought he looked awful, but thought, *Well, I can always tell Mrs. Denham that he's an artist, an eccentric one at that.* Aloud he said, "All right, come along. We'll get a good dinner out of this if nothing else."

The two made their way through the center of New York. In spite of its high population Matthew noticed that there was a rural air about the place. He even saw cows being driven through the streets to a common pasture west of Broadway. Pigs and chickens were a common sight along the road, which was simply a muddy thoroughfare. There were no sidewalks, and he later learned that the streets had to be cleaned by the householders. The street-lighting was also done by the citizens. One householder in every seven hung out a lantern before his residence, and six of his nearest neighbors shared with him the expense of keeping the light burning.

"This is the place, I think," Matthew said, stopping in front of a sturdy house of Dutch pattern on Williams Street near the corner of Wall. The house they paused before was as rigidly rectangular as a barn. It had no projecting wings, or bow windows, or frills of any kind. However, it was well proportioned, and the bricks used to build it were of various colors—yellow, brown, blue, and red arranged in different designs. The decorative brick gave the house a certain air of lightness and charm.

"This is a Dutch house!" Vandermeer announced. "I've seen many like it in Antwerp, back at my home!"

"Well, Manhattan was settled by the Dutch, and there's still a lot of Dutch people here," Matthew said. "Come along."

As they mounted the little porch, which Vandermeer called a stoop, Matthew felt an excitement at seeing Abigail again. They knocked on the door, and it was opened almost at once by a Negro woman wearing a gray dress with a white apron and a white cap.

"Yes, sir?" she said.

"My name is Matthew Bradford. This is Mr. Vandermeer. I believe Mrs. Denham is expecting us."

"Yes, sir, she is. Will you come in?"

As the two men entered, the woman took their hats and said, "If you'll come this way, Mrs. Denham will be right down. You can wait in the parlor." Matthew and Jan were ushered by the servant into a large parlor filled with fine old, dark furniture of mahogany and walnut. Along one side of the wall, two high windows allowed light, and a huge fireplace occupied one end of the large room. The sunlight touched a series of fine porcelain statuettes on the mantel, causing them to gleam richly, and at the other end a harpsichord with a small stool sat beneath a grouping of paintings.

Vandermeer went at once to examine the paintings, and turned, saying with some surprise, "Yah, these are good paintings! I'm surprised!"

"Why should you be surprised?"

"Most people buy a picture of horses jumping over fences and call it art. These," he turned to move his round, stubby hand in a sweeping gesture, "these are fine paintings. Mostly from England, I think."

They were examining the paintings when a woman with beautiful silver hair and quick brown eyes entered the parlor. She was in her middle sixties, Matthew judged, rather small boned, and carefully dressed in a pearl gray gown with delicate lace at the neck and sleeves. "Mr. Bradford? I am Esther Denham."

"I'm happy to meet you, Mrs. Denham. May I present my friend, Mr. Jan Vandermeer."

Vandermeer bowed deeply from the waist, and his eyes danced. Waving at the paintings he said, "Your paintings, they are very fine, Mrs. Denham."

Esther Denham smiled at the abruptness of the man. Her quick eyes took in the rather outlandish dress of the one, and the careful dress of Matthew Bradford, but she said only, "They were collected by my husband. He had quite good taste, I think."

"It was so kind of you to invite us, Mrs. Denham," Matthew said at once. "I've only come to New York recently, as Abigail may have told you."

"Yes, so she said. She and her mother will be down soon. I thought we might have an early dinner, then afterwards, we can come back in here and you can talk to us about painting. I understand you're a very fine artist."

Matthew flushed and shook his head. "Mr. Vandermeer is the expert. I'm only a pupil, I fear."

"Dot is right!" Vandermeer cried, nodding vehemently. "But one day he will surpass the master! You watch what I tell you!"

At that moment Abigail and her mother entered the parlor, and both men turned toward her. Matthew's eyes lit up, and he realized at that moment how much he had wanted to see her again. "Abigail," he said, going forward, "it's so good to see you!"

Abigail took Matthew's hand and smiled. "It's good to see you too, Matthew."

Matthew turned and said, "Mrs. Howland, I trust you're well?"

"I'm feeling better, Matthew. It's nice to see you."

Matthew said, "May I introduce my friend and teacher, Mr. Jan Vandermeer."

As soon as introductions were made, Mrs. Denham said, "I think we will go to the dining room now. I hope you two are hungry. We've prepared too much food, I'm sure."

Jan Vandermeer laughed loudly. "You ask two poor, starving artists if they're hungry? My dear lady, artists are always hungry, but it is good for us to suffer! Otherwise how could vee be artists?"

They moved into the dining room, which was furnished with a magnificent sideboard on which sat an array of silver trays and drinking vessels. The table was covered with a white cloth with candelabras on each end. Underneath it was a crumb cloth to protect the dark blue checked carpet beneath. As they sat down Matthew knew enough about furniture to recognize that the chairs were genuine Hepplewhite.

Mrs. Denham said, "I think we will have the blessing before the first course. Mr. Bradford, would you be so kind?"

Taken completely off guard, Matthew bowed his head and in a rather stumbling fashion asked the blessing. Of course, in his home he was accustomed to such things, but he had somehow not expected it of Mrs. Denham. He could not tell why. When he looked up he smiled at her and said, "That reminds me of my home. I don't think we ever had a meal in my life when my father didn't ask the blessing or ask one of us to do it."

"I'm glad to hear it, sir. Your father is a wise man."

The meal began with soup, which was then followed by fish, so fresh and white and flaky that it fell apart under the fork. Then there was a joint of mutton and also cuts of beef. Served with the tender meat were sauces, vegetables, which were crisp and well-done, and three different kinds of bread. They were served cider, which was evidently brought up from a cellar, for it was cool, and sparkling, and fresh. Finally for dessert there were several fresh fruits and custards.

During the meal Matthew had cast his eye whenever possible at Abigail. He was grateful for the presence of Jan, who dominated the conversation, having an opinion on everything that Mrs. Denham mentioned.

Abigail was wearing a pale green dress, and her hair was done up in a ravishing new hair style. She wore a pearl on each ear, and the rosy light of the candles brought a glow to her smooth skin. She said little, but Matthew was pleased that she seemed glad to see him, and he wished that he could enjoy the meal with her alone.

After the meal they went into the parlor, where Jan talked enthusiastically about the paintings. He admired the pictures, pointing out the flaws and the virtues of each. Finally he came to one, a portrait of Mrs. Denham herself, probably done ten years earlier.

"Now this is a really fine piece of work. May I ask the artist?"

"Gilbert Stuart, Mr. Vandermeer. He was a close friend of my husband's."

"Indeed, a fine, powerful portrait!" Vandermeer exclaimed. "He

116

could compete against the finest of the Continent, I think!"

Abigail said in one of the few silences that Vandermeer permitted, "How is your family, Matthew?"

"Not too well, I'm afraid. There's some kind of an epidemic going around Boston. You're fortunate that you got out when you did."

"Oh, I'm so sorry to hear it!" Abigail said. She was sitting next to Matthew on one of the two couches in the parlor. Leaning forward, she touched his hand and said, "I hope it's not serious."

The touch of Abigail's hand on Matthew's sent a thrill through him. He wanted to take her hand, but did not. "My cousin, Clive Gordon, has come from Halifax to take care of them."

"Oh yes. His father is in the British army, isn't he?"

"Yes, he is, Mrs. Howland."

"How sad that families are pitted against one another in this terrible war. I hope it will soon be over."

"No, it will not be over soon!" Vandermeer announced in a voice as solid as granite. "Have you not heard about the meeting in Philadelphia?"

"What meeting is that?" Mrs. Denham inquired.

"The meeting of the Continental Congress," the artist nodded. "Everyone thinks they will declare this country independent from England!"

"It'll be a shame if they do," Abigail shook her head. "They could never stand against the full force of the English army. No nation on earth could. Why, England has the most powerful and trained army in the world—and the most powerful navy as well!"

Talk went around the table about the revolution, and finally Mrs. Howland excused herself and went to bed. Esther took Jan off to show him the different pictures in the house, and for a moment Abigail and Matthew were alone. Abigail said, "Come, it's stuffy in here! Let's go out to the garden."

"All right."

Matthew followed Abigail out through a pair of double doors and found himself in a delightful garden lit by a single lantern that shed its feeble light over the orderly rows. "This is beautiful!" he said. "Mrs. Denham must love flowers."

"I believe she does. She's a very fine woman."

Abigail moved closer to Matthew as they stood there speaking of the flowers, and knowing men as she did, it was simple enough for her to draw him on. Even as she did this she had a sudden thought of Nathan Winslow—how she had convinced him that she was in love with him—and the thought of that deception came with a painful start, which surprised her. She had never thought much about what kind of woman she was, but now that the world had fallen to bits about her she was forced to think. In the days since she left Boston, she had wondered over and over again how she could have become so despicable as to deliberately plot to entice a man to fall in love with her in order to manipulate him. Time and again she had almost decided it was more than she cared to do, but there was no other route of escape. She had no finances, no prospects. She and her mother were totally dependent upon the kindness of her aunt; therefore, she turned to Matthew and lifted her face, saying, "I've missed you, Matthew."

The slight touch of Abigail's body as she turned to him, the soft quality of her voice, and the faint perfume that was like an intoxicating drug seemed to draw Matthew Bradford. Almost without thinking he put his arms around her, drew her close, and kissed her. Her lips moved under his, and he felt her hands go behind his neck. There was an alluring quality in her that he had never known in any woman. She was a beautiful young woman, and her touch seemed to take his breath. Her lips were soft under his, and he held her almost fiercely, half expecting she would pull away. She did not, but held the kiss, adding the pressure of her own lips. When he lifted his head he said, "You are the loveliest thing I've ever known!"

"Thank you, Matthew." She moved back then as he reached for her, knowing that it was time to let him think about what she was and what he was. They went back into the house finally and met the others.

After the two men left, Esther said, "That's a fine young man. That artist friend of his, he's amusing, and I suspect a very fine artist."

Abigail responded, "Yes, Matthew comes from a fine family. They're patriots, of course. His older brother is with Washington here in New York."

"Have you known him long?"

"Yes, Aunt Esther, for some time. I've always liked him."

Esther Denham asked no more questions, but her sharp brown eyes had observed how the two young people had watched each other across the table. She was also aware of the flush on Matthew's face as they had come in from the garden and could pretty well tell what had happened. "Well," she said, "we will have to have him here again, and Mr. Vandermeer, of course."

Abigail gave her aunt a grateful look. "You've been so kind to us," she said. "I don't know what Mother and I would've done if it hadn't been for you."

Esther came forward and kissed the young woman on the cheek. "It's a delight to have you here. I was terribly lonely until you came. I hope you and your mother will stay a long, long time."

As she turned and left the room, Abigail suddenly felt a sense of distaste for herself. "What kind of a woman am I who can deceive a man so easily—and Aunt Esther, too. If she knew what was in my heart, she would throw me out at once." But she knew that was not true, for she had discovered quickly that Esther Denham was a woman of deep Christian character, and she could tell her aunt's faith was real and genuine. Turning, she moved across the parlor and went to bed at once. For a long time she lay there thinking of how odd her fate was, and for some reason she felt terribly discouraged and despondent as she thought of the future.

10

A Small Piece of Paper

AS SOON AS THE *Lone Star* anchored in the harbor, Clive disembarked and hurried to the Bradford household. When he knocked on the door it opened almost at once, and Daniel grabbed his hand, relief washing over his face. "Clive, my boy, I'm so glad you've come! Come in—let me take your bag."

"How are the sick folks, Uncle Daniel?"

"Not as well as I'd like." Daniel nodded toward the stairs. "Come along, I've kept a room on the second floor for you. You'll be staying here, of course." He moved up the stairs quickly and Clive followed him. When they reached the room at the far end of the hall, Daniel opened the door and waved Clive inside. He found a pleasant room containing a rather ornate bed with a canopy and a fine washstand with a china pitcher and basin on its polished surface. "Make yourself at home. You may want to lie down and rest," Daniel said. "I know it has been a hard trip."

"No, I'd really rather see my patients first."

Daniel nodded quickly. "Come along. I think they're all awake by now. I've kept them in separate rooms." He led the way to the next door, knocked on it, then opened it. "Sam! The doctor is here," he said as he entered the room, followed by Clive.

Sam, who was lying in bed, lifted his head and muttered, "Hello, Clive. Glad you came. I'm pretty sick."

"We'll have to see what we can do about that." Clive sat down on the chair beside the bed, gave Sam a quick examination, and said cheerfully, "We'll have you fixed up in no time! I've got some medicine I want you to take."

"Does it taste bad?"

"All medicine tastes bad! That's part of the reason it's good for you." Clive grinned. He took a glass, mixed a potion from the supplies he had

120

brought from Halifax, and watched as Sam gulped it down and made a horrible face. "You'll be coming around soon," he said. "You won't feel as bad as you do now."

"That's good," Sam muttered. "I hate to think I'd feel this bad the rest of my life!"

Clive rose and the two men left the room. Again Daniel knocked on the next door, and when a voice said faintly, "Come in," he opened it. The two men stepped inside, and Clive moved to where Rachel was lying in a single bed, just under a window. The light came in and touched her face, and Clive saw at once she had a gaunt look about her. Her features were swollen and she licked her lips almost painfully.

"Hello, Rachel," Clive said. He put his hand on her forehead, took her temperature, then examined her carefully. They were, of course, the same symptoms that Sam had, which he had expected. She was, however, feeling much worse, and although he spoke cheerfully to her and gave her encouragement, when he stepped out of the room he shook his head. "She's lost too much weight. She's got to eat more and drink more liquids."

"She can't keep much down." Daniel shook his head and bit his lower lip. "I'm worried, Clive, and Jeanne is the worst of all. She's across the hall here." He stepped to the door, knocked on it once, waited, and when there was no answer knocked again. "She's like that sometimes. Just passes out."

Opening the door, Daniel stepped aside and showed Clive into the room. It was decorated with a feminine touch with yellow curtains and delicate ornaments on top of a chest alongside the wall. Clive, however, did not notice this. He stepped up immediately to bend over the young woman who lay in the bed. Jeanne's face was pale, and her breathing was very shallow. "Jeanne—" he said quietly. She did not move, and he put his hand on her forehead, noting that she had a higher fever than either Sam or Rachel. He picked up her limp arm, felt her pulse, then turned to Daniel. "Has she done this often?"

"Almost every day she has trouble like this. I wanted to send for Dake, but, of course, he couldn't leave his unit." Daniel looked at the young man and wanted to ask questions, but he refrained until the two had stepped out into the hall.

"What do you think, Clive? What is it?"

"It could be cholera," Clive said, "or half a dozen other things. These plagues are all about the same. I'm glad you sent for me, Uncle Daniel. They do need quite a bit of care."

Daniel drew a deep breath and expelled it. He shook his head. "I'll be your nurse. You just tell me what to do. I'll do the praying and you do the doctoring," he said, attempting a smile. He knew as well as Clive the dangers of such sicknesses as these, and as the two men stood there quietly speaking of treatment for the patients, it took all the faith that Daniel Bradford had to believe God for three miracles.

𝕋   𝕋   𝕋

Clive entered the room to find Jeanne sitting in a chair beside the window and said at once, "You shouldn't be up, Jeanne!"

Jeanne Corbeau Bradford smiled up at the tall, young physician. "You know what I've been thinking about, Clive?" she said, ignoring his gentle rebuke.

"I don't know—about what?" he said. He took his seat on the bed facing her and noted with relief that her eyes were clear and she seemed to be free from fever. The past few days had been difficult for him, especially when treating Jeanne. He had to remind himself constantly that thinking of the past was futile now. Yet even as he sat there, memories came flooding back as he thought of the days in the woods that he had spent with Jeanne and her dying father.

Jeanne was wearing a blue robe over a nightgown, and her curly black hair was cropped rather close. She had strange violet-colored eyes, the most beautiful Clive had ever seen. He remembered how he had been almost shocked when he had seen them. "What were you thinking of?" he asked, to drive the thoughts of the past away.

Jeanne smiled and cocked her head to one side. "I was thinking about how I found you so sick in the woods, and *you* were the patient then and *I* was the doctor. Do you remember?"

"Yes, I do," Clive said rather shortly.

Surprised at the brevity of his reply and the tone of it, Jeanne said, "What's the matter, Clive?"

"I just . . . think we'd better not discuss those days."

Jeanne understood at once. She knew she had hurt this man by her choice to marry Dake, yet great affection for him still remained and always would. Now she put out her hand and he took it. "You and I would never have been happy, Clive. You're going to be a great doctor and have a practice in London. You'll be among great society people. That's not for me," she said simply. "I like the woods. I like to go out in the morning and see where the deer have come up close to the cabin. I still like to hunt and to fish. It's the sort of thing you could do, but you would never feel yourself fulfilled."

Clive understood with part of his mind that Jeanne was right. He had always known this. Even when he had felt most in love with her he knew there was a dark foreboding in his mind about their future together. He was not a woodsman and liked his nature tamed—a cultured, cultivated garden perhaps, with all the flowers in neat orderly rows. He liked his hedges neatly trimmed and all in order. Jeanne, on the other hand, liked the wilderness, the wild tangles of the deep woods—the free running rivers that cut serpentine paths through the land. Clive thought of their differences for a moment, then smiled, "Perhaps you're right, Jeanne." He hesitated, then said, "Are you happy?"

"Very happy. I found a good husband, and we'll have a good life together when this war is over." She smiled gently and said, "And you'll find a wife who knows how to dress and do all the things that the wife of a famous surgeon in London must do."

The two sat there talking for a while, and from that moment on Clive felt a release in his spirit. All the sadness and grief that had been burdening him since Jeanne had chosen to marry Dake seemed to fade. It gave him a lighter look at life, and all that were in the house noticed that he seemed to be more cheerful than when he first arrived.

T   T   T

"Go to Philadelphia?" Micah was surprised. He looked up from the forge where he had been working on the latest attempt to create musket barrels and stared at his father. "What in the world is in Philadelphia? We're too busy here at the forge!"

Daniel had a sheet of paper in his hand. "I wrote to Benjamin Franklin in Philadelphia about a month ago. You know what trouble we've been having with this firing mechanism. I don't think we're ever going to get it right. Well, everyone knows Dr. Franklin is the most able inventor in the Colonies." He held the letter up and grinned. "I just wrote to him and asked if he would help. The letter came just this morning. He says for me to come and we'll talk about it."

"I doubt if you'll be talking about muskets, Pa," Micah said, shaking his head. "They're having that big meeting of the Congress, aren't they?"

"Yes they are, but Dr. Franklin says for me to come anyway. I don't know how that man does all that he seems to get done! He invents things, is into politics up to his ears, and runs his printing business. I don't think there's another man on this continent like him, or in Europe either for that matter. Anyway, I can't leave with a house full of sick people, and I can't leave the foundry either. So I want you to go and talk with Mr. Franklin."

Micah considered his father's request for a moment. It was typical for Micah to take his time, for he was methodical in all things, quite unlike his twin Dake who threw himself into any adventure impulsively. Finally, Micah nodded. "I suppose that would be best, Pa. When should I leave?"

"Right away! As soon as you can. I think it'd be quicker to travel by horseback rather than take the coach, but you can be the best judge of that. You'll need to take plenty of money for the trip. I'll go by the office and get it."

Daniel returned to the office and obtained the cash for Micah's journey. He was about to return to the workshop when he heard a knock at the door. "Come in!" he said. When the door opened, Cato, the butler for the Fraziers, stood there. "What is it, Cato?" Daniel asked.

Cato, a tall, distinguished black man, said, "It's Mr. Frazier, sir. He's taken a turn for the worse. Miss Marian wants to know, will you come?"

"Of course. How did you get here, Cato?"

"I rode one of the horses, sir."

"Come along, then. My horse is already saddled. I'll go with you."

"Yes, sir!"

Daniel delivered the cash to Micah and shook his hand, saying, "I think you ought to leave right away, son. Write me as soon as you get to Philadelphia."

Impulsively he hugged the young man, and then turned and walked away. He mounted the fine buckskin mare that was his favorite, touched her with his heels, and said, "Come on, Caesar!" The horse left the stable yard at a smooth gallop, and Cato followed on his horse as best he could.

When they arrived at the Frazier home, Cato said, "I'll take care of the horse, Mr. Daniel."

"Thank you, Cato." Daniel ran up the steps and knocked at the door. It was opened almost instantly by Hattie, the cook. "Miss Marian say for you to go up to Mr. John's room, sir."

"Thank you, Hattie!" Daniel quickly moved down the hall to the end, where he knocked on the door and entered when a voice indicated, "Come in!" Stepping inside he saw Marian leaning over her father, and moved to stand on the other side of the bed. "I came as quickly as I could!" Looking down he said, "How are you, John?"

John Frazier was not an old man, only sixty, but bad health had drained him of his vitality. His eyes were sunk back in his head, and his skin had the texture of pale clay. "Glad—to see you, Daniel," he wheezed.

There was a rattle in his chest, and alarm rose in Daniel. He had known of Frazier's poor health, but this bout seemed worse. Looking across at Marian he said, "Have you called the doctor?"

"Yes, he's been here once, and he's coming back later this afternoon.

You sit down and talk with father. I'll go make him some tea and broth. He's hardly eaten anything."

When Marian left the room, Daniel sat down and for a time spoke quietly, trying to encourage Frazier. In truth, he was worried, for he had great affection for John Frazier. Frazier had taken him in to the foundry when he'd had little to offer except the strength of his hands and the willingness to work hard. Now, he was half-owner, and for all practical purposes had complete authority. John had never questioned anything he ever did at the business, and the two had become very close friends.

Frazier lay quietly, seeming to labor for breath. Finally after a time he opened his eyes and looked up and whispered, "Daniel, I must talk with you." He took another deep breath, held it, and expelled it, then moved his hand in a helpless gesture. "I may not live, Daniel." When Daniel started to protest he shook his head. "I'm like an old animal; I know I'm going to die. I don't fear death, but it's Marian I'm worried about."

Daniel leaned forward to catch the words, which were very faint. "What can I do, John?" he asked quietly.

"Leo will get all the property when I'm gone. That's the law. Women have no protection." He hesitated and then reached out his hand. When Daniel Bradford took it he squeezed it with surprising force. "You must help her when I'm gone—protect her, Daniel."

The man's words brought a sense of uncertainty and doubt to Daniel. He shifted uneasily, then shook his head. "She has a husband, John."

"No!" The word came explosively, and John's grip tightened on Daniel's hand. "Leo will destroy her! You know what he is better than anyone. You must help her, Daniel!"

"Of course, I'll do what I can. You know that, John."

"You must do everything! I can't tell you how, but I've known for a long time that you two love each other—oh, I know it hasn't been a worldly thing! You're both honorable Christians. I can see it in your eyes, there's no guilt nor shame—" The sick man paused for a while; he had lifted himself in his vehemence and now lay back, seemingly exhausted. "Promise me, Daniel," he whispered.

Daniel saw that his friend was slipping into some sort of coma or sleep, so he leaned forward. "I promise, John. I'll do everything I can for her!"

When Marian came back into the room with a tray, she saw her father asleep. Daniel rose and said, "I think sleep might be the best for him."

Marian stood there, trouble in her eyes. "He's very ill," she murmured. Then looking up to Daniel she said, "Did he say anything?"

Daniel hesitated, then the basic honesty that was in him came forth. "He asked me—to look out for you."

Marian's eyes went to her father. She loved him dearly and knew that she would not have him for long. "That's like him," she whispered. "He's always put me first." Then she looked back, and even in her sorrow there was a tremulous smile on her generous lips. "And will you look after me, Daniel?"

"As well as is in my power, Marian." He did not say more, and the two turned away from the moment. Their emotions were deep. These two felt things strongly, but the barrier of Leo Rochester stood between them, and they knew better than to remain on dangerous ground.

🛡   🛡   🛡

Micah Bradford reached Philadelphia on the twenty-eighth of June and found America agonizing over independence. It had been months since Thomas Paine's *Common Sense* had swept across the Colonies, but as the summer heat came to Philadelphia, Congress could not quite bring itself to declare the Colonies an independent nation no matter how hard John Adams pushed and shoved. It teetered on the bank like a swimmer afraid to plunge into a raging torrent.

At this point in history, King George III of England made perhaps the greatest mistake of his reign. Parliament had voted to raise an army of fifty-five thousand men to come to crush the rebellion in America, but the men of England did not rally to the cause. Among the officers of the Royal Army and Navy there was much sympathy for the Americans. The war against America was not popular with the citizens of England. They felt, in effect, they were fighting against themselves—for these, after all, were Englishmen.

King George, faced with failure of his own people to rise to the occasion, went looking for hirelings. He found them among the principalities of Germany. Eventually some thirty thousand German mercenaries were hired, most of them from the Hesse-Cassel regions, who came to be called Hessians. Britain agreed to pay all the expenses of the Hessians as well as thirty-five dollars to their prince for each soldier killed, twelve dollars for each one wounded, and over five hundred thousand dollars annually to the Hessian government. With this last act, George III convinced most Americans that there was nothing left to do but cut the umbilical cord and declare their independence.

As Micah arrived in Philadelphia he noted at once the excitement everywhere. He had no trouble at all locating the home of the famous Benjamin Franklin, and although he rather doubted his welcome, he was pleasantly surprised. Knocking on the door of the yellow brick, two-story house in the center of town, Micah was ushered into the parlor by a diminutive servant and found Benjamin Franklin unable to rise.

Franklin, sitting in a chair, his right leg on a cushion, looked over his spectacles and said, "Good day, sir! You find me unable to rise to the occasion. You are Micah Bradford, I take it?"

"Yes, Dr. Franklin. My father has written you—"

Franklin waved his hand. "Yes, I'm very interested in your father's proposal." He winced as he moved his foot and muttered, "Blasted gout, what a time to be laid up! Sit down, Mr. Bradford, I have something that you'll be interested in!"

Micah sat down, and Benjamin Franklin nodded to the servant, saying, "Bring that folder over on the desk, Simon!" When he had it safely in his hand he opened it and said, "I've been doing some work on this firing mechanism for the muskets. I think I have come up with something very interesting." He started to rise and then cried out in pain. "Oh well, perhaps you will come and look over my shoulder!"

"Of course, Dr. Franklin!" Micah rose with alacrity, and soon the two men were pouring over the drawings, clear and meticulously executed on the sheets within the folder.

"This ought to work splendidly!" Franklin said. "I hope it will be of some use to you and your father!" He frowned then and handed the folder to Micah. "Take it home with you!" He added as an afterthought, "If I'm not mistaken, General Washington is going to be desperately in need of muskets very soon."

"How do things look with the Congress, if I may ask, Dr. Franklin?"

Franklin scowled. "You may ask, but I am afraid I have no easy answer! Adams wants the Colonies to be unanimous in their stand against England, but some of the Colonies are holding out, I'm afraid. New York, Pennsylvania, South Carolina, and Maryland are all on the fence. We must bring them in!" he exclaimed. "Will you have tea?" he interrupted himself. For the next thirty minutes Micah Bradford enjoyed the privilege of listening to perhaps the greatest mind in America speak freely about the problems of revolution and independence. Franklin was apparently speaking without any intention of stopping when the servant came in and said, "Mr. Adams is here—Mr. Sam Adams, I mean, Dr. Franklin."

"Have him come in!" Franklin said. His house was open to all visitors, and when Samuel Adams entered, Micah stood up at once.

Sam Adams said, "Why, Micah, I didn't know you were in Philadelphia." He came forward and offered his hand. Samuel Adams, the shabby, intense, master propagandist of the revolution was not handsome, but he had an intensity unmatched among men. His brother, John

Adams, was cultured, highly educated, and an aristocrat in every sense, but plain Sam Adams had been the spark that had ignited the revolutionary fervor. He had swayed Boston, played upon it like an instrument, bringing on the reaction of England, who sent General Gage and an army to quiet the firebrand.

"It's good to see you, Mr. Adams. I've just come from my father to talk with Dr. Franklin about our plan to build muskets."

Adams small eyes glowed with revolutionary fervor. "Fine—! Fine, my boy! We're going to need all the muskets we have!" He turned to look at Franklin and said, "Are you ready to go, Doctor?"

Franklin groaned and looked at his servant. "Bring the sedan chair to the door, Simon!" he said. He got to his feet, fumbling for his crutches. At once Micah leaped forward and handed them to him.

"Here, sir, let me help you!"

"Thank you, young man!" Franklin made his way painfully to the door, and the two men followed him. Two men carrying a sedan chair were there to meet him, and Franklin, groaning, got into the chair and said, "I'll be a little bit slower than you, Sam. You tell them I'll be there!" He turned his eyes and said, "You'll be around, will you not, Mr. Bradford? I'd like to talk some more to you about this factory your father's going to start."

"Yes, sir, I can stay as long as you please."

Sam Adams took Micah's arm. "If I remember right, you're quite a scholar! I need a scribe for the next few days. Could I press you into my service?"

"I'd be happy to serve any way I could, Mr. Adams."

"Come along!" Adams said impatiently, and he practically hauled Micah along the streets, headed for Independence Hall.

🔔　　🔔　　🔔

Micah Bradford never forgot those first days in Philadelphia, when a new nation was birthed. Every day Franklin was carried in a sedan chair to the State House by two paroled convicts, and was helped inside by Micah, who had an opportunity to see the new government in action. He noticed that there was an irresolute air about this Second Continental Congress. It approved what was called the Olive Branch Petition, which appealed directly to George III against Parliament. It was an effort at peace but was doomed from the start. The king refused to receive the petition and instead called on Parliament to put a "speedy end to these disorders by the most decisive exertions." The news that England had hired German mercenaries to quell the rebellion stunned even the moderates, and they realized that they were engaged in more than a family feud. "Nothing is left now but to fight it out," said Joseph Hewes of North Carolina.

An effort began to set forth the position of the Colonies in a formal document. The committee to draft a declaration was formed, and Thomas Jefferson was chosen to do the actual writing. Micah was standing close beside the small group, along with Sam Adams. Jefferson, a tall, red-headed man, looked at John Adams and said, "You really ought to do the drafting, Mr. Adams!"

"Oh no!" said Adams.

"Why will you not? You ought to do it."

"I will not!"

"Why, sir?"

"First, you are a Virginian, and a Virginian ought to appear at the head of this business. Second, I am obnoxious, suspected, and unpopular. You are very much otherwise. And finally my third reason; you can write ten times better than I can."

Thomas Jefferson was perhaps the most remarkable man of that congress. He was indeed a fine writer, although a poor orator. He had a high voice and stammered considerably. Nevertheless, he was the right choice to draft the declaration. His document was based on George Mason's famous Virginia Bill of Rights, which, in turn, relied almost entirely on John Locke. When Jefferson submitted his draft to Adams and Franklin for their criticisms and suggestions, forty-eight changes were made. Adams was deeply impressed by the language of the declaration. Franklin proposed the most changes.

Micah was rather amused at the witty explanation that Franklin gave Jefferson, who was somewhat chastened over so many alterations.

"I remind you of a hatter," Franklin said, his eyes twinkling, "who was about to open his shop. He made a sign that read, 'John Thompson, Hatter, makes and sells hats for ready money,' but his friends declared 'hatter' superfluous because there was a picture of a hat on the sign. 'Makes' was not necessary, because the buyer should care less who made them. He also didn't need 'ready money' obviously because no one bought hats on credit." Franklin's lips turned upward in a smile. "Only, 'John Thompson sells hats' was left, and these words also vanished after it was argued that 'sells' was redundant because no one gives hats away, and 'hats' was not needed because of the picture. So, nothing was left but the name. So you see, my dear Mr. Jefferson, my changes are not quite so radical as these."

Mr. Jefferson took the changes in good grace, and the Declaration of Independence was complete. Jefferson read it aloud in his high-pitched voice. "We hold these truths to be self-evident, that all men are created equal, that they are endowed by their Creator with certain inalienable rights, that among these are life, liberty and the pursuit of happiness."

Micah heard them read and thrilled to them, despite his own uncertainties about revolution. "By George," Micah Bradford murmured. "That says it complete! What I've always thought life should be like— life, liberty, and the pursuit of happiness." He found himself stirred by the Congress and by the great men he watched and heard speak in great ringing words, and he found himself more and more in sympathy with what these men were trying to do.

🜊   🜊   🜊

On July 1, 1776, John Adams arose, confident that the vote on declaring the Colonies free and independent would pass unanimously. But a canvas showed that there were still only nine colonies in which a majority of the delegate supported the measure. Maryland had swung toward it, but South Carolina had defected under pressure from Edward Rutledge. While Delaware was evenly divided, Caesar Rodney, known to be a friend of independence, was home at the bedside of his ailing wife.

Standing close beside Sam Adams, Micah heard Adams say to Franklin, "We've got to get Rodney here! He can swing Delaware, and without Delaware we're lost! I'll send someone after him if you think best."

"Do so at once!" Franklin exclaimed.

That night a courier rode ninety miles to Rodney's home with a plea for him to return to Philadelphia the next day to cast his crucial vote. New York, its delegates still claiming their instructions were to oppose independence, abstained from voting. Pennsylvania, no longer similarly bound, nevertheless, was in opposition by a vote of four to three. The Quaker ruling class was responsible for this.

But Richard Henry Lee of Virginia persuaded Rutledge to drop his opposition if both Delaware and Pennsylvania voted approval. Next, a deal was made, which was typical of Adams. John Dixon and Robert Morris were persuaded not to take their seats officially the next day. Pennsylvania would thus be in the affirmative three votes to two.

On July 2, Congress convened again. Franklin was there, his gout-swollen foot propped up on a stool. Jefferson was pacing the floor, his face drawn with the strain. John Adams and others could hardly bear the tension. Rain lashed the windows, and all hope seemed to be gone, then finally a cry came out, "He's come! There's Rodney!"

Almost every delegate except Franklin came to his feet as Caesar Rodney entered the hall, spattered with mud and soaked to the skin.

130

He had a cancer sore on his small, round face that was hardly bigger than a large grapefruit, and he was livid from his hard ride.

"We can do it!" Franklin whispered. "Now we can do it!"

Rodney's arrival put Delaware into the affirmative column. Afterward Pennsylvania followed suit, and South Carolina came back aboard. Although New York still abstained, the Colonies' assembly notified Congress on July 19 that it now favored independence unanimously.

On July 4, all the delegates to Congress—except John Dickinson—approved the Declaration of Independence. John Hancock, as president of the Congress, signed first with a great bold flourish that was to make his name synonymous with the flamboyant signature. He declared loudly, "There, I guess King George will be able to read that!" One by one the others all signed. Radicals, moderates, and conservatives all united in their determination to form a free and sovereign new nation.

Micah was standing beside Sam Adams, and he saw tears running down the older man's face. Adams had fought for this for years, and now he whispered, "Under God we will have a new nation. . . !"

11

BETRAYED?

AND SO THE COLONIES had a Declaration of Independence—but paper declarations do not win wars—armies accomplish that. Though the Second Continental Congress had proudly declared their independence, the entire revolution was in a state of flux.

George Washington, listening to very bad advice, had sent Benedict Arnold with a small, makeshift army to capture Quebec. The quixotic notion that Canada could be easily conquered, the leaders found hard to shake off. The fortress city of Quebec had cast its shadow on a generation of American colonists, and it seemed plausible that they might seize it and add it to their own territory.

On the last day of the year 1775, Arnold and his ragtag army fought their way through bitter winter weather and, in a raging blizzard, launched surprise attacks on the city, but Montgomery, the commander of the French forces in Quebec, was killed and Arnold wounded. A counterattack on the leaderless American forces turned the tide. Throughout the bitter winter Arnold clung to his lines around the city, but spring brought heavy reinforcements of British troops and ended all American hope for a great northern victory.

At the same time that American survivors of this foiled invasion were trickling back to Fort Ticonderoga, the British admiralty dispatched an expedition against the southern colonies. Sir Peter Parker led an impressive force of ten fighting ships, plus transports, for Sir Henry Clinton's twenty-five hundred troops. Parker and Clinton decided to attack Charleston, the South's leading port. Guarding the channel into that harbor was a log-and-earth fort on Sullivan's Island commanded by Colonel William Moultrie. On June 28, 1776, the great ships closed in and unleashed a furious cannonade. The fort, however, made of palmetto logs and sandy earthworks, simply absorbed the shots and shell. The fire from Moultrie's guns gave Parker's fleet a fearful pounding. That night, after suffering a painful wound, Sir Peter Parker withdrew, and a great American defensive victory gained two years of peace for the South.

Thus the score was one to one, a victory apiece for the British and their American cousins. Now, like a game of chess, the moves would begin, and the game seemed uneven. On one hand was England, the empire, the most powerful nation on the face of the earth with the mightiest navy and the largest army; on the other hand stood a group of disunited colonies divided by politics, religion, and sometimes enormous distances, with no standing army and no navy at all.

The British political scene at this time seemed to balance out any disadvantages the Colonies faced. George III was not only hated by everyone in the revolution, but his popularity even among his family and subjects waned. George III was not born in the happiest of homes. Queen Caroline, the wife of George II, said of her son, "My firstborn is the greatest liar and the greatest beast in the whole world, and I wish, I most heartily wish, he was out of it!" Her greatest solace on her deathbed was, "I shall never see that monster again!"

On October 25, 1760, George II died, and young George became King of England. A queen was found for him at once, a young German lady named Charlotte. They settled into a happy domesticity, and George started trying to act like a king. He loved nothing better than mingling with his subjects as "Farmer George." He believed, absolutely, in the divine right of kings—which was unfortunate, for that particular doctrine was on the verge of going out of favor. By the time the war with the Colonies came, he had surrounded himself with a group of close friends whose advice and influence would sink all the empire's efforts to conquer the Colonies.

The prime minister throughout the revolution was Lord North, a fat, amiable man who hated trouble. While he was at Oxford his tutor told him, "You are a blundering blockhead, and if you were set in the office of prime minister, you would be exactly the same!" North admitted later, "It turned out to be so!"

The actual conduct of the war was primarily in the hands of George Germain. He had been born Lord George Sackville and was a proud and arrogant man who had once been sentenced to death by a court-martial for cowardice. By contrast with Lord North, who was liked by even his political enemies, Lord George was disliked even by his political friends.

The leadership of the army was weak, but the condition of the most powerful navy in the world suffered also. Commanding the British naval forces, Lord Sandwich, first Lord of the Admiralty, was a bit of a rake—a tall, shambling, weather-beaten man who looked as if he had been hanged and cut down by mistake. Seeing him walking afar off, an acquaintance said, "I am sure it is Lord Sandwich for, if you will observe, he is walking down both sides of the street at once." Sandwich was fairly capable, at times, but the British fleet had been badly neglected since the end of the Seven Years War.

Opposing the British forces was George I—George Washington of America. The burden of independence fell upon his shoulders, and this tall, quiet man came into his position as commander in chief with many good qualities and a few bad ones. He was incapable of fear, everyone reported, and he did not always fight wisely, but always bravely. He had experience on the frontier, and by the time the revolution exploded he had married a widow, Martha Dandridge Custis. He was one of the wealthiest men in the Colonies, and his chief interest was his plantation at Mount Vernon. On leaving for the First Continental Congress he had made his gesture. He was a gambler by vocation and knew the odds of war, and he made the decision to risk everything he owned on the Continental Army, such as it was. Although the Declaration of Independence was signed, the British had dispatched the mightiest expeditionary force in history toward the Colonies. Sir Peter Parker brought his beaten men back from Charleston, and General Howe awaited the sign to move toward New York. There was tension in the air of the English-speaking peoples, and no one knew what to think of the situation—of the sudden longing for freedom and independence that had exploded in the thirteen colonies of America.

While the British prepared to strike against New York, and George Washington's untrained forces prepared to receive them, Katherine Yancy tended to her father and uncle in Halifax. True enough, she was conscious of the great movements that were stirring. The warships at the harbor were constantly being supplied with stores from the mainland, and James Steerbraugh hinted several times that he would soon be leaving with the fleet.

Katherine had become very fond of the tall, young lieutenant. He had been helpful since Clive had left, but Katherine missed Clive. She was somewhat shocked at how much, indeed, she missed him. She did find time to go, more than once, to the Gordon home, but her uncle grew steadily worse, and she spent much time searching for good food that might help him regain his health.

On July 6 she received a distinct shock. She had gone around the small shops, gathered some fresh vegetables, what little fruit was to be had, and made her way to the prison, which actually was an old warehouse. There were no windows in the sides, and light filtered through only the front and the back where two panes each had been cut into the ends.

The entrances were guarded by red-coated marines who had learned to know Katherine. One of them greeted her as she approached that morning. "Good morning, Miss Yancy!" He hesitated, then said, "I'm sorry, I have bad tidings for you."

At once Katherine thought of her uncle. "Is it my uncle Noah? Is he taken bad?"

The marine shifted nervously and did not meet her eyes. "I couldn't say, miss. You see, your father and your uncle were taken back to the *St. George* just early this morning."

Katherine stared at the marine without comprehension. "Back to the hulks! But why?"

"I don't know, miss."

"Who ordered it?" Katherine demanded.

"I have no idea, miss. You'll have to ask the officers."

Katherine went at once to the headquarters, where she learned that James Steerbraugh was gone for two days. She asked to see General Howe, and was told that he could not see her at the present. She waited all day at the headquarters, and finally when the sun was almost set, the sergeant came out and said, "General Howe will see you now, Miss Yancy."

Katherine entered the general's office and demanded directly, "General Howe, why have my father and uncle been moved back to the ship?"

Howe looked at her with some surprise. He had been in meetings for the past several days, and his mind was completely taken up with the hundreds of decisions that had to be made before the fleet left Halifax. "Why, I'm certain I don't know, Miss Yancy! I hadn't heard of such a thing! There must be a good reason for it, though."

"My uncle is in very poor health!" Katherine said. "I beg you, General. Let them be returned to the prison!"

General Howe ordinarily was a kindhearted man, but he was tense, for he had received orders from London that seemed to him impossible to carry out. His nerves were on edge, and he said sharply, "I'm sorry, Miss Yancy, but I cannot undertake to fulfill your request. It's possible that all the prisoners have been returned to the ship because the fleet will be sailing soon and they must, of course, go back with us."

"But you may not leave for days or even weeks!"

"I cannot discuss this matter with a civilian! Excuse me, I'm pressed for time!" Howe swept by the young lady. He felt sorry for her, but this was one minute detail that he felt his officers could better handle, and he fought down an irritation at this interruption.

Katherine felt helpless as the general left. She knew that there was only one thing possible, and she steeled herself to do it. *I'll have to go see Banks*, she thought. *And I'd rather die!* She made her way to the prison again and asked the same marine who had informed her of the change, "Could I see Major Banks?"

"I'll see, Miss Yancy." The marine left and soon returned to nod at her, saying, "Yes, you may go right in. You know where his office is, I believe?"

"Thank you, Sergeant."

As soon as she entered Banks' office, she had harsh memories of her last visit here when he had put his hands on her. Banks was sitting at his desk and looked up with what seemed to be surprise.

"Well, Miss Yancy, we meet again!"

"Major Banks, why have my father and my uncle been moved back to the *St. George*?"

"Why, I only heard about it myself this morning."

"Were they moved there by your order?"

"Oh, dear, no!" Banks got up and approached Katherine. He seemed to be relatively sober and said, "It was none of my doing, I assure you!"

"But you're in charge of the prisoners!"

"I have been forced to accept the assistance of Mr. Gordon. I think you know that!" There was a bitterness around his tiny, pursed lips and he said, "It was his father, the colonel—and he has interfered in my department—not for the better, I'm afraid. Your 'friend' Clive has asked Colonel Gordon to speak to General Howe, and he did, I'm sorry to say."

Katherine could not understand what the officer was saying. "What does that have to do with my father and my uncle?"

"Why, they were moved back to the hulks by Mr. Clive Gordon's request—his order was in his father's name, but it was his doing."

"I don't believe it!" Katherine spoke before she thought. "He wouldn't do that!"

"No? I assure you he did. Look—" Banks turned, walked back to his desk, opened the drawer, and pulled out a piece of paper. "Here is the order! It was here when I arrived this morning."

He handed the paper to Katherine, who quickly read it. "Have the prisoners, Amos and Noah Yancy, removed from the base prison back to the *St. George*." It was signed, "Clive Gordon."

Katherine stared at the sheet of paper, then lifted her eyes. "I can't understand this!"

Banks reached out for the paper, saying, "I must have that for my records!" Taking it, he put it back in the drawer, then turned to face her. "I'm afraid you don't know the young man's reputation! It's not very good where women are concerned. I think he was toying with you!"

Katherine found this completely unbelievable. She stared at the major and said, "Why do you say that?"

"Why, it's a matter of common record! He's been known to chase women before."

Katherine's head was swimming. She could not believe what was happening. "You could reverse his order, couldn't you?"

"No, oh, dear me, no! You saw what happened when I crossed Mr. Gordon. He threatened me with a duel. He's a hotheaded chap as well as a womanizer, and if I did this I would be crossing the colonel, his father."

Katherine stood there, her mind numb. She tried to think of something to say, but nothing came. Finally she said, "Major, could I have your permission to visit my father on the *St. George*?"

"Why, as I've always said, Miss Yancy, I want to be helpful! I'll give you a pass, of course, then later we can meet to discuss some better arrangements."

It sounded like something all too familiar to Katherine, but she accepted the pass that the surgeon scribbled out. As he handed it to her, he patted her shoulder and said, "Don't feel too downhearted! Many young women have been deceived by handsome young men before. You go along and see your father, and I'll speak with you later to see if . . . if the visits can be continued."

Katherine left the prison feeling like a trapped animal. She could not understand why Clive Gordon would do such a thing. She made her way at once to the docks, where she obtained a passage to the *St. George* with one of the fishermen.

When Lieutenant Smith saw the pass, he said, "I'm sorry to see them come back. They had to carry the old gentleman aboard. He was unable to walk."

Katherine allowed herself to be escorted to the cabin that had become familiar to her on her previous visits. She clasped her hands tightly together, trying to make sense out of it. When her father came in, she saw at once that he was troubled. "Father!" she said, going to him and putting her arms around him. He looked tired and worried. "Why has all this happened?"

"We weren't told anything, Katherine!" Amos Yancy said. The two sat down in the hard chairs while they spoke. "I'm worried about Noah! He's worse. I don't think he can stand life down in the hole."

"Why did he do it?" Katherine burst out.

"Who?" her father asked in bewilderment.

"Clive Gordon! The surgeon tells me it was by his orders that you were brought back!"

Amos Yancy was too tired to think straight. He was worn down by the long imprisonment, and now worry for his brother clouded his mind. "I don't know, my dear. We must simply trust God."

The two visited for a while and finally Katherine rose and said, "I'll try to get you moved back, but General Howe won't listen to me, and I don't think Major Banks will either. I'll do the best I can for you, though."

"I'm sure of that, daughter."

Katherine left the St. George, and as soon as she stepped ashore she stood there uncertainly. There was nothing really she could do, and for a long time she walked along the rocky shore seeking desperately to find some way to help her father and her uncle.

The sky was gray that day, and a storm was blowing up far out at sea. She saw dark clouds rolling along majestically, but with a menace in them. The gulls followed her, crying harshly as they swooped nearby looking for scraps. She ignored them and tried to pray, but she was not very successful. God seemed to be locked away somewhere from her. The heavens were brass, and her pitiful attempts to call on God seemed to be vain words, even to her.

Finally she turned homeward and thought about Clive. "I was wrong once before about a man," she said, thinking of Malcolm, her former fiancé. "I put my trust in him and he failed me. Now, here's another one I shouldn't have trusted." She was not thinking too clearly, for bitterness welled up inside her toward Clive. She made her way back to the inn, but it was dark and she went to bed at once.

For two days she went back and forth to the ship, each time receiving worse news from her father about his brother.

On the third day she had just risen and gone downstairs when she saw the tall form of James Steerbraugh. He caught her eye and came to her quickly. Removing his hat, he asked, "May I see you, Miss Yancy?"

Fear rose in Katherine and she said quietly, "Yes." They took a seat at one of the tables. There were no customers there, and even the innkeeper had stepped into the back room.

"I have bad news for you, I'm afraid." The fine eyes of Steerbraugh were filled with compassion, and he said, "It's your uncle. He passed away last night. I just got word and I came right here."

Katherine was flooded with memories from her childhood. "I remember riding on his shoulders," she said quietly. "He loved children, and he spoiled me hopelessly. He was such a good man, and to die like a dog in the bottom of that foul ship...!"

Steerbraugh could say nothing to this. He asked, "Would you like to go to your father?"

"Yes, I would!"

The two made their way to the ship, where Katherine was soon speaking with her father. Amos seemed almost calm. It was as if a burden was lifted. He said once while they were talking quietly, "He was so ready to go, Katherine. Almost the last thing he said to me was, 'I'll be seeing my Lord Jesus soon. I'll tell Him you'll be along one day.'" He looked at Katherine and nodded. "It's a good thing, daughter. There was no hope for him really."

"I know. It's just—" Tears came to her eyes and she dashed them away. "It's just that I'll miss him so!"

"Aye, so will I." He looked at her carefully, then said, "Now, listen to me, daughter. There is something you must do. You must take Noah home for burial."

"No, I must stay with you!"

"You can do nothing for me, but you owe this to Noah! I would do it if I could, but since I can't it's up to you."

They talked for some time, and slowly Katherine began to see that this was the way it would have to be. "All right, Father," she said. "I'll make the arrangements."

🛡   🛡   🛡

The arrangements were difficult, and if it had not been for James Steerbraugh, Katherine would have been helpless. She found him a friend, indeed, and he took care of all the details. He came to her at the end of the second day and said, "Miss Yancy, I've taken care of everything. The ship will be leaving tomorrow. It will stop at Boston. Your uncle's body has been embalmed and placed in a casket."

"I'll pay you, of course, all the expenses!"

"Don't speak of that! I'm glad to help. I'm just sorry it's come to this."

"You've been so kind, not like—"

When she broke off, Steerbraugh blinked with surprise. "I'm not like who?"

"Not like your friend Clive Gordon." Steerbraugh tried to speak, but she said, "No, I don't want to talk about it!" She put her hand out, and he took it at once. She squeezed it, saying, "Thank you so much for your many kindnesses! I'll be on the ship tomorrow. I don't know if we'll meet again, but I'll never forget you, Lieutenant."

The next day at noon the freighter, with the unlikely name of *Blue Skies*, pulled out of Halifax headed for Boston. It was loaded with supplies that would be purchased by the patriot cause, but Katherine was not thinking of that. She was thinking, as she stood in the bow watching the gray water part and the white bubbles that clung to the sides of the old freighter, *I wish father were with me!*

She thought then of her uncle down below and of the loss she had suffered. Finally she thought of Clive Gordon, and her lips tightened. *I'll never trust another man as long as I live!* she thought with more bitterness than she'd ever known. She knew that was wrong, for she had seen the courtesy of James Steerbraugh, but she was not herself. Betrayal twice in a row had been too much for her, and she stood there holding the rail until her knuckles grew tight, thinking of how she had given her trust and admiration to a man who had turned against her.

12

"HE'S A MAN, ISN'T HE?"

LEANING BACK IN HIS Windsor chair, Clive Gordon surveyed the Bradfords that had gathered at the breakfast table and felt a glow of satisfaction. Daniel, of course, sat at the head of the table with Micah on his right hand, directly across from Clive. These two, naturally, were strong and healthy, but it was the other three Bradfords who brought a special pleasure to the young physician. Sam was shoveling pancakes down his throat so fast that there was some danger of choking, but he washed them down with huge drafts of milk. Beside him, Rachel, her cheeks having regained their glow of health, was eating eggs and ham with obvious relish. Across from her sat Jeanne, wearing a very attractive green dressing robe. She was faring well with a large bowl of mush over which she had poured a liberal dose of molasses.

"Well, I wish all my patients would recover as well as you three!" Clive said after taking a sip of the strong coffee in his mug. "That's what a doctor likes to see."

"That's what I like to see, too!" Daniel said. His face was tanned and he held a piece of pancake speared on the end of his fork. Pausing before he put it into his mouth, he looked fondly around the table and said, "You've done a fine job, Dr. Gordon! I'm going to recommend you to all my friends."

"They won't be able to afford him!" Micah grinned. He looked across the table at Clive and said, "The first thing a successful doctor does is raise his fee so that he doesn't have to fool with common folk like us, just the aristocracy!"

A laugh went around the table, and Clive took it good-naturedly. He had become very fond of these American relatives of his and was looking forward to seeing his own family so that he could tell them about how well he had fared with them.

It was a pleasant breakfast, with light streaming in from the window to the left of the room and through the Dutch door with the top swung open. The smell of the new earth that had been broken up for a garden floated in from the outside, and it was cool and pleasant in the cheerful kitchen where they had gathered around the circular table for their morning meal. Finally Micah began to speak of the meeting in Philadelphia. He held them spellbound, tossing around names such as Thomas Jefferson, John Adams, John Hancock, and, of course, Benjamin Franklin.

Finally Sam interrupted to say, "I should've gone with you! I would have if I hadn't been sick! Dr. Franklin's an inventor like me!"

Micah grinned broadly. "Well, at least his stoves don't blow up like some of your inventions do!" Then when he saw irritation cloud his young brother's brow he said quickly, "You know I was just teasing! You and Dr. Franklin would get along very well, I think. He's a tinkerer if there ever was one—just like you!"

Mollified, at least momentarily, Sam speared the last morsel of pancake with his fork. He shoved it into his mouth, and Rachel said, "Sam, don't take such big bites! You never taste anything! You're like a snake. You gobble things down as if someone's going to take it away from you."

Sam paid his sister no heed whatsoever. "What does it mean, Micah, the Declaration of Independence?"

Micah's brow furrowed, and his mild hazel eyes grew thoughtful. He ran his strong hand through his straw-colored hair and, as was customary, thought for a moment before he spoke in a gentle drawl. "I suppose, Sam," he said finally, with regret tingeing his tone, "it means that we'll fight a war to separate ourselves from England."

Sam picked up the glass of cider, drained it off, and set it down firmly before looking at Clive. "What does that mean to you, Clive? Does it make you mad like it does old King George?"

"Sam, don't be impudent!" Daniel said sharply.

But Sam shook his head and shrugged. "Well, Clive's an Englishman, isn't he?"

Daniel Bradford said firmly, "So am I, Sam, and you heard what I said. We'll have no more discussion of this!"

Clive at once spoke up. "I suppose we'll have to discuss it; everybody else is in the Colonies—and at home in England, too." He looked at Sam and said, "Frankly, Sam, I think England is making a terrible mistake!"

"You do?" Sam's eyebrows lifted. "Well, why don't you do something about it?"

Clive laughed abruptly. "You mean I should go home and walk into the palace and grab King George III by the scruff and tell him, 'Now look, George, you have to stop that foolishness over in the Colonies, you hear? It's got to stop!' "

Laughter went around the table and Jeanne said, "But surely there's somebody over there to tell the king what an awful mistake he's making!"

"I'm afraid not! All his advisors are fools except for William Pitt, and George won't listen to him." Clive thought about the morass of English politics and said, "It's so simple when you think of it. North America, this country America, is the most valuable possession England has, and because she wants to collect a few pounds in taxes she's throwing it all away. Why, if she would be reasonable and accept America as Americans on equal terms, a kingdom could be forged that would keep Europe in peace for generations. France or Spain wouldn't dare attack if America and England united. America with all her resources, and England, with her powerful armies, would be an unbeatable combination."

Daniel listened carefully as the young man spoke. Finally he said with sadness marking his voice, "I'm afraid you're right, Clive. England's too bullheaded to listen, and it's going to be a long hard war. I wish your father were somewhere else, in India perhaps."

"So does he, Uncle Daniel!" Clive shrugged. "But a soldier goes where he's ordered, you know that."

"Yes, I know that. Still, it's a tragedy, and I shudder to think about Dake being in a battle with his blood kin on the other side. It's hard on your family, I know."

Rachel saw that the conversation had taken a turn that saddened Clive and her father, so she changed the subject abruptly. "I've been thinking about the Yancy family you spoke of. The young woman whose relatives you helped." She looked at her father and said, "Do we know them, Pa?"

"Yes, we do. Didn't you see Katherine at the wedding?"

"I don't know. If I did, I don't remember ever seeing her. Have I met the Yancys before?"

"Yes, we all met them when George Whitefield had the meeting here, remember? Everybody came, and we ate once at a tavern with several families who were attending the meeting, including the Yancys. You were very young then, and Sam there was no more than a baby, still crawling around." Daniel laughed at Sam's reaction and said,

"They were Congregationalists, I think."

"That's right!" Clive said with interest. "Katherine mentioned that. You do remember them?"

"Now I do! You had some talk with her father, didn't you, Pa? You were talking about the sermon and how Whitefield was different from any minister we had ever heard."

"Yes. I really enjoyed talking to Amos Yancy," Daniel said. "He was a tall, well-set fellow with brown eyes and curly brown hair. And his wife's name was Susan."

"That's right!" Clive said, excitement touching his eyes. "Well, this is interesting! I'll have to tell them when I get back to Halifax."

"I remember Katherine, now," Rachel continued. "She was about my age, I think. We sat together at the inn and talked about boys, if I remember. Both of us were just learning they were different from girls." She grinned roguishly at her father, who winked at her. "She was a pretty girl. I was envious of her! She still is I take it, cousin Clive?"

Clive was embarrassed and said merely, "You don't have to be envious, Rachel. You're every bit as attractive as Katherine!"

The breakfast ended, but later that morning Clive came upon Jeanne in the garden. She was sitting on a wooden bench that Sam had built, and Clive asked, "May I join you, Jeanne?"

"Of course, here, sit down!" She had changed clothes and was wearing a sky blue dress, and she wore no bonnet on her head. Her short, black, curly hair that Clive had always admired formed ringlets that framed her face, and her large violet eyes, as always, attracted him. "I don't know some of these flowers. I know these—they're primroses. And we call these four-o'clocks."

Clive picked one of the small blossoms—long tubes with a fragrant smell. "Why do you call them that?"

"Oh, because they open about four o'clock and don't close until the next morning." She named several more flowers, then Clive mentioned the ones that grew in England that he liked particularly.

A brown thrasher alighted in a hedge, twitching his tail and staring at them with bright eyes. They laughed at his antics and finally began talking about their experiences in the past. Clive began, for he had been somewhat troubled about his romance with Jeanne. Finally he said, "I suppose, Jeanne—what I'm saying is I made a fool out of myself over you! I can see now that Dake's the husband you need, although you'd be a prize for me or any other man."

Jeanne listened to him quietly, then hesitated only for a moment. "I think you're very interested in Katherine Yancy, aren't you, Clive?"

"What makes you think that?" Clive demanded rather defensively.

He picked up a stick and tossed it at the brown thrasher, which flew off ten feet, then came back arguing vociferously at the interruption. "I find her attractive, of course; she's a very pretty young woman."

"I think it's more than that!"

Clive shifted uncomfortably in the seat. She had touched on a sore spot with him, and finally he turned to her and said in a half-ashamed tone, "I guess I must be a faithless man, Jeanne. You're right, I am attracted to Katherine. Here a short time ago I was in love with you—or thought I was, and now I think I'm in love with her. I must be a womanizer!"

Jeanne reached over and put her hand on Clive's. Squeezing it she said, "You're not a womanizer, far from it! You're a gentleman in every sense of the word."

"Then, why don't I know when I'm in love?"

"I think it's hard to know love, Clive!" Jeanne tried to frame her thoughts. She was not an eloquent young woman, but things were very simple to her. She loved her husband, Dake. She loved the out-of-doors, and she loved God. Now, trying to explain the complexities between men and women was suddenly difficult for her. Finally she said, "I think part of the love between a man and a woman has to be—well, *admiration*. I always had such an admiration for you."

Clive looked at her with astonishment. "Well, that's what I felt for you, Jeanne! I think I admired you more than any woman I'd ever seen. You were so strong and handled hard things so well. That was what always impressed me about you."

"I think this is what attracts you to Katherine Yancy, isn't it? You said so before."

"Why . . . I believe that's right! She *is* a strong woman. Not many could have done what she's done." He began to talk enthusiastically about Katherine's struggle to help her father and her uncle. Finally he said, "It's hard for me to tell. She's very attractive, and a man is drawn to that. Good looks aren't everything, but they certainly don't hurt. It's what she is that has drawn me to her, I think. Is that love, do you think, Jeanne?"

"I think it can be part of it. Are you going to see her again?"

"Yes, I'm going back to Halifax right away, probably the day after tomorrow. There's a ship leaving then. I'm concerned about her father and uncle. Neither of them is in good condition." He rose and said, "It will be hard to leave here. You and the Bradfords have made me feel like part of the family."

Jeanne rose and said, "You are part of the family, Clive." Looking up at him she smiled and said, "I'm glad we've had this talk. I think it might have helped clear up something in your mind."

He leaned down suddenly and kissed her on the cheek, a brotherly kiss. "Yes it did! I feel much better now, *cousin* Jeanne. You are a discerning young woman."

☫   ☫   ☫

The two men who walked along the streets of Boston, headed for the foundry operated by Daniel Bradford and John Frazier, could be mistaken for nothing else but clergymen. Both wore the customary suits of solemn black, broken by the whiteness of the stocks at their throat, and both had a serious look on their faces. Asa Carrington, at fifty, was the older of the two. He had black hair and eyes, was no more than medium height, but was strongly built. He moved quickly, purposefully, this pastor of the Methodist Church of Boston, and when he spoke his voice was deep and full. "You'll like Boston, and your new church is a fine one! I'm glad you've come, Devaney."

Reverend William Devaney, six inches taller than his Methodist friend, was the new pastor of the Congregational Church in Boston. He was a tall man, angular, no more than thirty years old, and there was an innate dignity in him. He had dark blue eyes, dark blond hair, and rather craggy features. "It will be quite different from the small village where I've been pastor for the past four years," he said. He looked at his new friend and said, "It's kind of you to introduce me around, Asa."

The two men had become close friends, and it had been helpful indeed for Devaney to get an introduction to the city of Boston. The Methodist pastor knew everyone, and Devaney had already met the mayor of the city council, and now he said, "I understand the Fraziers are staunch members of my church, although I've not met them yet."

"Well, John Frazier is an invalid. He has only the one daughter as I mentioned, Lady Marian Rochester, married to Leo Rochester."

"What sort of people are they?"

Asa Carrington hesitated, but only for a moment. "You'll find Marian Rochester to be an outstanding member of your church."

Noting the omission of the husband, Reverend Devaney looked at his companion. "And her husband?"

"Well . . . Sir Leo is not a church man. I tell you no more than is common knowledge. He's not a man that is admired. Oh, he's rich, of course, but has a bad reputation for gaming, gambling and—well, other things."

Devaney was an astute young minister and knew that "other things" probably meant consorting with women; however, he did not press the

146

issue. He stored the facts in his mind and said, "Is that the foundry ahead?"

"Yes, it's owned jointly by John Frazier and by one of the members of my own church, Daniel Bradford." He hesitated again and said, "William, I hate to plunge you into wheels within wheels, but the situation is—well, *complicated.*"

"Complicated how?"

"There are rumors around that Daniel, who came to this country as an indentured servant for Sir Leo and has worked his way up to half-owner in this factory . . ." The Methodist preacher hesitated, then said, "I'm not one to bear rumors, but there are some about Marian Rochester and Daniel Bradford."

"That's unfortunate."

"There's nothing to them, I'm convinced!" Carrington said quickly. "You know how rumor mills are; every city has them. I just tell you this because I know you'll hear it, and I want to assure you I'm convinced Daniel Bradford is an honorable man, and Marian Rochester is a woman I cannot presume to praise too much. She's put up with a terrible life from her husband, and now her father is dying. She has to rely on someone, and Frazier's very fond of Daniel, not only as a business partner, but he sees him as a son. Come along, I'll introduce you."

The two ministers entered and found Daniel working at a forge with his son, Micah. After the introductions were made Daniel said, "I'm happy that you've come, Reverend Devaney. It's been hard on the Fraziers not having a pastor, although our own pastor has been good to visit them."

Devaney was favorably impressed with the Bradford men. He spoke carefully to them of the Fraziers, of his having to make adjustments, all the time studying Daniel Bradford's face. What he saw pleased him, for there was a basic and inherent honesty, almost nobility, in Daniel's face. He could not imagine such a man to be involved in anything scandalous with another man's wife.

After a time Devaney said, "I begin my new duties on rather a sad note."

"How is that, Reverend?" Daniel inquired.

"A funeral, I'm afraid."

"Oh, you've had a loss in your church family?" Reverend Carrington asked. "That's not the best way to start, is it? Anyone I know?"

"I don't know them personally, of course. A gentleman named Yancy. I've met the family. The funeral is tomorrow."

"I am acquainted with some Yancys—but they have been in Halifax."

Devaney stared at Bradford. "Well, it must be the same family. This man's name was Noah Yancy. He died in Halifax, and his niece, I understand, who was there, brought the body back."

Daniel quickly questioned the minister, and as soon as they left he said, "I've got to go tell Clive about this, Micah! You can get by without me for a time."

Leaving the foundry he walked quickly home. It was too short a distance to even bother with a horse. He found Clive out in the garden in the backyard, where he was speaking with Rachel and Jeanne. "Clive!" he said, "I've got some news for you! Not very happy news, I'm afraid."

Clive rose at once, asking quickly, "What is it, Uncle Daniel?"

"Was the name of the man you treated in Halifax, Amos Yancy's brother, Noah Yancy?"

"Yes!" Seeing his uncle's face rather troubled, he said, "What is it? What's happened?"

"I'm afraid he died, and Katherine has brought the body home." He quickly told how he had heard the news from the new minister of the Congregational Church.

"I must go at once! This is terrible!" Clive said as soon as Daniel finished.

"Do you know how to get to the Yancy place?"

"No, but I'll find it!"

"I think you should go by the Congregational Church. The minister told me he was going back. In any case, someone can help you under these conditions. Take my horse—the mare!"

"Thank you, Uncle Daniel!"

As Clive left, Daniel said sadly, "Too bad! It bothered Clive; I could see that."

Jeanne said, "He was just talking this morning about going back to see if he could help the two men." She hesitated, then added, "And he was anxious to see Katherine, too."

👑 👑 👑

Katherine had arrived at Boston only two days earlier, and that late at night. The previous day she had spent taking care of the affairs and comforting her mother, who was deeply grieved over the loss of her brother-in-law. Susan had been very attached to Noah, with a deep affection for him, and now it seemed her nerves could not stand the strain.

Katherine had taken over everything, including making the funeral arrangements. She had stayed at the church most of the morning, greeting friends of the family who had come by to offer their condolences, and had finally left at two o'clock in the afternoon. She had found her mother asleep, and she, herself, was weary and drawn. The trip had been hard on her, for it had been a rough crossing and she had been sick for the first part of the voyage, unable to eat. The strain of worrying about her father was always with her, and she went into the kitchen to fix a cup of tea. After fixing the tea, she sat there wearily, her mind clouded with thoughts. She heard a knock at the door, and since the servant had gone to the market, she rose and moved to open the door, assuming that it was another neighbor who had come to offer help.

When she opened the door she stood there absolutely dumbfounded, for it was Clive Gordon who stood there wearing a dark blue suit, his hat in his hands, and his eyes fixed on her.

"Katherine, I just heard about your uncle! I'm so sorry."

Katherine could not think for a moment. She had wondered how she would react if she ever saw Clive Gordon again, and it was worse than she had anticipated. She stared at him coldly, bitter thoughts flashing through her mind, but all she could really remember was that he had failed her. Coldly she said, "Mr. Gordon, I have nothing to say to you!"

Clive stared at her with astonishment. "Why . . . why, Katherine, what do you mean by that?"

Katherine's voice was as cold as polar ice. "You killed my uncle, and you will probably be responsible for the death of my father! I hope I never see you again!" She shut the door abruptly and turned and put her back against it. Her limbs were trembling, as were her hands, and tears of anger sprang to her eyes. She ran out of the hallway, ignoring the knocking on the door and the sound of Clive's voice pleading. She went to her bedroom, fell across the bed, and tried to stifle the sobs that rose in her breast.

T   T   T

Rachel stood outside the small red-brick house, and when the door opened she asked quietly, "Miss Yancy?"

"Yes, I'm Katherine Yancy."

"My name is Rachel Bradford. I believe we met once some years ago!" Rachel saw the doubt in the young woman's eyes and said, "It was at a meeting when George Whitefield came to Boston. Our two families met at the Pigeon Inn. You and I sat together and talked about the meeting. I've never forgotten it, though it was a long time ago."

"Oh, I do remember that! Won't you come in, Miss Bradford."

"Thank you!" Rachel entered the house and was escorted to the parlor, where the two women sat down. "I've come to offer my condolences on your loss, Miss Yancy."

"Thank you, it was kind of you to come—especially on such a brief acquaintance and so long ago."

Rachel had talked to Clive and had been shocked at the utter bewilderment and pain that she had found there. She had listened carefully, but saw that Clive was only confused by Katherine Yancy's behavior. "I thought I'd done the best I could for her, but she acts like I'm a murderer!" he had said. He had been as one stricken, and Rachel had decided to take it upon herself to make a visit. Now as she sat there, she knew she had to be absolutely honest. "I wouldn't have come on such a slight acquaintanceship, but I've come on behalf of a relative of mine."

"A relative, Miss Bradford?"

"Yes, my father's sister is Lyna Lee Gordon, and her son is Clive Gordon." Rachel saw the shock touch the eyes of the young woman and said quickly, "I've been very ill recently, along with my younger brother and my sister-in-law. My father sent for Clive to come and care for us. He stayed with us until we were all well."

Katherine sat there listening in a state resembling shock. She had known that Clive was going to treat his family in Boston, but to see the young woman before her brought everything back clearly.

"I'm afraid I have nothing to say about your cousin!" she said briefly.

"Would you mind if we talked about it? Clive is very distressed!"

"I have nothing to say about Clive Gordon!" Katherine said. She felt a moment's pain at the thought of the loss of her uncle, and somehow she had tied his death inextricably to Clive Gordon. She said, "If he hadn't put my uncle back on that prison ship, my uncle would be alive today!" She did not really know if this were true, for her uncle had been very ill even in the prison inside Halifax. But bitterness had gripped her, and she had linked Clive Gordon and Malcolm Smythe together as men who could not be trusted.

"I can't believe that my cousin would do anything dishonorable!"

Furious anger rose in Katherine and she said bitterly, "He's a *man*, isn't he? And if he's a man he can be unfaithful!" She stood to her feet, saying, "I'm sorry, and I thank you for coming, but I cannot discuss Clive Gordon!"

Rachel saw the hopelessness of remaining and she said, "I offer the sympathy of my family, my father, and my brothers."

"Thank you!"

The words were brief, and Rachel had no choice but to leave.

T   T   T

The funeral was well attended, but Katherine was not really aware of the crowd. She did hear some of the sermon by Reverend Devaney. She believed with her head all that he said—that there would be a time when all the righteous would come forth out of the grave, and her uncle would be one of them. But that was dry doctrine to her. All she knew now was bitterness, that he was dead, and that nothing could bring him back.

At the cemetery the body was lowered into the grave, and Katherine stood there listening as the Scriptures were read. She was conscious of the blue sky overhead, the birds reeling about in wide circles, the smell of the fresh earth, and of spring, but it meant nothing to her.

Finally she lifted her eyes and saw Rachel Bradford standing, waiting to speak to her. Forcing herself to be polite she said, "I thank you for coming by. It was kind of you, Miss Bradford."

Rachel said, "I'm sorry for your loss." She hesitated, and then said quietly, "Clive has gone back to his family."

Katherine didn't answer, and finally Rachel moved away.

Later that afternoon, when the grave was filled in, Katherine came back to the cemetery, drawn there by some strange impulse. She stood over the grave, raw and red, a mound that covered one whom she had loved dearly. Bitterness came to her. It was mixed up somehow with a fear for her father. *He may die too!* was the thought that was constantly with her.

She thought of Clive and of all the Scriptures she had heard about forgiveness. She thought about something that Rachel had said during her visit, that bitterness can only destroy. She knew it was wrong, and yet somehow she could not put away the anger and the bitterness within her. She lowered her head and tears ran down her cheeks—yet she could not find a gentleness in her for Clive Gordon—and she knew she never would forgive him.

PART THREE

—

FIGHT FOR LONG ISLAND

August—September 1776

13

ABIGAIL AND MATTHEW

THE WORN OAK DESK was piled high with maps of every sort, and light from the small window threw a pale illumination over the one that had gained dominance on top of the stack. Standing behind the desk, Colonel Henry Knox allowed his large gray eyes to run over the lines that delineated the streets of Manhattan. Knox's left hand was braced against the table as he leaned over it supporting his ponderous bulk. He weighed over two hundred and fifty pounds and swelled the fabric of his pale cream waistcoat. The blue frock coat with the golden epaulets, the wide white collar turned down, was buttoned tightly just under the white ruff of lace at his throat. Knox's other hand was kept on his hip, just under the edge of the frock coat. He had been shot there in a hunting accident and lost several fingers, so he usually kept it half hidden.

Henry Knox was one of those men who loved war even though he was not a soldier—at least not at first. He had been a successful bookseller in Boston, but had delighted in stories of war, and had become an expert in the history and use of artillery. His hobby had become his profession when he had been hastily added to George Washington's staff and sent to Fort Ticonderoga to bring back cannon to Boston. Henry Knox might not have had a military background, but then neither had anyone else in Washington's ragtag army.

Knox's quick eyes ran to and fro outlining the problem before him with a keen, analytical mind. He studied the shape of Manhattan Island, and a sense of foreboding rose in him. "It's nothing but an island!" he said, noting that the boundary of one side constituted the East River, and the other side the Hudson River. Instantly he knew that the mighty warships of King George's navy could not be prevented from sailing up either side and pounding Manhattan with its cannons.

155

A knock disturbed the colonel, and looking up with some irritation, he barked, "Come in!"

When the door opened and a young man entered, however, a pleased smile turned the corners of Knox's lips upward, and he at once moved around the desk with a great deal of grace, which some heavyset men possess. "Micah—" he beamed. "Come in!" He extended his hand, shook Micah Bradford's hand, pumping it enthusiastically. "I just received your letter yesterday! You made good time! Here, sit down. There's some of this cider left. Let me pour us a drink. We'll toast your new service in the Continental Army!"

Micah Bradford was very glad to see Henry Knox. The two had been good friends for a long time. Micah was the reader of the Bradford family and had haunted Knox's bookstore since adolescence. The huge bookseller had taken to the young man, and the two had spent many happy hours together talking of books and poring over the latest volume of poetry or history.

"It's good to see you, Colonel Knox! My father sends his best wishes!"

"Ah, yes, and how's the musket factory coming along? I'm very interested in that—but I'd be more interested if he would begin to manufacture cannon!" Knox bustled around pouring the clear cider into two pewter mugs, then motioning for Micah to take one, he took the other. He held his glass out, which Micah touched with his own, and beamed. "To a happy military career for my young bookworm!"

Micah took a long drink, then shook his head. "Not a very long career. Only ninety days, Colonel."

"Well . . . well, we're grateful for that! Right now we need every man we can get to hold this place."

"You think it's going to be difficult?" Micah asked, setting his mug down.

"I think it's going to be *impossible* if the British send as many ships as I think they will."

"What does General Washington say about this?"

Knox shrugged his burly shoulders. "He's very sensitive to the desires of Congress. He says that Congress wants New York held, and His Excellency is determined to do so if possible."

"What's so difficult about it, Colonel Knox?"

"Why, it's completely indefensible! Come here, I want to show you something." Knox drained the remains of the cider, slammed the mug down, then moved back behind the desk. "Look at this!" he said, pointing a blunt finger at the outlines of New York. "We can be surrounded, cut off, and annihilated. That's what's the matter with it! I wish we could leave and make our stand somewhere else."

For some time the two men spoke of the battle that was to come, until a knock on the door interrupted them. When Knox barked out a command to open it, a young lieutenant came in at once, his eyes glowing with excitement. "Colonel Knox, the British fleet—it's beginning to arrive!"

Knox frowned and shook his head. "I wish they'd given us another month to fortify the city. Come along, Private Bradford, we'll have a look at the lobsterbacks and their ships!"

As the two men made their way down toward the harbor, Micah asked, "How many troops do we have for the defense of the city?"

"Counting every man jack of them, about nineteen thousand."

"Why, that seems like a great many!"

"Not enough, and they're not trained! Almost all of them are infantry—and half of those are militia," Knox scowled. "They're poorly armed, poorly equipped, and poorly trained." He glanced over and said, "Your brother Dake is here, isn't he?"

"Yes, sir! He's signed up for the duration with the regulars, the Continentals."

"Well, they're the best of the troops. If anything will save us, it will be the Continentals."

As the two men moved toward the docks, they noted the soldiers digging furiously, throwing up barricades. Knox stopped twice to give directions to the officers in charge. Finally they reached the dock and stared out over the water. Micah was shocked at the number of sails that covered the gray ocean. He said nothing, and it was Knox who began counting the masts out loud. The count went on for some time, and he finally said, ". . . forty-four, forty-five. I guess that's the lot of them, but there'll be more to come!"

There was a grimness on his round reddish face, and he shook his head. "By the time they all get here we'll have our hands full."

Sir William Howe had arrived with only three ships, but soon forty-five more appeared, and soon after eighty-two more. Howe had brought with him nine thousand three hundred men from Halifax. They landed on Staten Island and set up camp. Soon Sir William Howe's brother, Sir Richard Howe, appeared from England with another hundred and fifty vessels and more troops. Next came Sir Peter Parker with Clinton's expedition to Charleston—fresh from failure, and burning to wipe it out. A month later, Colonel William Hotham arrived with thirty-four more ships, twenty-six hundred elite troops from the Guards Brigade, and eight thousand Germans.

By the time they were all ready, the British forces mustered thirty-two thousand men under arms—horse, foot, and artillery—supported by twelve hundred guns from the warships, and ten thousand sailors. By then, so many transports and lesser vessels had arrived that they whitened the water.

It was the biggest and most expensive expedition that Britain had ever sent overseas. They had spent the staggering sum of eight hundred and fifty thousand pounds to organize and supply it. The Americans were now facing the most powerful armada ever assembled under the British empire!

$$T \qquad T \qquad T$$

Abigail Howland had fallen into a comfortable pattern during her brief stay in New York. After the hardships of the siege she had endured at Boston, her aunt Esther's house seemed to be an island of paradise. She loved the house itself, which was well proportioned and built following the Dutch fashion, one of the narrow ends of the house facing the street. On the warm summer evenings it was the custom for everyone in the neighborhood to sit outside, and even though the drums of war were sounding, there was lively singing and front-door parties that Abigail thought very pleasant.

The house itself had four rooms on the ground floor—a parlor, a dining room, a library, and a kitchen. Above, on the second floor, there were six bedrooms, and over them was an attic used by the servants. There was a cellar for the storage of household supplies, and just outside the kitchen door, a woodshed—a dark, roomy place in which a whole winter's supply of wood for heating and cooking could be kept.

On the roof there was a cupola—a sort of covered balcony that could be reached by the stairs. Already Abigail had found this the most pleasant place to stay in the cool, cobwebby hours of the morning. She had come up now to sit there with her aunt, and the two watched as the street below began to come to life with the morning activity.

"It's so different with all the soldiers here," Esther Denham said quietly, looking down as a troop passed, followed by a caisson and cannon rumbling over the cobblestones. She was wearing a light tan dress cut in a simple fashion, and wore a white bonnet, even indoors, as was customary with her. Her silver hair peeped out from under it, and she turned to smile at her guest. "You came at a very busy time, Abigail," she said quietly. "Ordinarily things aren't quite this busy in New York, but then we didn't have a war going on."

"I suppose I'm used to it, Aunt Esther," Abigail answered. She looked down on the narrow street below and thought about the difficult months she had spent in Boston uncertain of their future. Turning to her relative she smiled. "It's been so good to be here. Mother and I were in a bad condition back in Boston."

"It's been good to have you. I've been lonely these recent years. It's nice to have company again."

Esther Denham was a widow and had only one living daughter who lived in Pennsylvania. She was married to a merchant in Pittsburgh, and Esther had not seen her in over a year. There was a wistfulness in her face as she said, "I miss Aileen and my two grandchildren very much."

"Have you ever thought about going to live with your daughter and her family?"

"No, that wouldn't do! They have their own life, and this is home to me. I've spent almost my whole life here in this house. It would be too hard for me to leave it."

The two women sat there speaking quietly. Below in the kitchen, the servants were getting breakfast ready, but just now there was a quietness in the cupola, and it was pleasant to sit there with no responsibilities, nothing to do. At least it was so for Abigail. She had started coming up early in the morning only a few days earlier, invited by Esther, who had said, "I always begin my day there. Just a quiet time, just me and the Lord."

Abigail had been put off by the reference to God, but she had joined the older woman out of a desire to start the day differently. She had expected to be preached at, but it had not been like that. Esther had simply read one of the psalms and had made a few comments on it, then had bowed her head and prayed a brief prayer. Relieved, Abigail had joined her, and now as she sat there she was thinking how unusual it was for her to join anyone in what amounted to a religious exercise. She did not like church—what she had seen of it—and avoided it whenever possible. It had been necessary to make a show of appearing at the services, for her family had been rather strict about this.

Now Esther opened the Bible on her lap and without comment read a portion of the Psalms. It was the thirteenth psalm and it began, "How long wilt thou forget me, O Lord? Forever? How long wilt thou hide thy face from me?"

The words caught at Abigail, and she listened more carefully than was usual for her. When Esther closed the Bible and Abigail observed, "That's not a very happy chapter, Aunt Esther. It sounds like the psalmist is complaining to God."

"I'm sure that's true. That's one of the things I find attractive in the psalms. David and the others who wrote these songs were very honest. Sometimes they seemed to be downright angry at the Lord—as in this one. You can almost imagine," Esther said with a smile, "David shaking his fist and shouting, 'God, are you going to leave me like this forever? What's wrong with you?'"

The thought intrigued Abigail. "I never thought of that. He doesn't sound like a very holy man."

"David was a man after God's own heart," Esther said quietly. "But he was a man not only of great passions but of unbridled ones sometimes. He wept, he cried, he laughed, he danced, he loved God with all of his heart, though he often failed Him."

"Why did God love David so much?"

"I think because David loved Him so deeply. Secondly, I think because he was a great repenter."

"That's a strange thing to say—a great repenter."

"It's true enough, though. David sinned greatly, but the instant he recognized it he turned from his sin and cried out to God. I think that's something all of us need to learn, don't you?"

Abigail hesitated. She could not well agree with her aunt honestly, for she had never denied herself anything. In all truth, she had never been very sorry for anything she had done. Thinking back quickly she remembered how sorry she was that she had been caught on several occasions—but the thought of being sorry for the sin itself was a novel idea to her. "I suppose so," she said noncommittally, "but it doesn't sound like David was getting along with God."

"No, at this point I think he was not," Esther nodded. She let the silence run on and seemed to be meditating thoughtfully over the words on the page. She ran her fingers over the lines again and said, "That's clear from the second verse: 'How long shall I take counsel in my soul, having sorrow in my heart daily?' Those aren't the words of a happy man!"

"I don't understand it. I thought God's people were supposed to be happy."

"There's a difference I think, Abigail, between happiness and joy."

"Oh? I thought they were the same."

"Not really. Happiness is that good feeling we have when everything is going right—when we're not sick, and when we have plenty of food, a roof over our heads. When things are going very well, then we have this feeling of happiness."

"But what is joy, then, Aunt Esther?"

"I think that's the experience we have in our hearts when things go completely wrong—and still, we are not disturbed in our hearts. It is like happiness—but it is not dependent upon outward circumstances. I think that's how the martyrs could endure the flames; even though God

160

had taken away everything in this world that brings happiness, He had given them the joy of His own presence in their hearts when they faced death."

Abigail listened carefully as her aunt spoke, but it made little sense to her. She finally was glad when her aunt closed the Bible and said, "I think we must pray for all the soldiers who will soon be fighting." She bowed her head and prayed a simple prayer. She ended by saying, "And bless Abigail, Lord. Touch her heart in a very special way and lead her in the way that is right, and I ask this in the name of Jesus. Amen."

Abigail was not at all sure of her feelings concerning this prayer— so personal! Something was stirring within her at the reading of the Bible. She could not explain it, but ever since she had begun reading with her aunt there had been a restlessness in her. More than once she had decided not to come again, but there was something in her aunt's calm assurance that intrigued her. Now she said, "Tell me some more about our family."

"You were so interested in them that I brought you a letter. This is from my mother, Rachel Winslow Howland. It was written to a friend while Rachel was in prison in Salem waiting to be tried for the crime of witchcraft."

"That was all such a long time ago. It's hard to believe in those things anymore."

"It was real enough for them. Gilbert Winslow was there, and he was an old man at that time. Let me read you some of what your grandmother says." She took up the piece of single sheet, handling it carefully, and read:

My dear Emily,
　　It appears that God may be about to take me out of this world. Five others from the prison were executed yesterday for witchcraft. One of them a very elderly woman, two very young men. The judges are sparing no one, and I am prepared to hear their judgment. I write these words to let you know that my faith has not been shaken. God is here in this dirty, foul prison. It is as though He had lit a lamp in my heart and lighted the dark places. If I go to be with the Lord God tomorrow, I will meet my Beloved. It will be a celebration for me, and I wanted you to know how glorious it is to be able to face death with joy. He has given this joy to me unexpectedly. I always was afraid of death, even the thought of it—but now that it is here, I feel the presence of the Lord Jesus Christ in my heart, and I go to meet Him with victory in my spirit.

　　　　　　　　　　　　　　　　Your friend,
　　　　　　　　　　　　　　　　Rachel Winslow

After Esther put the letter down carefully in her lap, Abigail shook her head. "I don't see how anyone could face death like that. I couldn't!"

Esther began to speak of the power of God to calm troubled spirits. Finally she said, "I'm not sure that I have dying grace now, but I don't need it. God gives us grace as we need it, not when we don't." She sat there quietly and asked finally, "What about your spiritual condition, Abigail? Are you at peace with God?"

Abigail was shaken by the simple, direct question as she never had been by any sermon. Somehow Esther's words brought a sense of fear, for she knew that she was not at peace with God. Almost abruptly, in order to shut off the feelings that were raging through her, she said, "God has no use for me!"

"You're wrong there, my dear!" Esther said quietly. "God so loved the world that He gave His Son, and you're part of the world. He loves you. We have the cross of Christ to prove God's great love." She began giving her own testimony on how she had found God.

Abigail was glad when the servant came to announce that breakfast was ready. She arose at once and went down the stairs, determined not to come back and listen to more of her aunt's preaching. It had frightened her and stirred things within her heart that she could not explain. "I know why I've come here," she said. "I'll do what Leo asks, and then I won't have to stay in this place any longer. . . !"

☙   ☙   ☙

Abigail slipped into the new dress that her aunt Esther had insisted on buying her. It was a formal gown of watered silk taffeta in the empire style. The neckline was quite low, and the small dainty sleeves stopped at the same level as the necktie. She admired the rose satin ribbon that bound in the sleeve and the neckline, and looked down to the bottom of the skirt decorated with four flounces of lace, topped by rows of tiny silk ribbon florets. She slipped her feet into her satin slippers, picked up her fan and her bag, also made of satin, and wrapped a paisley stole around her shoulders. She took one quick look into the mirror, admiring the necklace that her aunt had insisted she wear, a double strand of pearls with a large rose quartz, and earrings of rose quartz to match.

Leaving her room she encountered her mother, who said, "My, what a beautiful gown—and you look so well in it!"

"It is beautiful, isn't it? And so nice of Aunt Esther to buy it for me. We had such fun shopping!"

"Oh, I forgot to tell you! A letter arrived by post yesterday. I put it on the card table in the hall."

"Thank you, Mother. I'll take it with me!"

"Where are you going this time? You and Matthew have been very busy for the last week. I think you've been somewhere every day and most of the nights."

This was true enough. Matthew had appeared and invited Abigail to spend an afternoon with him nearly a week ago. Since then he had been back every day enjoying several meals with the family and attending church with them two days earlier on Sunday.

"I think we're going to his studio or his apartment that he shares with his friend," Abigail said. "I'll tell you about it when I get back!"

She moved into the hallway, picked up the letter, and stopped abruptly. She recognized Leo Rochester's handwriting. For a moment she was tempted to return it, for she did not want to read it. Nevertheless, she knew that it must be done. Opening it quickly, she scanned the lines:

My dear Abigail,

I have been waiting anxiously to hear from you. I am anxious to hear how our project is going. Also, I inform you, that if you need more funds, write me by post and I shall see that they are supplied. I am sure you are making progress, and I will expect to hear good news from you very soon.

Leo Rochester

Abigail slipped the letter into her reticule and left the house. The coach was waiting, and she gave the address to William, the driver, and then got inside. As the carriage rolled along over the cobblestones, she paid little attention to the activities on the streets, for she was thinking of Leo Rochester and their "project."

It had seemed logical enough, and possible enough, back in Boston—this convincing Matthew to do what Leo Rochester wanted. After spending a great deal of time with Matthew, however, Abigail felt less certain. She had learned to like him immensely, far more than she had ever thought she might. There was an openness and an honesty, yet a sense of humor that made Matthew a charming and delightful companion. He had spent the more recent years in England and kept her amused with countless, interesting stories of which he seemed to be filled.

I wonder if I can do it? she thought as the carriage pulled up in front of a building.

"Here we are, miss," the coachman said. Jarred out of her thoughts she got out of the carriage and said, "You needn't wait, William. I'll take a carriage home."

"Yes, ma'am!" William spoke to the horses, and the carriage pulled away.

Abigail looked at the building, then started up toward the door. She heard her name called and looked up to see Matthew leaning out of the window.

"Stay right there!" he yelled. "I'll be down to escort you up!"

Abigail smiled at his exuberance and realized that his yell had introduced her to the neighborhood. A small detail of soldiers laughed at her, and one of them said, "You better come and go with us, missy! We'll show you a good time!"

Abigail could not help smiling as the sergeant dressed the man down. *Soldiers are the same everywhere*, she thought. It had been the same in Boston whenever she went out on the street. Everywhere she had gone, she was constantly accosted by the British troops.

The door opened and Matthew came out at once. He was wearing a simple black broadcloth coat with white knee britches. His eyes were alive with pleasure and he reached out and took her hand. "Just on time!" he said. "Vandermeer and I have been planning for your visit. Come upstairs!" Matthew talked incessantly as he led her up the stairs. When they reached the top, he opened the door and ushered her into the apartment.

Vandermeer, who greeted her at once, was well dressed, as far as he was concerned for the visit of Abigail Howland. He had heard much about the young woman and had dredged up a colorful waistcoat, containing all the hues of the rainbow, and a pair of baggy trousers that were much the vogue in Holland, though seldom seen in England. His round moon-face beamed and he said, "Ah, Miss Howland, so happy to see you again! Just in time for tea and cakes!"

"We'll be going out to eat later on," Matthew said as he led her to a table covered with a rather ancient white tablecloth.

Jan began pouring the tea and gave neither of his companions time to speak. "You haf completely captivated our young friend, Miss Howland. I think he will never make an artist until he stops thinking so much of you!"

Abigail had liked the Dutchman from the first. There was an openness and a cheerfulness about him that could not be withstood. Smiling at him she asked, "Can't a man court a woman and be an artist at the same time, Jan?"

"I do not think so! Art takes everything!"

"What about yourself, Mr. Vandermeer? You do not have a sweetheart?"

Vandermeer found this amusing. He gestured enthusiastically with his hands and spoke in explosive bursts as was his custom. "I haf a million sweethearts, but they are all on canvas! Look at this!" He ran across the room, ripped a canvas from a stack, and came back holding it up. It was a portrait of a young peasant girl, apparently painted on the Continent. She was pretty and had a roguish expression on her face. "Here! Is she not beautiful?"

"Very pretty! Was she your sweetheart, Mr. Vandermeer?"

"It does not matter what she was. Whatever she was," Jan exclaimed almost violently, "she is not like this! In fifty years, she will be old and white haired and stooped, and perhaps with no teeth! But this one here on the canvas, ah, she will be just the same, yes?"

"I suppose so!" Abigail laughed. "But you can't cuddle up to a piece of canvas in a frame!"

"You are romantic!" Vandermeer grinned. "Most young ladies are!"

"I rather agree with Miss Howland, Jan," Matthew said quickly. "Flesh and blood is better than cold paint!"

Vandermeer held the picture up and shook his head. "You will never be an artist until you get that idea out of your head!" he exclaimed. "Everything changes but art. It always remains the same!"

"I don't think that would be good if people remained the same," Matthew said. "It's natural enough to be young, and naturally we grow old. Would you always have us stay sixteen years old?"

For nearly an hour the philosophical argument about youth and age and life went on. Abigail found herself, without difficulty, entering into it. It was refreshing to be listened to, able to talk in the company of men and be respected—which had not always been the case. Some men she knew had no respect at all for a woman's judgment. Looking over at Matthew she was impressed at how different he was from most other young men she knew. He was completely different from his brother Dake, and from Daniel Bradford. Now that she knew the truth about his birth, this did not come as a great shock.

However, he was not like Leo Rochester either. As the two men continued to fire barrages of arguments at each other she thought, *He looks like Leo somewhat, but there's a goodness in him that Leo doesn't have.* She thought he must have gotten that from his mother, and finally when the argument was referred to her she pulled her thoughts back together and laughed. "I can't settle all of your arguments. I think you both are pretty foolish anyway."

"You are right! All artists are foolish! Ve haf no sense at all in a practical way!" Vandermeer admitted, laughing at his own shortcomings.

Later on in the afternoon the three of them went for a walk throughout the city, then returned for a brief meal that Vandermeer fixed. He was actually a good cook, and the leg of mutton was expertly done with spices that he would not reveal. After the meal, Matthew said, "I must take our guest home, Jan."

"You must come back many times!" Vandermeer said, smiling as he shook the hand that Abigail offered him. "Matthew is a foolish young man, and it will take both of us to get him reared properly! You will teach him about love, and I will teach him about art!"

After the two had left, they went to a park and sat down for a time. It was a quiet place, giving the impression of being out in the open countryside. For a time they sat and talked, and then Abigail said regretfully, "It's getting dark. I must be getting back, Matthew!"

"I suppose so!" Matthew said rather grudgingly, then turned to her. "Stay just a while longer!"

"Well, not for long," Abigail said. She was aware that Matthew was very vulnerable in many respects. His years on the Continent had not made him into an accomplished ladies' man, as it might have many. There was an innocence in him, and she knew she had gained some power over him. Again she thought of Leo's note, and when Matthew suddenly reached out and took her in his arms she yielded herself to him.

As he kissed her she was suddenly confused by several things. She had been kissed before, naturally, and was not inexperienced in love. Nevertheless, there was something in his embrace and in his kiss that was somehow different—or at least so it seemed to her. There was a response in her as his arms pulled her closer, and his lips sought hers with passion. She gave herself to him, but at the same time she was aware of a disturbance within her own heart. *I'm doing this just for money*, she thought with a stab of disgust. *That makes me little better than a prostitute!*

Suddenly she pulled away, confused by her own thoughts, and stood to her feet.

"What's the matter? Have I offended you, Abigail?"

"No . . . no, you haven't, Matthew, but I think it's better that we go home now."

"As you say!" He found a cab, and the two rode quietly back to the Denham house.

When he walked with her to the door after the carriage stopped, she put out her hand and said, "Good night! It's been delightful!"

"Will I see you tomorrow?"

"If you like!" She smiled then and turned and entered the house. When she went to her room, she undressed quickly and put on her nightgown and got into bed. She sought sleep for some time, but it did not come. Her thoughts were ragged and wild, and she almost cried aloud as she thought, *What else do I want! I was ready to marry Nathan Winslow just to have security. Now all I have to do is nod and I'll have Matthew. He'll have a title someday. I'll be Lady Abigail Rochester!*

But these thoughts did not please her. Restlessly, she turned and buried her face in the pillow, trying to blot out the thoughts of what she had been and what she was now. Somehow, even in the midst of this, she was conscious of the quiet voice of her aunt reading Scripture to her, and this was even more frightening.

For the first time in her life Abigail felt completely and totally helpless. She was a self-sufficient young woman, able to manage her own affairs—or so she thought. But as she lay in bed, memories came to her that she hated—things that she had done, how she had used people. And for the first time in her life Abigail Howland prayed a sincere and earnest prayer. It was short and came out almost in the form of a cry, "Oh, God—don't let me be so awful!"

14

A Dream Out of the Pit

AFTER MICAH LEFT to serve with Colonel Knox in New York, Daniel Bradford found that he had to work twice as hard at the foundry. He had not known how much Micah had taken the burden from him, until at the end of the first week he had found himself red-eyed from lack of sleep and unable to think clearly as he went about his work. He rose before dawn and by noon had done a full day's work. Snatching a bite of food as he could, he doggedly moved through the rest of the day and often did not get home until well after dark. Rachel scolded him, and Albert Blevins, the tall sour-faced bookkeeper in the foundry, told him bluntly one afternoon, "You're going to kill yourself, Daniel, if you don't learn how to take some rest!"

Looking up from the piece of white-hot iron that he had been pounding with a sixteen-pound hammer, Daniel blinked and found that his throat was so dry he could not speak. He put the glowing iron on an anvil and pounded it into shape, then dipped it into the barrel of water. The water reminded him that his throat was dry, and he moved across and lifted a bucket, drinking directly from it thirstily. The water ran over his chin and down the leather apron he wore, but he did not heed it, so delicious was the drink, even though it was tepid.

Blevins watched all this with a jaundiced eye. He had been with the Frazier Ironworks long before Daniel came, and at first he had been skeptical of the new partnership. He was devoted to John Frazier and had been afraid that the younger man would edge his master out. However, through the years he had been satisfied to see that Daniel Bradford's devotion to Frazier was second only to his own. Now he was anxious that Bradford would put himself into a state of exhaustion and said with a snappy tone, "Go home, Daniel! Take a long bath, crawl in between some clean sheets, and sleep for twenty-four hours!"

Looking across the smoky blacksmith shop, Daniel grinned wearily. "You're worse than a mother hen, Albert! Hard work never killed anybody!"

"Where did you ever get a crazy idea like that? Hard work has killed more people than wars. It just takes a little longer than a bullet to do it!" He came across and put his hand on Daniel's chest and shoved him. He was a frail man, and Daniel was sturdy, thick with muscle, and he could not move him. Doubling up his fist he struck him hard in the chest and said, "Go home! Spend some time with your son and daughter! Go out and get drunk. Do something besides work!"

"I don't think the last would answer," Daniel shrugged. Weariness struck him like a club, and he suddenly realized it was hard just to keep standing. "But I think you're right. I may come in late tomorrow."

"Good! That's showing some sense!"

"Have you heard from John today?"

"I got a note from Mrs. Rochester. She says the doctor was there, and he's not any better."

"I think I'll stop off on my way home." Then seeing the glint of disapproval in Blevins' eyes he said, "Just for a few minutes, I promise!"

"I know what your promises are worth like that. You'll sit there and talk with him for two hours!"

"Not that long, Albert. He's not able to talk that much." He looked over at the tall, thin man with the cadaverous face and shook his head. "I'm concerned about John, and so are you."

Blevins held Bradford's glance and nodded. His lips going tight, he said, "He's not doing well, Daniel. Go by and see him. Your visits cheer him up a great deal."

It was over an hour later before Daniel walked up and knocked on the door of the Frazier house. Again he was surprised at how tired he was. "Must be getting old," he muttered. "I can remember the day I could work like a mule for a week." He was still a strong man, he knew, and at forty-six could work most of his younger employees into the ground. He was thinking how age comes up, sneaking around the corner, and touches you instead of announcing itself.

When the door opened, Cato stood there, his teeth grinning. He bowed jerkily and said, "Yes, sir, Mr. Bradford. I'm glad you come!"

"How's Mr. Frazier, Cato?"

Cato reached out and took Daniel's hat and shook his head sorrowfully. "Not too well, I'm afraid. He's awake though. You can go right up."

"Is Mrs. Frazier with him?"

"No, sir! She's gone to see the Williams family down the street. They lost their little girl day before yesterday."

"I'm sorry to hear it. I was hoping she would pull through."

"Yes, sir, we all was hoping that, but she didn't make it. The funeral will be tomorrow I 'spect you will want to go."

"Of course. I'll go on up then, Cato."

"When you come down I'll have a bite fixed for you to eat. I 'spect you ain't had no supper yet."

"Don't bother, Cato."

"It ain't no trouble, sir. You visit a while with Mr. Frazier. It always helps when you come to see him."

Daniel nodded and went at once to the sick man's room. He found John Frazier sitting up reading in bed. He looked, in fact, better than he had the last time that Daniel had come, and he said cheerfully as he entered, "Well, if you keep improving like this, you'll be out chopping wood!"

A slight smile tugged at John Frazier's lips. He knew Daniel always put the best face on things and put the book aside. "Sit down, Daniel. Tell me what's been happening at the foundry! How's the musket enterprise going?"

Daniel sat down and for some time chatted with Frazier. He studied the older man without seeming to, noting that Frazier's color was somewhat better. He did not mention Frazier's sickness, for there was nothing to be said about it. He enjoyed the talk, for he had always had a special affection for John, and was grateful to him for giving him a start in a growing business.

Frazier enjoyed the visit too, but after thirty minutes he seemed to tire. "I just can't seem to gain any strength, Daniel, but the doctor has got me on a new medicine." He reached over and picked up a brown bottle and grimaced, pulling his lips back to show his distaste. "It tastes horrible! I think Dr. Bates thinks that the worse the taste, the better the medicine."

"Bates is a good man!"

"Yes, he is. He's done all he can. Well, go along. You look tired, Daniel."

"I think I will. Blevins was telling me I need to take it a little bit easier."

"So you should. You'll wear yourself out if you don't slow down. I remember," Frazier said with a sad look in his eyes, "when I could work like that. Enjoy it, Daniel, it'll soon be gone." Then he caught himself and laughed shortly. "There I am talking like a prophet of doom—but

170

you mind Blevins. He's got a lot of wisdom in that skinny skull of his."

Daniel shook the frail hand and said, "Let's have a prayer before I leave."

Frazier looked up quickly. "That would be good, Daniel!" As Daniel prayed, John held to the strong, powerful hand with both of his as if to draw strength from it. A fleeting thought came to him—not a new one, for he had it often: *If only Marian had married Daniel.* When the prayer was over he whispered, "Thank you, Daniel, that helps a lot."

"Good night, John." Daniel left the sick man's room and went down the hall. He turned into the kitchen where Cato was sitting on a stool, holding a cup of something.

"Yes, sir, Mr. Daniel, you set yourself right down here. I done got some pork chops cooked up, and some of Lucy's fresh baked bread, and some of them field peas you like so much."

Suddenly hunger struck Daniel like a club, and he sat down and fell upon the food that Cato set before him, washing it down with long drafts of fresh milk. At some point Cato warned him, "Don't eat too much! We got fresh apple pie, just like you like, Mr. Daniel!"

Daniel pitched into the pie and finished it off with a cup of hot black coffee with three heaping spoonfuls of sugar in it. Leaning back he shook his head. "That's the best meal I've had in a spell, Cato! Thanks a lot!"

"You're welcome, Mr. Daniel!"

Daniel rose and left the kitchen, but as he turned into the hall he encountered Leo Rochester. He stopped abruptly and said, "Hello, Leo."

"Hello, Bradford."

Rochester was wearing a dark green dressing gown over what appeared to be some thin clothing. His hair was mussed, and there were dark circles under his eyes. "I couldn't sleep," he muttered. He shook his head, pulled his shoulders together, and said, "Come into the study." Without waiting for an answer he turned, and Daniel followed him down the hall. They turned into the walnut-lined study, where two lamps burned over the mantelpiece, casting an amber light over the desk and the horsehair furniture. "You want a drink?" Leo asked, picking up a bottle from the desk.

"No thanks, I've just eaten, and it's late!"

"Sit down!" Leo said. He, himself, turned and dropped into a chair, poured a drink, and held it up to the light, examining the amber color of it. "The doctor tells me," he remarked, "that I'm not supposed to do this!"

"Better listen to your doctor."

Leo lowered the glass and looked over it at Daniel. "I never was much for listening to advice," he said, then downed the liquor. His shoulders shuddered as the jolt of the alcohol hit him, and he leaned back in the chair. "I guess I look like death warmed over," he remarked, a sarcastic tone in his voice.

"You don't look very well, Leo. You've been having some kind of trouble. What is it?"

Leo Rochester considered the broad shoulder, the deep chest, and the thick neck of Daniel Bradford, and for a moment envy ran through him. He had always been envious of Daniel Bradford, not just of his strong body—but more of the spirit that the man had. Now, his own physical problems had stripped him of much of his own strength, which had been considerable. He locked his fingers together and leaned back into the chair. "I don't want to talk about myself. How's John?"

"Not too well. Have you talked to Dr. Bates lately?"

"Marian has. She says he doesn't hold out a great deal of hope. John's just wearing out."

"Yes, I think you're right, and unless God intervenes I fear he won't last."

His remark caught at Leo Rochester. He leaned forward, placed his elbows on the table, and locked his fingers together. Placing his chin on them he considered Bradford with a speculative look in his blue eyes. His brown hair had fallen over his forehead, but he did not notice. A silence fell across the room, and Leo seemed unaware of it. From somewhere out in the hall a large clock was ticking, counting off the moments in a sonorous fashion. Leo finally said thoughtfully, "You really believe that, don't you, Daniel?"

"Believe what, Leo?"

"That God's interested in us!"

"Yes I do!"

"Why should He be interested in a bunch of creatures like the human race? There's not much to us, Daniel, even the best of us."

"I disagree, Leo." Daniel's voice was calm. He was accustomed to Leo's poking fun at his religion and had long ago refused to let it bother him. "I think you know better, really. What about your own father? He was a good man, and you know it!"

Leo suddenly grinned. "You would bring him up! I could bring up a thousand men who are not what they ought to be—but you're right about my father. He was a good man! I can't deny it."

"I shouldn't think you'd want to!"

Leo was caught in some sort of inner turmoil. He had hated Daniel at times, but still there was something in the man he was drawn to. Ever

172

since Daniel was a mere boy, he had tried to shake Bradford's rocklike Christian convictions. He had treated him shamefully, almost in an inhuman fashion, and still Bradford refused to strike back. Leo leaned back and said, "I've been thinking about the past a great deal. You and I have been tied together in rather strange ways, haven't we, Daniel?"

"Yes, we have."

"Do you remember those times how I lied to you and Lyna and made you both think the other was dead? Does that still grate on you a little bit, Daniel?"

"Not anymore." Daniel shook his head and added, "I hated you when I first found out about it, but that's gone now."

"Nice to be able to think like that . . . to forgive. I don't find it so easy."

"It's not easy for any of us!" Daniel sat back and looked at the ravaged face of the aristocrat before him. Dissipation had marked Rochester's face with coarse lines, and there was disillusionment in the eyes that were now sunk back into deep sockets. He had watched Leo destroy himself for years, and there had been times, as Leo too had admitted, that Daniel hated Leo. Now, however, he felt a strange compassion come over him, and he said, "God's not like we are. For some reason that I can't understand, and perhaps no one else, He *is* love. And, therefore, He forgives. I think we've got to grasp that about God even if we can't understand anything else."

"And you really believe the things these Methodists have been spouting about—that you must be born again?"

"Yes, I do! A man is naturally bad. That's why the Scripture says, 'All have sinned, and come short of the glory of God.' "

Leo considered this, then reached out suddenly and poured himself another drink from the bottle. He held it for a while and then downed it, shuddering again. "I'll agree with that. We've lost the glory of God, all right—if we ever had any! Go on, tell me some more," he said.

There was a jeering note in Rochester's voice, but Daniel took him at his word. For some time he sat there telling how Jesus Christ had come into his heart. How that since that time he had been different. He spoke slowly, deliberately, and in the background he heard the clock ticking out in the hall. It was the first time Leo had ever listened to him, and the thought came to his mind like a white-hot iron, *Why, he's dying!* Bradford was astonished at that but then he thought, *Men die every day, women and children, as well.* Leo Rochester had been a part of his life for so long that he had become a fixture—although one that he had to learn to endure. Now, looking at the weakness of what had once been strong hands, and noting the color of Rochester's face, Daniel somehow knew that this was his opportunity.

He spoke slowly and calmly, quoting many Scriptures, and finally when Leo did not speak he said, "We've never talked about these things, have we, Leo?"

"No!"

The brief word was enough to reveal some of the condition of Rochester's mind. The fact that he would listen, Daniel understood, was almost a miracle. He said, "I think it's good for all of us to stop and think about God. I wish I'd done it earlier. I wish you would now, Leo."

Leo Rochester was strangely quiet. He sat there listening as Daniel spoke about man's need for God and pressed the question upon him. But finally Leo brusquely said, "Good night, Daniel!"

Daniel hesitated. He wanted to say more, but he saw the adamant look in Leo's face. Rising, he said quietly, "It's been good to talk with you, Leo. Maybe we can do it again sometime."

"I said good night!"

There was a sharpness in Rochester's voice, and Daniel shrugged and left the room. Leo sat there for some time after the door slammed. He poured another drink and was about to lift it to his lips when Cato crept inside and said, "Can I do anything for you, Mr. Leo?"

"No! Good night, Cato!"

"Good night, sir."

Leo sat there holding the glass. It gave forth shimmering amber light as it reflected the lamps burning on the mantel. He did not drink it, however, but sat there quietly. His heart seemed to beat strongly enough, but he knew that was an illusion. Sooner or later it would either quietly cease to beat or would explode with one massive burst. Fear came to him then, which was something he could hardly bear. He had never been afraid of anything, but now he knew that this was something he could not buy and something he could not arrange.

He thought again of the words of Cato—*Can I do anything, Mr. Leo?*

It was as if the words had been spoken aloud, and he whispered huskily in reply, "No, Cato—nobody can do anything for me!"

🆃   🆃   🆃

Leo Rochester was not the only person in the Boston area who was suffering from an attack of fear. Katherine Yancy had gone to bed early, for she had been sleeping poorly recently. She wanted to go back to Halifax to find her father to do what she could for him, but everyone said that the British would be leaving there and moving back to New York. She was afraid that she would get there only to find that the fleet had

174

sailed, bearing the prisoners away. Every day she had gone down to the harbor, noting that many ships were beginning to gather there, mostly men-of-war, and, of course, there was no way to contact them.

Katherine had eaten a light supper and gone to bed just after dark, but she had tossed restlessly until finally troubled dreams began to come to her. Usually she slept dreamlessly and awoke instantly refreshed and ready for whatever the day might bring. However, now she tossed and turned and muttered. Sometimes she came almost to the surface of consciousness and was aware of herself. Several times she almost decided to get up, but then dropped back off again into that part that lives just below the consciousness.

Finally she began to feel an ease, but just as she did, a cry came to her in her dream. It seemed to come from nowhere, and she felt herself wandering through a dense and thick woods. The branches reached out and grabbed at her hair, and briars tore at her hands and ripped her clothing. She did not know where she was, and the darkness frightened her. It was not an ordinary darkness. It was even darker than the darkest midnight down in a coal mine where no light can ever strike. She found herself crying out and whimpering with fear, for she suddenly remembered as a child she had been afraid of the dark.

The cries that she heard seemed to come from up ahead, and there seemed to be a tiny glow of light in that direction. Stumbling over the broken ground, her feet aching from rocks that cut her feet, she felt herself bleeding as the thorns struck her face. Fear rose in her, for she could not see, and the only sound was an unseen man's voice crying for help.

Finally the light grew brighter, and eagerly she pressed forward. The walking seemed to be easier and she was aware of huge, old trees that towered over her with trunks as large as small houses. Out of the darkness she sensed a presence of evil around her. She looked around and saw red eyes gleaming with a malevolent burning fire. Frightened, she stumbled forward toward the light.

The light seemed to swell, and suddenly she was aware that the land before her fell suddenly away. She halted abruptly and moved forward until she came to stand on the edge of a tremendous precipice. The land fell away down . . . down . . . down, but she was not looking far below where it ended with craggy rocks like teeth along the bottom of the tremendous canyon. Her eyes were fixed on a man who was hanging from a ledge not five feet away. Her first thought was, *He's falling. I've got to help him!* She moved forward and knelt, saying, "Reach up, let me help you!" She could not see his face because he kept it turned away, but his cries seemed to be fading. She called again, "Let me help you—!"

And then he looked up, and she saw in her dream that it was Clive

Gordon. His fingers were torn and bloody as he held on to the cruel stones. His face was contorted with the effort of simply hanging on, for if he released his grip, Katherine saw, he would fall to his death. He looked up at her saying nothing, but his lips formed her name—*Katherine!*

Katherine knelt there on the precipice, looking down into Clive's face. The wind was rising from somewhere, keening and howling behind her, and she felt the red eyes glowing as they burned in the darkness behind her. She was frozen in time and space. How long she knelt there in the dream looking down at the agonizing features of the man below, she could never tell.

Then Clive whispered, "Help me, Katherine!"

And then Katherine felt hatred well up inside her, bitterness like a bile in her throat. She clenched her fists together and shook them, suddenly crying out, "Go on and die—you deserve it!"

And then—Katherine awakened with a jolt. She was whispering, "No, no, no!" And suddenly her whole body ached, for she was tense in every muscle. Throwing the cover back, she stood up and found that her legs were trembling, as were her hands. She held her palms on her temples and moved over to stare out the window. The moon was shining mildly and she saw it reflect on the street outside, but she could not remain standing and collapsed, falling to the carpet on her knees, holding to her head and rocking back and forth.

She was horrified. The dream had torn at her and shaken her, and now she recognized that it was somehow more than a nightmare. For a long time she knelt there rocking back and forth, and finally she whispered, "Oh, God, forgive me, forgive me. . . !"

𝕿　　𝕿　　𝕿

A pale sun was beating down on the waves as Katherine reached the docks and stared out over the sea. She had been up for hours, walking back and forth in her room, still shaken to the depths of her heart by the nightmare that had come to her. She had dressed and fixed breakfast for her mother, then left, unable to carry on a conversation. As she stood on the dock watching the British ships dot the green water with their white sails and their tall masts, looking much like a forest, she did not know why she had come here. For a long time she simply stood and watched the soldiers as they worked on the fortifications and thought of the battle that was to come.

She was more concerned, however, about the battle that took place in her own soul. Katherine Yancy was a spiritual woman. She knew what it was to pray, and since childhood had been taught the things of

God from both her father and mother. Now she seemed to have had a horrifying look into the depths of her own heart—and it was like looking into a bucket full of crawling, slimy things—ugly and hideous!

She thought again of how she had cried out in hatred and whispered hoarsely, "It was only a dream!"

But somehow she knew that it was a dream that held a meaning, and the meaning was connected somehow with her treatment of Clive Gordon.

"Why, hello, Miss Yancy!"

Quickly Katherine turned and found Rachel Bradford standing regarding her. "Hello, Miss Bradford!" she said rather stiffly. She remembered the last time she had seen Rachel at the funeral and how coldly she had treated her. Shame came to her, and she dropped her head. Finally she lifted her eyes. "Miss Bradford, I must apologize for the way I spoke to you at my uncle's funeral."

"Don't speak of it, Miss Yancy!" Rachel said at once. "It was a hard time—and still is, I'm sure."

"I thank you, but my behavior was unforgivable."

Rachel noted something different in the young woman's demeanor. It was hard to explain, but the last time she had seen Katherine Yancy there had been a burning anger in her eyes. Now, however, Katherine was somehow broken. "Could we walk together for a while?" Rachel asked quietly. "I like to walk and look at the sea."

"Why, yes, of course. . . ." Katherine said at once. Part of her wanted to refuse, and yet she felt so bad about the way she had behaved to Rachel Bradford that she knew she must somehow make it right.

The two women strolled along the harbor. The fishermen were bringing in their catches, and the two women watched, although both of them had seen it many times before. They talked about the war, and Rachel informed her about Micah's enlistment in the army. "So I have two brothers now with General Washington!" she said.

Katherine wanted desperately to say something about Clive Gordon. Already she knew that somehow she would have to deal with her attitude, and the thought had come to her that perhaps she could write him a letter. It would be a difficult thing to do, but she knew that somehow she would have to deal with her feelings toward him.

"I suppose Mr. Gordon has gone back?"

"Why, as a matter of fact, he hasn't!" Rachel answered.

Instantly Katherine turned to look at the young woman. "You mean he's still in Boston?"

"I don't have very good news, I'm afraid. You know the sickness that affected me and my brother and sister-in-law? Well, we've all recovered, but Clive came down with it just as we were getting well."

"I'm . . . sorry to hear it!"

Rachel blinked with surprise. This was not the same attitude she had sensed in the young woman before. "He's not doing very well, and I'm worried about him. So is the doctor."

Abruptly Katherine stopped and turned, and when Rachel did the same, she noticed that Rachel looked tired, almost exhausted. "You look very tired, Miss Bradford."

"Please call me Rachel. Yes, I am tired. Several people have come down with the sickness in our neighborhood—dear friends. Those of us who are well are trying to nurse them as best we can. Since Micah has left, it's been very difficult."

Katherine thought only for a moment, then she spoke impulsively. "If you would tell Mr. Gordon—" She broke off abruptly and bit her lip. She could not bring herself to say anything more, and finally said, "I must be going home. Good afternoon, Rachel!"

Rachel stared after her, mystified and puzzled. Finally she turned and made her way home, wondering what was going on in the mind of Katherine Yancy. *She's changed so much,* she thought as she made her way along the half-deserted streets. *I wonder what's happening to make her seem so different?*

♦ ♦ ♦

Katherine arrived at home, cooked a lunch for her mother, and then finally went out to sit in the garden. Plato came to throw himself at her feet. He looked up at her with his big eyes, and she leaned over and ruffled his fur. He growled deep in his throat and Katherine said, "I wish my problems were as simple as yours, Plato. As long as you've got something to eat, and aren't hurting, and get a little attention now and then, that's all you require, isn't it?"

Plato suddenly reached out and took her hand between his huge jaws and squeezed slightly. It was a trick he had done from the time he was a big-footed mongrel puppy that her father had brought home. He had soon become Katherine's dog. Now suddenly she fell down beside him and hugged him hard. Plato looked somewhat surprised and moved to lick her face. For some time she sat there hugging the huge dog, then finally she left him and went inside.

All afternoon she thought about her dreams, and when twilight came she put her coat on and said, "Mother, I'm going out!"

"When will you be back? It's getting late!"

Katherine hesitated, then said, "I may stay the night with a friend. I'm not sure. James and Jewel will be here if you need anything." These

178

were the servants that came on a part-time basis—Jewel to take care of some of the cooking, and James to chop the wood and do the man's work.

"All right, dear!"

Leaving the house, Katherine went at once across town, coming to stand at last before the door of the Bradford home. She took a deep breath, knocked, and saw the surprise wash across Rachel Bradford's face as she opened the door.

"Why, come in, Miss Yancy!" Rachel said.

"You may as well call me Katherine!" Stepping inside, Katherine suddenly found it difficult to say what she had come to say. Taking a deep breath, however, she straightened her shoulders and said, "I've come to help, if I can, Rachel."

"Help? Why, help in what way, Katherine?"

"I can see you're very tired. You're barely over your sickness yourself." Katherine hesitated for one moment and then said, "I want you to let me help with the house—and with nursing Clive Gordon."

Shock came then to Rachel Bradford, but she concealed it as well as she could. Of all the things she had expected, Katherine's sudden appearance and sincere offer to help took her aback. However, she smiled and said, "How kind of you, Katherine!—and I will not say no! Come along, we'll sit and talk about it awhile."

The two women went into the parlor and sat there for some time talking. Finally Katherine could not keep silent. "I may as well tell you. I have been perfectly horrible to Clive. We were very close in Halifax. I grew upset with him, and have been very bitter, but I want to make it up—if he'll allow me."

A smile touched the soft lips of Rachel Bradford. "I think he'll be very glad to see you. Come along. I think he's awake."

As Rachel rose and turned to leave the room, Katherine stood up and followed her, but she dreaded the scene that was to come. She knew that deep down inside she still resented Clive Gordon for what he had done to her uncle, but she had come this far and now she prayed, *God help me to go as far as I have to go. I can't stand another horrible dream like the one that's been haunting me.*

15

God Isn't Far Away

GENERAL WILLIAM HOWE'S BROTHER, Admiral Richard Howe, arrived off the coast of New York after a three-month's voyage from England. His fleet consisted of a hundred and fifty ships with a reported fifteen thousand reinforcements aboard for his brother, General Howe. Howe's secretary, a man named Ambrose Serle, described his emotions upon arrival after the tedious voyage in his journal:

> This morning, the sun shining bright, we had a beautiful prospect of the coast of New Jersey at about five or six mile's distance. The land was cleared in many places, and the woods were interspersed with houses, which, being covered with white shingles, appeared very plainly all along the shore. We passed Sandy Hook in the afternoon, and about six o'clock arrived safe off the east coast of Staten Island. The country on both sides was highly picturesque and agreeable. Nothing could exceed the joy that appeared throughout the fleet and the army upon our arrival. We were saluted by all the ships of war in the harbor, by the cheers of the sailors all along the ships, and by those of the soldiers along the shore. The soldiers and sailors may have been cheering the arrival of Admiral Howe's fleet, but even more they were giving vent to their happiness over the fact that that very day at noon the British warships the *Phoenix* and the *Rose* had forced their passage up the Hudson in despite of all the batteries.

When the heavily armed ships passed up the river, the cries of the unhappy Americans rent the air. General Washington was disgusted with the spectacle of his soldiers. He observed a number of them walking along the banks of the Hudson gazing at the ships as if they were at a show of some kind. Washington was not known for outbursts, but during this period some of his staff observed that he was unhappy enough to give vent to his rage.

Admiral Richard Howe, unlike his pleasure-loving brother, was a generous and liberal man. He was a Whig who had hopes of inducing the Americans to see the folly of their ways. He had also arrived in New York empowered to offer peace terms to the Colonies in hope of preventing a full-scale revolution. His first step was to send Joseph Reed, who had returned to the army as adjutant general, a letter. Reed did not reply; instead he forwarded the letter to Congress. Two days later, after his arrival, Admiral Howe decided to arrange an interview with Washington, the American commander in chief. What followed was a comedy of manners.

Lord Howe sent a flag of truce up to the city. He also sent the captain of his flagship, the *Eagle*, with a letter to the commander in chief. He was met by Colonel Henry Knox and Colonel Reed. The captain said, "I have a letter from Lord Howe to Mr. Washington."

"Sir," said Colonel Reed coldly, "we have no person in our army with that address."

"Sir, will you look at the address!" the officer said.

Reed looked at it, and it was simply addressed to George Washington, Esquire. "I'm sorry! No sir, I cannot receive that letter."

"I am very sorry," the officer said, "and so will be Lord Howe, but any error in the superscription shouldn't prevent them from being received by General Washington!"

Colonel Reed then said, "You are sensible of the rank of General Washington and our army?"

"Yes, sir, I am! I am sure my Lord Howe will lament exceedingly this affair, as the letter is quite of a civil nature and not a military one! He laments that he was not here a little sooner."

Knox and Reed simply refused to receive a letter that did not acknowledge their commander in chief as General Washington. They bowed and left the captain of the British navy standing there. But Lord Howe was a persistent man. He tried once again two days later, but the peace talks came to nothing, as everyone quite expected.

General Washington had worries of his own—for the sails in the harbor were as thick as the wings of birds of prey. Moreover, sickness decimated his ranks. To oppose an enemy force that now exceeded thirty thousand, Washington now had but ten thousand five hundred men in the posts around New York, and about three thousand seven hundred of these were sick and unfit for duty.

Shortly after this, forty more ships arrived to bolster the British force. Washington was perplexed at the enemy's failure to attack. He deemed it wise to send his headquarters' papers to the Congress at Philadelphia for safekeeping. He finally came to the conclusion that rainy weather was postponing the attack, or else the enemy was awaiting still more forces.

The weeks of waiting ground sharply on the nerves of the British troops, but they availed themselves of daily amusement offered by Staten Island, a land of Tories. The Hessians arrived and were spoiling for a fight. In fact, the entire British army seemed confident that the disorderly, untrained troops of America could not stand against them. Every soldier was eager to teach the colonists a lesson they richly deserved.

🔔 🔔 🔔

Abigail Howland could not remember a time in her life when she had been so utterly confused of mind. She continued to meet with Esther in the mornings, saying little, but listening as her hostess quietly read from the Scripture and drew lessons from it that Abigail had never considered. She had always thought Christians dull and hypocritical, but she could not claim this for her aunt. She had learned well the generosity of the older woman's heart, and her reputation among the servants and the neighbors was impeccable. Everyone knew that Esther Denham was a woman of godly character—this Abigail could not deny.

One Sunday she went to church with Esther, as had become the custom with her and her mother. She sat there in the high-back pew listening as the preacher spoke on a rather alarming subject, "Prepare to Meet Thy God."

It was, however, not a hell-and-brimstone sermon such as Abigail had heard a few times. The minister, a tall man with steady brown eyes who wore the vestments of a man of the cloth as if he had been born to it, said in the midst of the sermon, "These words usually are accompanied by warnings of the pits of hell and the fate of the unbeliever. I would have you hear them this morning as a gentle call from a loving God. He is calling you to prepare. That is why Jesus Christ came into the world, to prepare a way for those that do not know God so they can find Him. And now that that way has been prepared through His blood, the only preparation we can make is to confess ourselves unable to forgive our own sins and free ourselves from them, and to look to Him to do that."

For some time the minister spoke of turning from sin and turning to God. He quoted liberally from the Scriptures, and Abigail, by the end of the sermon, was totally miserable. She could not understand what was happening to her, and that afternoon she kept to her room, unable to keep her countenance before her mother or her aunt.

Finally after the sun went down, she went to supper and managed, though with great difficulty, to keep her turbulent spirit from showing. Carrie Howland remarked on how much she enjoyed the sermon, and Esther said eagerly, "Yes, it was a fine sermon, wasn't it? Reverend Johnson is such a gentle, loving man. It's so good to see a man like that proclaiming from the pulpit."

Abigail said nothing as the two women continued to discuss the sermon. She excused herself as soon as possible and went to bed early.

The next morning she arose, dressed, and at ten o'clock Matthew came to take her out for a drive. As usual they drove by the harbor to take a look at the fortifications and the excitement of the soldiers. She had never seen so many different colors and kinds of uniforms in her life, and she remarked on this to Matthew. "Why don't all the soldiers have the same kind of uniforms, I wonder?"

Matthew answered, "I think it's because they come from different states. Each state chooses its own uniforms. Colorful, isn't it?"

"It must be very confusing. All the British wear the same color uniforms, don't they?"

"I think not! The Jaegers, for example, wear green uniforms, I'm told. And the Black Watch, the Scots regiment, wear kilts!"

"Kilts—you mean like little skirts? How funny!"

"I'm told they're not very amusing! They're called the 'Ladies From Hell,' they're so fierce in battle," Matthew remarked. They were driving along, looking out over the ocean, and he turned, suddenly stopping, and took her by the arm. "Look at that! It's a beautiful sight, isn't it, Abigail?" He swept his arm to where the armada of ships formed out in the harbor, looking like a forest of bare trees. The sails were all furled, and they could see, even at this distance, some of the British sailors as they moved about the decks. "I'd like to paint that, but it would be hard."

"Jan would ask you what it would all mean!" Abigail said. From the several times she had been in the company of the Dutch artist, she had absorbed some of his theories concerning art. "According to him, every painting has to mean something."

"I'm not sure he's right about that!" Matthew shrugged. "Some paintings just *are*! If you paint a picture of a dog, it's because people like to see pictures of dogs. It doesn't have to mean anything."

"Jan would have your head for that!" Abigail said. She looked up at him and smiled slightly. She made a fetching picture there in the morning sunlight. She was wearing a pale apricot dress and a straw hat with a wide brim, as was the fashion of the day. Her complexion was flawless, and there was something in her hazel eyes that expressed the light that lurked within her. She made a most attractive picture to young Matthew Bradford.

He looked at her suddenly and, without preamble, said in a husky voice, "Abigail—"

Caught by his tone, Abigail looked at him. "Why, what is it, Matthew?"

"Marry me, Abigail!"

Abigail was aware of the sound of the lapping of the waves on the piers, and of the harsh cries of the sea gulls far down the beach. She was aware, as well, of the hard blue sky above and the dark green of the sea. They met in a line straight as a knife's edge out of the horizon. Something inside her said, *This is what you've always longed for! Now it can be all yours—money, position, everything. . . !* The thought came to her strongly as a physical blow, and she knew that a few days earlier she would have at once accepted Matthew's proposal.

Now, however, she found herself hesitating. When she said nothing, Matthew took her arms and looked into her face, saying, "Marry me, Abigail, I love you! I want you to be my wife."

Abigail opened her lips to say, "Yes, I will marry you"—but somehow the words would not come. She was confused and knew that somehow her confusion resulted from the days she had spent in Esther Denham's company. She had become dissatisfied with what she was—the deceit she was carrying out—and she remembered suddenly the words of Paul Winslow, *I've seen the hard beauty on the outside, but deep down there's another Abigail Howland, a better Abigail.* Desperately she sat there trying to think, wondering at herself for hesitating, but somehow she could not make up her mind. Matthew was speaking, and she heard him say, "We can take Leo's offer, after all he is my real father; I believe that. It was hard for me to accept at first. It wouldn't mean that I wouldn't love Daniel and the family any less, but it would open up a whole new world for me—and for you, Abigail."

"Matthew!" Abigail said, struggling for words. "We haven't known each other very long." It was not what she wanted to say, but she looked up at him and could only add, "A couple ought to know each other better than we do!"

Matthew shook his head stubbornly. His hands tightened on her arms and he said with force, "I know I love you! All that matters is, do you love me? Do you care for me at all, Abigail?"

Abigail could not meet his gaze. She dropped her head, thinking of Leo's offer that she had so eagerly accepted back in Boston. She had, in effect, agreed to betray this man who stood there with love in his eyes, and on his face, and in his voice—to betray him for money. Now she could not bear the moment any longer. "You will have to give me time to think," she whispered. She managed to lift her eyes and say, "You're such a fine man, Matthew, but this is too important to decide right now!"

Matthew did not speak for a moment, then he nodded. "I see you're not certain about me, but you will be, Abigail!" He smiled then and looked suddenly very handsome as the wind blew his hair, and she was conscious of the fact that here was a man that she could love. Strangely enough, she had never thought about the long-term side of marriage. Always it had been pleasure for a moment, and security. Now those two things somehow did not seem as important, and she turned the moment away by saying, "Let's go to the park."

"All right, but I promise you, you're not going to have any rest. I love you, Abigail, and I'm going to marry you!"

🦁   🦁   🦁

For two days Abigail listened as Matthew continued to press his case. More than once she decided to accept his offer. Once she even got out a sheet of paper and started to write to Leo of what had happened—but somehow she could not bring herself to do it. She became nervous and even irritable, and finally her mother said, "I don't know what's the matter with you, Abigail! You ought to be having the time of your life with a fine young man like Matthew, but you're as snappy as I've ever seen you!"

Finally, in desperation, Abigail decided to talk to Esther. She could not talk to her mother. They had never been intimate, and even now she did not feel comfortable speaking of something like this to her. She waited until the next morning when the two went to the cupola for their usual morning tea and time of quiet conversation. Abigail waited until Esther had finished reading the psalms and said the prayer, then before she could change her mind said almost desperately, "Aunt Esther, there's something I have to tell you!"

Turning to her niece with some surprise, Esther said, "Why, what is it, child?"

Abigail hesitated for only one moment, then she began. "You don't know me, Aunt Esther. All you know is what you've seen since we've been here—but I'm not what I seem."

"I think few of us are."

"*You* are!" Abigail said. She bit her lip, then straightened her back as if she were marching in front of a firing squad. "I'm going to tell you what kind of a girl I've been. . . ." She began to speak with an effort, going back to her childhood, and for the first time in her life she confessed things that she had known about herself. She spoke of her selfishness, how she had cheated her way through life, how she had learned to manipulate people when she was little more than a child. She seemed to hear her own voice as if it belonged to someone else speaking of what a terrible young woman she had grown into. Finally she related how she had had an affair with Paul Winslow and how she had betrayed him to snare Nathan Winslow when the tide of politics changed suddenly. Finally she said, "I came here under false colors, Aunt Esther. Leo Rochester hired me to come to be nice to Matthew Bradford. He wants something from him, and he thinks I can help him get it."

Finally Abigail ceased. Her hands were clenched around the handkerchief that she had pulled at as she related her story, and her lips were drawn tightly together. She dropped her head, and there was a moment's stillness, then she looked up and there were tears in her eyes. "That's what kind of terrible woman I am, Aunt Esther!"

Esther's voice was filled with compassion. "Why are you telling me all this, Abigail? You didn't have to."

"I don't know!" Abigail shook her head and dabbed at her eyes with the handkerchief. She almost never cried, and was somehow resentful and ashamed that she was crying now. It hurt her pride. Straightening up, she stared out at the street below for a long time. "Matthew asked me to marry him two days ago," she finally said, then turned to look at Esther with a tragic expression. "It's what I've always wanted. He'll come into a fortune. I can't tell you about that now, but I could have everything I've always wanted."

"Do you love Matthew, Abigail?"

The question seemed to disturb Abigail tremendously. She stood up suddenly and began to walk about the cupola wringing her hands and keeping her face turned away from Esther. Finally she stopped and turned to face her aunt. "How can I know?" she asked in desperation. "I came here to betray him for money, and now he says he loves me—and I believe he does! It would be so easy just to say yes, but somehow I can't do that!"

"Come and sit down. I want to talk to you, Abigail," Esther said quietly. She waited until the young woman came, then said, "You may not know what's happening, but you've been very unhappy lately, and I've watched you."

"I've been *miserable!*"

"I think it's the Spirit of God striving with you, Abigail. That's the way it happens. We will never come to God as long as we are happy and content. It's only when we become discontented and know something is wrong that we begin to reach out to Him. I think God has been touching you, stirring your spirit—Christians call this sort of thing *conviction*. It simply means that you are becoming aware of what you are, and God is doing it!"

"Why is He doing it? Why doesn't He leave me alone?"

"Because He loves you, and He wants to make something much sweeter, and finer, and nobler out of you than you have ever been."

At once Abigail thought of what Paul had said about a better woman being deep inside of her. She shook her head and whispered, "I can't go back and redo all the things that I did that were wrong. I can't, Aunt Esther!"

"You can't undo the past, but that's the part that Jesus plays. He takes us where we are and forgives all of our sins, and then He gives us the power to live a good and holy life. We could not do it ourselves."

"I can't believe it. God's a million miles from me!"

"God isn't far away! The kingdom of God is within you, Abigail. Jesus said, 'I stand at the door and knock. If any man will open the door, I will come in.' I'm going to ask you to do that right now!"

Abigail stared at her aunt with shock and disbelief. "Ask me what, Aunt Esther?"

"I'm going to ask you to open the door of your heart and let Jesus Christ come in."

"I don't know what you're talking about!"

"Jesus said, 'You must be born again.' By that He simply meant that you must become a different person. Just like a baby is a brand-new human being. All old things will pass away. You will be a new Abigail, a sweeter, finer woman than you've ever known possible. That's the work of God to make you like himself. . . ."

When Abigail failed to respond, Esther continued, "Abigail, did your father ever tell you much about your grandmother, Rachel?"

"No, not really. He just said she was a foolish old woman who died with nothing to show for her life."

"Well, Saul was wrong about that. I'm sad to say that I agreed with him for many years. Your grandmother was one of the finest Christian women you could hope to meet. We've already talked about the struggles she faced living in the Plymouth colony. She always stayed true to her God, no matter how difficult the circumstances. She even faced down an Indian to save someone's life.

"She took after her grandfather, Gilbert Winslow. He was one of the original pilgrim settlers that landed at Plymouth Rock in 1620. He was acting as a spy for the Crown at the time to gain information about the actions of the 'feared' separatists, the pilgrims. He was converted after coming to America and became a wonderful preacher. He had pretended to be one of the pilgrims and had fooled many of them before he was converted, including your great-great-grandmother, Humility Cooper Winslow. Our family, the house of Winslow, is filled with many men and women of strong faith in God. It pains me to have to say that for a long time I was not one of those. Saul and I both went in different directions from what our parents wished.

"I still remember how your father and I used to mock our cousins, William, Mercy, and Adam, for their beliefs. It wasn't until after I was married that I began to see the futility of striving for things of this world like money, power, and position. My husband, George, and I had worked to amass a small fortune, before we lost everything in a bad business venture. It was then that I remembered everything I had been taught by my parents. I encouraged George to attend some church services with me. We were both wonderfully and miraculously converted in a revival service. We then began to live for the Lord, and through His infinite mercy, He saw fit to restore our fortune, which we always tried to use to help those less fortunate. I think God wanted to see if we would still serve Him after getting our money back, and I can thankfully say that with His help we remained true to our commitment to Him.

"Abigail, I am not proud that it took me so long to come to the Lord after all He had done for me, but I am thankful that He forgave me even after all the times I had mocked Him and those who chose to serve Him. Please don't waste more of your life like I did. Accept Him now. He is always ready and willing to open His arms of mercy and forgive His lost children."

For over an hour Esther spoke softly, answering questions, reading Scripture, quoting many verses from her heart. When Abigail became frustrated and almost angry, Esther patiently would bring her back to the thought of giving her heart to God.

Finally Abigail said, "I don't understand any of this, Aunt Esther! I'm tired, and I don't know what to do!" Then suddenly she began to weep in earnest. All of the pressures, all of the fears, and all of the anxieties suddenly burst over, and she simply wept. She was aware that Esther had come and put her arm around her, and she turned to the older woman and clung to her as a child clings to its mother. The storm in her heart continued for a long time, and finally she drew back and drew a shaky breath. "I don't know what to do, Aunt Esther! Tell me—help me. I can't go on being what I have been!"

"Then it's time to be what you have never been—a child of God. Let me read you a few Scriptures, and then we're going to pray." She read several passages from the Bible, speaking of turning from sin, and of the blood of Jesus, and finally she said, "We'll pray now. Abigail, you must speak to God in your heart exactly as if He were here. As I pray, you call upon the Lord, and He will enter and do a work in you."

Esther began to pray, and Abigail prayed, too—not aloud, but in the depths of her heart. She never remembered all that she said. She was sure it was not eloquent. She did remember once crying aloud with her voice, "Oh, God, help me, I'm such a wicked girl! Help me to be good, in Jesus' name!"

Soon it was over, and Abigail found herself completely drained. She had wept in deep repentance for all the things that had led her so far from God. But now her face relaxed, and she could feel the tremendous tension give way to a deep inner peace. She looked at Esther with wonder in her eyes and whispered, "I feel so . . . so *clean*, Aunt Esther!"

"Yes, I can see that! There's a difference in you. You're at peace with God now." She kissed Abigail and said with joy and tears in her own eyes, "Didn't I tell you?"

"Tell me what, Aunt Esther?"

"Didn't I tell you that God isn't very far away? Now you've found Him, and you must never turn Him loose. Be obedient to Him."

"I don't know how."

"I will teach you, and the Holy Spirit will teach you. That's what He's here for."

The two women sat there for a long time, and finally they rose. Abigail knew, as she left the cupola, that her life would never be again what it had been before!

16

A Man Can't Erase the Past

THE ATTACK CAME WITHOUT WARNING, even without a hint. Leo Rochester had risen from his bath and was putting on his clothes. Sitting on the bed, he drew on first the white stocking that came up over his knee and had reached down to pull the second over his toes. He had pulled the stocking up over the heel, and it fit so snugly that he grunted as he gave it a firm tug.

Somehow that tug seemed to have pulled something loose inside his chest, for he felt a pain that started somewhere deep inside—a dull ache that he had learned to recognize with dread.

Loosing the stocking, he straightened up and sat on the side of the padded Windsor chair, his face pale, and his eyes wide with shock. The pain seemed to swell inside him as if he had swallowed some kind of monstrous seed that was now exploding into growth. It pushed at the walls of his chest, and the throbbing of his heart was like a mighty engine churning in his ears. He held his breath and prayed that it would go away, but it did not. A tiny needle-sharp pain began at the top of his left shoulder. It increased in magnitude, feeling as if someone were shoving a white-hot stiletto into his flesh. It moved down to his biceps, then his forearm, and then his fingers, so that the whole arm was one seething mass of agonizing pain. Gasping, Leo fell back on the chair, closing his eyes. The pain gnawed at him, but even as he sat there, it began to recede. It took the same route that it had taken. First his fingers were freed from the agonizing grip and became numb. Next the whole arm was numb, and the throbbing in his chest mitigated somewhat. He grew nauseated and thought that he would vomit. Swallowing hard, he sat very still and waited for it to pass.

Finally, his brow damp with perspiration, he drew his right hand shakily across it and took a cautious breath. He had the familiar sensation that something in his chest was made of fragile glass and that a sudden movement would shatter it into a thousand shards, destroying everything within him.

Finally the nausea left, and he became aware that, at least this time, he was spared. He rose, and as he did so, his left arm seemed to flop like a lifeless member. Standing in the middle of the room, he tried to lift it. He grunted and strained with all of his might, but all that he achieved was a slight twitching of the hand and a slight bend at the elbow.

"It can't go on like this!" Rochester muttered. He had put his sickness out of his mind as best he could, although he knew it was just lurking, waiting to attack him. Now he stood there uncertainly, and finally, for lack of anything better, he bent and managed to get the stocking up over his knee with his right hand. But as he looked at the rest of his clothing, he knew they were too much for him. Standing, he moved to the door and called out, "Cato—Cato. . . !"

The servant had been just down the hall polishing silver, and he arose at once. He moved swiftly down the hall, where he found Sir Leo standing in the doorway of his bedroom. "Yes, sir?" he inquired. "Can I help you, Mr. Rochester?"

"Come in here!" Leo said quickly. When he stepped back, and after Cato entered the room, Rochester said, "I've got to have help. I've injured my arm. Help me get my shirt and britches on!"

"Why, yes sir, Mr. Rochester!" At once Cato went to the heavy clothes press and said, "You want this shirt, sir?"

"Yes, and those dark gray britches."

As Cato was assisting Rochester to dress, he asked, "How did you hurt your arm, Mr. Rochester?"

"I took a fall from my horse! It'll be all right."

Finally Rochester was completely dressed, including the small waistcoat that Cato had been obliged to button. He slipped on his frock coat and reached out for the tricorn hat and put it over his head. He hesitated one moment, and then said, "Cato, make a sling out of something. Something to put my arm in so it won't be giving me any trouble." He assisted Cato in picking out a square of cloth and making a neckerchief. When it was tied around his neck, he put his arm in it and nodded with some relief. "There, that'll do until it gets better! Go tell High Boy to bring the carriage around. I want to go to town."

"Yes, sir!" Cato said, then left for the stables.

Leo left the house walking very carefully and climbed awkwardly

191

into the carriage using his one hand. He seated himself with a sigh of relief, and soon after the door slammed he stuck his head out. "Take me down to Jefferson Avenue, High Boy!"

"Yes, sir, I'll do that! Get up there, you hosses!"

Forty minutes later Leo was climbing the stairs to the office of Dr. Henry Settling. He entered the narrow reception room and found, to his relief, that there were no patients there. It was too early in the morning, he supposed, and he called out, "Dr. Settling!"

Almost at once the door opened and Henry Settling came out. He had apparently been about to leave, for he had on his street clothes, which consisted of a dark brown suit and a frock coat that he had not buttoned. He held his hat in his hand, but when he saw Rochester, he immediately put it down on a table and said, "Sir Leo, you just caught me. I was just about to go out. Come in!"

Leo stepped into the inner office and once again noted how crowded it was with rows of cabinets containing the paraphernalia and instruments of the medical trade. He was usually slightly disgusted by the acrid smell of chemicals, but this time he did not notice it. "I've had another attack," he said bluntly. "Worse than the others. . . !"

Settling, at once, took off his coat, saying, "Sit down here, and let's have a look at you!"

"I can't use my left arm too well," Rochester said.

"Let me help you with it."

With the physician's assistance, Leo managed to get out of his coat, and soon sat with his shirt off before the doctor. This time the examination was more thorough; Settling took so long that Leo grew irritable. Settling was listening to his chest for what seemed to be an interminable time, and Leo finally demanded, "Well, what's wrong with me?"

Settling straightened up and stroked his Vandyke beard. A careful light had come into his light blue eyes, and he spoke slowly. "You had another attack. I'm sure you must realize that."

"What does that mean?"

"I'm afraid it's not good news, Sir Leo." Settling said, "Let me help you get dressed." As he helped Leo fasten his clothing, he spoke in a moderate tone. Settling was used to delivering bad news, as all doctors have to be. He never liked doing it. It was the one part of being a doctor that he would have assigned to another if that had been possible, but he had learned to recognize fear, for it became almost palpable in many people. Settling saw it there now in Leo, so strongly that he could almost smell it. Behind the eyes of the aristocrat lurked a mindless, screaming fear that had to be imprisoned as a madman in a cage. He spoke soothingly, but he was aware that Rochester was not at all fooled

192

by his bedside manner. He finally said, "Your condition is not as good as it was when you first came here."

"Well, I know *that*!" Rochester tried to move his arm and found that he had regained some use of it. "My arm's better now!" he remarked. "What happened to it?"

"It often happens with heart problems. You have some kind of a stoppage in your blood stream, I would think, and when that's shut off you lose the use of one of your arms. Hopefully, you'll gain the use of it back completely."

Leo flexed the arm again and decided to leave it in the sling until he regained better use of it. Awkwardly he struggled back, and Settling moved forward to help him get it in a comfortable position. Then Leo turned and faced the doctor squarely. Though the fear gnawed inside him, Leo Rochester was no coward. He was an utter realist who prided himself on looking things straight on, taking the facts as he found them. "Am I going to die, Settling?"

Settling did not hesitate a moment. He had been asked this before by patients and had a stock answer. "We've all got to do that, Sir Leo."

"I don't want any of your blasted philosophy!" Leo snapped harshly. "I mean, am I apt to drop dead before I get back home?"

For one minute Settling hesitated, then said, "I can't give you the answer to that. I've known men in worse condition than you who have lived many years. They took their problem as a warning and did all they could to modify it. I've already told you that it depends to a great extent on how well you take care of yourself."

Something left unsaid in the physician's words caught at Leo. "So I notice that you say that I won't drop dead."

"That's always a possibility. I've known men who've never had a pain in their lives. Young men, apparently healthy, who suddenly, without cause, died of a massive heart attack. I wish I could give you guarantees, Leo, but there are none in this life."

"Well then, give me your sermon again on how to take care of myself." Leo listened as the doctor repeated his instructions about diet, staying away from strong drink, and getting plenty of rest. It was, he knew, the same speech the doctor had delivered to many people. Finally he asked, "What would be the risk in taking a sea voyage?"

"A sea voyage? Where do you want to go?"

"I'd like to go to England."

Settling shrugged. "I see nothing against it as long as you don't hit a storm at sea, or run into something unexpected. Are you planning on leaving right away?"

"I'm not sure."

"See me before you go, and I'll do the best I can to get you some tonic."

Leo left Dr. Settling's office, got into the cab, and said, "Drive around by the city hall, High Boy!" He settled back again, and when the carriage stopped, he got out and went into a small red-brick building across the street from Boston's city hall. He was greeted there by Dawkins, the family lawyer, a short fireplug of a man with flaming red hair—what was left of it—and spent an hour in the inner office going over business. By the time he had emerged, it was nearly noon. He got back into the carriage and said, "Take me home, High Boy!"

"Yes, sir! Get up there, you hosses!"

𝕋   𝕋   𝕋

Dinner had been a quiet affair, and Marian was pleased that her father had been able to come downstairs to the table and eat. "It's so good to have you here, Father," she said. "Here, try some more of these beans. Hattie made them especially for you! She knows just how you like them."

John Frazier smiled and accepted another spoonful of the beans that she placed carefully on his plate. He speared a few with his fork, put them in his mouth and chewed them, then nodded, "Hattie always could make the best beans in the world! I wonder how she seasons them?"

"I don't think she'll tell anybody that!" Marian smiled. "It's her secret formula." She was wearing a pale yellow dress with light green trim, and her hair fell down her back in a most attractive fashion. "She's got a surprise for dessert, too!"

John Frazier was enjoying the meal tremendously. He did feel better, and these days he seized times like this eagerly. Looking around he said, "I always liked this room. I remember when your mother and I were building the house, we had some rousing arguments over the wallpaper."

"Who won?" Marian asked, knowing his answer.

"Oh, she did, of course! She always knew how to have her own way out of me—exactly as you do!" He looked over at Leo, who was sitting across the table, his arm still in a sling. "I'm sorry about your arm, Leo. I've never known you to fall off a horse before."

Leo looked up from his plate, for his thoughts had been far off, and he caught only the last part of Frazier's words. "It isn't serious," he murmured. "I'll probably take it out of the sling tomorrow."

"Did you go see Dr. Settling?" Frazier inquired.

"Yes, I did. He's not concerned about it."

194

"Good man, Settling," Frazier said. He had become somewhat of a connoisseur of doctors since his illness, and for a while spoke of the virtues of Leo's physician. Then he inquired, "Have you heard any news of the action in New York?"

"I don't think the battle has started yet," Leo said. His brow furrowed and he shook his head. "I don't think the colonists will have much of a chance against King George's army. I understand it's a formidable array of force that General Howe will command." He spoke for a while about the revolution, but his mind was obviously not on it. He got up finally and said, "I'm going to read for a while in the study. I'm glad you're feeling better, John."

"Why—thank you, Leo." Frazier watched as his son-in-law left the dining room, then turned to face his daughter. "Leo's looking very poorly, isn't he, Marian?"

"Yes, I'm glad he went to see the doctor." She was fairly certain, however, that whatever he had done to his arm, it had nothing to do with falling off his horse. He had lost weight, and there was a lifelessness about him that was foreign to his character. "I think he's more ill than he lets on."

"He was always such a big, bluff, strong fellow," Frazier murmured. The thought came to him, *What if he should die before me?* But he put it aside, saying, "Well, at least you're healthy, and I've never seen you looking prettier, Marian."

"Why, thank you, Father," Marian smiled. She rose and came over, then bent down and kissed him. "You sit right there. I'm going to get you some of that custard that Hattie worked so hard on."

She left the room and soon returned with a cut-glass deep dish, which she set before her father. Handing him a silver spoon she said, "Now, you start on that, and I'll get some for myself."

The two sat there enjoying the custard, and finally Frazier sat back and sighed with pleasure. "It's been good, coming to the table and sharing a meal with you and Leo."

"It's been good to have you! I'm praying that you'll get well and get out of that bed again." There was a longing in Marian, for she loved her father dearly. She thought back again to the days when he had been strong and lively; they seemed almost like a dream now, but she did not let him ever see the doubts that came to her. "Now, do you feel up to a game of checkers?"

The evening passed, and finally, when her father retired to his room, Marian returned to the parlor. She sat there for a while reading, then was surprised when she looked up to see Leo enter. Putting the book aside she asked, "How does your arm feel?"

"Well enough." Leo sat down across the room from her on one of the couches. He was silent, and there was a heaviness in his manner. Finally he said, "I went to see Dawkins today. I made some arrangements with him."

"What sort of arrangements, Leo?"

"Oh, just things that need to be taken care of. The deeds to some of the lands I bought last year in Virginia. I had to have him write letters—oh yes, I made a new will."

Marian's head lifted at this. She made no comment, except to say, "What was wrong with the old one?"

"I've never been satisfied with it." Leo crossed his legs and stared down at the soft satin slippers that he wore for comfort in the house. He touched one of them and ran his finger along the seams, then looked up abruptly. "I made sure that you'd be well cared for if anything happened to me."

Marian flushed slightly. It was the first time he had ever said anything about the possibility of his death to her, and she knew that it was not accidental. "I hope," she said quietly, "that I never have to think about that."

Leo straightened up then and gave her a direct stare. "Marian, do you love Daniel Bradford?"

Instantly Marian grew fearful. "Leo, we've talked about—"

"I'm not accusing you of having an affair with him!" Leo said quickly. "You've assured me often enough that you haven't."

"And do you believe me?"

Leo slowly nodded. "Strangely enough I do. I think I always have." He smiled suddenly at a thought that touched him. "I think Bradford's too much of a holy man to try to steal another man's wife."

"Don't mock, Leo!"

"I'm not mocking," he said, shrugging his shoulders. "I'm just thinking what I've always felt. He's always been that way, ever since he was a boy—and I've had a wry sort of admiration for him. Oh, I've hated him at times and wanted to kill him when we were younger, but that's all over now!"

"I'm glad to hear that, Leo!" she said quickly, hoping he would not press her further on the matter.

"I asked you if you loved him."

"I don't have any right to love him, Leo, nor he me—but that's not an answer." She hesitated, then said, "It's difficult to explain. I've always admired Daniel. The very qualities that you've made fun of, I've found very—well, attractive. He's honest, he's been faithful to his wife, he's a good family man." Suddenly she looked straight at him and said,

"I think I admired him most because he never did try to take advantage of me!"

"If he had tried, would you have surrendered?"

Marian Rochester had a streak of honesty that ran broad and was strong as an iron bar. Without blinking she said simply and plainly, "I don't know, Leo."

Leo Rochester stared at her and finally grunted, "Well, that's honest enough for me!"

"I'm married to you, Leo, and as long as we are alive I'll be your wife."

Leo Rochester found this statement interesting. It was simply a re-statement of the marriage vows, but he was thinking more deeply these days than he had in the past. He sat there quietly, considering his wife and knew that her beauty was little less than it was when he had first seen her. Now, at forty-one, she was still the same tall, well-shaped dark-haired beauty he had married. A pang came to him, not physically, but thoughts of what might have been. Slowly he got up and said, "You wouldn't have given in to him, not you!"

"I'm glad you think so, Leo."

"You're too much like him. You're a puritan to the heart—just like he is. The two of you are a pair." He turned and left the room, and she heard his footsteps as he moved down the hall. She sat for a long time, wondering at the strange scene that had passed. A sense of foreboding came to her, and she considered her life, how it had been, but did not permit herself to think of the future. The clock ticked out in the hallway, and she slowly picked up the book and began reading again.

𝕋   𝕋   𝕋

Clive Gordon had been asleep, but a sudden jerking of his tall body brought his head in contact with the hard maple headboard. The solid *clunk* sounded loud to his own ears, and he grunted aloud and reached up to touch his head.

"Clive, are you all right?"

The voice came from his left, and he turned quickly to see a figure outlined there. He could not see the face, for the lamp was behind the woman, forming a golden aureole around her head. He squeezed his eyes together and shook his head, which aggravated the ache that came from the blow he had taken. He opened his lips, which were dry as toast, and croaked in a voice that he did not recognize. "Where— who—?"

A cool hand touched his forehead, and twisting in the bed, his body was wet with sweat. He felt that his skin was tight and dry, so hot had

197

it become. "Water," he croaked again and tried to lick his lips. The woman left, and he heard the sound of water pouring from one vessel to another, then she was back again. He felt an arm under his back, pulling him upward. "Sit up," the voice said. He felt the cool glass against his lips and gulped thirstily. He was trembling so much that his teeth chattered against the glass, and some of the water ran down his chin and dripped onto his chest. Reaching out he grabbed at the glass and turned it upward, for it was the most delicious thing he had ever tasted.

"Be careful, you'll strangle yourself, Clive! Wait just a minute, and you can have more."

Clive felt the hand on his back. He could speak more clearly now and asked, "Rachel, is that you?"

"No, it's not Rachel."

Clive lay back down and watched as the woman turned her back. She returned to the washstand where she poured water from a pitcher to fill the cup. When she turned again he saw her face, and shock washed over him. "Katherine!" he whispered.

Katherine moved and helped him up again. His flesh felt hot beneath the thin shirt he wore, and the shirt itself was soaked and damp. She said quietly, "Drink this!" She waited until he gulped the water down, then still holding him said, "I'm glad you're awake."

"Katherine, what are you doing here?"

"Helping Rachel," she said quietly. "Your nightgown is soaked." She put the glass down on the table, then felt his forehead. "I think your fever has broken some. It's been so high, we've all been afraid for you."

"How long have you been here?"

"I just came tonight. Now, we've got to get you a dry nightshirt on. Can you sit up?"

"Why . . . yes."

Clive was not thinking clearly. He sat there while she tugged the nightshirt upward, pulling the sheet up over his lower body, then said, "Lift your arms." When he obeyed, he felt the shirt go over his head. He shivered, for suddenly the room seemed cold. Staring with fever-bright eyes, Clive watched as she removed a nightshirt from the chest against the wall, came back, and said, "Now, lift your arms again." When he obeyed, she slipped it over his head, and then said, "Now, do you want to lie down?"

"No, let me sit up!"

Katherine put a pillow behind him, then moved away. Drawing up a chair she sat down and looked directly at him. "You've been very sick. I'm sorry."

Clive could not believe what was happening. The sickness had come on him slowly, and he had remembered how he had thought to fight it off, but then the high fever had come, and it had been a nightmare. Now, waking up to find Katherine taking care of him was a distinct shock. He said nothing for a long time, and neither did she. Finally she leaned forward and asked, "Clive, are you awake enough to understand me?"

"Why, of course. My head is beating like a drum, but what is it?"

Katherine had prepared herself for this moment. She had always known that she would have to do it, and she saw that even now he was not in complete control of his faculties. "I wanted to tell you," she said with some hesitation, "how I'm sorry I treated you so badly." He started to speak, but she shook her head and cut him off. "I don't know why you did what you did, but you were kind to me in Halifax and to my father and uncle, and I'm grateful for that."

Actually Clive was understanding very little of this. He was dizzy, and his head ached, and a chill was coming on. He began to tremble, and he could not make sense out of what Katherine was trying to say. He stared at her with a lack of comprehension, and then sickness came upon him.

Katherine quickly helped him lie down. He shook so violently it frightened her, so she began to put covers on him. As she sat beside him she thought, *I've told him how I feel.* She knew she would have to tell him again when he had recovered, but somehow it would be easier now.

T   T   T

She had gone to sleep sitting in the chair, and now she woke up with a start, for she heard him calling out. "Clive—" Her neck ached, but she ignored it as she rose and bent over him. "Are you all right?"

Clive muttered and threw his arms about. He was, she saw, having some kind of a nightmare. He was mumbling something she could not understand.

Leaning forward she whispered, "Clive, wake up. You're having a nightmare." But he was too deeply caught by the dream. She heard him say, "We'll get you out, Amos. I'll get you out of here. . . !"

The words caught at her. He was speaking her father's name, promising to get him out. It had to be a dream of the time when he had helped them in Halifax, and suddenly she was glad to know that at least in his dreams he was still faithful! She stood over him and listened as he mumbled over and over again, speaking of some of the things that she recognized. She heard her own name called more than once, and finally he dropped off into a fitful sleep. She stood there looking down on his thin face outlined by the yellow gleam of the lamp. He seemed very young, and she could not see the traces of deceit she had blamed him for. Finally, she took her seat again and sat there until dawn watching him and thinking of what had happened between the two of them.

⊺　　　⊺　　　⊺

The next morning, at ten o'clock, Clive awoke. His fever had broken and his eyes were clear. He called out, "Katherine!" but when someone came to the door he saw it was Rachel. At once he asked, "Was Katherine here last night, or was I having a nightmare?"

Rachel came over and put her hand on his forehead. A smile touched her broad lips and she said, "Yes, she was here. She's gone home now, though. How do you feel?"

Licking his lips and taking stock of his condition, Clive said, "Much better. The fever is gone—although it was bad last night. It happens like that sometimes, doesn't it?"

"Yes, it did with me! Could you eat something?"

A ravenous hunger suddenly arose in Clive and he said, "Yes, anything!" As she started to leave the room he said, "Is she coming back . . . Katherine, I mean?"

"Yes, she said she'd come back to help take care of you tonight."

Clive slept most of the day, but he ate several times, and by the time the shadows were beginning to fall, he was feeling much stronger. He managed to get out of bed and put on a robe that belonged to Daniel Bradford. Since he was six feet three and Bradford was somewhat shorter, it did not fit him well, but he was able to take a few shaky steps back and forth and laughed aloud. "I'm going to make it!" he said with satisfaction. He had not been at all sure of that, for he had seen others go down and not recover from whatever this sickness was that ravaged Boston.

He was sitting in the chair staring out the window when he saw Katherine approach. He straightened up and watched as she moved to the entrance and was admitted by Rachel. Turning to face the door, he waited expectantly. Soon enough it opened, and when the two women came in, he ignored Rachel, saying, "Katherine!" But then he could think of nothing else to say.

Katherine was embarrassed as well, but seeing this, Rachel said, "Sit down, Katherine. I was about to bring his supper in. I'll bring yours too, and you can eat together. Move that table, will you?"

"All right, Rachel."

Glad to have something to do, Katherine moved the table over and then pulled the chair across from Clive. "How are you feeling?" she finally asked.

200

"Much better!" He stared at her so directly that she blushed. "I thought I was having a dream last night."

"You did have a dream, several of them," Katherine said. "Do you remember any of them?"

"A dream? I remember some nightmares, and being so hot I thought I was going to catch on fire. Then I woke up and there you were."

"Do you remember what I said to you?"

"Not very much."

"Then I'll have to say it again." Katherine was more at ease now. She had spoken to him about this once, although he didn't remember it. "I treated you shamefully when you came to Boston. I think I hated you, Clive."

Clive shook his head. "I never understood why you were so angry."

Katherine looked at him, tilting her head to one side. It was an attractive way she had. She studied him carefully and saw nothing but a genuine bewilderment in him. "Don't you really know why I was angry?"

"I haven't the foggiest idea!"

"When you left Halifax," Katherine asked, "did you leave any orders concerning my father and my uncle?"

"Why, no! What sort of orders do you mean?"

Suddenly Katherine saw that he was telling the truth. There was a bewilderment in him that she could not mistake. "I went to see Major Banks at the hospital and discovered that my father and my uncle had been moved back to the hulks."

"Back to the hulks? Why, that's impossible!" Incredulity showed itself plainly on Clive's face. "I can't believe it!"

"I went to see Major Banks—" Suddenly Katherine hesitated, for looking back she saw clearly what had happened. Slowly she said, "He showed me an order that he said was written by you. It ordered my father and my uncle back onto the *St. George*."

"I never gave such an order! I never wrote it, Katherine!"

"I . . . I see that now, Clive. It was all Banks' doing!" Anger flared through her, not at Banks, but at herself for being beguiled by the man. "I was a fool to believe him. I've never seen your handwriting, so I didn't question it, and he kept it. He must've written it himself!"

"I see why you were so angry," Clive said. "Anyone would be."

But Katherine was shaking her head almost violently. "I can't *believe* I was so foolish! I never believed anything he said before, and I never trusted him. Somehow it just never occurred to me that a man would do a thing like that!"

"He's a bitter, vindictive man, Katherine," Clive said.

The two sat there, and suddenly Katherine could not meet his eyes. "I'm . . . I'm so sorry, Clive."

He reached across the table; her hands were folded on it clenched tightly together. He took them, pried them apart, and held one of them in his own. "Don't grieve yourself," he said, and gentleness ran through his tone. "All the evidence pointed against me."

The touch of his hands on hers was warm, and she remembered how it had been with him before. How she had admired him and trusted him, and how kind he had been to her and to her relatives. Tears came to her eyes, and she whispered with bitterness, "I was hurt by a man once. Do you suppose I'll go on distrusting every man I meet?"

"You can't live without trust, Katherine, and you won't. It's not in you to be like that."

Startled, she looked up and met his eyes. Most men she knew would have been at least victorious to have been proved right. Many would have even been harsh and condemnatory, but she saw nothing of this in Clive Gordon. He was smiling at her now, and suddenly a heavy weight lifted from her shoulders. She whispered, "You're so kind, Clive!"

His hands tightened on hers, and he lifted them suddenly and kissed one hand. She flushed and dropped her eyes. She could not speak for a moment, for the fullness in her throat. Finally, she looked up and found that somehow all of the anger and bitterness had dropped away from her. Blinking her eyes to clear them of the tears, she said softly, "Will you let me start all over with you, Clive Gordon?"

Clive looked at her, then kissed her hand again. "We'll both start over," he said, his eyes warm and confident.

17

DISASTER FOR HIS EXCELLENCY

FINALLY, EVEN THE CAUTIOUS General William Howe was ready to make the advance, the first step against the conquest of New York. On the twenty-first day of August 1776 British officers began loading troops onto the ships at Staten Island. They swung east to Gravesend Bay, where they were well out of the range of Washington's cannons. A great thunderstorm interrupted briefly, but the complicated maneuver went smoothly. The British troops were ferried ashore in seventy-five flatboats, eleven bateaux, and two galleys, all built specifically for this invasion.

The landing made a splendid sight. The vessels spread acres of white sails to dry in the bright sunlight that followed the storm. Long Island glittered, the hills and fields a bright green. By noon fifteen thousand men with all their arms and supplies were landed, and rank after rank of brightly arrayed British regiments advanced smartly in time to the beat of the drums and the tinkling of the fife. The British objective was the American position on Brooklyn Heights.

Brooklyn's defenders, less than eight thousand in all, occupied a series of posts on a broken ridge nearly two miles in front of the main fortifications of the village. Despite being outnumbered, Washington's troops had an advantage in holding higher ground than the British. Once again the British, as at Breed's Hill, would have to march up a hill into the guns of the Americans.

General George Washington had faced the problem of how to stop the overwhelming troops of England with foreboding. Finally, he had entrusted the command of his troops to an Irishman from New Hampshire, General John Sullivan. Then Sullivan was replaced, by the order of Washington, with Israel Putnam. Between the two of them they arranged a forward line along a bluff overlooking Flatbush where the British were camped. The Heights were broken by several roads and passes, and the Americans carefully guarded the three western ones. Jamaica Pass, on the east, was left guarded only by a small picket.

Early in the morning General Howe called his officers together. When they were standing before him he said, "Gentlemen, we are ready to do our duty!" He had stretched a map of Long Island and its environs out on a table. "You see here, our adversary has put their line across this area. Here is the battle plan. The Hessian troops will mount noisy demonstrations against the western end of the Heights, here near Gowanus Bay and the two center passes. Meanwhile, Lord Cornwallis and Sir Henry Percy, with ten thousand men will sweep to our right. You will fight your way through and come around behind the rebels." Howe looked up with satisfaction in his eyes. "We will trap them, I believe, gentlemen. Are there any questions?"

Sir Henry Crutan said with exultation, "We shall have them, General. The war will be ended here today!"

"It very well might! Washington, I'm told, is a fox hunter," Howe said, and a smile lifted the corners of his lips. "We shall drive the fox to cover, and then take him, and this little demonstration among the Colonies will be over. We can get back to being Englishmen as usual!"

        🜨   🜨   🜨

Dake Bradford was on the left flank of the American line. He stood there beside Silas Tooms, and his heart beat faster. "I keep hearing firing down to our right," he said.

Tooms nodded, his jaw tight with tension. "I reckon that's right. They're hitting Sullivan hard down that way." He stared out into the morning across the fields, expecting to see the red flash of troopers. "I expected them to hit here before now," he said, a puzzled look in his eyes. "I wonder where they are?"

Thad Mobrey, a sixteen-year-old who had joined only the day before, said, "Let 'em come. We'll stop 'em, won't we, Sergeant?"

Tooms gave Mobrey a look of disgust. "Just be sure you don't turn and run, Mobrey, when you see the lobsterbacks coming!"

"Run!" Mobrey said and laughed loudly. He shook his musket and said, "That'll be the day when Thad Mobrey runs from a bunch of lobsterbacks!"

The tension built as the firing on the right grew louder. Dake grew thirsty but discovered there was no water to be had.

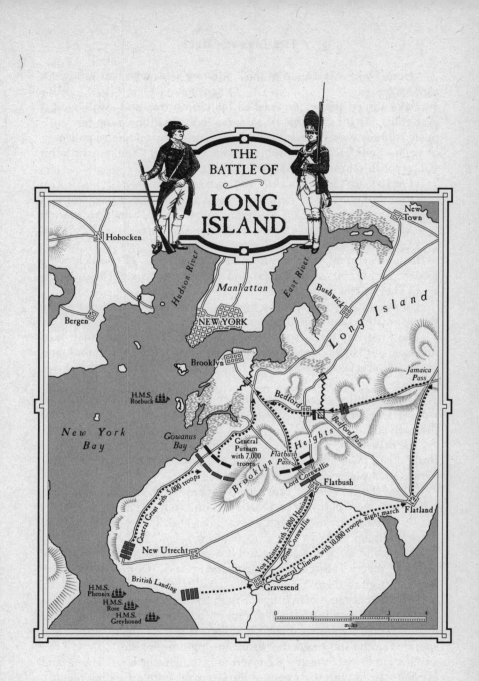

"Here, Dake, have a sip of this!" Mobrey said, who had brought a canteen.

Dake sipped the water, washed his mouth out, and swallowed it gratefully. "Thanks, Thad!" he said. He looked at the young boy curiously. Mobrey was slight, not over five six or seven, and had a pale mop of yellow hair. He looked about fifteen years old. "You're a little bit young for this, aren't you, Thad?"

"I'm sixteen," Mobrey said. "That's old enough!"

Dake thought of Sam, who was the same age as this boy, and was suddenly very glad that his younger brother was not here. He started to answer Mobrey when a yell went up from his left.

"To the rear, the Redcoats, we're flanked!"

Instantly, Tooms whirled and narrowed his eyes. He was chewing tobacco and spat it out on the ground. "There they come!" he said quietly. "They've got us boxed."

He was exactly right. Howe and his troops had mousetrapped the whole position, and now the trap was sprung!

The American officers did what they could. They pulled their men into line, but Howe simply rolled up their left flank. Dake, Tooms, and Mobrey stuck close together while falling back, but Dake saw that it was hopeless.

The ground was almost totally covered by impenetrable brush woods. The greater part of the American riflemen could not defend themselves.

The British line marched on inexorably, and finally when the militia could stand it no longer, they broke and ran despite the officers' desperate attempts to get them to stand.

"They shouldn't have run," Thad Mobrey said. His face was pale, but his lips were tight. He had loaded his musket, and he peered across the field that was now covered with smoke. "Look, I never seen no soldiers like them. . . ."

Tooms and Dake looked up, and it was Tooms who said, "That's the German Jaegers." His voice was grim and he said, "Our boys will never stand in front of them."

The Jaegers came marching through the drifting mist of the morning, their green uniforms blending in with the trees and bushes. Their drums played a steady cadence, and their bright bayonets dipped and sparkled in the sun's rays that broke through the smoke.

"It's Hessians!" the cry went out and the farmer boys, young and untried, stared with wide eyes at the Germans with an aching fear.

They tried to make a stand, but it was a thin little ragged line. Suddenly they heard the drums of the Redcoats coming from behind them.

Dake whirled around and yelled, "They're coming from the other direction!" He sighted his musket on a tall German and pulled the trigger. The rifle kicked and he saw his man go down. Frantically he reloaded.

"We can't stay here!" Thad Mobrey said, his voice trembling.

"Take it easy, son!" Tooms said. "We'll get out of this."

But men were streaming by, mostly young farm boys who had never fought in any battle before, except for the few who had been at Breed's Hill. Overcome by fear and panic, they threw down their muskets and ran. The officers pleaded with them, trying to stop them, but they blindly dashed away. Thad Mobrey stood, and, trembling, his face began to twitch. Dake said, "We'll handle it, Thad—" but Mobrey threw his gun down and started to run. Dake started to run after him, but Tooms grabbed him and pulled him back.

"You can't stop him, Dake! Come along, they're making a little stand over there."

But Dake was watching as the Americans ran away. He saw that they were trapped. The Germans were yelling and laughing as they ran after the fleeing men. The Germans were yelling, "Yonkee! Yonkee!" and then Dake saw Thad trapped and flanked by two groups of German Jaegers. Thad turned to run, stumbled, and a big German came forward and held his gleaming bayonet high. He rammed it into the boy's back and laughed as he did so.

Dake only had time to see the boy writhe like a cut worm as the Jaeger yanked the bayonet out and plunged it in again and then again.

"Let's go, Dake!" Tooms said.

Dake blindly obeyed, and the two found themselves fighting for their lives. It went on for hours between the wooded lines that tried to hold in the American base fortification.

General Sullivan was found in a cornfield trying to hide, but he was captured by three blond Germans who dragged him to his feet and hauled him off. General Sterling was also captured, and still the fighting went on. Only on the American right, where the Maryland and Delaware Continentals, the best-furnished troops in the army, fought, was there anything like success, but by early afternoon the battle was all over. More than three hundred were killed, and a thousand Americans were captured. British and German losses were less than four hundred.

The British were exultant, for they were now directly in front of the American fortifications on Brooklyn Heights. All they had to do was make one more push, and the army of General George Washington would be gobbled up—and the American Revolution would end!

As the wounded, exhausted American soldiers struggled back, Dake found himself wondering if it had all been in vain. He and Silas Tooms had survived, along with most of their squad, but it seemed hopeless. "I don't see how we can stand another attack, Silas!" Dake panted glumly. He looked around at the gruesome wounded, many twitching with pain, and some dying even as he watched. "They're going to hit us one more time, and then we'll be done for!"

As George Washington, from his vantage point, looked over the ghastly scene, he noted the British converging on an open plain below. *They make a rather beautiful sight,* he thought, *British in red, Hessian regulars in blue, and Jaegers in green.* They fanned out like the spokes of a multi-colored wheel, almost like a rainbow. They had stopped firing and ignored Washington's feeble cannon fire. It was the largest army Washington had ever seen gathered together in one place, and he watched as the preparations for the final charge were being made.

"Now they will attack!" Washington said grimly to Knox, who was standing by his side.

Micah had served as Knox's aide throughout the battle, and now he saw that Washington's face was grim and unrelenting. He glanced down below at the thousands of red and blue and green coated soldiers, admiring the way they marched in perfect unison. But then he heard Washington say with a note of relief and incredulity in his voice, "Look, Knox, they're not going to attack!"

The big man stared at the British forces, and whispered, "What is happening, sir?"

"General Howe has decided not to attack, not today anyway, unless it's a trick. Perhaps he's going to try a sneak attack tonight under cover of darkness."

"I don't think he'll do that, sir. A frontal attack and he'll have us."

Washington suddenly became all action. "Double the sentries! Rum and water for every man! The men must return to their formations, and all must be fed."

Micah was kept on the run then, for Knox utilized him, as he did every man he had, in getting the guns pulled into position. Washington moved through all the encampment, and it was a miracle how he was able to pull the army of wounded and terrified men together again.

Down below, the officers of General Howe were perplexed and angry. Howe had called off the attack, and Clinton and Cornwallis both pleaded with him to make one more effort.

"Sir!" Cornwallis said urgently. "They are waiting for us! They're in our hands. All we have to do is attack and we'll finish this thing once and for all!"

But General William Howe had a long memory. He was thinking of how at Bunker Hill, the British troops had marched up into the guns of the Americans and had been cut to pieces. True enough, the army in front of him seemed to be beaten, but he knew that the Americans, like a wounded bear, could turn, and he could not spare any more men. Some might ignore the fact that it took a year to train one British soldier and cost hundreds of pounds to get him to this point, but he could not afford to do so. Besides, he was a careful man, one who could analyze the situation carefully.

Pointing upward to the hill he said, "Look there, gentlemen, there is the enemy. Over there is the East River and there is the Hudson. Our ships can pull in and cut them off. In the morning we will send the ships in, and we will gather them up."

General Clinton disagreed. "I wish we would go now, sir, and finish it off!"

But Howe said, "The men have been marching for sixty-seven hours under a sixty-pound pack. They have fought a battle for six hours, running up and down hill, and they are exhausted. In the morning they will be fresh. We will attack in the morning!"

So the British sat down to rest, and the shattered and frightened Americans began pulling themselves back together again. Washington took command and wasted no time on attempts to fix the blame for their defeat. It was obvious to him that the battle had been lost by Sullivan's failure to hold Jamaica Pass, but he did not give the slightest hint of the serious predicament that he and his tiny army were in. Instead, by his powerful physical presence alone, he inspired new courage in his men. He moved throughout the camp, overseeing the construction of a new fortification, visiting guard outposts, speaking encouragingly to his men in the trenches. Finally he looked up, his attention broken by a roll of thunder and a bank of dark water bearing clouds that moved over Brooklyn and Long Island. A thought began to form in his mind, and he withdrew to his camp, letting it take form.

Morning had worn to midday, and now midday into a rainy, humid afternoon. Dake found Micah, and the two brothers embraced each other. Micah cried out, "I'm glad you're all right, Dake. I was afraid for you!"

Sergeant Silas Tooms stared at the two men. "Well," he said, "I must be seeing double. I guess I lost my wits after that last battle."

"This is my twin, Micah," Dake grinned. "This is Sergeant Tooms, Micah."

Tooms studied the faces of the two young men, so identical, and then said, "Well, you'll have somebody to talk to when they put us into a prison camp."

"It won't come to that!" Dake argued.

"Tell me why it won't!" Tooms spat out. He pulled his hat off, and water ran down his face in rivulets. He was a hard-bitten man, tough in bone, muscle, and mind. Now he looked around and said, "They got us boxed. Look, troops over there—over there, and over there!" He swung his arm around and said, "And over there, nothing but water! The lobsterbacks have got us!" He put his hat on again and shook his head dourly. "I reckon that's why that British general wasn't anxious to attack. He can take us anytime he wants to."

Washington's staff felt about the same way. General Putnam came over, and when Washington asked how many men they lost, he said, "I don't know, but we're hurt sore." He studied Washington, marveling that a man could be composed with such staggering odds outnumbering him. *It'd be better*, Putnam thought sourly, *if he had cursed and raved a little bit at what's happened*. Aloud he said, "It'll be dark soon, sir. They may attack again."

"They may," Washington agreed.

"We're in no condition to resist another attack, Your Excellency."

Washington turned his cold gray eyes on Putnam. He said in a hard tone, "If they attack, we will fight again!"

"Yes, sir!"

Washington walked back and forth, his mind moving from one possibility to another, and rejecting them one at a time. "There must be something, even now when things seem to be at an end!" He knew that the men were all watching him, and through the gathering dusk he could see the hundreds of white faces of the soldiers waiting—expecting him to do what seemed impossible. Slowly it came to him that there were only two alternatives. The first was to surrender, and something in him longed to give up, to get rid of this cowardly rabble he called his army, to go back to Mount Vernon and Martha. This was the obvious way, but he never allowed it to rise in his mind, but put it down firmly.

The second alternative was to fight. He could gather his troops together, and when the British attacked at dawn, they could all die for their country. He knew that the officers, men like Henry Knox and Israel Putnam, loved the thrill of danger. They would follow him into utter defeat, but he knew that the fight would not even be glorious. The army would turn and break at the first British charge, and nothing would be accomplished. The revolution would be lost.

One other thought kept nibbling at his mind, and he allowed it to surface. *Retreat*. Retreat would save his army—at least for a time. If he could get the men away, he had a chance—and America had a chance. But retreat seemed to be the only alternative that was utterly impossible.

"Retreat!" he said aloud, and his mind fluttered like a bird in a cage. He looked up at the dark sky, swept the confusion of the stricken battlefield. The only thing that stopped them from deserting now was the cold waters of the river that lay at their backs. "Retreat!" he said half aloud.

It began raining in earnest as he walked through the camp. He reached one of his officers, General Mifflin, who was, at thirty-two, his youngest general. The young man had not been in on the battle yesterday, and now he spoke carefully. "I'm sorry that we took such losses, sir."

Washington nodded. "We will fight again!" he said.

"Yes, sir, of course!"

Washington and Mifflin walked slowly along, speaking to the men from time to time. Washington noticed that boats were sliding back and forth across the East River. As he always did, he admired the men who rode, as he admired all men who did things well. Observing more closely, he saw they maneuvered the boats with such skill that he said, "They know about boats."

"Yes, sir, they do!"

They know about boats. Washington studied the men in the boats. They were leather-skinned, long-faced Yankees, and there was a uniformity in the blue jackets and stained oilskins most of them wore. This was the one thing that his army lacked for the most part. At least these men skillfully, easily maneuvering the boats were one of a kind. "Who are they?"

"They're part of Glover's regiments. Marblehead fishermen, I think. Maybe they can't fight, but they certainly know boats. They been fishermen all their lives."

Washington's mind leaped at the statement. "How many are there?" The rain was pouring down now, and when Mifflin said six or seven hundred, he suddenly knew what had to be done. For ten minutes he paced in the pouring rain.

Putnam, who was old and tired, came down the slope to join them, and Mifflin glanced at him past the big man. Putnam finally said, "I don't think they'll attack today. Why should they fight in the rain when they can sit in their tents and wait for the weather to clear?"

Suddenly Washington lifted his head, and there was a light in his gray eyes they had not seen. "We won't retreat, gentlemen. We are going to bring over reinforcements, and we're going to take our sick and wounded back to New York!"

"Back across the river, sir?" Mifflin asked in confusion.

"Yes!" Washington pointed to the Marblehead fishermen. "I want you to get every boat on this river, everything that floats. I want boats brought down from the North River, every fishing boat you can lay your hands on, and I want every one of them brought to the Brooklyn shore."

The men looked at him and Mifflin said, "But what for, sir?"

"We're going to withdraw to Manhattan."

"The entire army, sir?"

"Yes, the entire army."

♜   ♜   ♜

The Marblehead fishermen all had the look of men of the sea. They marched with a sailor's rolling gait. True enough, they wore cocked hats to the line, along with short blue jackets and loose white trousers. They spoke a language all their own, the language of the sea, of storms, sails, and ships.

Stocky John Glover, their colonel, was on hand on the dark night of August 29, and he was jubilant that he and his men were on the water again. They had taken charge of the small boats that Washington had collected. Now they brought them bobbing up to the Brooklyn Ferry Landing. Men bent beneath loads of baggage and equipment, marching silently down to the waiting boats. The army began to come like phantoms, silent, words softly spoken and whispered even. The rain came down in torrential sheets, for which they were all profoundly grateful. For a while it seemed they could not make the crossing, the tide was so strong—then suddenly the wind veered to the southwest and subsided.

Washington had visions of thousands of panic-stricken men fighting madly into the boats when the order to retreat was given. When his officers mentioned this, he had said, "You won't tell them. Order certain regiments to be relieved, one by one. Let them think the rest are holding the line."

And strangely enough, and miraculously enough, this was the way the massive retreat happened. When Washington moved later down to the waterfront, he was amazed by the number of boats the Marblehead men had gathered. They came out of the murk of fog and rain, in an endless stream driven by the wind, commandeered by laughing fishermen. The laughter sounded strange to Washington. He had not heard much of that lately. As the boats came in, Glover had them moored and beached and stripped of all gear; then he ordered them to wait.

Knox came to ask, "Sir, what about my guns?"

"Spike them!" Washington said.

"Where are we going to find more guns if we spike these?"

Washington said nothing, and Knox argued, "An army fights with guns!"

212

Washington turned his eyes on the big man. "An army is men. We'll get more guns, Colonel."

"Yes, sir!"

It was astonishing how well the scheme worked. Throughout the night, every regiment, when it was told to leave, thought that it was the lucky one, that they would not have to bear the brunt of the English attack. Slowly they all made their way down into the boats, and when it was close on morning, the fog began to lift. The British had not caught them, which was a miracle in itself. One ship, up the East River, would have revealed the whole scheme, but they had not come.

George Washington waited until all the boats were loaded. Knox was sitting in one of the boats as it rocked with the swell of the tide. His eyes were on Washington, who was marching along the shore. Knox said to Micah, "He won't leave until the last man's loaded."

Micah Bradford watched George Washington as he advanced. "That's right, he won't." His heart suddenly was filled with devotion for the big man as he approached. *I did the right thing*, he thought, *joining with General Washington*. He watched as Washington stepped in and sat down.

"We're ready to go," he nodded to the sailor.

The tiller man finned it off, and his oars scooped at the water. The boat glided out into the river, and Micah saw with astonishment that George Washington was already sitting limply, his head on his chest. He was asleep!

Knox said, "Well, Bradford, he's still got his army. We'll see now what he can do with it. . . ."

ONE BRIGHT STAR IN THE HEAVENS

MICAH ACCOMPANIED COLONEL KNOX after they disembarked from the boats of the Marbleheaders. They were the last of the whipped and exhausted troops to arrive on the East River shores and stagger through the narrow streets of Manhattan. The weather was unseasonably cold, and the fog sent a chill through his bones as he accompanied the colonel through the groups of wounded that lined the streets.

"The surgeons are going to be busy, sir!" Micah murmured.

Knox cast his glance at the surgeons moving among the scores of wounded men. "You're right!" he said shortly. He shook his head and muttered, "It never should have happened."

Hundreds of wounded now lay in rows through which the two men made their way. Micah winced as he saw bloody heads and the stumps of severed arms and legs being stuffed into canvas sacks. It was a gruesome sight, and he said, "War isn't really very glorious, is it, Colonel?"

"Not this part of it."

The two men made their way toward headquarters. The moans of the sick and dying were an anthem of pain that made an accompaniment to the clash of the guns being moved and the rattle of iron wheels on the cobblestones. Micah noticed, with a sense of cynicism that was not his custom, that there were few citizens lining the streets to see the fighting heroes home. When Micah and Knox reached Washington's headquarters, which were in Richmond Hill, they found the small group of officers gathered in the comfortable house. It was a massive framed building with a portico supported by two ionic columns decorated with carved pilasters. From the second floor, out of a railed balcony, one could see for a great distance.

The meeting began when Israel Putnam said, "Sir, we must evacuate Manhattan immediately!" Putnam was stout and strongly built, with a remarkable head of bushy white hair. Now he shook his massive head, saying, "It's impossible for our forces to defend sixteen miles of coastland!"

Washington, himself, was confused. The disaster at Brooklyn had shaken him, but not a man knew it, for he kept his usual calm demeanor. "Congress has ordered that New York be held at any price, at all hazards!" he said firmly.

After some discussion the generals all agreed that the obvious military decision was to move north into the rough, hilly northern end of Manhattan Island. Washington pointed at the map, saying, "Nine thousand troops will withdraw to Harlem Heights. Five thousand will remain in the city proper, and we will strengthen Fort Washington and Fort Lee." There was some talk but little argument, for Washington's officers had learned to give their advice and counsel and then wait for His Excellency, General George Washington, to speak.

After Washington had left, Knox said to General Greene, "I think he'd be calm if the sky fell in on him."

Greene, the tall, balding ex-Quaker, nodded slowly, "I think it *has* fallen on him."

🦁   🦁   🦁

For three weeks Washington watched the army of General Howe, expecting each day that the attack would come. Howe, however, did little. He went back to Staten Island and waited, planning his next move. Washington had spent the time trying to plan for the defense of New York. He could not bring himself to give it up, and in the midst of his confusion committed himself to one of the worst military decisions he made during the entire revolution. He left some of his army in the city at one end of Manhattan, and some of it he posted up in Harlem at the other end. The weak part he put in the middle, using his poorest troops in the most critical place.

On the night of September 14, British frigates crept up the East River and anchored off Kip's Bay. The shore was held by several regiments of Connecticut militia who had scratched out only a shallow ditch along the water's edge. The leader of the Connecticut troops, a Major Gray, was disgruntled, as were his men. They were tired and angry, and confident that nothing could happen to them. Most of them slept during the night, which was as black as ink. The East River was hidden in the murky darkness. At some point someone said, "There be someone out in that river!"

"Shall we give them a volley?"

"What for? They can't see us."

When the gray of dawn lit the eastern skies, the Connecticut men saw four mighty ships of the line anchored prow to stern with broadside spacing them, guns rolled out, and gunners standing by. The sun broke through the mist and cast an enchanting halo about the ships of war, and the Americans stared in horror and astonishment.

Then on the British deck pipes began to twitter, and wide flotillas of marines began to move toward the shore. Major Gray gave a hoarse command, but no one heard an American musket fire, for at that moment one of the British officers cried, "Fire!" and an inferno of round shot and grape shot struck the Connecticut men. The poor patriots never saw the ships of the line again. A solid wall of smoke formed in the river. They tried to run, but their weapons were ripped from their hands by the solid blast of grape that rained down on them. They tried to rise up, but the shells tore them to pieces. They tried to crawl to their friends, and saw that their friends were lying dead.

Finally they did what frightened men will do. They began to run. They left the belching guns behind them, but they saw columns of men marching in close order, and someone cried out, "Hessians!"

The big guns had ceased their fire, but the decisive shout from the Germans rang out, "Yonkee! Yonkee! Yonkee!" They plunged away, these men from Connecticut, but knew that they were doomed as the Hessians marched forward, crying, "Yonkee! Yonkee! Yonkee!"

The town of New York was clustered tightly on the southernmost tip of Manhattan Island. It was full of crooked little avenues and ordinarily was a bright, cheerful town. Israel Putnam had been assigned by Washington to defend the city itself, but the general was awakened from a sound sleep by a young man named Aaron Burr, who burst in, saying, "They've landed!"

"The British?"

"Hessians, too, on both sides of the Island!"

"How many?" Putnam demanded.

"I don't know—thousands!"

Putnam shook his head. "They couldn't have landed!" he insisted. "If they have, we're caught like rats in a trap!"

"They're on both sides of the Island coming toward the middle. We've got to get through before they close the door."

Putnam thought for only one moment, then nodded. "Get the men together. You'll have to lead us out of here, Burr!"

"Yes, sir! We've got to hurry or we'll wind up in a filthy British prison!"

✠   ✠   ✠

Washington had been awakened by the crashing of the guns. He had leaped to his horse and recklessly driven the animal, clearing a wall with a bound, then a brook, then a fence. He saw the army coming toward him, running and straggling. Pulling in his horse, he tried to talk to them, but there was no recognition in their blank eyes. They swarmed past him, ignoring his commands. "I'm your commander. I'm your general! Get behind the stone walls and use your guns!"

But the men swarmed past him like rabbits, and Washington knew a moment of rage. He drew his pistols, but the guns misfired. He flung the pistols at them, then drew his sword. Riding among them, he struck at them with the flat of it, begging, pleading, but they ran on. Still, Washington rushed across the field like a madman, his voice raging.

Then he paused helpless. He braced himself in the saddle, and looking up he saw the column of the British marching smartly only a few hundred yards away. Yet he didn't move. He felt that he was dead, and wondered vaguely why he could still hear and see. The British were only a hundred yards away now.

"Come away, sir, please!" General Mifflin was beside him, along with others begging him to retreat. "Please, come away, Your Excellency!"

Washington slowly turned his horse and rode away in front of the advancing British troops.

✠   ✠   ✠

The long column crawled over the road like a scarlet snake. General Howe rode at the head of the column, he and his aides all mounted on white horses. All around them were evidences of the Americans' headlong flight: old bayonets, knapsacks, muskets, hats.

They rode on and the heat increased. Their beautiful pressed, colorful uniforms became limp and wet. They were herding a long group of American prisoners, clusters of dirty, frightened boys, and one of Howe's officers stared at them, saying, "Stubborn beasts!"

Howe felt no hate. He simply wanted to end this stupid war so that he could return to England. It was almost over now, he knew.

One of his officers said, "We can have them all before night, General. They're probably ten thousand."

"A good catch," Howe nodded, taking off his hat and wiping his brow.

"Yes, sir, but we must hurry!"

"Oh, there's plenty of time."

"Well, of course, sir, but a few of them are across the Island. We could cut them off, you know."

"I suppose. You know I'd give my soul for a drink." He pointed to a pleasant Georgian house set back off the road. Two colored servants were occupied in taking down wooden shutters, and he asked idly, "Do you suppose they'd offer us a drink?" Without waiting for an answer, he started his horse for the house and the staff followed him.

Several ladies sat in front of the house, but they rose to greet the British officers. General Howe swept off his hat, and all three ladies were impressed by his good looks. One was blond and blue-eyed, with hair like combed flax. They were all quite pretty.

"My dear ladies, I wonder if we could prevail upon you for water. William Howe at your service."

"Your Excellency!" the three ladies said and dropped very graceful curtsies.

"I am Mrs. Murray. This is Miss Van Clehut and Miss Pinrose. Please, gentlemen, come into my humble house."

Howe and his officers dismounted and followed the ladies into the house. They were all relaxed, and by tea time Howe had finished his third bottle of claret.

"But we are rebels, you know," Mrs. Murray said roguishly.

"Bosh, there are no more rebels," General Howe smiled genteelly.

There was some talk of the war. All the time General Clinton was urging Howe to get on with the battle. However, Clinton was persuaded to give them a little music, so he sat down at the clavichord, playing and singing very well indeed. The hot afternoon passed as pleasantly as any late summer afternoon. Finally the clock struck five, and Howe looked outside. "Well, dear me, I've lost track of the time! We must be on our way. Thanks, Mrs. Murray, for your gracious hospitality."

And so the afternoon passed, and Mrs. Murray's tea party kept General Howe busy. Mrs. Murray was a devout patriot, but did not really know what a service she was doing for her country and for General Washington. While the British generals enjoyed their afternoon tea, George Washington and his ragged troops passed north and found refuge behind the lines at Harlem Heights. There Washington worked ceaselessly, under a driving rain that almost drowned his poor half-dressed men. He was thinking, *We've got to do something to put a spark of light in the men. They must have some sort of a victory! They can't go on fighting, and retreating, and losing. There's got to be one bright star in the heavens for them to look to!*

That bright star came on September 16. A Colonel Knowlton and his rangers, about one hundred twenty of them, made a valiant foray against the British. Knowlton was a favorite of his superiors and the idol of his men. Erect and elegant, he was a tall, handsome man in his late thirties.

Knowlton and his rangers stood off nearly four hundred light infantrymen for half an hour; then they heard the squeal of bagpipes, which warned them that the famous Black Watch regiment was hard on its way. Knowlton ordered a careful retreat. As jeering scarlet lines poured into the valley, Washington came up to stand beside Knowlton just as a British bugler stood up in full view and blew the fox hunters' call that always announced the end of a chase, for it meant, "The fox has skulked into his den."

Exhausted and his nerves on edge, Washington felt the sting of disgrace. Rage suddenly brought color to the face of Washington. It was an insult to the Virginia aristocrat to hear the hunters' call.

He turned to Knowlton and said, "Knowlton, are you afraid?"

"No, sir, I'm not afraid of anything on the green earth!"

"Could you take a party down to that valley and come in behind those—fox hunters?"

"Yes, sir, I can do it!'

"Then try it! Take a regiment with you, some Virginia men and Major Leitch."

As soon as Knowlton left, Washington turned and said to General Mifflin, "I want a frontal attack in that direction!"

Mifflin nodded and turned away, glad that he was given a chance to show that he was not afraid either.

Knowlton led his men and the Virginians through the hills. Soon they encountered the enemy, for a German officer spotted them. *"Was ist das?"* the German cried. Then the cry, "Yonkee! Yonkee!" went running down the line of Jaegers. The Germans advanced and a blaze of musketry crashed into the faces of the Americans. Knowlton fell dying, but as his lieutenant stooped beside him, he managed to say, "Tell the general I wasn't afraid."

In the meantime, Mifflin had led two hundred Massachusetts men head on into the fray. They started across the valley, and Washington spurred down toward him. They watched as the men attacked, and then suddenly from the right came another sound of musketry.

"It's Putnam coming up with another five hundred!" Washington cried. There was a crashing sound and he saw Knox and young Micah

Bradford coming with their light field pieces. The men, seeing the re-inforcements, scrambled over the stone wall and charged the British in-fantry. They forced the British back, and Washington followed, yelling and laughing, as they routed the enemy.

The single column of British light infantry had expected no oppo-sition whatsoever. Now, they faced what seemed to be a screaming mob of lunatics. The column gave way, and then—for the first time British regulars forgot their guns. They threw them down and turned in re-treat.

"We did it!" Micah gasped, turning to General Knox, who was watching the British troops run away. "We stood up against British reg-ulars!"

Knox could not speak, he was so moved, and then General Wash-ington came up. His face was alight with joy, and he said, "Well, this was one bright star in the heavens!"

T   T   T

Not a drop of rain had fallen in New York since the stormy night when the American army had retreated to Harlem Heights. It was very dry now, indeed, and practically the only pure drinking water to be found in New York was in the Collect Pond, north of the Commons. All the rich families purchased pure spring water from peddlers who hauled it in carts and stopped at their back doors.

Most of the houses in the city were wooden, and most roofs were shingled with cedar. They had been baked by the blistering summer sun and now were dry as toast. Many of the trees that had long shaded the city streets had been cut down by the troops, both British and American. There were many wretched dwellings in the city, and in narrow lanes and in filthy, crooked alleyways the poor made their homes in log huts with dirty floors and rickety wooden tenements of three or four rooms.

On Friday afternoon, September 20, a hot wind began to blow from the southwest and increased until it was almost a gale force. As dark-ness fell, the winds whipped the branches against the windows and tossed dry leaves and blew dust into the eyes of those who made their way along the darkening streets.

In the dark hours of the night somehow a fire started. Many of the New England soldiers were eager for the city's destruction. General Greene had reminded General Washington that two-thirds of the prop-erty in the city was Tory owned. Militarily it made sense to raze the city. Why willingly hand over comfortable quarters to the enemy when you were quartered in leaky tents in Harlem Heights?

Somehow several fires started simultaneously in the crowded

downtown streets. One began in a house of prostitution on the wharf near Whitehall Slip. It spread immediately to an adjacent tavern, burning through the flimsy wooden structures. When it hit the kegs of hard cider and sawdust, it sent both buildings up like exploding bombs. The explosion scattered blazing sparks to the tinder-dry roofs of the dwellings next door. Soon another fire broke out in the Old Fighting Cocks Tavern on the Battery, then in a crowded inn on Broadway called the Whitehall.

All of the church bells had been carried away by the retreating population, so there was no way to spread the alarm except by women's screams. Fire companies—all volunteer—soon arrived, but they were disorganized and undermanned. The engines and pumps were out of order, and water itself was in short supply.

Soon women and children rushed out of burning houses to watch helplessly as flames leaped from roof to roof. Soon a wall of fire moved hungrily up the entire Island. It sucked the air from the narrow streets and alleyways, and rickety tenements went up like kindling. Showers of sparks fell everywhere, and men and women formed almost useless bucket brigades.

Horses trapped in their stables shrieked in fright. Some broke free and stampeded through the streets. Some people trying to flee ran barefoot through the fire, beating at the sparks that fell from the sky and ignited their hair and nightdresses. A warehouse full of guns and gunpowder on Stone Street blew up, turning the immediate neighborhood into an inferno.

Matthew Bradford was awakened by the sound of people crying. He jumped up, shouting, "Jan, something's happening!" The Dutchman came out of his bed, and the two ran to the window. "The city's on fire!" Matthew cried.

Jan stared blankly at the street, then nodded slowly. "We must get what we can out of here! Never mind the clothes. Take the paintings."

The two men took the best of their paintings and left the building just before it was swept by a solid sheet of flame.

"Jan, I've got to go see about Abigail! Those women are all alone in that house, and it's right in the pathway!"

"Ya! I will go with you!" Vandermeer nodded.

The two men made their way to the Denham house, and not too soon. They piled their paintings in the front yard and rushed up, where they were met by a frightened Abigail. She had been watching the fire advance, and even now it was next door.

"Oh, Matthew!" she cried. "I'm so glad you've come—and you, too, Jan!"

"We've got to get out of here!" Matthew said. He glanced at the fiery wall that was even now catching the house on fire and said, "Where's your mother and Mrs. Denham?"

"Aunt Esther's gathering her valuables."

"There's little time for that!" Vandermeer said. "But I vill go help!"

The three of them rushed inside, and soon were all engaged in helping Esther Denham gather her priceless family paintings and photographs and letters.

"We can't take any more. The house is on fire now!" Matthew cried.

But Esther begged for just a little more time. She had the servants gathering her family silver, and then the cry came, "The porch is on fire! We've got to go!" Jan had come in and picked up the bag. "Come, Mrs. Denham. Nothing's worth losing your life for!"

Esther stood looking around the room that had been her life for so long. Soon it would be nothing but ashes, and she hesitated for one moment.

Abigail came over and put her arm around her. "Come along, Aunt Esther," she said quietly.

"All right, Abigail."

The two women got as far as the porch. The others were already outside when suddenly Esther remembered. "Oh, I forgot my mother's portrait!" She rushed back inside before anyone could stop her.

"Matthew, go get her!" Abigail cried. She looked up and saw that the entire top of the house was on fire and in danger of caving in.

Matthew dropped the sack he was carrying and, without hesitation, dashed back into the house. The smoke was so thick it burned his eyes, and he called out, "Esther—Esther, where are you!" He got no answer, so he dashed into another room—just in time to see the ceiling begin to cave in. He also saw Esther Denham, who was evidently blinded by the smoke, groping her way across the room.

An ominous creaking came from overhead, and suddenly without warning, the beams gave way. The whole upper floor seemed to fall in, and Matthew saw one of them, a heavy timber, strike the elderly woman. It merely grazed her shoulder, it seemed, but it knocked her to the floor. It was on fire, and quickly he leaped forward, pulled off his coat, and smothered the blaze that licked at her clothing. Picking her up, he forced his way blindly through the smoke. The fire was crackling and roaring behind him, and he barely managed to make it out of the house before the whole structure collapsed.

Abigail came forward. "Matthew, are you all right?"

"Yes, but Esther was hurt, I'm afraid! Let's get away from the house." He carried the injured woman out into the street, and then paused.

"We've got to get her out of here!" he said.

Esther began to move her head and open her eyes. She was dazed, but quickly her wits returned to her. "Abigail!" she cried and reached out her hand.

"Yes, Aunt Esther, what is it?"

"Is the coach out of the carriage room?"

"Yes, it is!" Abigail had seen one of the servants bring the coach around to the street, so the horses were already hitched to it.

"We must go to Boston!" she said.

"Boston?" Abigail was amazed. "Why would we want to go to Boston?"

"I have a house there. Just a little place, and no one's living in it." Esther Denham looked at the house that had been so precious to her and shook her head. "There's nothing left here."

"But you're hurt, Aunt Esther."

"Get your mother, we must go! There's nothing left here in New York!"

Matthew said quickly, "That might not be a bad idea, Abigail. I'd better go with you! It wouldn't be safe for you to travel alone."

"Ya!" Vandermeer said. "I vill also go! We can paint in Boston as well as New York!"

It was decided, and the carriage and the extra wagon made its way down the streets. The houses were blazing on each side, and Esther sat huddled close to Abigail, who had her arm around her shoulder. She had not been badly injured, but the thought of losing her home and all her treasures made her turn and look back.

Abigail knew her aunt was hurting and she whispered, "I'm sorry, Aunt Esther, but you lost everything."

Esther Denham turned and the light of the blazing fires illuminated her fine-boned face. "I haven't lost everything," she whispered quietly. "I still have Jesus, and I'm looking for a city that has better foundations than a little village like New York!"

The small procession moved out of the city, and finally onto the country roads. They made their way along quietly. Matthew and Jan drove the wagon behind, which contained the few possessions they had been able to salvage. Neither of them said anything, but as they looked back they saw the sky lit with the fires that were consuming the city.

"Well, I suppose Howe will have the city, but it will be nothing but ashes," Matthew remarked.

"Ya, that is so!" Vandermeer agreed.

As the flames leapt into the sky, lighting it up, Esther Howland Denham looked back once more—then said goodbye to earthly possessions.

PART FOUR

THE FALL OF FORT WASHINGTON

October—November 1776

19

BACK TO BOSTON

THE DEVASTATING FIRE THAT LEVELED over five hundred houses in New York had an unexpected side effect. Many victims of the inferno left the city seeking refuge with relatives in the outlying districts, and some even migrated to other states. This exodus soon caught up with the small band that Matthew led. The first day they were passed by wagons loaded with furniture salvaged from the fire. Some rode horses, carrying only what they could stuff into saddlebags. As they watched this rather grim flight Matthew shook his head. "It's going to make things a little bit harder, Jan."

"Why's that?" The roly-poly Dutchman was not a man to worry past the next meal. However, it was going on toward dark, and this was becoming a concern for the artist.

"I think it's going to make it harder to get a place to stay at night," Matthew nodded. Looking up at the sun he said, "We can travel for maybe another three hours; then we'd better find something."

"Ya, but in the meanwhile I will see what we can find to eat! Pull over under the shade of those trees, Matthew!" When Matthew obeyed, the Dutchman jumped in the back of the wagon and began digging through the pile of boxes, bags, and assorted plunder. Lifting up a basket he said, "Aha, now ve will haf a picnic!" He leaped to the ground, walked back to the carriage, and lifted up his hand. "Now, ladies," he beamed, "I invite you to join me for a little banquet!" He assisted Abigail and her mother to the ground, and then said, "Mrs. Denham, would you like to get down and walk a little?"

"You know, I really think I would." The falling beam had grazed Esther Denham's left shoulder, and she had such difficulty using her left arm that Abigail had fixed a sling for it. Nevertheless, with the sturdy Dutchman's help, she got down out of the carriage and arched her back, sighing with relief. "This is good, Jan," she said.

227

"Come mit me!" he said, and led her over to the shade of the tree. "This time I will be the host!" As the ladies walked around stretching their cramped muscles, Vandermeer laid out the food that he had hastily stuffed into a large basket on his last trip into Esther's house. Ruefully he wished that he had salvaged more, but he made the best of it. "Come," he called, "ve will have our little banquet!" The others came to stand before Jan, and he put his eyes on Mrs. Denham, saying, "I will ask the blessing, no?" Without waiting for permission he bowed his head and asked a most proper blessing. When he looked up and found Matthew staring at him with surprise, he said, "You did not think Jan could do that? I tell you my father and my mother were fine Christians! I would hope some of it rubbed off on me! Now, we have baked chicken, pickles, French bread, and a meat pie. Here, let me help you, Mrs. Denham!" He sat down beside her and, to the amusement of the other women, treated her like a child. Since she could use only one hand, he cut her food into small pieces and put it onto a plate, also seeing that she had plenty of the cider, which he had brought in a large stoneware jug.

"You're a very fine host, Jan," Esther said, staring at him. She was exhausted, and the pain from her injury nagged at her, but she did not let it be known. "I'm glad to hear that you come from a Christian family."

"Oh, ya, mine uncle he was a *predicator*—that is a preacher. My parents thought they would make a minister of me, but such was not to be!" He sighed heavily and shook his head. "Now I am a simple painter and a disappointment to my parents!"

Esther put her hand out on his and said quietly, "You're not a disappointment to me, Jan."

Jan's face flushed, but then he smiled. "Maybe I'm not a complete failure." He glanced over to where Matthew and Abigail were sitting off to one side and said, "That pair, they would make a fine couple!"

"I think they might. Abigail just recently found her way." Esther thought of Abigail's past and studied the girl's face. "She's such a beautiful girl, and her life's been wasted up until now."

"Matthew, he is foolish with love for her! I never saw such a lovesick duckling!" He chuckled deep in his chest and said, "He dreams about her whether he's asleep or awake, but that is the way it should be between young lovers, ya?"

"Ya, indeed!" Esther smiled, continuing to watch the pair as they talked and enjoyed their meal.

After the meal they rested for a time, lying on quilts and blankets that Jan and Matthew had pulled out of the wagon. It was indeed refreshing, but then they loaded up, pulled out, and rode for another three hours. Finally they came to a small village and Jan said, "I will go see about rooms at that inn."

Matthew waited until Jan came back and noticed that he was frowning. "No room for us in the inn?" he asked.

Jan looked at him. "You know the Bible, too! Well, they say they will make places for us, but it will not be pleasant."

The innkeeper was an enormous woman who did not believe in bathing often. The aroma from her sweaty body was forceful enough to make Matthew blink when he drew near to her. She had a strident voice that would stop hair from growing, and she negotiated the prices in a bullying way.

"We've got plenty already stopping here, so if you want to stay you'll have to pay for it!"

"We'd be glad to pay," Matthew said quickly. "Do you have a room for these ladies? My friend and I can manage anywhere."

"They'll have to share it with some others. You ain't the first to get here, you know!" The woman was taller than Matthew, and her fingers were like miniature sausages. Her nails were bitten to the quick, which accounted for them having no dirt under them, but the dirt seemed to be everywhere else. Her dress had almost lost its original color by food that had been allowed to dry across her massive bosom. She wiped her runny nose with her sleeve and said, "The women can have the room downstairs. You and your friend, the Dutchy, can bunk with the fellers upstairs!"

None of the women had ever had such an experience as they had that night. The small room had three beds in it, so there was barely room to walk between them, and there were already five other women in the room. The stench of unwashed bodies seemed to fill the place, and Mrs. Howland's face grew very pale. "I believe I'd rather sleep out in the wagon," she murmured.

Abigail agreed with her. "We'll stay here tonight, but tomorrow we'll have to find something better." She bargained with the other tenants so that the three of them had one of the beds, and somehow they made it through the night—despite the fact that one of the women snored so loudly that there was little chance of a sound sleep.

Up in the attic the men fared little better. Their bedfellows were every bit as unwashed and prone to snore as those below. However, they made the best of it. Corn-shuck mattresses were their lot, placed on the hard boards that composed the floor. Matthew shook his head doubtfully. "This is pretty rough, Jan. I hope the women are better off."

"I don't think they will be! Bad on them, although it doesn't matter so much for us! Ve must do better tomorrow!"

They arose at dawn and shuddered at the cold, greasy pork chops that were offered for breakfast. Instead, they made the main part of their meal on hot mush with butter and salt, which they washed down with a great deal of the strong tea that their hostess sloshed out of a huge urn.

During the days that followed, Matthew learned to begin looking for an inn early. More often than not, he managed to find an acceptable place for the women, while he and Jan slept in the wagon, or under it if it happened to be raining. The roads were bad, and several times Matthew wished that he had arranged for a sea voyage—but the die was cast and they made the best of it.

On the last night of their trip, just outside of Boston, they found a respectable inn with good accommodations for the women. The cooking, too, was better than usual, and after the evening meal Abigail and Matthew stepped outside. Ragged skeins of clouds were scudding across the gray skies above. The smell of burning leaves brought an acrid odor to them, a smell that Matthew always liked. He leaned his back up against a big oak tree and stared upward, thinking of what might be coming, then turned to look at Abigail. "It's been hard on you!"

"Harder on mother and Aunt Esther," Abigail said. She was wearing a gray dress of simple cut, which now was sadly in need of washing, but there was no chance for that. Even in this rather worn garment she made a fetching picture. She was not wearing a bonnet, and her hair cascaded down her back. She reached up and touched it and made a face. "I'd give anything to wash my hair!"

"We'll be in Boston tomorrow; you can do it then. It looks pretty to me, though." Matthew stepped closer to her and ran his hand over her hair. "I'd like to see you all dressed up in a beautiful gown, and wearing diamonds, at a ball. We'll do that someday."

This had been Abigail's dream once, but now she was disturbed to find that that sort of thing did not matter too much to her. "That would be nice," she murmured. She turned to study Matthew, examining his face rather curiously. He was not a large man, though taller than average, but hard living had pared him down so that he seemed to be almost gaunt. He was wearing butternut trousers, a white shirt with fluffy sleeves, and a leather vest cut off at the shoulders. He wore brown stockings and scuffed leather shoes with pewter buckles. His hair was light brown and blew with the wind, and as always, the light of quick intelligence shone in his blue eyes.

He looks like Leo, Abigail thought with a sudden start, *but he's not like him—not really*. She had thought much about Leo Rochester and his offer

230

to her, and as the days had gone by, Abigail had become more and more aware that she had been wrong to accept it. She had spoken once to Esther about how she grieved over her past. Her aunt had said quickly, "You can't go back to the past. God has forgiven you for all of that. Now what you must do is live for Jesus Christ today! The past is gone forever, Abigail!"

Her aunt's words had comforted her then, but now as she looked at Matthew and saw that he was considering her with an admiring light in his eyes, she was confused and wondered if she ought to tell him of Leo's plot. She almost did as they stood there. The impulse came to her abruptly, lingering on her lips. Matthew saw that she was about to say something and waited—but at that instant Jan came out of the inn and joined them, speaking jovially of their safe arrival in Boston.

And so the moment passed away. Afterward, Abigail wondered what it would have been like had Jan not come out of the inn at exactly that moment.

𝕋   𝕋   𝕋

"Well, I guess we just about made it, Jan." Matthew Bradford drew a sigh of relief as he pulled the team up in front of the red-brick house that set back from the streets farther than most. The horses were willing enough to stop, for Matthew had driven them hard for the past four hours, anxious to get the women into shelter before nightfall. A cold wind was sweeping in from the west, and Matthew glanced up at the threatening skies. "May be snow in those clouds," he muttered, "but we're all right now!" He turned the team into the narrow lane beside the house and, reaching the carriage house, jumped to the ground. Moving back to the buggy, he looked up into the wan face of Esther Denham and said quickly, "We're all right now, Esther."

Esther Denham had been hanging on to the seat as the buggy had bounced over the rutted roads for the past few hours. Her face was set and pale, but she had not complained. She looked at the house and asked, "Where is this, Matthew?"

"Why, this is my home," he said. "Here, let me help you down."

"We can't all pile into your home like this unannounced!"

Matthew laughed. "We're not much for formalities around here. Unless father's taken in a lot of extra company, there'll be plenty of room. Come now, let me help you down." Matthew helped the elderly lady down, and when she staggered slightly, put his arm around her. "Can you help your mother, Abigail?"

"Of course!" Abigail leaped to the ground, then turned to her mother. In truth, she herself was exhausted, but she had youth and strength on her side. "Come along, Mother, we'll soon have you into a nice comfortable bed." She helped her mother to the ground and followed Matthew as he led Esther to a door on the side of the house.

Jan had immediately begun to unhitch the horses and soon had both teams inside the small barn. He found the feed bin, gave them a generous portion, then hung the harness up before turning to go to the house. When he stepped inside the door, he called loudly, "Hello!"

Matthew appeared at once, with a young woman by his side, and said, "Come in, Jan!" He waited until the Dutchman was inside and said, "This is my sister, Rachel. Rachel, this is Jan Vandermeer."

Rachel smiled and offered her hand. Jan took it and bent over it with a flourish, kissing irrepressibly. She smiled at his exuberance and said, "My brother's told me so much about you."

"And I haf much to tell you about him!" Jan smiled broadly.

"Come along," Matthew grinned. "I'll show you where you'll be sleeping, Jan! You'll have to share a room with me."

Matthew turned and led Jan to a room on the second floor pleasantly furnished with a trundle bed. Matthew nodded at it. "Did you ever see one of these?"

"See one? It was a Dutchman who invented trundle beds! I vill take the bottom part!"

"We'll let the ladies get all cleaned up. My brother Sam has invented a newfangled kind of bathroom," Matthew said. "You have to heat the water outside, then it comes in through pipes."

Jan was interested in such things and followed as Matthew went outside. There was a large iron tank next to the house with a firebox underneath. Quickly Matthew built a small fire, fed it steadily until it grew larger, then turned to say rather wearily, "Well, that's all there is to it! There'll be hot water soon." He rubbed his face, the stubby bristles rasping under his fingers. "I'd be glad to get a bath and a shave!" he said. "It's been a rough trip."

Inside, Abigail and her mother were in the large bedroom that Rachel had shown them to. It was actually a master bedroom, the largest of the six in the house. "Pa would want you to have this!" she had said. "He sleeps wherever he is when he gets tired. Sometimes I wake up to find him on the floor in the parlor with a book beside him."

All of the women had protested, but Rachel had smiled. "Abigail can sleep with me. We have a guest, Mr. Clive Gordon, in one bedroom, but we'll make out fine, won't we, Abigail?"

Abigail was not prone to argue. The trip had worn her down, and she could not but express her gratitude to Rachel.

After the unpacking was done, Rachel led Abigail to the special bathroom, where she gestured toward a large copper tub. The two older ladies had already washed their faces and collapsed into bed, but Abigail had mentioned that she'd love to have a full bath. Now, as Rachel explained the apparatus, Abigail looked curiously at the tub and at the plumbing that young Sam Bradford had installed.

Rachel leaned over, turned a valve, and suddenly water began trickling in from the pipe. Steam began to arise at once, and Rachel laughed at the astonished expression on Abigail's face. "This is my brother's invention. Sam is a specialist in them, I suppose you might say! Here are the towels, and we always place this rug on the floor so when we step out we won't get water on the carpet. . . ."

As soon as Rachel left, Abigail removed her soiled clothing and lowered herself gingerly into the hot water, then gave a sigh of relief. She had filled the tub almost full, and now lay completely submerged in it. It was an exquisite sensation, and she closed her eyes and allowed herself to enjoy the pleasure of the moment. After she had soaked for fifteen minutes, she sat up and picked up the bar of scented soap that Rachel had left and soaped herself completely. After this she washed her hair, then rinsed it. Stepping out of the tub she pulled the metal flange away and saw the water begin to form a small whirlpool as it drained away. This fascinated her. She also saw, with chagrin, that she had left a line of dirt in the tub. Quickly she grabbed a small towel and washed it out.

"It looks like pigs have been bathing in this!" Abigail laughed to herself. Toweling herself off, she put on the clean undergarments and the dress that Rachel had furnished, then left to go back to the bedroom. With a feeling of exceptional good will, Abigail sat there beside the window drying her hair, brushing it and combing it. When her hair was finally dried she fixed it quickly, pinning it up. Just as she finished, Rachel entered to say, "Pa's home, and supper's ready. I bet you're starved!"

"I could eat anything!" Abigail nodded. "The food's been just *awful* in the inns where we've stayed."

The two young women left the bedroom, went down the hall, and Abigail was greeted by Daniel Bradford. "Well, Miss Howland," he said, "I'm very glad to see you!"

"It's so good of you to have us, Mr. Bradford. I trust we won't be an inconvenience for too long."

"Don't be foolish!" Daniel shook his head and smiled. "We're always glad to have company. You've met my son Sam?"

Abigail advanced at once to the young man who was watching her carefully. He had auburn hair and was rather strongly built, and at the age of sixteen looked extraordinarily like his father. "Sam, I must thank you for your invention. It was lovely having a hot bath! I think you're a genius!"

Sam grinned suddenly and winked at her. "I've always thought so myself. Maybe you could sort of spread the word around with Pa here, and the rest of the family!"

A laugh went up from the others who had gathered at the table, and Daniel Bradford said, "Well, let's sit down and see what kind of a cook that daughter of mine is!"

"Mrs. White cooked most of it, Pa!" Mrs. White was the housekeeper, and just as Rachel spoke she entered the dining room bearing a large tureen of soup that gave off a delicious odor.

"And what's that, Mrs. White?" Daniel asked.

"Turtle soup! Sit down and eat before it gets cold!" She was a short, broad woman with crisp brown hair and decisive ways. "Hurry up, now! I'll bring the rest of it after you've said the blessing—and make it a short one!"

Laughter filled the room again as Matthew said, "She's the real head of this household. The rest of us just mind her!"

Daniel said, "Clive, I believe you've met Miss Howland."

Clive Gordon had risen when Abigail came in. "We've met before, at an officer's ball when I was here in Boston. How are you, Miss Howland?"

"It's good to see you, sir, and how are your family?"

"Very well, I trust."

"Mr. Gordon came to doctor us all and got sick himself," Sam announced. He seated himself firmly and said pertly, "Remember what Mrs. White said about the blessing, Pa. Make it a short one!"

"A longer blessing wouldn't hurt you any, boy!" Daniel said with a smile that pulled the corners of his lips upward. He bowed his head and said, "Lord, we thank thee for this food. Amen."

The brevity of the blessing caught Sam off guard, and he sat there for one minute before realizing it was over. His head flew up, and his eyes blinked with shock. "Well, Pa, you didn't have to make it that short!" Then he immediately held his soup bowl out and filled it with the large dipper.

"Make yourselves at home," Daniel said. "Just watch Sam, and you'll see our expert on good manners around here!"

They all laughed, for Sam was slurping his soup energetically and noisily. He paused long enough to say between bites of the fresh bread that had been served with the soup, "The Chinese say that you're sup-

234

posed to eat food real noisy when you're a guest to show that you enjoy it."

"You made that up, Sam Bradford!" Rachel said indignantly and looked over at their guest and shook her head. "He's always making things up! When he doesn't know something he just makes up a story!"

During the course of the meal, which everyone was enjoying, Esther said, "I hope I'll be able to move us all into my house. I haven't been there in many years. It was rented out for a time, but not lately."

"Where is it, Mrs. Denham?" Daniel inquired.

"Over close to the older Catholic church, St. Luke's."

"I'll find it tomorrow, Mrs. Denham," Matthew said, "and get you moved in as soon as possible."

Clive listened as talk ran around the table, and finally he excused himself and went to his room. After he left, Mrs. Denham looked at Daniel and said, "He is your nephew, sir?"

"Yes, his mother is my sister. His father is a colonel in the British army in New York now." There was a sadness in his tone, and he shook his head. "Not an easy thing to think I have two sons there with Washington. They may be facing my brother-in-law in battle at this very moment."

A silence went around the table, which Matthew finally interrupted, "Well, come along into the parlor." The group moved in there, where they had a pleasant enough evening. They were all tired, however, and went to bed early.

🦁   🦁   🦁

The next day Matthew rose early and went at once to locate the house. He found it easily enough, then went to the foundry, where he found his father already at work. "It's a mess, Pa!" he said. "I think the Redcoats stationed some of their men in there during the occupation. All the windows are broken out, and the furniture is wrecked—they left it practically a garbage dump!"

"We'll have to fix it quickly!" Daniel said decisively. "You take Sam and whoever you need from the foundry to get it cleaned up. Buy new furniture if you have to."

Matthew nodded and said, "That's what I expected you'd say, Pa. Poor lady—she lost almost everything in the fire."

"Did you see your brothers while you were there in New York, Matthew?"

"No, I didn't. I asked about their units, but they were always up in the north part of the Island. Have you heard from them?"

"Nothing lately, of course. We're all concerned about them and I know you are."

Matthew hesitated, then asked, "Have you seen Leo, Pa?"

"Yes, as a matter of fact I have. I was out to see John not long ago. I stayed a little bit late, and Leo and I had quite a talk." He studied Matthew carefully and asked, "Have you given any thought to Leo's proposition?"

Instantly Matthew looked up, his eyes locked with his father's, and he hesitated uncertainly. "I . . . I haven't thought about it a great deal." Defensively he added, "I've been studying hard with Jan, and then the fire came, and trying to get the women here—" He broke off uncertainly, then shrugged his shoulders. Weariness swept across his features, and he finally said, "I just don't know, Pa—it seems like I can't make up my mind. I wish things were more simple." Bitterness ran through his words, and he turned and stared out the window at the men who were unloading a wagon. The scene did not seem to interest him, and he turned back to say, "I'll have to think about it a great deal."

A great pain came to Daniel Bradford then. He loved this boy, no less than he loved the children of his own blood. He had loved his mother, and he saw her now in Matthew. Seeking for some way to make the choice easier, he said evenly, "Whatever you do will make no difference in the way I feel about you, Matt. I hope you know that."

Matthew could not speak for a moment. "I know that, Pa, and it wouldn't make any difference about the way I feel about you either—but when a man changes his name—I don't know, it frightens me a little bit to think about it for some reason."

"You'd still be who you are. Nothing's going to change that. You pray about it, son, and do what you think is right." For a time Daniel stood there gazing at this young man who was going through such a difficult time. Finally he added, "You could do a lot for people with the money. I don't deny that. And your years in England have given you a sympathy for that country that none of the rest of us have."

"Don't say that, Pa!" Matthew said quickly. "I don't want to be classed with those who are coming to take over. I'd like to see America a free country!"

Daniel smiled and slapped Matthew on the shoulder. "I think you will see it, but it's going to be a long, hard struggle. I worry about Micah and Dake in the army—and soon Sam will be in there." He hesitated, then added, "I think I've got enough sons in this fight. Maybe the best thing would be for you to go back to England and finish your studies."

Matthew shook his head hesitantly. There was an uncertainty in him that he had lived with for months, ever since Leo had first told him the truth about his birth. Finally he said wearily, "I don't know, Pa. We'll just have to see."

🛡️   🛡️   🛡️

Matthew found that the house took more work than he'd thought, but between what he did with Sam's help and several of the workmen, they put Esther's house back in good condition.

Sam took a special delight in it, and when they went to get the ladies two days later, Sam gave them a tour through the dwelling. He pointed out all the work they had done, and when he had finished he said, "I hope you like it, Mrs. Denham."

"Why, Sam, it's perfectly wonderful. It looks better than it did years ago! I'm very much afraid I'm going to have to give you a reward."

Sam perked up at once, expecting money. Esther came over, reached up and pulled his head forward, and kissed him on the cheek. When she saw the chagrin in his face she laughed aloud, reached into the reticule tied to her wrist by a small chord and pulled out a gold coin. "There, Sam, that's a little bit more substantial than a little old woman's kiss!"

Matthew helped Sam carry in all of the belongings that they had brought from New York, and when it came time to leave, he said, "You'll need a man around here, maybe two men. Anything you want, I'll be handy and so will Sam."

"Where is Jan?" Abigail asked curiously.

"Oh, he's found a little romance of his own at the Elkhead Tavern, a little barmaid there that he's romancing. She's about a foot taller than he is, which makes it a little bit hard." The thought of the two together made him laugh, and he said, "We'll go visit them soon. You'll enjoy Jan's courtship, Abigail!"

"All right, that'll be fun!"

When the two left, the women moved through the house, and it was Esther who said, "I don't know what we would've done without them!" She looked curiously at Abigail and said, "Have your feelings about Matthew changed?"

"I don't know. I'm afraid I don't know myself, Esther."

"Well, don't you worry one bit," the older woman said. Then she brightened up and said, "But you will know yourself. I know things are going to be fine with you and him."

🛡️   🛡️   🛡️

Two days after Abigail and her mother had moved into the house with Esther, Leo came to the front door. Abigail answered the door and found him standing there, a heavy overcoat covering him down to the tops of his boots. The temperature had dropped, and the threat of snow was in the air. "Oh—come in, Leo!" she said quickly.

Rochester entered and removed his hat. When he turned to her, she was shocked to see how drawn his face was. He had lost so much weight that when he took off his coat she noticed how his clothing hung on him. He had always been so well tailored that his appearance came as quite a shock. However, she only said, "There's a fire in the small parlor. Come, and you can thaw out."

"Thank you, Abigail." He moved to the parlor, asking, "How's your mother?"

"She's doing very well." Abigail turned to him and motioned toward one of the overstuffed chairs in front of the fire. When he sat down she poked the fire logs and sent up a swarm of sparks, then turned and said, "We got here just in time, it seems. It would've been terrible to have been caught out on the road in weather like this. I think it's going to snow."

"Yes, I think it might." Leo's voice was idle, and he sat there staring into the fire wordlessly.

"I'll get you something hot to drink, tea perhaps."

"That would be nice."

Abigail moved into the kitchen where she found the other two women working on supper. "It's Mr. Rochester," she said. "Come in and meet him, Aunt Esther."

"Oh, not now, I'm not properly dressed!" Esther protested. "Perhaps later."

Abigail took one of the trays, and after the water was boiling on the stove, she made the tea, then moved back into the parlor. Setting the tray on a small table, she poured the tea and passed one of the cups to Leo.

"Thank you," he said and sipped at the tea.

Abigail said, "I've been meaning to send you a note, but since we got back it's been all I could do to keep the house running." She expected him to comment, but he said nothing.

Finally Leo looked up and said, "I suppose you've heard, I've been ill?"

"Yes, Matthew told me. Have you seen him since we got back?"

"No, I haven't. Is he here?"

"Not yet, but he should be anytime. He usually comes in about this time of the day." She sipped her own tea, then struggled to find some way to communicate with Rochester. He would not, she understood, be sympathetic with her new desire to lead a better life. He was not a man of God, and had little sympathy for things of the Spirit. She remembered suddenly how once at a party they had made fun of a raw preacher, and shame washed over her as the scene came back before her eyes. She sat there sipping tea, talking about how they had gotten settled, and how fortunate they were that Mrs. Denham had had a place to flee to in Boston after the fire.

Finally, Leo looked up at her. He set the teacup down and said, "I have been expecting to hear from you about your progress with Matthew." He waited for her to answer and when she did not, he said, "What's the matter? He *is* in love with you, isn't he?"

"I . . . I'm not sure, Leo. He seems to care for me."

"Well, what's the problem? Has he asked you to marry him?"

"Yes, he has, but—"

"Why haven't you told me this?"

Abigail looked at his face and saw that his eyes were sunk deeper in his head. She noticed also that he had difficulty using his left arm. All this came to her while she desperately tried to find an answer to his question. Finally she said simply, "I can't go through with our agreement—I just can't!"

Leo stared at her with incomprehension. This was his last hope! He knew that his health was growing worse constantly, and if ever he was to have his way with Matthew, it would be through this girl. Anger now touched him when he realized the thing he wanted the most was being dashed by her stubbornness. "What's the matter with you, girl?" he asked roughly, gesturing impatiently with his right hand. "Long as I've known you, you've wanted money, position, and fine clothes. Now, it's right in your grasp. What is it? Don't you like Matthew?"

"Oh yes, I do! I like him very much, but I can't marry him just to— well, just to get the money!"

"It never troubled you before!" Leo said shortly. "What's gotten into you?"

Abigail drew a deep breath, and then said, "Something happened to me in New York. I know you're going to laugh, but I was converted while I was there, Leo." She tried to say more but realized that anything else would be superfluous. She sat there and saw shock, amazement, and then scorn sweep over the craggy features of the tall man. Before he spoke, she knew what he would say.

"So, you're becoming another one of these puling Christians! Well, what's wrong with that? I guess he's probably a Christian himself, isn't he? His father's practically a saint—the whole family is. That ought to make things even better."

"I . . . I just can't—"

Suddenly she broke off at the sound of the door slamming, and she heard Matthew's voice calling out. "It's Matthew!" she said. "Please don't say anything to him about—what we've talked about!"

Matthew suddenly appeared at the door and said, "Abigail, I wish—" He turned and saw Leo and said quickly, "Why, I didn't know you were here, sir!" He came quickly and offered his hand. He was shocked at how Rochester had deteriorated in the period since he had seen him last. He tried to allow none of it to show in his face. "I'm glad to see you. May I have some of that tea, Abigail?"

Abigail said, "Yes, of course!" She poured him some and then said, "I'll let you two talk."

After Abigail had left the room, Matthew spoke rapidly. He was nervous and hardly knew what he was saying. Leo sat there and listened to him quietly, trying to digest what he had just heard from Abigail. He inquired finally, "How have your lessons gone with Vandermeer?"

"Oh, very well, sir! He's a fine painter, and I'm learning a great deal. He's here with me, did you know?"

"No, I didn't know that. Why haven't you come to see me?"

"Well, I had to get Mrs. Denham and Abigail and her mother settled. The house was a wreck." He went on to explain how he and Sam and some of the others had put the house together and said, "I was coming by tomorrow. I should have sent you a note, I know."

Leo said without preamble, "I want you to give me an answer, Matthew." He struggled for a moment about what he wanted to say next. He hated speaking of his own health, but now there was no way out. "I've—not been feeling well."

"I'm sorry to hear that, sir. You've been to the doctor?"

"Yes, they're a worthless lot! I've never been one to think a great deal about the future—but according to the doctor, it's time for me to be thinking seriously about taking care of myself."

Matthew could not think how to answer that. He heard the wind blowing against the panes, sweeping around the eaves of the house, carrying dead leaves that rustled crisply. Finally he said, "You really should. You're not looking well at all."

"What's your answer, Matthew? I don't have time to waste." He glanced toward the door and said, "What about Abigail. Are you fond of her?"

"Yes, I am. I've asked her to marry me."

"You could take better care of her if you had money. Her mother's a widow now. She's going to need care, too."

"I can't let that be a factor, sir."

240

Never had Leo Rochester felt so helpless. All he wanted lay here within his grasp! He felt again the fragile beating of his heart. He had begun to imagine it was skipping beats, but he was not sure if that were actually so. As the fire crackled, and the leaves swept around outside the house, all punctuated by the ticking of a clock on the mantel over the fire, he realized he was powerless to gain his ends. Finally he looked up and said, "I can do no more, can I?"

"I really don't think so, sir. I must have a little time."

Leo's thin lips grew tight. He stared at this son of his, thought of his life for a minute, and finally got to his feet. "I must go." He let Matthew go with him to the door and help him on with his coat. He settled his hat on his head, then looked at Matthew Bradford and said almost desperately, "Time is just what I don't have, Matthew." He turned then and left the house. The door closed behind him, and he looked up at the sky that was beginning to show tiny flakes of snow. It was a long winter coming on, he knew, and he felt in his heart that the coldness of it had already touched him.

20

LIFE IS MORE THAN ART

AFTER THE DEFEAT that Washington suffered at Brooklyn Heights—then later on the Island of Manhattan—many felt he should be replaced as commander in chief of the American forces.

As if in answer to this desire, General Charles Lee descended upon the beaten army that languished on the island. For weeks his coming had been anticipated. Mr. Lee, his supporters pointed out, was everything that the commander in chief was not. They told of how he had repulsed a British attack on Charleston. They wrote about his military history in Europe, and insisted that the Continental Army would not have been beaten in Brooklyn if General Lee had been there to lead them. Soon some were pushing all the blame for every mistake onto the shoulders of Washington of Virginia. And Washington agreed with many of the comments. He knew, only too well, that as a military man, Charles Lee was everything that George Washington was not. He had a deep and sincere reverence for Lee and had constantly written him telling him of his confidence.

Lee was now coming to Harlem, but many of Washington's officers did not share their commander's evaluation of the skinny general. Knox fairly bristled with dislike for Lee, General Putnam sneered openly, and General Nathaniel Greene proclaimed that he would not trust Lee to command a squad!

When Lee arrived at the encampment on Manhattan, those who had not seen him were astonished by the man. He brought a dozen dogs with him, yapping at his heels, and his appearance was not impressive. He was tall and extremely skinny. He spoke with a high-pitched voice, blinking his eyes rapidly, and had a nasal drawl. He seemed to have an affectation of seeing only what he wanted to see, whether the object was a hundred yards away or right under his nose.

For all his mannerisms and ugliness, Lee was a good soldier—far more experienced than anyone else in the American army. He had been born into battle, and all of his forty-five years he had never known any other life but the army. He did not fight for a cause, but because soldiering was his trade, he accepted the admiration that came from some as if it were his due.

Lee had not been at headquarters for more than two hours before he demanded a counsel of war. The officers came without eagerness into the dining room of the Morris house, which Washington had made his headquarters. They were taken aback by Lee's sprawling in the commander's seat at the head of the table. Washington stepped back in the shadows, effacing himself as Lee began to speak with a corrosive expression. "Blast it all!" he said. "We must get out. There's no other way to it! This place is a filthy trap, and if those lobsterbacks only had sense to put a ship up the river, they'd have us already!"

"We've held them for weeks!" Putnam growled.

"There's no way in the world to take Fort Washington!" Greene pointed out.

"Oh, you simpletons!" Lee drawled. "Ten soldiers could work and drive you out of here in an hour!"

They wrangled and almost came to blows shaking the frail table. It even came to the point where they were speaking of duels and challenges, calling each other names. Lee had only one answer for all of this. He called them, "Simpletons!"

Coming out of the shadows, Washington said quietly, "General Lee is right! Sooner or later we'll have to leave New York and retreat. Perhaps we'll try to hold Fort Washington and Fort Lee. I don't know yet, but when I went away from home I thought it would be for a little while." He hesitated and a quietness settled on those gathered in the room. "But it will not be for just a little while, gentlemen. We will be gone from our homes for a long time." His voice grew more firm and he said, "We will retreat, if we have to, over the mountains. Why, there's a forest there that's twice as large as Europe itself! Someday we will become an army, and then we will not run away anymore!"

In the days to come Washington had to repeat those words to himself many times. "We will not run away, we will not run away, we will become an army." And he tried to make an army. He took what measures he could conceive of, patching the ragtag organization together, lecturing, advising, scolding, and pleading. All the while Lee drifted through the camp like a guest of honor telling endless tales of his experiences on the battlefields of Europe. And the Yankees loved it—some of them. They loved his cleverness and his obvious hints about who would be the commander in chief in time to come.

Men deserted by tens and twenties and fifties. When some of them were brought back, the commander in chief grimly ordered them to be whipped until the blood ran in rivulets down their backs. Day after day there was a steady plague of mutiny, desertion, thievery, and complaint. And all the time, the entire army waited for the British to come—as they surely would.

T　　　T　　　T

Winter began to close its icy grip on Boston, and as Katherine Yancy came into the house, her face was ruddy with the touch of the cold wind that was whipping across the streets. Slipping out of her coat and gloves, she went to the kitchen and put the parcels of food on the table. The fire was going down in the stove, so she rekindled it, thinking quickly of the menu for the day. After the fire was burning sufficiently, she heated water and made tea, then she put together a bowl of mush, added butter and salt, and putting it all on a tray she moved out of the kitchen and to the room that her mother was occupying.

When she went in she found her mother still in bed. "Get up, Mother!" she said. "I fixed you some fresh mush." Susan Yancy had been ailing for some time. The doctors could find nothing specific wrong with her, and she had tried not to complain. Now she got stiffly out of bed and let Katherine assist her as she put her arms through a warm wool robe.

"You shouldn't be cooking breakfast for me. I don't eat that much," she said.

"Sit down, Mother," Katherine said. "Try to eat all this if you can. It will be good for you. I'm going over to the Bradfords' this morning. I'll fix you something for lunch and put it on a tray."

"How is the young man?" Susan Yancy inquired as she sat down and began to sip the steaming tea.

"He's doing very well, but I'm really going over to see Rachel this morning. We're going to put some things together for the children at the orphanage."

After she had seen that her mother was comfortable, Katherine left for the Bradford home. When she was welcomed in by Rachel, she said, "It's getting colder all the time. I shouldn't be surprised if we didn't have snow this week!"

"Come into the kitchen. We'll sit down and talk for a while." Rachel smiled. "Your nose looks like it's frozen."

The two young women went into the kitchen. They had become close friends, and Katherine had been able to come over often. For a while they spoke of the small things that occupied the lives of women who keep house, and finally Clive walked in the door. He was thin, and the traces of his illness showed in the hollows of his cheeks, but there was a clear look in his blue eyes, which lit up at once when he saw Katherine. "I thought I heard you, " he smiled. "How's your mother?"

"Not too well, Clive!" Katherine admitted. "She just doesn't seem to be able to get her strength back."

"This has been a bad time for Boston!" Rachel shook her head. "I can't think of a house that hasn't had someone down sick."

"Maybe I ought to set up practice here!" Clive grinned. He took his seat at the table with them and accepted the cup of tea that Rachel poured and put before him.

"You might get plenty of patients, but no one has any money!" Katherine shrugged. "The town's not the same since the occupation."

Clive did not respond to that. There was still an awkwardness between the two of them, which neither of them had been able to overcome. Since their reconciliation, the two had become close, but there was always the matter of the revolution between them.

Now as Clive sat there looking at Katherine's cheeks, which were reddened by the cold, he admired her features again. He especially liked the way her eyes crinkled when she laughed. Her eyes almost disappeared, and he had said once, "I don't see how you can see anything when you laugh; your eyes are closed!" There was a goodness and a fullness about this girl that he had found only in Jeanne Corbeau, and now he sat there comparing the two women. As Katherine and Rachel talked he suddenly felt foolish, as he often did when he thought about Jeanne. He could not get it out of his mind that he had been too quick to make up his mind that he was in love. He knew now that Jeanne had married the right man, and he was happy for her.

"Well, I've got to clean the house. You two sit here and talk for a while," Rachel said briskly.

When Rachel left the room, Katherine gave Clive a critical look and said, "You look stronger. How do you feel?"

"Much better! It's nice to be taken care of. Rachel's a good nurse, and I'm fortunate to have been here when I got sick."

"Have you heard from your family?"

"No, the mails aren't running too regularly. The last letter I got, they were fine." He hesitated, then said, "They mentioned you—how much they missed you."

Katherine dropped her head, unable to meet his eyes for some reason. "You have a fine family," she said.

They talked for a time and finally Katherine said, "I must help Rachel. We're getting a few things ready to take to the orphanage. We'll have to be gone most of the morning collecting them from the neighbors."

"I wish I could go with you, but I have an errand of my own. Through the mail, of course." He sounded mysterious, and when she asked him what it was, he merely shrugged his shoulders and said, "Oh, just something I'm involved in."

He rose when she stood up and came over to stand beside her. She looked up with surprise. She always liked to do that—look up at him. She had always thought herself too tall for a woman and for years had stooped to make herself seem shorter. Her father had said roughly, "Stand up, girl! God made you tall and strong; now thank Him for it!"

It gave her a feeling of femininity to look up at a tall man, and she rather liked it. A fleeting thought crossed her mind that this may have been part of her problem with Malcolm Smythe, but she put it aside as foolishness. *He's fine looking*, she thought, noting his regular features. She liked his hair, which was red and rather long now. *I've got to give him a haircut*, she thought, and then wondered at herself for considering such a thing. *It's as if I've taken him over.*

"I've been thinking about our time in Halifax, Katherine. We had good times there."

"Yes, we did, Clive."

He said no more but suddenly reached out and took her hand. He held it, looking down at it for a moment, then squeezed it and left the room abruptly.

Katherine stared after him, then said aloud, "Well, I wonder what that was all about!" Then she turned and left the room herself, her mind filled with the errands she and Rachel must attend to.

🔔   🔔   🔔

"Are you warm enough, Esther?" Matthew Bradford had stopped by early Sunday morning at the request of Esther Denham. She had asked him to take her to church, and he had been pleased to do so. He had ushered her to his buggy, and now he tucked the blanket around her, adding, "I felt some snow earlier. It might be falling fast by the time church is over."

"I'm fine, Matthew," Esther said. She looked back in the rear seat where Abigail and Jan Vandermeer were sitting. The two of them had grown to be great friends. Vandermeer had been a good influence on the whole family. He was filled with enthusiasm and seemed to wake up every morning shouting, filled with plans, his clothes smudged with the paints that he constantly worked with. She turned and said, "I've missed going to church."

"Well, you'll hear a good preacher this morning. I haven't been as faithful as I should, but as far as preachers go, I think Reverend Carrington is top drawer!"

"I must have good preaching!" Jan insisted from the backseat. He reached forward and slapped Matthew on the back so hard the young man wheezed. "Good preaching should be like good art—strong, powerful, and lots of it!"

Matthew spoke to the horses, and by the time they reached the church, tiny snowflakes were stinging their cheeks, getting somewhat larger. He stopped in front of the church and leaped out and helped the ladies down. Then he drove around to the side of the church and tied the horses to the hitching post, noting that the crowd would be small today. When he entered the building he heard Jan's booming voice. Reverend Carrington was standing in front of the round-bodied Dutchman, smiling slightly.

"I expect a good sermon, Reverend!" Jan exclaimed. His blue eyes were crackling with excitement, and he said, "I like my art and my preaching strong! Let us haf the full gospel, sir!"

Reverend Asa Carrington was amused by the man. "I'll do my very best, Mr. Vandermeer! It will be good to know that at least one member of the congregation won't fall asleep!"

"Asleep in church? You point them out, and I vill wake them up!" Vandermeer nodded vehemently. He turned around to see Matthew, then said, "Come, we get seats up front where we can hear the good minister!"

Reverend Asa Carrington was a fine minister. Abigail sat listening to the sermon, drinking it in. She had discovered since becoming a Christian that the Bible, which had always been a dead book to her, had now suddenly come alive. She had discovered also that there was a special pleasure in listening to preachers—some of them at least. She had heard Asa Carrington before, and as he spoke that morning on "Christ in you, the hope of glory," she thought how different things were for her. It came to her that the last time she had been in this church, she had sat beside Nathan Winslow. Her face flushed as she remembered, with shame, how she had tried to trap him into a marriage simply to escape from difficult circumstances. But that soon passed, and sitting between Matthew and Esther, she enjoyed the sermon thoroughly.

Matthew was very much aware of the young woman at his side. He had watched her carefully since first meeting her, and was firmly convinced that he was in love with her. Now there was a pride in him as he saw her fresh beauty, and the thought came to him, *I think she's the most beautiful woman I've ever seen!* Looking across the room, he saw his own family sitting together as they usually did—at least part of them. He missed Micah and Dake, and from the look on his father's face, he knew that same thought was in him.

After the sermon was over, they returned to the Bradford house, where they ate a lunch of cold chicken, cuts of beef, and bread baked the previous day. Rachel heated up a huge pot of beans, and as they sat around the table, Daniel and Jan discussed the sermon.

Daniel Bradford liked the Dutchman—as they all did. He was amused at the interpretation that Jan put on some of the pastor's remarks, and finally said, "Were you converted at a young age, Jan?"

"Converted? I'm not converted, Mr. Bradford!"

The remark brought the attention of all of them, for Jan certainly gave the impression that he was a converted man. When he saw their surprise, he spread his thick hands out and said, "I am going to be converted one day, but I haf never done it yet!"

Matthew exclaimed, "Why, I'm surprised, Jan! I thought you were a Christian."

"I am making up my mind!" Jan said. He began to tell them how he had been brought up in a Christian home, but had gotten far away from God. "I went to Paris, and if a man wants to get away from God, that's the place to do it!" he said explosively.

"But what are you waiting for?" Daniel asked with some bewilderment. "You know the gospel. And you obviously are aware of the dangers of waiting to become a Christian."

For once Jan Vandermeer was speechless, perhaps for the first time since Matthew had known him. He sat there saying nothing for a time; then he said, "You are right, no doubt, Mr. Bradford! Many are fools like me who let their opportunity pass until it is too late!"

Abigail was sitting on Jan's right. She turned and there was affection in her large eyes. "I know what you mean, Jan," she said. "I got far away from God, too. So far that I was afraid that God wouldn't have me!"

Jan turned to her, interested in her remark. "You could not haf been such a sinner as I was!" he declared firmly.

Abigail could not speak, so full was her throat with emotion. She was aware of Matthew's eyes on her, and the shame of how she had tried to deceive him was cutting inside her like a sharp razor. She could not find words to answer, and it was Matthew who said quietly, "I think men are greater sinners than women!"

Abigail glanced up quickly, catching Matthew's eyes. It was a kind thought on his part, and she at once felt a warm glow at his thoughtfulness.

After the meal they went into the parlor, where they enjoyed

Rachel's singing. Finally, they had a visitor. Katherine Yancy came in, and everyone noticed how Clive, who had said very little during the meal, at once became very animated.

"Come in! Come in, Katherine!" Jan boomed. "Now we will hear you sing!"

"Oh, I'd rather not!" Katherine said, but the Dutchman would not be put off. He led her over to the harpsichord, practically plunked her into the seat, and gave her no choice. "Now sing!" he commanded.

Katherine laughed and shook her head. Vandermeer's manner was abrupt, but she rather liked it. She sang two songs, and then refused to sing more, despite Vandermeer's urging.

When she took her seat, Clive crossed over to sit beside her as the others listened to Vandermeer speak with great authority on everything under the sun. Clive turned and surprised her by saying, "I'm going to be leaving soon."

Quickly Katherine glanced at him. "Why, you're not able to travel, Clive!"

"Something important has come up. I got a letter today that could be very significant." He saw the question in her eyes and said, "It's something that I must do." He hesitated for one moment, then said, "Katherine, you've become very important to me!"

Suddenly Katherine knew a start of agitation. She had learned that this tall Englishman had a way of putting his heart into simple words. Looking at him, she saw that his eyes were intense, and that he was waiting for her reply.

"Clive—" she said hesitantly. "You mustn't—you mustn't feel too strongly about me!"

"Why not? Is it the revolution?"

"Well, yes!" Katherine said.

"Revolutions come and go, but love is forever!"

Katherine looked up quickly. It was strange the way he had put it, but she said at once, "But the revolution is here, and you and I are divided by it. The Bible says that two must agree or they can't walk together." She looked over quickly and noticed that the others were paying them no attention. "You mustn't think about me like that, Clive! You'll be going back to England, and I must stay here. I couldn't be happy in England."

Clive Gordon did not answer. For a time the noise of the room floated over them, but they were intensely aware of only each other. Finally he said, "Katherine, I know you trust God, and now I want you to learn how to trust me!"

It was an enigmatic remark that Katherine could not fully grasp. She saw that there was something in his eyes that she could not quite explain. During his illness she had learned to take care of him, almost as if he were a child, but now he was no child, but a tall, strong man. And he was saying something to her that she could not grasp. She was thankful when she heard her name spoken.

"You must settle an argument, Katherine!" Jan boomed. His voice always dominated the room, and he said, "Which is more important, art or life?"

Katherine was still thinking of the strange statement that Clive had made and stared for a moment, trying to put Jan's words into focus. "Why, I think life is more important, of course."

"No, you are not correct! You sing well, but you do not understand art!"

"Look at that picture!" Jan waved his hand at a picture of a young girl. "There she is! Who is that young lady, Mr. Bradford?"

"Her name was Amy Templeton. She was a good friend of ours years ago. She grew up with Matthew. You remember, don't you, Matthew?"

"Of course," Matthew said. "A sweet girl. It's a shame she died so young."

"Ah, she is dead! That is too bad, but there is the picture!" he said. "So she is not gone at all!"

"But that's only a picture!" Katherine said. "I don't know the girl, of course, but a picture is not as good as having a person."

Jan got up and began to pace the floor. He was wearing a mismatched suit that consisted of a coat of a strange yellowish color, trousers of a faded plum tint, and a shirt that should have been thrown away, as it had traces of crimson paint on the collar, but none of this mattered to Vandermeer. He walked over to the picture, gesticulating wildly, and said, "Art is for the purpose of freezing things so that they will stay the same! This young girl was captured by the artist's brush on that day! Now, it is sad that she is gone—but there she is!"

Katherine listened as Vandermeer went on speaking with great enthusiasm. When he paused slightly she said, "But life isn't like that, Jan. Things change! We wouldn't want things to always remain the same. If that were true, a baby would always stay a baby, and as sweet as babies are, we want them to grow up. That's part of life."

Vandermeer loved to argue. He said, "Of course, they must grow up, but when the artist steps in he will take just a tiny part of life, and he will fix it so that it will never change! That young girl—look at the eyes how they glow, and the lips how soft they are, and the hair! See how the artist has caught her there at a moment so that she will never change! That is why Matthew must paint you very quickly, Abigail!"

He turned to the girl and said, "As beautiful as you are, young lady, I regret to say one day that your hair will grow silver, and the beautiful form will not remain so!"

"That wouldn't matter to me!" Matthew said. "I've already painted a portrait of Abigail—though you could do better." He thought of what Jan had said, then shook his head in disagreement. "That's just part of love, Jan. You love people when they grow older, just like you do when they are younger—even more, I think."

Abigail turned to look at him quickly but said nothing.

Katherine, however, was aware that something seemed to be wrong with Jan's thinking. She argued for some time with him, and the Dutchman chortled with delight. He did not seem to care whether he won or lost the argument. It was the lively discussion itself he liked.

Finally Katherine said firmly, "I like your paintings, Jan, but we have to grow up!"

"Ah, but growing up means pain. You have no idea how much pain I went through growing up! I still see men and women everywhere, and they give each other pain, even when they say they love each other!"

"That's better than being frozen!" Katherine said firmly. She thought for a moment, and then feeling Clive's eyes upon her, she said quietly, "Life is more than art!"

Finally the meeting broke up, and as Katherine was leaving, Clive came to take her hands. "This is goodbye for a while. I'm afraid I may not see you again for a time." He smiled at her, adding, "I liked what you said to Jan. You are a very wise woman, Katherine—and a beautiful one, too."

Katherine's lips turned upward in a smile. "Perhaps you'd better have Jan paint my picture. According to him, I'll soon be a tottering old woman, and all that will be left will be a picture of me as I am now."

"That's not a bad idea, his painting your picture—but I liked what you said about life being a process." He held her hands for a moment, then suddenly raised them and kissed them. "Goodbye, Katherine! You'll be hearing from me."

Katherine left the house, wondering at the strangeness of the conversation. As she made her way home, she seemed to feel the pressure of Clive's hands on hers, and she wondered at the strength of her feelings for the tall, young Englishman.

21

LYNA HAS A DREAM

THE *PORPOISE* LEFT BOSTON, its hull packed with salted cod. Clive Gordon had been fortunate in securing a place on the small freighter. He had heard that it was going to touch in New York to deliver part of its cargo to the British quartermaster in Howe's army, and Clive had at once gone to the captain.

"We're not a passenger ship, Mr. Gordon," the doughy Captain Millford told him brusquely.

"I realize that, Captain Millford, but I very much need to get back to my family in New York. Just put me anywhere. I promise I won't interfere with your passage!"

Millford had reluctantly agreed, and Clive had made the journey in relative comfort. The sea was calm, but the snow that had been threatening Boston came floating out of an iron gray sky the first day out. He had stood in the bow watching the flakes, some of them as large as shillings, as they fluttered down. They disappeared as soon as they touched the water, and as he stood there he was mindful of the brevity of human life. His sickness had not frightened him, but it had made him keenly aware of how fragile life was.

The prow of the *Porpoise* rose and fell, and as Clive held on to the rail he thought steadily of Katherine. An image of her face formed in his mind, and he was amazed at how clearly he could recall every feature. He could also recall practically every conversation he had ever had with her, and he found pleasure in going over them repeatedly. It had been more of a shock when she had turned on him than anything that had ever happened to him, and now he knew a moment of gratefulness that they had resolved their differences.

The snow did not last long, and by the time the *Porpoise* pulled into the harbor at New York, the weather had turned somewhat better. He said goodbye to Captain Millford and clambered down the side into the small dory that bobbed over the tops of the waters as the oarsman sent it toward the shore. Stepping out on the dock, he looked around and was taken aback by the large number of soldiers that he saw. The Redcoats were everywhere, and he could tell there was an excitement in their behavior. He was still somewhat weak from his sickness, so he motioned to a carriage, which pulled up beside him at once.

"Yes, sir, gov'nor?" the cabby asked alertly. He was a muscular man wearing a multicolored wool coat, and a soft-brimmed felt hat pulled down nearly over his bright blue eyes.

"I need to go to army headquarters."

"Get right in, gov'nor!" The cabby said, "Take you there in two shakes of a duck's tail!"

Twenty minutes later Clive dismounted from the carriage, paid the driver, then turned toward the large building that was obviously some kind of a headquarters. The British flag flew at the top of a staff that was mounted on the second story, and as he went up the steps he stopped in front of one of the two guards who were standing guard with their muskets. "I'm looking for Colonel Gordon. Can you tell me where I might find him?"

"He's right inside, sir, on the second floor."

Clive mounted the steps slowly, though he was satisfied to find that he had regained most of his strength. He still was conscious that he had lost weight, but he knew that he could gain that back. When he reached the second floor, he tried the first door, and was informed that Colonel Gordon was at the end of the hall. Moving down, he opened the door and stepped inside. He saw a familiar face and smiled. "Hello, Corporal Cummings!" he said. "Is my father here?"

Corporal Cummings, a diminutive young man no more than twenty, had looked up with surprise from the papers scattered on the desk in front of him. "Why, yes, sir, Mr. Gordon! He'll be glad to see you!"

"Does he have someone with him?"

"No, he doesn't. I think you could just go right in!"

"Thank you, Corporal!"

Clive advanced to the door behind the corporal, which led to some kind of inner office, knocked, and then stepped inside. He smiled at his father, who looked up, and Clive saw the astonishment sweep across his face. "The bad penny back again, Father!"

"Clive!" Leslie Gordon leaped to his feet, stepped around the desk, and came at once to give Clive a mighty hug. "Where in the world have you been? How are you? Are you over your sickness?"

Clive laughed. "Well, I'm fine—if you don't crush me!" He smiled at his father and said, "I'm very well. I just got in. I probably smell like fish—that was the cargo."

"Sit down! Sit down, my boy! Your mother will be excited to hear this. Have you been home yet?"

"Not yet. I wanted to come and talk to you first."

"Well, we have been concerned about you. It was a pretty bad sickness, I take it?"

"Not very pleasant, but God brought me through it. It's been a sad time in Boston. Quite a few have died."

"How are Daniel and his family?"

"Completely recovered." Clive took his seat and leaned back in the hard-back chair. "Micah and Dake are in the army with Washington. I suppose you knew that?"

"I knew about Dake. I thought Micah hadn't made up his mind about this war, what to do about it."

"I suppose he has. At least he's signed up for ninety days."

The two sat there talking for some ten minutes, then Leslie Gordon leaned back and clasped his hands, studying his son carefully. "What about Katherine Yancy? Is she all right?"

"Well, yes, sir, she is." He hesitated, for he was not at all certain how his father would receive the news that he had come to give him. To put the matter off he said, "How is the army positioned?"

Leslie Gordon's face clouded. "We should have ended this thing before! We had them whipped, but General Howe called off the attack. Nobody knows why."

"What's the situation now, sir?"

"We're getting ready to move out in a day or two, I expect. The men are ready to end it. They want to go back home to England." The long features of Colonel Gordon grew sad, and he shook his head thoughtfully. "I'd like to go myself, and I suppose you're ready to go, too?"

"Well, I'm not sure," Clive said carefully. "I've been thinking a lot about that."

Instantly his father understood that this reluctance of Clive to leave America was connected with the young woman who had become such a vital part of his life. He almost reminded the young man that it had not been long since he had been just as interested in another young woman, but he restrained himself. "This would be a good country once we put this rebellion down—when things can get back to normal."

"I really came back with an idea, sir." Clive hesitated, then said, "I'd like to do something for Amos Yancy."

"Ah, you're still there, are you? Well, I don't think you need worry about it. Once we bag Washington's army, there'll be an armistice, and

I'm sure all prisoners will be released."

"I hope so. Is there no way he could be released now?"

"Not that I can think of at this point. The general is too busy to even approach him with it."

Clive thought about that for a moment, then said, "I suppose so. I think I'd better get home and see Mother."

"Good! She'll fatten you up a little bit. You've lost weight."

"Will you be home later?"

"Of course—that is if we don't decide to attack, but that's not likely for a few days. Go on now! Tell her I said to kill the fatted calf for the prodigal!"

Clive left, and as his father had known, Lyna Lee Gordon overwhelmed him. She and Grace hugged him until he had to protest, "You're going to break my bones! Give a fellow room to breathe, will you?"

They welcomed him home, along with David, who was equally glad to see him. Clive was tired after his long journey, but that night after the others had gone to bed, he and his mother sat talking before the fire for some time. He had always been able to talk about himself with her, and now he did not realize how much of himself he was revealing.

Lyna sat there looking at this tall son of hers, thanking God that he had survived the illness. She was well aware of how often Katherine Yancy came into the thread of his dialogue. She was a discerning woman, and her son was very precious to her—as were all of her children. *He looks so much like Leslie,* she thought. *And he's like him, too. Naive and he doesn't know very much about women.* She thought of how in her attempt to escape from a lustful master, she had disguised herself as a young man and entered into the service of Leslie, then a young lieutenant. She had fallen in love with him while he had no idea that she was a young woman. *When he did discover it, however,* she thought suddenly with a smile, *he certainly made up for lost time.* And now this young son of hers, who looked so much like his father, was falling in love, too. She listened as he told of the misunderstanding that had come between him and Katherine, and then how he desperately wanted to help Katherine's father gain his freedom.

Finally, Clive stopped and looked surprised. "I always did talk to you too much!" he laughed, half embarrassed. "Don't you get tired of hearing all of my problems?"

"No, I never do!" Lyna looked at him as the fire threw its reddish reflections across his face, making his craggy features seem even more pronounced. She was apprehensive, for she knew the gap that existed between those loyal to the Crown and those fighting for their freedom.

She also knew from her acquaintanceship with Katherine Yancy that there was little likelihood that the young woman would ever join herself to a man who was loyal to the Crown.

Finally she said quietly, "Katherine's a fine young woman. You think a great deal of her, don't you, Clive?"

"Why, yes I do. Do you like her, Mother?"

"Very much!"

"How do you think I could help her father? I thought about it, and there seems no way."

"We'll pray about it. With God all things are possible!" Lyna said. She rose then, kissed him, and went to bed. Clive sat before the fire for a long time after that, and as he had seen Katherine's face in the sky on the ship, now he seemed to see it in the flames of the fire. Finally he got up and went to bed, remembering his mother's words, *We'll pray about it*. He smiled and muttered, "That's what she always says."

🔔   🔔   🔔

Lyna was tossing on her bed, half asleep, half awake. Leslie had left early before dawn. He had whispered to her, "You sleep as long as you can. No reason for you to get up." He had kissed her, then left, and she had dropped off back into a deep sleep. For some time she lay there sleeping quietly, and then she began to dream. In the dream she remembered again how she had met Leslie. The dream came to her in sharp, clear fragments, some of which were frightening, and others were very joyous. She did not dream often, and it disturbed her somehow when she did.

Finally, that part of the dream ended, and other images began to form in her mind. It was not a clearly oriented dream, and the chronology of it seemed all wrong. She threw her hands up over her head, striking the headboard, and this seemed to pull her out of the dream. But, as such dreams are, she lay there for some time neither sleeping nor fully awake, and still the figures appeared. She seemed to see Clive's face, tense and drawn—and then the face of the young woman that he was in love with. Others came, and a voice seemed to speak, but she could hardly make out the words.

Finally she awoke with a start and sat upright in bed. She had been wearing a cap, but it had come off in her tossing, and her hair was falling down her back. She sat there trying to put the pieces of the last dream together, for somehow she felt that it was important.

Oh, God, help me to know the interpretation, if there is one!

She prayed this prayer, feeling somewhat foolish. She had never had a dream that meant anything. She had heard of others who had, and, of course, knew well the Bible stories of those to whom God spoke in dreams. Now she sat there quietly praying and waiting as she had learned to do when she was uncertain. Slowly the dream began to fall into place, and astonishment came to her. She sat there for some time, and then finally threw the covers back. Quickly she dressed and went down to the room that David shared with Clive. She knew that a cannon shot in the room itself would not awaken David, so she stepped inside and moved over to where Clive lay sleeping on one of the single beds. "Clive," she whispered, "get up!"

Clive was a light sleeper. His eyes flew open, and when he saw his mother he was startled. "What is it—is something wrong?"

"Get dressed, I have something to tell you," Lyna said quietly. She turned and left the room, going into the kitchen, where she stirred the fire from the ashes that she had banked the night before. Soon it was burning cheerfully, and she began to move about pulling together the materials for a breakfast.

Clive came in, his face troubled. He was stuffing his shirt down in his breeches and came to her at once. "What is it, Mother? Is something wrong with Father?"

"No, nothing like that." Lyna said, "Sit down, Clive, I want to tell you something." She waited until he was seated, then came over to stand before him. "I don't put much stock in dreams. I don't have many dreams as a matter of fact—but I had one early this morning that I think has a meaning."

Clive's interest was caught. He had never known anyone who had a dream that actually meant something. "What sort of a dream was it?" he asked.

"It was about you, Clive," Lyna said. She reached up, touched her hair, then shook her head. "It wasn't very clear at first, then it came to me sometime early this morning. I think the sun had already begun to come up, but I wasn't fully awake."

She began to describe the dream to him as best she could, and found it very difficult. Clive listened, and finally he said with puzzlement, "I don't really see that it means anything. Naturally you were interested in me and in Katherine and in her father."

"I think I know what it means." She came over and pulled her chair closer. Her eyes were bright and her lips were parted with excitement. "Here's what I think it means, Clive. . . ."

🃏   🃏   🃏

"Well, Clive, you're here bright and early this morning. I didn't expect to see you!"

"Father, I want to talk to you. I have a favor to ask."

"Well, of course!" Leslie stood up at once behind his desk, for he saw Clive was tense. "What is it?"

"I want you to arrange an exchange, sir."

"An exchange—what sort of an exchange?"

"I want you to get Amos Yancy's release in exchange for one of our men held prisoner by the Americans."

Leslie stared at Clive and wondered what had brought all this on. "That would be very difficult," he said. "What made you think of such a thing?"

"Actually, it was Mother who thought of it." Clive hesitated, but he knew his mother would certainly tell her story to his father when he got home. "Mother had a dream this morning, and that was what she saw in the dream. She saw all of us, me and you and Katherine and her father, and then she saw me bringing a man out of the American lines. Then she dreamed that you unlocked a door and Amos Yancy came out of a cell."

"Your mother dreamed that?" Leslie was genuinely surprised. "She doesn't dream much that I know of."

"No, but she says she thinks it's more than just a dream." Clive's face was intense, and he asked with an earnestness in his voice, "It could be done, couldn't it, sir?"

"Well, there *are* exchanges made all the time. Usually it isn't too complicated, but now with a battle shaping up, it would have to go through certain channels of command. And how do you know the Americans would exchange one of our men for Yancy?"

"I don't know that, but I'm going to find out. I can't think of any other way, so I'm going to believe in Mother's dream or vision, or whatever it was."

"Well," Leslie said, troubled by what he had heard, "I'll do what I can, son, you know that. But it will take a miracle."

Clive suddenly smiled. "Well, Father, there are precedents, you know." He turned and walked to the door. When he got there, he looked back over his shoulder. "You start getting the paperwork. I'm going to talk to the Americans."

"You're going over to the American lines?"

"Yes, that's what I'll have to do!"

"But you might get shot! They're not very careful who they shoot at. They're expecting us to attack at any time."

"I'll be careful!" Clive shut the door, and left his father standing alone in the room. He made his way out of headquarters, his mind buzzing with the plan. It wasn't a plan, really, but he knew it was something he had to do. He made his way to a livery stable, and when the hostler came to meet him he said, "I want to rent a horse."

Ten minutes later he was mounted on a fine gray mare. He rode north, headed for the lines that his father had mentioned the previous day. He had no idea of how he would get through his own lines, and certainly none of how he would cross over to the American side without getting shot at. All he knew was this was something he had to do.

22

"A Man in Love Does Very Strange Things"

THE HARSH OCTOBER WIND was sweeping across the Heights where the American army stretched out waiting for the British attack. Overhead a flight of noisy crows split the air with their harsh calls, then settled down on a cornfield and pecked at the stalks.

Dake watched, without interest, as the birds darkened the sky, then fell to the ground. Turning to Micah, who had come from his position with Knox's guns to visit, he said, "I wish they'd come on. I'm tired of this waiting!"

Micah wore a heavy blue woolen coat that reached to his knees, and he had procured a fur cap that came down almost over his ears. It was like one he had seen Benjamin Franklin wear once, and he rather fancied it. "I wish I had some mittens made out of fur to go with this cap," he murmured. He blew on his hands, which were rough and bruised from handling the guns of Henry Knox, then followed Dake's gaze down the hill. They could see the British sentries moving faintly, the red of their jackets making colorful splashes against the specter gray of the earth. He pulled off his cap and rubbed his head for a moment, then pulled it back on. "General Knox says he doesn't know what they're waiting for. They could have hit us anytime."

"I wonder what General Washington thinks?"

"I don't know. Nobody knows that, I guess."

The two stood there talking quietly, stamping their feet from time to time to get the circulation going, and Dake suddenly slapped his hands together in an impatient gesture. "I'd hate to die at a time like this!"

"A time like this?" Micah stared at Dake with surprise. "What do you mean by that? Anytime is a bad time to die!"

Dake was wearing the makeshift uniform of the Continental Army. It wasn't much, but he felt a little pride in the difference between it and those worn by the militia. He ran his finger along his musket, lifted it, and sighted it down the hill. The range was too far, of course, and he put it down, then turned to say, "I guess you're right. There aren't many times when a man wants to die, but it's just—"

Suddenly Micah smiled, "You're thinking about Jeanne."

"Yes!" Dake flashed a grateful smile at this twin of his. Though they were far different in many ways, still there was a link that bound them together. And sometimes they seemed to know what the other was thinking. "I want to take care of her. I want us to have children, and then grandchildren. I'm looking forward to being a crotchety old grandfather someday!"

Micah laid his hand on Dake's shoulder. "You'll make it, Dake," he said gently. He received a shy smile from Dake, then said, "I got to get back. We're going to have more practice with the guns—not that we ever shoot them; not enough powder for that." He turned and walked away, saying over his shoulder, "Don't get into any trouble while I'm gone."

Dake grinned, then turned to look back down the hill. For the next two hours he entertained himself by passing along the lines. Someone had brought up some beef, and he helped make a fire and boiled the meat. After it was done, he and Sergeant Tooms took their portion, lay it on a slab of thick brown bread, and moved over to sit down on the log of a fallen elm tree.

"I don't see why we're hanging around here," Tooms complained. He bit off a portion of the beef, chewed it thoroughly, then swallowed it. "If it was me, I'd get this whole army off of this island quick!"

"Maybe you're right!" They had gone over the argument many times, and Dake had no inclination to argue further. He was aware that something was happening down the hill. In the distance he saw a horseman break out of the English camp and move slowly toward the American lines. "Look at that! Maybe he's coming to surrender the army!" he grinned.

Tooms finished his beef and bread, and then stood up. Grasping his musket he said, "Let's drift over and see what's going on."

The American sentries down the way had seen the solitary horseman leave the British lines. Their sergeant said, "You all primed, men? We may have to shoot that limey out of his saddle just to teach him a lesson."

"He ain't wearin' no uniform, Sarge!"

"Well, he's a spy then. We ought to shoot him anyway!" a continental said.

"Shut your mouth!" Sergeant Oaks said. He was a tall, weather-beaten man from Delaware, and now stood up to get a better view of the horseman. "I don't know what he is! Maybe he's bringing a message over! Anyhow, I'll talk to him. You fellows get back to your post! I'll handle this."

Clive Gordon had kept his eyes on the line of American soldiers along the top of the ridge. He had encountered some difficulty passing through the English line, but had had the forethought to bring a pass from his father. That had scarcely been enough, but he had simply talked his way into passing through the lines. Now he saw a tough-looking sergeant and half a dozen Continental soldiers spread out awaiting his arrival. As soon as he got close, he pulled his horse up and said, "Good afternoon, Sergeant!"

"What's your business!" Sergeant Oaks snapped. "This is no place for a civilian!"

"I'm here to see General Washington!"

A laugh broke out among the soldiers, and a short, stubby one with a full beard said, "You're gonna have tea with him, limey?"

"I have business with the general." Actually Clive had no hopes at all of seeing General Washington, but he had thought by showing a little audacity it might make his case stronger. At least he might get to see one of Washington's lieutenants.

"Well, you ain't going to see him! Turn around and get back there!"

Clive did not move but stepped off his horse and came forward, leading the animal. "It's highly imperative that I see someone in authority!" he said. "I have urgent business."

"You got any papers?"

Clive shook his head. "None that would interest you."

The sergeant stood there arguing, and Clive's heart sank. It was fairly clear he was not going to be admitted. He had stiffened himself for resistance, intending to get himself arrested if necessary, when suddenly, to his surprise, a voice said, "That's all right, Sergeant Oaks, I know this man."

Oaks turned around to see who spoke and instantly said, "What are you doing here, Private Bradford? Get back to your place!"

But relief washed over Clive as he saw Dake Bradford. "He'll vouch for me!" he said. "We're relatives!"

Oaks looked at the tall Englishman doubtfully. "That can't be!" he said.

"Yes, it is!" Dake said easily. He carried his rifle in the crook of his arm and nodded his head toward the civilian. "This is Clive Gordon. He's my cousin. His mother is my father's sister." He did not ask what Clive was doing there but turned to the sergeant and said, "I'll be responsible for him, Sergeant!"

"Well, he'll have to leave his arms here."

"I'm not carrying any weapons, Sergeant."

"All right then, but, Bradford, you go right to the lieutenant. He's supposed to handle things like this!"

"All right, Sergeant, I'll do that!"

Turning, Dake walked away, and Clive quickened his pace until he caught up with him. "I'm glad you came along!" he said as soon as they were out of earshot. He looked along the line and saw that every soldier seemed to be eyeing them with curiosity. "I guess you don't get many visitors around here—not from our side!"

Dake said, "Not many." Then when they had passed through a grove of trees he pointed over to where a group of tents had been set up. "We'll have to go see the lieutenant. The sergeant will check on that." He turned to face the other and asked directly, "What are you doing here, Clive?"

Clive had considered what he might say when it came down to it and had decided that simplicity was the best thing. "I want to get a man exchanged, a prisoner in the hulks."

"One of our men?" Dake spoke sharply. "Why would you be interested in an American prisoner?"

"He's the father of a friend of mine."

"What's his name?"

"Amos Yancy."

"Yancy? I don't know any Yancys."

"I thought you might. The family's from Boston. Your father knows them slightly, and Rachel as well."

"Who are they?"

Clive stood there in the cold wind explaining who the Yancys were, and he saw skepticism on Dake's face. "Why are you so suspicious, Dake?"

"Because you're an Englishman. Your father is a colonel in the English army. I can't understand why you'd be so anxious to get an American out of prison."

Clive hesitated only momentarily, then he made a helpless gesture with his hands. "Well, to tell you the truth, Dake, I'm in love with his daughter."

Dake stared at Clive unbelievingly. It had not been that long ago when the two of them had been fiercely competing for the attention of

Jeanne Corbeau. Dake had been rather shocked when Jeanne had chosen him. Clive Gordon had money, education, was a doctor, and had a fine career ahead of him, while Dake had a job in a foundry. Now he asked, "What do you mean you're in love with her?"

Instantly Clive knew what Dake was thinking. "I don't mind saying it, Dake," he grinned sheepishly. "I've said it myself. I thought I was in love with Jeanne, but I see now that I wasn't. I talked to her about this not long ago."

"You talked with Jeanne?"

"Yes, I went there to take care of your family. You heard about that? Jeanne was very sick, as were Sam and Rachel."

"I did get a letter from Pa about that."

"Well, I got sick after they got well, and Jeanne helped take care of me." He shook his head and said, "I can see how it would never have been good for me to marry Jeanne. I'm a city man, and she loves the out-of-doors. Besides, she's so crazy in love with you I wouldn't have had a chance."

Dake grinned suddenly and felt much better. He had thought wildly for one moment that Clive had come here to tell him some bad news about Jeanne. Relieved that his family and Jeanne were doing fine now, he said, "I'm glad we got your approval, cousin!"

"You've got a fine wife there. She's worried about you, though."

"Well, I'm worried about myself." Dake looked back toward the hill and shook his head. "What's this girl's name?"

"Katherine Yancy."

"Well, why did you come over here?"

"Dake, I've got to have a man, an English soldier that you've captured to trade for Amos."

Dake looked at him and began to laugh. "I swear, Clive, I thought Sam could come up with the most harebrained schemes in the world, but this beats all! You want to ask our officers to give you an Englishman so you can trade him for an American? Why, they'll never do it!"

"They might. I've got to try! Amos is in bad shape, Dake. I don't think he can live much longer if he doesn't get out of that foul prison ship! I know! I know—!" He put up his hand as Dake started to speak. "We're the ones that began making prisons out of leaky old ships, but that's none of my doing, and I'm against it!"

Dake stood there listening while Clive pleaded his case. The more he listened, the more he was certain that it would never work, but a scheme began to form in his mind. "I'll tell you what," he said, "there's one man that can do you some good."

"And that man is?"

"Colonel Knox."

"Is he your officer?"

"No, but Micah's serving under him. Come on, we'll go let Micah in on all this, and he can get you in to see the colonel."

"What makes you think Knox would listen more sympathetically than some others?"

"From what Micah says, it's just the kind of thing he would listen to. He's a great big fellow. He knows guns better than anybody in our army, but more than that, Micah says he's downright romantic!" A wry grin twisted Dake's lips, and he shrugged his broad shoulders. "It looks like it's going to take somebody romantic to listen to your proposition. Come on now!"

T   T   T

"Let me get this straight," Micah said, "you want me to get Colonel Knox to release a prisoner that we've taken so that we can give him to you, so that you can take him back over the line and trade him for an American that we don't know, and that we may never see?"

Clive stood before Micah and shrugged helplessly. "I know this all sounds crazy, but it's all I can think of to try. Armies do trade prisoners. They're exchanged all the time!"

"Yes, but it takes a mountain of bookwork, and the lobsterbacks aren't going to be interested in making any trades. They're more interested, right now, in wiping us out."

"Will you at least take me to see Colonel Knox so that I can ask him myself?"

"Oh yes, I'll do that. That won't be hard. Come along!"

Micah led them through the camp to a line of guns that the men were drilling with. Micah walked up to the colonel and said, "Colonel Knox, could I trouble you for a few moments?"

"What is it, Corporal Bradford?"

"There's a man here, an Englishman, that I would like for you to hear. Actually, he's my cousin."

"Your cousin?" Knox was wearing an outlandishly colorful uniform. He favored such things, and now as he turned he looked enormous as he eyed the tall Englishman standing beside Dake. "Is that your cousin there?"

"Yes, sir! I must warn you, he's a little bit romantic."

Knox's eyes twinkled. He kept his maimed hand inside his coat, but his interest had been captured. "Well now, we shall see about that!" He moved across the ground lightly, for he was very agile despite his large size.

"Colonel Knox, this is my cousin Clive Gordon. His father is Colonel Leslie Gordon of the Royal Fusiliers."

"Indeed, and you are not in the army yourself, Mr. Gordon?"

"No, Colonel, I'm a physician. I appreciate your taking time to speak with me. I have a rather audacious request."

"I see! Well, let's have it!"

Clive immediately plunged into an explanation, speaking rapidly. He even rose to heights of elegance when he spoke of the poor condition of Amos Yancy and the terrible conditions of the hulk where he was kept prisoner. He finished by saying, "I have come on the hope that you would exchange one of the English soldiers for this man."

"And why have you done all this? Is he a relative?"

Instantly Clive recalled Dake's word about Knox being a romantic. "I'm in love with his daughter, sir." He embellished the story somewhat, telling how the two had met. Finally he said, "I know this sounds foolish, but a man in love does very strange things."

"Indeed, so I've heard, and do in part believe," Knox said. He laughed and his huge belly shook as he said, "I did some foolish things myself when I was your age, Mr. Gordon."

"Do you think there's any chance at all, Colonel Knox?"

Knox thought hard for a moment. "It would be very difficult. Every time we try to trade one of their men for one of ours, they make impossible demands. They want us to give them a captured general for every private that they have. The trades are supposed to be equal, that is a lieutenant for a lieutenant, a private for a private."

"This man was probably not even in the army! He was at Bunker Hill in the first action. I think he was just part of the local militia."

"That makes no difference. He's been treated as a soldier!" Knox said rather brusquely. His mind was racing, for he was a quick-witted man. He studied the young man carefully and liked what he saw. He had had many friends among the British officers in Boston, General Gage being among the best. Many of them were unhappy with the way England treated America, and this young man was not in the army.

The three men stood there waiting, and finally Knox made a sound of surprise. "Ah," he said, "a thought comes to me! We took a lieutenant captive a week ago, a Lieutenant Harrison. I've spoken with him, and it seems he's one of General Howe's aides."

Hope came to Clive at once and he said, "Are you thinking perhaps you could exchange him for Amos Yancy?"

"I think it might work. I will have to cut some corners and see that some papers are burned. Actually, we can't use the fellow. He just clutters up our way. He's nothing but a clerk. He won't be doing any fighting, I found that much out. Yes," he said pensively, "I think it might do." He studied young Clive Gordon and said, "Come along, I will see what can be done."

"Thank you, Colonel!" Clive hurried off with the colonel, and Dake and Micah stood regarding them.

Micah pulled off his fur cap, tossed it up in the air, and caught it. He grinned, saying, "Well, Clive is right about one thing."

"What's that?"

"A man in love does do very strange things!"

🦁　　　🦁　　　🦁

General Howe had just finished his dinner and was in a rather good mood. He looked across at Colonel Leslie Gordon, who stood facing him, his son Clive at his side. Leslie had said when he had entered, "Sir, this is my son Clive. I think you may have met him."

"Yes indeed! He's done some fine work helping our surgeons!"

Clive said, "Thank you, sir. I don't want to take up much of your time. I believe you have an aide, a Lieutenant Harrison."

"Yes." Howe's face fell. "A very fine young man—a distant relative of mine by the way. Too bad, he was captured last week."

"Yes, sir, I know. I've been across the American lines. They're willing to exchange Lieutenant Harrison."

"Indeed! That would be excellent!" Howe's face grew puzzled. "May I ask how it happened that you were in a position to negotiate such an exchange?"

"I have a friend, a young woman, whose father is in the hulks. You may remember the name Amos Yancy."

Howe's brow furrowed. "Yes," he said hesitantly, "it is familiar, but I don't recall."

"You may remember that the surgeon and I had some difficulty over the man. I had him taken off the hulks, and then Major Banks had him sent back."

"Oh yes, I do remember. Unfortunate affair. I remember the young lady, too. Very attractive, very attractive, indeed! What is this you're proposing?"

"It's very simple. Colonel Knox, who is in charge of such things, said he will exchange Lieutenant Harrison for Mr. Yancy."

Howe looked at the young man, his mind working quickly. He was a ladies' man himself, and every bit as romantic, in one sense, as Henry Knox. A smile tugged at the corners of his lips and he said, "I believe such an exchange would be mutually beneficial. You may work it out with my adjutant." He put his hand out and said, "I am grateful to you

267

for your service. Have you considered, perhaps, a commission as a surgeon in our own army?"

Clive hesitated. "It's a possibility, sir. My father and I have talked about it."

"Well, I hope you decide to join. We need fine young men like you. My thanks again for your help! Take care of it, Major Burns."

As soon as the visitors were gone, Howe turned to a tall colonel who had been waiting patiently. "Well now, that's a relief. I'll be glad to have Harrison back."

"Yes, sir, he'll be most welcome. Now, have you decided about the attack?"

"The day after tomorrow if the weather is fine." Walking over to a map he said, "We will take the men here"—he pointed to a spot on the upper end of the Island—"and land them, then come around behind the Americans. You will accompany General Cornwallis, advancing upward."

"We'll have the men trapped. There's no way for them to go."

"Exactly! Well, Colonel, it'll all be over soon."

𝕿   𝕿   𝕿

Amos Yancy looked up when a voice said, "Come along, Yancy!" A hand seized him and pulled him to his feet. His bones ached, but he withheld the cry of pain that leaped to his lips.

"Where are you taking me?"

"Don't ask questions, just come along!"

Stumbling as the burly guard pulled him across the floor and through the massive oak door that slammed behind them, which was locked by a sentry, Yancy shivered in the cold. But that was nothing new. He shivered all the time. He had chills and fever, and knew that he could not last much longer. Every day the cry, "Throw up your dead!" echoed, and he had helped to deliver the bodies of some of his best friends out on the deck for burial in the sea, sewn in a canvas sack with a cannonball at one end. It was midafternoon, and the sun was not bright, but after the darkness of the hold, it almost blinded him.

"Come along there, pick your feet up!"

Doing his best to keep up with the guard, Amos wondered what could be happening. He hoped briefly that perhaps Katherine had returned. He had given up, almost, thinking about that, and had resigned himself to die.

"In here, step lively!"

Stepping inside the cabin, the door slammed behind him. There stood the captain of the *St. George* and a tall man whom he had seen

He stared at him, squinting until finally he made out the features. "Dr. Gordon!" he said.

"Yes, I'm glad to see you, sir, and I have good news."

"Good news?"

"Yes!" Clive had come aboard the *St. George* with the papers signed by General Howe himself. The captain had been shocked but pleased. "You've worked hard enough to get this one off," he said. "I'm glad of it. He's in poor shape, I'm afraid, as all of them are."

Now Clive came over to stand beside the smaller man. He was emaciated and was trembling through the thin shirt that he wore. "You're going home, Mr. Yancy," he said quietly. He saw the head snap back and unbelief wash across Yancy's face. "Yes, it's true enough. You've been exchanged for an English prisoner, but you can't go like that. Here, I brought some warm clothes for you."

His mind reeling with unbelief, Amos Yancy allowed the tall doctor to help him put on the warm woolen clothes. They felt so good after the rags he had worn, and finally he murmured in a whisper of wonder, "I can't really believe it!"

"You will. We'll stop at an inn and spend the night. You can have a warm bath. We'll get you shaved—then we'll head for Boston in the morning." He smiled and said, "You'd like that, I know."

Amos was silent for a long time, it seemed. Slowly it began to sink in, and he trembled, not from the cold, but from relief. "That will be good, Doctor!"

Clive took his arm. "We'll take it slow. You'll be with your wife and daughter soon, and you'll be well, too."

Amos Yancy reached out and touched Clive Gordon on the chest to assure himself that this was real. He smiled tremulously and whispered, "God has delivered me, my boy—that will make me well!"

🦁 🦁 🦁

Howe's plan to attack should have worked. There was, as a matter of fact, nothing to keep it from working. It was fairly simple. He sent a large force through the East River into the Sound, and a flanking attack on Westchester. All the British troops had to do was to dismount from their boat, march overland, and form a line of battle. The poor, ragged troops of Washington would be trapped. They had an enemy advancing from their rear, and they could not run forward because Cornwallis and the other half of the army was positioned there.

It should have worked—but it did not.

The boats crept up the East River under cover of night. It was a foggy night, and they did not land at the planned destination, but in a soggy, swamplike area where the troops had to dismount and wade through the cold water. It was not an auspicious beginning, and almost accidentally their flanking movement had been spotted. A young boy had seen them land and passed the word along to some of the sentries, who at once went to General Washington. Washington had not expected a flanking attack. He went to study his map, and no way of escape occurred to him. He was caught; there was no way to escape—except one. A faint possibility began to grow. He thought slowly, *If I were to pick up this army and move slowly and deliberately, there would not be a mass retreat with my men losing their heads. If I could get them packed together, men crowding each other, and know that there was a solid rear guard behind, it might work—but first someone has to hold off this flanking attack.*

He put his finger back on the map at the spot where it might be held. The Delaware and Maryland troops had held once at Harlem Heights against unfavorable odds. They might hold again. Suddenly he thought of the Marblehead fishermen who had brought them off from Brooklyn, across the East River. He had been impressed with them then, how they moved slowly, methodically. He had seen them with oars in their hands, and he wondered how they might fare with muskets.

"Send for Colonel Glover!"

Shortly Colonel Glover entered, a man of Washington's age. He had very light blue eyes, and his lips seldom broke into a smile. There was a Yankee air about him, and he spoke in a nasal voice but moved with a certainty that Washington liked.

"Colonel Glover, your men can handle boats, but can they fight?"

Glover stared at his commanding officer. "Yes!" he said simply.

Washington liked that single word, that one monosyllable, for it had the confidence of granite from the cliffs in Vermont. Washington pointed at the map. "The British have landed here. I want you to hold them until I get the army past them. Can you do it?"

Again Glover looked at the map, and again he said, "Yes, Your Excellency."

"It may take a while to get the whole army out of here. We'll have to do it slowly, and in order. I don't want the men in a panic." Again he asked, "Can your men hold them?"

And again Colonel Glover looked Washington full square in the eyes. "Yes, sir!" he said.

They shook hands, and Washington smiled then for the first time in a long while. "I'll give you some extra men from the Continentals," he said. "A few that will serve as the rear guard once the army has made its way out."

🐾   🐾   🐾

Dake was one of those selected to join the Marblehead fishermen in their attempt to stop the British. He and Tooms were tapped by their lieutenant and soon found themselves joining Glover's men. They had three tiny field pieces with them, and finally Glover found a spot that suited him. They settled behind the stone walls and primed their muskets. Glover called his officers together, and Dake was close enough to hear his instructions.

Glover lit a pipe and nodded toward the sun that was rising over the Sound. "The British will be coming from there." He seemed to be through with his instructions, but he added, "We will wait here until the army of His Excellency passes by. Now, any questions?"

There were no questions and the men went at once to prepare themselves for the onslaught. Dake watched as they loaded the cannon, and was shocked at what he saw. They loaded the cannon, not with shot, but with rusty nails, bits of wire, old iron bolts, broken horseshoes, even pieces of glass and parts of pewter pots and pans. A cold chill ran down Dake's spine, and he turned to look at Tooms who had come to stand beside him.

"I never saw anything like that, Sergeant," he whispered.

"Me neither!" Tooms grinned as if amused. "That'll give the Redcoats something to think about when they meet a cannon full of that." They moved up and down the line and discovered that the fishermen had all sorts of weapons, none of them standards. They were not riflemen, but carried huge, wide-bore muskets that were stuffed with the same rusty nails, old wire, and any sharp bits of metal they could find. They went about their task as they would have gone about baiting hooks back on their ships in Cape Cod. Then they began to wait calmly for the enemy to make its move.

The sun came up, a blinding orb of red, and metamorphosed the Sound into what seemed to be a sea of blood. The British began marching in. Dake heard their fifes playing a fine high tune before he saw them. Then they came into sight, their drums beating, their shakoes swaying, and their glittering bayonets punctuating the morning air. If they knew the enemy lay ahead of them, they did not show it. They had been drilled for years, and as they marched forward every foot was in step, every line perfect.

Dake glanced down the line of fishermen and readied his own musket. He saw the three cannons, their mouths open as if hungry for the feast that awaited them, and again a chill ran down his back as he thought of the sweepings of the blacksmith's floor, the nails, and the broken glass that lay in the bellies of the loose guns.

When the British line was less than thirty yards away, the fishermen let go. The guns belched with a mighty roar, and the muskets went off. Dake saw the man he aimed at driven backward, and knew he had hit him squarely in the heart. For a moment smoke obscured the field, but as it cleared he saw the horrible scene unfold before him. The whole field was full of men squirming and screaming on the earth, their bodies riddled with rusty nails and bits of broken glass.

"Load again!" Glover's voice came down the line.

Surely they won't come back, Dake thought. His hands were sweaty, despite the cold, as he loaded the musket, then looked up.

"They're coming again!" Tooms exclaimed.

The British came again, straight and precise, as if nothing had happened. They stepped over the bodies of men bleeding and squirming, and once again were wiped out by the terrible rain of steel and glass.

All morning they attacked the position of the Marblehead fishermen, but Glover's men held them off. It was glorious—and it was murder. The rusty nails and bits of metal of the fishermen cut the Redcoats to bits. Only three or four of the fishermen had died, but by late afternoon, more than five hundred British and Hessians lay on that bloody field.

And then General Howe called it off, for he could not stand seeing his troops cut down so brutally.

Thus, the army of Washington was protected by a group of fishermen who held the skies up while the Continental Army of George Washington passed northward, leaving New York behind for the British.

23

END OF A MAN

FOR NEARLY A WEEK Abigail had been severely pulled emotionally. Her newly found walk with God had wrought a profound change in her spirit. She found this demonstrated most dramatically in her inability to go any further with Leo Rochester's proposition to use her to gain Matthew as his son. The nights had passed interminably as she tossed and turned, unable to sleep as she considered the enormity of her problem. She lost weight, and both her mother and Esther questioned her concerning her well-being. She had put them off as long as she could, but finally on the morning of October 19, she arose almost ill from struggling with the problem.

Wearily she got out of bed, moved across to the washstand, and began to prepare for the task she dreaded. Pouring the tepid water out of the ceramic pitcher into a bowl, she washed her face, holding the cloth in place to soothe some of the lines out. Her eyes were gritty from lack of sleep, and she felt totally unequal to the scene that she knew she was facing. Slowly she donned a simple light green dress without paying any attention to the style, worked lackadaisically at putting her hair up, and then chose a warm cloak and a wool bonnet. Snow had fallen two nights before and now lay six inches deep over the countryside.

Moving out of her room she was glad that neither Esther nor her mother had risen. She left a note on the kitchen table, weighed it down with a light blue china sugar bowl, then moved out of the house.

The sun was already rising, and the brilliance of its reflection on the snow blinded her for a moment. It seemed a magical world that she moved through. The sharp edges of the houses and the shops that she passed were rounded into smooth curves, and all the ugliness of the street litter was now concealed and camouflaged by a pristine whiteness of the blanket of snow that covered everything. A fanciful thought came to her as she tried to find a carriage to take her to the Rochester

273

home. *It's so much easier to cover up a dirty city with snow than it is to hide something horrible in your life!*

A carriage finally came along and stopped for her. Gratefully she got in, instructing the driver to take her to the Frazier home. Leaning back, she noticed that the fresh snow that had fallen throughout the night had caused the carriage to move along silently. She missed the clip-clopping of the horses' hooves and the noise of the iron-bound wheels bouncing over the rough cobblestones. It was a smooth, silent ride, and only the sibilant hissing of the wheels passing over the snow broke the silence.

"What will I say to him?" she murmured aloud and shook her head fearfully. She was determined to free herself from the agreement she had made with Rochester—but how to do this without angering him she had not yet determined. Now, as the carriage moved along past house after house, glittering with its gleaming mantle of snow, she began to pray. She longed for the faith of her aunt Esther, but she knew that she did not have it yet. Finally, all she could pray was, "Lord, I don't know what to say, but I know this is the right thing to do! So help me to get through this, please. . . !"

By the time the carriage had stopped in front of the Frazier house, she had achieved some measure of serenity. Stepping out of the carriage, she searched through her reticule, found a coin, and passed it along to the driver, who touched his hat and said, "Thank you, mum!" then spoke to the horses, which quickly stepped out and the carriage moved off.

Turning quickly and lifting her head with determination, Abigail made her way up the long walk that led to the house. She stepped up on the stoop, reached out and grasped the brass knocker, giving it three sharp raps. The sound seemed to echo in the silence of the frozen morning, and for one moment she was tempted to turn and flee. The door opened, however, before she could move, and a tall black man, wearing a black suit, white stockings, and a ruffled white shirt, asked, "Yes, miss. What may I do to help you?"

"I would like to see Mr. Rochester, if I may. My name is Miss Abigail Howland."

Cato hesitated, saying doubtfully, "It's a little early, ma'am, but I know Mr. Rochester's up. If you'll come in and wait in the parlor, I'll ask if he will see you."

"Thank you very much."

Cato took the young woman into the parlor, where he indicated a couch. "I just made the fire, miss. You best warm yourself. You may have to wait a time until Mr. Rochester gets dressed and comes down."

"I'll be fine—thank you very much!"

Cato left the parlor at once and made his way to Leo Rochester's room. He knocked on the door, and when a voice answered sleepily he stepped inside. Rochester had already risen and was sitting in a chair wearing a dark blue robe and a pair of matching slippers. "What is it, Cato?" he asked.

"There's a young lady to see you. She says her name is Miss Abigail Howland."

At once Leo became more alert. "Miss Howland, is it? Well, go tell her I'll be down in twenty minutes!"

"Yes, sir, I'll tell her that."

As Cato left the room, Rochester rose immediately. He'd had a restless night, but that had become commonplace now for him. He had already shaved, so he threw off the robe, tossing it across the bed, and dressed as quickly as his limp arm would allow in a pair of dark brown knee britches over tan stockings. He slipped into a white shirt but ignored the tie. It was very cold, so he put on a double-breasted waistcoat of a brown hue, then over this a frock coat that he did not button. He pulled on a pair of velvet slippers, gave his hair a few strokes with a brush, then left the room. He made his way to the parlor, his heart beating rather irregularly, he thought. This also had become commonplace, so he ignored it. Entering the parlor he saw Abigail sitting on the couch across from the fire. He smiled, saying, "Well, my dear, you're early this morning!"

"Yes, I know I am. I should have waited until later." Abigail stood at once and looked apprehensively at Rochester.

"Well, sit down, my dear. You needn't stand!"

"I . . . I have something important to tell you, Leo," Abigail said with some hesitation. Her face was rather pale, and she swallowed hard, trying to remember her resolution. Finally she said, "I have some news that you won't like, I'm afraid."

Leo blinked and stared at her, his good humor vanishing. "What is it?" he asked harshly.

"I've come to tell you that I . . . I can't go through with what I agreed to do—about Matthew."

Leo knew a flash of blinding disappointment. He knew that he was a sick man, and he also understood that his only hope of gaining Matthew's consent to become a Rochester lay with this girl. He was not a praying man, but he had thrown his spirit with all his force into willing Abigail to do as he asked. Now as she stood before him, pale of face, and with lips trembling slightly, a blind, unreasoning anger suddenly rose in him. This had happened to him many times during his life, but not so much in recent years. It had happened once when Daniel Bradford, only a boy, had crossed him, and he had thrown himself with a blind fury in an attempt to kill Bradford with his bare hands.

His voice was shrill as he ground out, "You're a fool! You gave me your word—and I demand that you do what you promised!" The girl began trying to speak, but Leo moved forward, took her shoulders, and began to shake her. "I won't be frustrated by a pious hypocrite like you!" he said furiously. The rage that crept up in him was like water from a dam that had broken. For weeks and months he had gauged everything in life by this one thing, and now he was being frustrated by this pale-faced girl who did not realize the enormity of what she was doing. He began to curse, and the impulse to slap her came strongly.

Abigail tried to speak, but he was too strong for her. There was a maniacal glaze in his eyes as she had never seen before, and she began to fear for her safety. "Please . . . please, Leo, don't—" But it was no use.

Leo was shouting now and shaking her violently. The rage that had come to him was like a red tide that rose, possessing him entirely, and he forgot everything except that he must make this girl do what he demanded.

Abigail put her arms out to push him away, and as she did, she became suddenly aware that Rochester had stopped shaking her. His hands were still on her arms, but his face suddenly turned pale as ashes. His lips opened, and he seemed to be gasping for air. Then with a hoarse cry he put his hands together over his chest, his eyes closing.

"Leo—what is it?" Abigail cried out.

Leo tried to speak but could not. He could only garble syllables, for the pain that had risen somewhere in the middle of his body was like an explosion. It shattered the frail tendrils of his nerves, and he felt the pain run down his left arm as it had before. But this was much worse than the last time—it was worse than anything he had ever known. He staggered forward blindly, thrusting his hands out.

Abigail tried to catch him, but Rochester toppled like a tree. His knees suddenly could not support his weight. He fell forward, and Abigail tried vainly to hold him. He was a tall man, however, and his weight was too much. She collapsed under his weight, and both of them hit the floor. "Leo!" she cried. "Is it your heart?" She saw him nod, and then his eyes rolled backward in his head, and he began to kick convulsively.

Abigail struggled to her feet, then ran at once to the door, calling, "Help! Somebody, help. . . !"

At once Cato appeared, his eyes wide with shock. "What is it, miss. What's wrong?"

"It's Mr. Rochester. He's having an attack. He needs a doctor!"

Cato stood immobile for one minute, then he said, "You go wake Miss Marian. Tell her I'm going to get the doctor. I'll be back as soon as I can!"

"Which is her room?"

"Upstairs, first door on the left!"

Abigail wheeled instantly and dashed to the stairs, scarcely aware of the slamming door as Cato left the house. She took the stairs two at a time, turned to her left, and rapped hard on the door, calling out frantically, "Mrs. Rochester—Mrs. Rochester. . . !"

"Yes!" came a voice from within. "Yes, what is it!"

"It's your husband. He's very sick!"

Almost at once the door opened, and Marian Rochester stood there wearing only her gown and a nightcap, but she was totally awake. "Where is he?" she demanded.

"Downstairs in the parlor!" Abigail said. "I came to talk to him. We were talking, and he had a terrible attack of some kind!"

"We have to send for a doctor!" Marian said at once.

"Cato's already gone. He said he'd be back with him as soon as he could get here."

"I must go to him!"

Marian paused only to get a robe, and Abigail followed her down the stairs. They rushed to the parlor, and Leo lay where she had left him. Marian fell on her knees and pulled his head up to her breast. She pushed his hair back, saying, "Leo! Leo, can you hear me?"

There was no response except for a mild fluttering of the eyelids.

Abigail stood there helplessly. She had the horrible thought that it was her visit that had brought on the attack. Unsteadily she whispered, "Is there anything I can do, Mrs. Rochester?"

"If you can pray," Marian whispered, holding Leo's head tightly, "you can pray that God will spare him."

The silence seemed deafening in the room, it was so thick. Only the sick man's hoarse breathing, rapid and irregular, broke the silence. The two women watched Leo's face, which was now twisted into an agonizing expression, and both of them prayed for Leo Rochester.

𝕿　　𝕿　　𝕿

Daniel had not been at the foundry for more than half an hour when Cato came rushing into his office. He gasped hoarsely, "Mister Daniel, it's Mr. Rochester! He done had a bad spell!"

For one moment Daniel Bradford could not speak. His first thought was, *If he dies, he'll die lost without God.* Aloud he said, "Is he alive?"

"Yes, sir. I took the doctor there, but Miss Marian said I was to come and tell you."

"I'll come at once, Cato!"

"Yes, sir, I got the carriage outside."

Twenty minutes later the carriage pulled up in front of the Frazier home, the horses covered with froth, for Cato had driven them hard. "I'll take care of the horses. You go on in, Mister Daniel!"

"All right, Cato!"

Daniel sprang from the carriage and ran to the front door. He did not knock this time, but opened it and stepped inside. He saw Marian standing with Dr. Settling and moved toward them at once. "How is he?" he demanded without preamble.

Settling tugged at his Vandyke beard, his eyes hooded and serious. "Not good, I'm afraid, Mr. Bradford. He's had a massive heart attack."

Daniel cast a quick look at Marian, noting that her face was as pale as he had ever seen it. She was holding a handkerchief in her hands, which she tugged at nervously.

"I'm glad you came, Daniel," she whispered.

"Is there anything I can do?"

Settling shook his head. "There's not much anyone can do in a case like this—except wait and pray."

Dr. Settling told them the details, at least as well as he knew them. "You're aware that he's had these attacks before?"

"No," Marian whispered, "I never knew that. He never said a word."

Settling gave her a surprised look. "But you knew he was ill?"

"Oh yes, I could see that—but he never said anything about heart attacks!"

"How long has this been going on, Doctor?" Daniel asked. He listened as Settling outlined Rochester's case, and when he was through Daniel said, "Isn't there any treatment, some sort of medicine? There must be *something*!"

Dr. Settling bit his lower lip nervously. He did not like to lose cases, but he had a premonition that he was going to lose this one. He had been worried about Leo for some time, and now he said in a weary tone, "We doctors can't do much. We can set a broken bone, we can bleed a man or a woman—but there's so much we can't do. Sometimes there's nothing we can do."

"And you think that's the case with my husband?" Marian asked directly, her face pleading as she turned to him.

Settling knew something about the marriage of this woman and Leo Rochester. He was aware of how Leo had mistreated her and was amazed to find that she still had this kind of compassionate concern. "I'm sorry, Mrs. Rochester," he said slowly, "but unless God does a miracle, your husband cannot live."

The words seemed to hang in the air. Settling shook his head and said, "There's nothing I can really do here. I'll go take care of the rest of my patients, then I'll come back as soon as I can."

"Thank you, Doctor."

As soon as the doctor left the house, Daniel said, "I think I'd better go get Matthew."

"I believe that would be best, Daniel. Leo's thought of little else these past days."

"I'll get back as soon as I can. Will you be all right alone?"

"Abigail Howland is here with me. She's sitting beside Leo now. Do you want to see Leo before you go?"

"No, I think it might be better if I go as quickly as possible." He left unsaid what was on his mind—that Leo might die at any moment. He looked at Marian, then said quietly, "I'm sorry about this, Marian."

"So am I, Daniel."

𝕿   𝕿   𝕿

Marian heard the door slam and heard Cato's voice. "That must be Daniel and Matthew," she said to Abigail. The two women rose and went out of the bedroom where they had been sitting beside Leo. The sick man had not spoken a word, but he was conscious from time to time.

When they stepped outside and moved down the hallway toward the two men, Daniel asked quickly, "Is there any change?"

"He's conscious, but only by fits and starts," Marian said. She looked at Matthew and said quietly, "I'm glad you could come, Matthew. I know Leo will want to see you."

Matthew had been deeply shocked by Daniel Bradford's news of Leo's sickness. At first he could not believe it, but then he remembered how badly Leo had looked physically over the past few weeks. The two had gotten into a carriage and returned at once to the Frazier house. Now that he stood before Marian, he found it difficult to speak. "I can't believe it's as bad as Pa says."

Abigail said nervously, "I'm glad you've come, Matthew. He did ask for you once when he woke up."

"Yes, he did!" Marian nodded. "Come along, he may be awake now."

The four of them made their way down the hall and turned into the room. Two high windows on one side allowed the bright midmorning sun to throw pale bars of light across the bed, falling across Leo's face.

They were so bright that Matthew could see the small motes dancing in them, but he was staring at Leo, whose lips were pale as clay. He saw that the sick man's eyes were closed, and for one sickening moment he thought Leo had died—but then the eyes fluttered open, and Matthew moved quickly to stand beside the bed.

"Do you know me, sir?" Matthew was the eyes flutter again, then open, and recognition come to them. "I'm sorry to find you so ill—but we must hope that you'll get better."

Leo Rochester was living in a strange world, one such as he had never known. He had awakened in bed, not knowing how he got there, and then it all had come rushing back. Now he was conscious of voices, of people moving, of the light that broke across the gaily colored quilt filled with reds and blues and yellows—but it was as if he saw through another man's eyes. Nothing was clear. The pain was still with him, that much was definite—but it was numb now, not sharp and keen and piercing as when it had knocked him to the floor.

He studied Matthew's face, striving to put everything together, then he whispered, "I'm glad you've come—Matthew."

"Is there anything I can do?"

Leo did not answer, indeed, did not seem to hear. His eyes were fixed on the face of the young man who bent over him. Finally he whispered, "You're very—like me, did you know that, Matthew?"

The remark brought a flush to Matthew's face. Flashing memories came to him of how he had first become aware that Leo was his father, so far as blood was concerned. Memories of how he had raged when he had discovered that Leo had forsaken his mother. He thought also of how for weeks he had been struggling with the offer of Rochester to make him his son, according to law—to hand him, as it were, a fortune, a title, and all that this world could afford. These thoughts came, not singly, but as bright flashes of scenes that struck against his mind. And now at the reminder that he closely resembled Leo, all of his thoughts coalesced on the one fact that he had not yet ever acknowledged Leo in any way whatsoever.

Awkwardly he reached out and picked up the hand that lay limply on Leo's chest. He held it and saw Leo's eyes grow suddenly surprised. "I am very like you, sir!" he said. "My mirror tells me that."

Leo felt the pressure of the young man's hand on his, and it moved him greatly. He was still not completely clear in his mind, but he knew that the face of that young man before him had goodness in it. There was honesty there, integrity, and for one moment bitterness came as he thought, *He got that from living with Daniel Bradford.* But then that thought passed away and he said, "You're not like me inside. That's . . . a good thing."

Matthew could not answer for a moment, but he was tremendously moved. He knew that this man was his closest link in blood in the world. He had half brothers and sisters, but this man—for all his faults—was his father. This was the man who had given him life. Matthew kept his hold on the limp hand and tried to think of something to say. It all seemed very inadequate now, and finally all he could do was murmur, "I'm sorry that I didn't have more time with you, but perhaps we shall yet. We must be hopeful."

Leo listened to the words but shook his head slightly. He himself recognized that he was a dying man. For some time he lay quietly, clinging to the hand of his son, and then his eyes dropped and he seemed to pass into a restless sleep. When Matthew tried to withdraw his hand, however, Rochester held to it tightly. Seeing this, Marian came over and, moving a chair closer, whispered, "Sit beside him, Matthew. He needs you now."

🦁   🦁   🦁

"Is he any better, do you think, Doctor?"

Marian had stepped outside with Dr. Settling, who had returned to examine Leo. It had been a long day for her. Twilight had come, and now the sun was going down, and there had been little change in Leo Rochester's condition. Marian kept her eyes fixed on Dr. Settling, looking for some sign of hope, but try as she might, she could not discern one ray in the gray eyes of the doctor.

"You must prepare yourself, Mrs. Rochester," Settling said gently. "I do not think he can last the night. His heart is shattered. I don't know what's keeping him alive now."

Marian stood quietly, taking in the doctor's words. She had expected no better news, and as he gave his advice about how things might be done, she realized that he was preparing her for the worst.

"Thank you, Doctor. I'd better go be with him."

"I think that would be best—he could go at any second."

Marian moved back inside and saw to her surprise that Leo was awake, and that Daniel had seated himself across the bed from Matthew. They made a strange tableau, these three men. She looked from one face to another, thinking how strange it was that Bradford and her husband had been drawn together in this final scene. Her gaze went to Matthew, and she noted the grief and uncertainty on his face, then she drew closer.

"We talked about this before, Leo," Daniel was saying quietly.

"About how a man needs God, and there's no better time than the present for any of us."

Leo seemed to be more alert and aware than he had been for the last two hours. He turned his head to study Daniel Bradford, and his voice was muffled by the pain. "I've lived a hard life, and an evil one in many ways."

Daniel said, "A man can change."

Leo Rochester had to struggle to form the words. "A deathbed repentance? No, I will not do it!"

"There's nothing shameful about that, Leo," Daniel said quietly. "You must have heard many times how as Jesus died, one of the thieves beside him on the cross didn't find it so. You remember? He said, 'Lord, remember me when you come into your kingdom.' Jesus told the thief, 'This day shalt thou be with me in paradise.' "

Leo's eyes were dim, and his features seemed to be collapsing, but stubbornness still dominated him even as his spirit was fleeing. "No—no!" he gasped. "That . . . would be the coward's way—to live for the devil all your life. Then when you're losing it to turn to God—and beg!"

"Leo, please listen to me!" Daniel leaned forward and there were tears in his eyes. "All of us have to beg. We're *all* beggars before the throne of God. Only His mercy saved any of us. There's no difference between you or anybody else. The Scripture says that all have sinned. We may not all have sinned alike, but we've all sinned. That's why Jesus died. . . ."

As Daniel pleaded with Leo to turn to God, Abigail stood behind Marian back in the shadows of the room. The lamp was lit now, and the light cast its golden gleams over the tableau before her. She was frightened, for she had never seen anyone die. She was more disturbed, and almost sick, at the thought that she might have been responsible, at least partly, for Leo Rochester's condition.

Once hours before, when his mind was clear, Rochester had put his eyes on her. Matthew had been sitting beside him, and Abigail had thought, *He's going to tell Matthew what I've done.* But Leo had only studied her carefully, giving her an enigmatic smile, then glanced at his son and said nothing.

Now Abigail watched as Daniel seemed to struggle, almost physically, to bring this man into the knowledge of God. She prayed as well as she knew how, and she could hear Marian praying over to one side, but it all seemed to be for naught.

Leo lingered on for nearly an hour. Finally they saw that he was adamant. He spoke in a hoarse whisper, his voice broken, his lips barely moving, "Daniel, I've always . . . hated you . . . for being what I . . . could never be!" He studied Daniel through dimmed eyes and shook his head. There was a bitterness in his lips, and he could say no more.

He turned to Matthew, and Matthew reached out with both of his hands and enclosed one of Leo's. Then Leo said, "You will have everything—even a title—if you want it. You can be Sir Matthew Rochester— or you can turn from it."

Then his eyes moved to Abigail. He seemed to see her alone, and he motioned to her with his head. Marian saw the girl stand back and said, "He wants you, Abigail."

Abigail started, then moved forward. She was trembling as she came to stand over Leo, who whispered, "Bend over—"

Abigail put her ear down to his lips that barely moved. She could not imagine what he wanted to say to her. She was aware that Matthew and Daniel Bradford had moved back, and then the hoarse whisper came. Rochester spoke in broken tones, but Abigail heard the words clearly: "Marry him, Abigail—keep your mouth shut—never tell him of our—arrangement. . . ."

Abigail waited, but he said no more. She straightened up and saw that death was coming. As she stepped back, her heart ached for this man who had never valued anything except the things of this world— and was now losing everything.

Marian stepped forward and fell on her knees. "Leo!" she whispered. "Leo!" She could say no more, for her throat was tight with grief.

Leo Rochester was almost gone, but he came back for one brief moment. He opened his eyes and tried to speak. Finally he said, "Marian, you . . . have been . . . faithful."

Those were Leo Rochester's last words. He closed his eyes, his body arched, and he seemed to fight for breath. He grasped Matthew's hand with a sudden surprising strength—and then his grip relaxed. His breath was expelled—and then he lay absolutely still in the finality of death.

Sick at heart, Daniel rose and walked blindly to the window. More than he had wanted anything in a long time, Daniel had wanted to see this man, who had harmed his family so much, find God. But Rochester had gone out into eternity without knowing Jesus Christ.

He turned back to see that Marian was crying. He wanted to reach out and touch her—but that would not be fitting. He took one last look at Leo Rochester and saw the face that had been so tense now relaxed.

Matthew stood beside the bed looking down at the face of his father. It all seemed unreal somehow, and finally one thought came to him: *I found you—and now I've lost you!*

24

THE SWEET AND THE BITTER

THE DEATH OF SIR LEO ROCHESTER had been a shock to many in Boston. He had not been a popular man, in one sense, for he had few close friends. He had, however, been a powerful and a wealthy man—and when death takes one of these, the world sits up and takes notice.

Those who had spoken most plainly about Rochester's faults while he was alive now mitigated their statements—at least in public. The news of his death meant a loss of income to some, such as the gamblers and the loose women of the town that had been beneficiaries of his wealth. They would certainly miss him in a pecuniary fashion!

Other more respectable people, such as his lawyer, his boot maker, his tailor, and those who served him in one fashion or another, would also miss the income that his death produced.

But there were others who were sincerely regretful, and one of these was Daniel Bradford. He'd gone over and over in his mind his history, remembering how Leo had caused him to be thrown into a dank and horrible prison in England when he was an innocent man. He also could not forget that for many years he had served Rochester as an indentured servant—also against his will. Despite himself, he remembered Leo's cruelty to Holly Blanchard, the young woman Daniel had married to give her child a name. Nor could he forget the cruelty toward Marian Rochester.

Still, for all of this, Daniel Bradford was deeply filled with regret. He had tried to comfort Matthew, explaining, as best he could, his own feelings. He saw that Matthew was more disturbed and fragmented by Leo's death than he was himself.

"It's natural enough that you should grieve, Matthew. For all his faults, he was your father, and I have to believe that he wanted the best for you. We didn't always agree. As a matter of fact, we rarely did—but I think as far as you were concerned, he was honest."

"He wanted a son more than anything else," Matthew said bitterly. "I could have at least been more understanding!"

"You can't torment yourself with what might have been! It was a hard thing for you to decide, and who knows, if he had lived you might have done exactly as he had wanted. In fact, you still could."

"Take the name of Rochester?" Matthew looked up. The two were standing alone in Daniel's office speaking quietly. It was after hours, and the two remained to talk. Matthew stared at Daniel and said, "I couldn't do that."

"You could if you think it's right. Personal things would be out of the way now. You mustn't stop on my account," Daniel said bluntly. "I know that's been on your mind."

Matthew nodded slightly. "It has. I'd have a new name. I wouldn't be Matthew Bradford, I'd be Matthew Rochester."

"Rochester is a good name. Your grandfather, Leo's father, was a fine man. I remember him well." He paused as memories from the past came to him, then said, "I think that's what Leo wanted—to see the virtues of his own father somehow come to pass in you."

Matthew was caught by this, for he had not considered it. "I never thought of that," he muttered. "Anyway, I can't think about it now. The funeral's tomorrow. I'll need more time."

"Certainly, that's only natural. But I just wanted you to know, Matthew, that this will be your choice. I'll love you, and you'll always be my son in my mind, no matter what name you call yourself. You'll still be Matthew to me!"

"Thank you, Pa," Matthew whispered, and suddenly he wished that his father would put his arms around him as he had when he was a small boy.

As if sensing this, Daniel moved forward. He grasped Matthew and hugged him hard. Matthew was slighter of form, and as he felt the strong arms of this man go around him, he thought of the thousand things that Daniel Bradford had done, how he had always been faithful, honest, and loved him without reservation. He felt tears beginning to rise and quickly shook his head. Stepping back he said, "I'll think about it, but I'll talk to you, Pa, before I do anything."

𝔗   𝔗   𝔗

Katherine Yancy had not been well acquainted with Leo Rochester, but when she heard the story from Abigail of how the man had died without God, it had disturbed her. The two women had talked about it, and it had been to Katherine that Abigail had finally revealed her fears. She spoke of how she had agreed with Leo to try to sway Matthew, not sparing herself.

"I . . . I agreed to make Matthew fall in love with me," she said stiffly, pain in her eyes. "I've not been a good woman, Katherine, and that was one of the worst things I've done."

"That's in the past," Katherine said quickly. "You're a Christian now, and that's all put away. And besides, you couldn't go through with it, could you?"

"No." Abigail shifted nervously in the chair she sat in, then added, "But, Katherine, I can't help feeling guilty over the fact that he had his attack over the news I gave him." She related how upset Leo had become that morning when she refused to do his bidding. When she finished, she looked up with some sort of sorrow in her eyes. "I feel I should have done it differently."

"You couldn't help what happened." Katherine comforted her as well as she could and finally said, "I think you should talk to your aunt Esther about this. I think she'll tell you that you have nothing to reproach yourself for."

"What about Matthew? Should I tell him what I did?"

Katherine almost spoke out, but then said, "It's easy for an outsider to make judgments, but I can't do that. I can't tell you what to do—but I believe God will tell you. We'll pray that you have understanding and wisdom, and when you do, whatever you do, it will be right."

Later that morning, after Abigail's visit, Katherine had moved about the house wondering if she had given good counsel. She wished she could have said more, but somehow there seemed nothing more to say. She was totally in sympathy with Abigail Howland. She had heard of the girl's bad reputation before, but Katherine was a firm believer in God's power to change people. Besides, she saw something new in Abigail that was pleasing to her. Abigail had a determination to go on with God, and all morning as she worked, Katherine prayed for the troubled young woman.

Just before noon, a knock sounded at the door. She called out, "I'll get it, Mother!"

Moving to the door, she opened it and stared speechless at the two men who stood there.

"Well now, daughter, you didn't expect to see me, did you now?"

"Father!"

Katherine threw herself forward, and her father caught her in his arms. Amos Yancy was smiling and patting his daughter on the shoulder, for she was weeping. He said, "Now, now, that's no way to take on. It's all over now. I'm home!"

Katherine pulled back and stared at him. "Pa!" she whispered. "How—" When Amos saw that his daughter could say no more, he turned her around, still keeping one arm around her. "There he stands, daughter. I believe you've met this young man?"

"Clive!" Katherine said and put her hand out. "Did you do this?"

Clive Gordon had been amply rewarded by the sight of the girl he loved so much in the arms of her father. "Well, I've done what any man would do," he shrugged finally.

"Amos!"

Amos looked up and saw his wife and rushed toward her. "I'm home, Susan!" he said.

Clive stepped forward and stood beside Katherine. The two watched as Amos and Susan Yancy embraced. Clive looked down to see the tears flowing down Katherine's face, and his own eyes were a little misty. He had gotten to know Amos Yancy very well on their trip from New York, and now as he watched the reuniting of this family, a sudden feeling of joy and pride came to him.

Katherine turned to him with wonder in her eyes. Her lips were tremulous, and she looked up into his face. "Clive, how did you do it?"

"I think the Almighty did most of it," he answered. He looked back at the couple who were still holding to each other. "They look very good together, don't they?"

"Yes, they do."

Katherine could not speak, her throat was so full, but she reached up and put her hand on Clive's shoulders, then she pulled him down and kissed him on the lips fully. "Thank you," she whispered, "for me, and for my mother, and for my father. Thank you so much, Clive Gordon!"

Amos turned to see his daughter kissing the tall Englishman, and he squeezed his wife and turned to wink at her. "Well now," he said, "could a man and his doctor get a bite to eat in this house?"

There was an instant bustling as Susan and Katherine pulled the two men into the kitchen, sat them down, and began rattling pots and pans, building fires, and making tea. It was a time of loud talk, and Susan Yancy came often to stand beside the chair her husband sat in, to touch his cheek, to smooth his hair back, to hold his hand.

Katherine was much the same, and finally after Susan had taken Amos off to put him to bed to rest, Katherine turned to Clive, saying, "How can I ever thank you?"

"Well, I can think of several ways," Clive grinned.

Katherine stared at him, and then shook her head. "You're a head-strong, willful man, Clive Gordon."

"That I am, and a man like me needs a headstrong, willful woman like you, Katherine Yancy!"

Katherine grew serious. She came to him, took his hand, and suddenly raised it with an odd gesture and kissed it.

"Oh, Katherine, you don't have to do that!" Clive protested, his face flushed.

"You've done so much, and I know you care for me, but—"

"Do you care for me?"

"I do, very much!" Katherine turned from him and walked over to the window. She stared outside at the sleigh that was sliding by in the snow, not seeing it really. She turned to him then and said, "Clive, we're so far apart."

"I know," he said. "I'm English and you're American."

"That's a big gap. Very big, indeed. This war's going to go on. Plenty of blood is going to be spilled on both sides. How would you feel if your father were killed by an American?"

"I would be grieved no matter whose hand killed him," Clive said evenly. He came to stand beside her. As he was very tall, he looked down, and then he reached out and touched her hair. Very gently he said, "It seemed impossible to get your father out of that prison, but I found out that with God, all things are possible. You know my mother had a dream in which God told her how to get your father out?"

"And I had a dream that showed me what I was so that I could forgive you."

"So God's speaking in dreams and visions, I suppose," Clive said. "But now you and I will have to believe that no matter how difficult circumstances get, we love each other. Somehow—someday, God will put us together."

"Do you really believe that, Clive?"

Clive Gordon took the young woman before him in his arms. He held her close, kissed her, and then said simply, "I believe it, do you?"

Then Katherine Yancy, who a very short time ago had determined never to trust a man, suddenly knew that this was one man she could trust her heart to forever.

"Yes, Clive," she whispered, "I believe that somehow it will happen."

🜚　　🜚　　🜚

The funeral of Leo Rochester was simple. The pastor had a difficult job, for he knew that the man who lay in state in the walnut coffin in front of the church had not been a man who had faith in God. Such times were always difficult, and Reverend Devaney, the pastor of the Congregational Church, did the best he could. He spoke for some time about the mercies of God, and mostly quoted Scriptures. As he looked out over the congregation, his eyes filled with compassion as they fell upon the widow dressed in black. He noted also the strong, stalwart form of Daniel Bradford, and recalled what the Methodist pastor had said about rumors concerning the two. Devaney was a man who had learned to believe what he saw, not what he heard, and he saw genuine grief in the face of Marian Rochester.

After the sermon was over, the congregation moved out to the small graveyard where a grave had been dug. The casket was lowered, and Devaney read more Scripture. The wind was moving slightly, swaying the bare black limbs of the trees overhead. The trees seemed to stir with the promise of life sometime in the far and distant spring. Overhead a ragged flight of blackbirds moved across the slate gray sky, and the gravelly sound of their voices came faintly to those who stood beside the open grave.

Finally the service was over, and people filed by to murmur words of consolation to Marian Rochester. She received them all with grace and dignity, the veil hiding her face for the most part.

Finally she turned, and Daniel Bradford longed to go to her—but he had more wisdom than that. He was glad to see Abigail Howland accompany her and said to Matthew, "I'm glad Abigail is staying with Marian for a while. She'll need someone. She shouldn't be alone."

Matthew nodded silently. He had been very quiet all day long, and he paused to take one look at the grave, then turned and walked away. Daniel wanted to go after him, but realized that this was one time that Matthew needed to be alone. Sam came up to stand beside him and said through cold lips, "Matthew sure feels bad, doesn't he, Pa?"

"Yes he does, Sam."

Sam asked directly, "Pa, was Mr. Rochester really Matthew's pa?"

"Yes, he really was."

Sam could not take this in. He shook his head finally and said, "That puts Matthew in kind of a bind, doesn't it?"

"I suppose it does." Daniel thought it might be good to prepare Sam, and he said, "He may be taking the name of Rochester."

"Why would he want to do that?"

"Well, Mr. Rochester didn't have any sons, Sam, and he wanted his own name to go on. He left most of his property, I understand, to Matthew, and a request that he take the name Matthew Rochester."

"Well, I don't think he ought to do it, Pa."

"You're very young, Sam. You know a lot of things now, but you won't be quite so sure of them before you're much older."

Daniel's voice was sharp, and Sam looked up with surprise. "Are you mad at me, Pa?"

"No! No, Sam, I'm not. Come along, we'll talk more about it at home."

🔔　　🔔　　🔔

Abigail knew that sooner or later she was going to have to tell Matthew the truth, and finally when he came to her two days after the funeral, she knew that it could not be put off any longer. She had stayed with Marian for these two days, and the two women had grown very close. Katherine Yancy had come by bringing Clive Gordon, and Abigail could see the way the wind blew in that direction. She and Esther had discussed it, and Esther had said doubtfully, "I don't see how they could ever marry. He's English and she's American."

"I know, but I'm just praying that God would put them together. They're so much in love."

Now, at three o'clock in the afternoon, Matthew came striding up to the door. Abigail had seen him out the front window, but she let him knock. She went to the door and admitted him, and saw at once that he was feeling much better than he had been during the funeral. "Come in, Matthew," she said.

"Hello, Abigail!" He smiled and reached out and took her hands. "My hands are cold!" he said.

"Come into the parlor. We've got a fire there and I just made tea. We've got some cakes that Mrs. Rochester and I made this morning."

The two moved into the parlor and Matthew sat down. He seemed much calmer now, but still there was a restlessness in him, and he asked, "Where is Mrs. Rochester?"

"She's gone out to do some business with the lawyer, I believe."

"How is she holding up?"

"She's very grieved over the loss of Mr. Rochester, but she's going to be all right."

Matthew seemed to be preoccupied with some thoughts, and his talk for some time was disjointed.

Finally he shook his shoulders together and said with dissatisfaction, "I didn't come here to eat cakes or drink tea, Abigail! I came to get you to marry me. You know I love you."

At that moment, Abigail knew exactly what she had to do. A great fear rose in her, but she fought it down and said quietly, "I have something to tell you, Matthew."

"Of course, what is it?"

"You may have heard some things about me, about the way I lived. I've been a selfish, thoughtless woman, and I want to tell you all of it."

"Do you mean about—?"

"Wait, let me tell you everything, Matthew. It's not pleasant, and I don't like to say these things, but I want to be perfectly honest with you. Will you listen until I'm through, and then you can say anything you please?"

"Why, of course, Abigail!" Matthew was somewhat shocked at the soberness of Abigail's tone, and he saw that her eyes were totally serious. He had been in a state of shock since the funeral, and still was to a great extent. He had one thing on his mind now, which was to carry out the wishes of Leo Rochester. He had made up his mind to that. He had also made up his mind to marry Abigail, and now he was curious as to what she might say. He knew, of course, that she had had an affair with Paul Winslow. That was common knowledge. He had thought that through in his mind, and now was sure that he harbored no unforgiveness or ill will because of it. Now he leaned forward and listened carefully as she told him the details of her life.

Abigail did not spare herself. She spoke clearly and evenly, though it almost tore her heart out to have to go over what she had been. She was fairly certain that he was aware of her behavior with Paul Winslow; nevertheless, she recounted it, and said, "I was very wrong, but God has forgiven me for it."

"And so do I. We'll put it behind us, Abigail!" Matthew said eagerly. "And that's what—"

"But that's not all." And now Abigail did hesitate. "I have to tell you that after the British left Boston I was destitute, my mother and I. She wasn't very well, and I was terrified. I didn't know what to do." She went on to speak for some time about her fear and uncertainty, and finally took a deep breath and went right to the heart of the matter.

"Just when I was most afraid, Matthew, I had a visitor. Leo Rochester came to me and said he had a proposition. Can you guess what it was?"

"No, I can't!"

"As you know, he wanted more than anything else for you to agree to take his name and to be his son."

"Yes, I know that, but what does that have to do with you?"

Now that the moment had come, for one instant everything in Abigail cried out for her to say anything but the truth. But she knew if she did, her whole life would be a lie. Taking a deep breath she said, "He wanted me to make you fall in love with me." She saw Matthew's face suddenly grow stiff, and his cheeks seemed to grow pale. Still she continued, "He gave me money to go to New York with my mother to live. We were going anyway to live with Aunt Esther, but he insisted that I try to influence you to get you to do what he wanted."

It was suddenly very hard for her to go on. Abigail saw the pain in Matthew's eyes and whispered, "I know this hurts you, but I must tell you. I took the money, and I came to New York with that in my heart, to make you fall in love with me, and to get you to do what Leo wanted."

Matthew seemed to be struck dumb. He stared at her in disbelief. Such a thing had never occurred to him! He had been attracted to Abigail long before he had found her again in New York. He thought of all the times they had had together, and there at that place, how she had filled his life with joy. Even as he thought of it he grew suddenly angry and said coldly, "So, that's why you were so ready to spend time with me?"

"Matthew—" Abigail began, but the whole truth was needed. "That was the way it was. I'm not proud of it, but I had to tell you." She was about to say that she had changed, and that her feelings for him had changed, but he gave her no opportunity.

Matthew Bradford was not in a sound, logical state. He had been distressed for some time over finding out the secret of his birth, a shameful secret it seemed to him. And then the strain of trying to decide whether or not to take Leo's offer had been bearing upon him hard. Then came the sudden death of Leo Rochester, and all hope of making an objective decision was gone, for the dying man's last request now lay heavily on him. In other circumstances he might have been cool and thoughtful, but now as he looked at Abigail, all he could think was, *She used me! She doesn't care a thing about me!*

Slowly he rose to his feet and said stiffly, "Thank you for telling me! It was kind of you!" There was a bitterness and a wry cynicism in his tone. He saw that his remarks hurt her and he said, "I will not impose on you any longer, Abigail. Obviously, you don't have to keep up the charade anymore."

"Matthew, it's not like that!" Abigail said. "Please, let's talk. . . !"

"I don't see that talk would help!" Matthew was gripped by an anger, such as he had never known. He turned and walked stiffly to the door and out of the room.

Abigail sat there hearing the door slam, and then tears came to her eyes and she began to sob.

She never knew how long she stayed there, sitting on the couch, her face buried in her hands. She was dimly aware that a door had closed, and she heard Marian say, "Abigail—?"

And then Abigail felt a hand on her shoulder, and she turned to Marian and suddenly threw her arms around her and began to weep afresh.

Marian Rochester held the trembling, weeping girl, and, like a mother, stroked her back and murmured comforting sounds. She made no attempt to discover what the trouble was at first, but finally Abigail began to speak. Marian listened to the choking sobs as the girl repeated what had happened, and then Abigail said, "Oh, Marian, I've lost him forever now!"

Marian said quietly, "Abigail, you've been faithful. You have done what you thought you should do, what God would have you do."

"But he doesn't believe me! He thinks that I didn't love him, that I was just after Leo's money."

"You know that that isn't so. It may have been once, but you wouldn't have told him if money were the only thing that mattered."

For some time the two women sat there, and Abigail's sobs began to grow fainter. Finally she groped in the pocket of her apron and found a handkerchief. She wiped her eyes and swallowed hard. "I'll never see him again—or if I do, he'll hate me. You should have seen the look in his eyes."

Marian Rochester had endured a life of sorrow and grief herself—living with a man who did not love her. And now her heart went out to this young woman who had thrown herself on God's mercies—and now it seemed that it all had been in vain. She tried to pray and ask for wisdom and finally she said quietly, "Abigail, you have been faithful. Now you must wait for God to be faithful. He never fails, not once, and someday you will look back and thank Him that you were honest, that you didn't shrink from doing this thing. God will honor you for it."

Abigail looked into the eyes of Marian Rochester. Hope was a cold, dead thing in her. She could not sense the presence of God. She realized now that she did love Matthew Bradford, that she had for some time, but he had looked at her with hatred, disdain, and bitterness. She knew she could not wipe that out from her memory, that expression on his face and the tone of his voice. She tried to believe the words of Marian Rochester, but it seemed impossible.

"I'll try to believe, Marian," she whispered finally. "But it's so hard."

Marian put her arms around the girl again and held her close. "It's always hard to believe God when the waters are deep and the night is dark," she whispered, "but somewhere, on the other side, you will find this God of ours never fails!"

25

WE'LL FIGHT AGAIN?

GENERAL HOWE WAS DISGRUNTLED when he discovered that the remnants of Washington's Continental Army had moved once more out of his grasp. Howe pursued doggedly, however, and on October 21, he found the Americans were digging in at White Plains. It took Howe another six days to reach this position. He prepared for a full-scale attack, deploying his whole army in the open before the eyes of the American troops. The next morning brought a confused fight. British and German troops drove the Americans off Chatterton's Hill, the right-flank anchor of their positions. Again some militiamen panicked. Some of the regulars did well, while others retreated prematurely. The British did not fare much better.

The Battle of White Plains was a confused and disorderly affair. Grant, the British general, contemptuous of American soldiers, suffered far heavier losses than was necessary. By the time the hill was finally taken, Howe decided to wait until morning before finishing the job. In the morning, however, it was raining heavily, and by the time it stopped, the rebels were gone again to another, and better, position three miles back. At this Howe gave up in disgust and returned to Manhattan.

George Washington never understood why Howe failed to deliver the blow that would have finished his army. Neither did anyone else ever understand. Some of Washington's officers made the wry remark that "General Howe is the best general we got in the American army."

Washington now was watching his men desert almost by the hundreds. His army had been split into three parts, one at Fort Washington in New York, one across the Hudson at Fort Lee, and the third part in Westchester. Washington went about his task as though he had won a victory. He inspected the regiments, and he wrote letters to Congress.

Among his officers and men he never showed anything less than total and absolute confidence.

On November 12, Washington rose one bright, cold morning and wished that he were back at his home at Mount Vernon. He loved the life of a country gentleman, and not a day went by but what he thought of the time that he might be permitted to return. For a while he went about examining different units and thinking about what General Howe's next strategy would be. One thing he knew, that somehow he would have to get his men out of Fort Lee and Fort Washington. They were strongly built forts, but he did not know if they could be held against the enemy's attack.

The next day he went to Fort Lee and discovered, to his amazement, that instead of beginning to withdraw the troops from Manhattan Island, Greene had reinforced them. He faced the handsome, young Quaker alone and said, "Nathaniel, what sort of insanity is this!"

"Sir, we can hold that fort!"

Washington had great confidence in Nathaniel Greene, and he did long to see Fort Washington defended, as Congress wished it to be held. After a moment or two he said, "Tell me the truth, Nathaniel, not what you think I *want* to hear. Can that fort be held?"

"Sir, we can hold it forever!"

"Never mind forever. Can you hold it for a month?"

"Yes, sir. Give us a chance and we can hold it!"

Three days later, General Washington received a message that General Greene should know the state of affairs at Fort Washington. At once the commander in chief mounted and made his way to the edge of the high cliff overlooking the Hudson River and Manhattan. From the direction of Fort Washington came the dull boom of a cannon. "Where is General Greene?"

"Across the river, sir."

"And General Putnam?"

"He's at Fort Washington, too, General."

Finally, unable to contain himself, Washington decided to cross the river. A boat was found, and he sat in the stern until they were halfway across the river. He heard the creak of oarlocks and called out, "Who's there?"

"General Washington, is that you?"

It was Nathaniel Greene, and the two men at once discussed the situation.

The geography of Manhattan was not complex. It was a finger of land, about two miles in width and fifteen miles long. The defense of this panhandle had been obvious to Washington. It seemed to be made for defense. What Washington did not know, what none of the American officers knew, was that General Magaw, who had been placed in charge of the defense of Fort Washington, had been betrayed. An American had gone to General Howe's headquarters and given him the complete plans of the fort. And now Howe, anxious to redeem his reputation, sprung the trap. British and Hessians had landed and surrounded the fort. As they did, the defenders fell back, often wounded, and out of ammunition.

As the two men sat in the boat discussing the seriousness of the situation, a furious roll of cannons split the air. "Get us to shore!" Washington commanded. As soon as the boat touched the shore, he leaped out. Instantly he saw a guard of Redcoats and long files of red-coated soldiers climbing up the path to the fort. The path that Greene and Magaw had assured Washington would not be taken!

Washington suddenly heard the cry of the big green-clad Jaegers calling out, "Yonkee! Yonkee!" And then they saw American soldiers fleeing in a panic from the Jaegers. Washington and Greene stared in horror as the Pennsylvania troops were flanked. They were pinned against the trees and driven screaming into the river, and there was no way for the officers to help as the Hessians began to shoot them, laughing all the time.

There was never really a question of defense. As Washington watched numbly, almost three thousand men of the American army and mountains of precious supplies fell into the hands of the British. The Hessians swarmed in from the south, others from the eastern approach, and red-coated troops marched up from the river. Soon it was all over, and Washington watched silently as the American flag was hauled down, and the British flag went up in its place.

𝕿　　　𝕿　　　𝕿

"And now Fort Lee is all we have left."

Dake Bradford stood beside Silas Tooms in the middle of Fort Lee, both bitter about the loss of Fort Washington across the river, and Tooms shook his head. "It was a foolish thing to try to hold these forts. The worst mistake George Washington ever made or ever will make! Three thousand of our fellows are on their way to prison camps. All those supplies, cannons, guns, ammunition of all kinds, uniforms—all gone!"

Dake swallowed hard, for it was a defeat that was hard to take. He was talking quietly with Tooms when he saw Knox stride across the open ground inside the fort. Behind him was Micah, and Dake went to him at once. "What's happening, Micah?"

"General Knox wants to take all the supplies out of the fort."

"Well, that makes sense," Dake said. "We've lost everything over in Fort Washington."

Micah looked over his shoulder. "I don't think there's time. The general says there isn't."

General Washington was facing Knox and General Greene, and Greene said bitterly, "There are reports of six thousand British soldiers. They've crossed the Hudson, five miles north of here. They are already coming to cut us off."

Instantly Washington demanded, "Evacuate the fort!"

"How can we evacuate, Your Excellency? We have no wagons, nothing to haul the supplies off."

"Never mind the supplies. Evacuate the fort!"

"But all the cannons, the provisions, what are we going to do?"

Washington's temper flew out suddenly. "General Greene, evacuate the fort and leave everything!"

"Sir, tomorrow we can have horses for the cannon."

General George Washington stared at him, his eyes flashing. "You heard my order! Right now!"

Greene began to yell commands. Knox came to where Dake and Micah stood. There were tears in his eyes and he said, "We've got to leave the cannons! We'll have nothing!"

Micah said, "Colonel Knox, we'll get them back."

"My beautiful guns!" Knox was mourning. "How can I leave them?"

Micah saw that the man was seemingly incapable of leaving the cannons and said, "Sir, we have to go—General Washington commanded it!"

Knox straightened up. "Yes, Corporal Bradford!" He stared around at men who were running and said, "Come, we must join them, we must not be taken!"

Washington fairly drove the men out of Fort Lee. He drove them as a cattle herder drives stock. When they fell or stumbled, he roared at them and whipped them with his quirt.

Dake and Micah were in that race, and even as they left Fort Lee and everything behind, Washington stopped and looked back to see the British Redcoats entering from the other direction.

General Greene came over to stand behind him. "Well, they have it, sir."

Washington said slowly, "You know, General, the symbol of Britain is the lion."

"Yes, sir, I know."

"There's a verse of Scripture that says that we shall tread upon the lion. It's in the ninety-first Psalm." Washington seemed to grow still.

297

"I've always liked that psalm. As a matter of fact, I've memorized it. Do you remember how it begins?"

"I don't believe so."

Washington quoted softly, "He that dwelleth in the secret place of the most High shall abide under the shadow of the Almighty." He continued to quote the psalm, word for word, and he paused and said, "The devil quoted part of this once to Jesus. Do you remember? It says, 'For he shall give his angels charge over thee to keep thee in all thy ways. They shall bear thee up in their hands, lest thou dash thy foot against a stone.'"

"Yes, sir, I do remember that."

"It's the next verse that I like, verse thirteen, 'Thou shalt tread upon the lion and adder: the young lion and the dragon shalt thou trample under feet.'"

The shouts of the British soldiers who had taken the fort came to them on the thin air. There were shouts of exultation and triumph, and Washington looked around and saw the beaten fragments of his army. He was quiet for a moment, and then he said, "One day, with God's help, we *shall* tread upon the lion. Your eyes will see it."

"Yes, sir! We shall indeed see our cause come to victory."

Micah and Dake were watching the British also. Dake said, "Well, they whipped us again!"

"No, they just took the fort—we're not whipped!"

Dake stared at his twin with surprise. He had not known the inner toughness of this brother of his. Micah had always been soft-spoken, thoughtful, but now there was a light in his eyes that revealed a determination that lay within him. "You're getting to be quite a bear cat!" he grinned. "You really think we can whip all those Redcoats?"

Micah nodded slowly. "With God, all things are possible. I believe God has put His hand on this land. He has a purpose for America. We'll fight again!"

"Well, let's get on with it, then," Dake said. He picked up his musket, slapped Micah on the back, and said, "Come along, brother. Tell me more about this purpose God's got for America."

🛡   🛡   🛡

Ten days after Fort Washington and Fort Lee fell, Daniel Bradford was alone. He had stayed at the foundry until dark, and finally sent the workmen on home. He and Blevins, as usual, had quarreled, saying that he would stay until the work was done, but Daniel had clapped him on the shoulder and said, "No, go on, Albert. We'll start again Monday."

It was late on Saturday, and after Blevins left, Daniel moved to his small office and sat down, looking at the drawings on the table before him. He had struggled hard with the problem of how to make a musket that could be produced for the troops of Washington. It was harder than he thought, and for a long time despair came upon him.

He had almost dozed off when a sound suddenly came to him. His head snapped up, and he was shocked to see Marian enter through the door.

"Marian!" he said, rising at once. "What are you doing here this time of the night?"

Marian did not answer. She was wearing a long royal blue cloak, and she removed it, putting it down on one of the chairs. She pulled off her felt cap, and her dark auburn hair fell down her back. She shook her head, and it caught the light of the lamps, giving off a reddish tint.

"You're working late," she said. It was not what she intended to say, but she needed time to catch her breath and to think.

"I know." He motioned toward the drawings. "I've been trying to put everything together so we can turn out the muskets, but I can't figure out how to do the rifling." He talked for a while about how to do the mechanism. "Nothing seems to work."

The two stood there for a while, and she shivered with the cold.

"Here, I've got tea! It's probably not very hot, but we can heat it up on the fire."

"That would be good."

Marian watched as he stirred the fire up and heated the water, talking about unimportant things. Finally when the tea was made, he poured it, and the two sat down in front of the fireplace and sipped at the rich, strong brew.

Daniel finally said, "I'm worried about Matthew."

"So am I," Marian said. "Has he said anything to you about Abigail?"

"He won't talk about her. Has Abigail said anything else?" Marian had shared with him the part of the story of how Abigail had confessed to Matthew that she had betrayed him and how he had stalked out angrily.

"He's young. He'll come around," Daniel said quietly. "Do you think he loves her?"

"I know she loves him!"

A log on the fire suddenly shifted and sent a myriad of sparks up the chimney. The crackling made a cheerful sound, and Daniel suddenly turned to look at the woman beside him. She met his gaze and he once again thought how beautiful she was. Her green eyes seemed enormous. Her heart-shaped face was the most attractive he had ever seen.

Finally he said, "You shouldn't be here, Marian."

"Because people will talk?"

"Yes, exactly that!" He stood up, and she stood up with him.

Daniel could not take his eyes away from her face. He whispered, "Years ago, when I was just a young man, a young woman came to the farm where I was an indentured servant. I took one look at her and I thought, *That's the most beautiful woman I've ever seen in my life!*"

"Did you think that about me, Daniel?" Marian's voice was a mere whisper, and she looked up at him, her lips parted slightly.

"I still think so—I always will."

Marian had come to see Daniel after spending several days wondering what her life would be now that Leo was gone. She had walked for miles in the cold streets of Boston, thinking, and had spent many more hours shut up in her room, unable to free herself of the questions that had come to her.

Suddenly she looked at him and put out her hands. He took them with surprise and found them warm and strong. He wondered at her impulsiveness, and he remembered that with one exception he never allowed himself to be alone with her after her marriage to Leo Rochester.

"Daniel—?" Marian hesitated then looked into his eyes. "Aren't you ever going to come to me, Daniel?"

"It . . . wouldn't be proper."

Marian increased the pressure of her grip, and there was an intensity in her that he had never seen before. "Do you love me?"

"I can't speak of that!"

"I realize you couldn't speak when I was a married woman, but I have no husband now."

Suddenly Daniel Bradford was aware of her as a woman in a way that he had not allowed himself to be. There was an intense femininity in her lips and her eyes, and he could only say, "It's too soon."

"We've wasted so many years, Daniel. We can't waste any more!"

She moved against him, something she had never done. Reaching up, she put her arms around his neck and pulled his head down. "I love you," she whispered, and then she kissed him.

Her lips were soft, and they moved under his. His arms tightened about her, and as she put herself against him he felt stirrings that he had fought against for years begin to rise up and to seize him. He was intoxicated with the smell of her hair, the touch of her soft form against his. She held him firmly, and when he increased the pressure of his lips she met him freely, fully. She withheld nothing, and he knew that this was her declaration of love in a way that she had never made before.

Finally, Marian pulled her head back and said, "We can wait a year to avoid talk—or we can have each other to love and cherish right now, very soon!"

Daniel found his hands trembling, and there was a weakness that he had not known was in him. More than anything under the sun, he wanted this woman, and he knew the courage it had taken for her to come.

"I should have been saying this to you, Marian! I shouldn't have made you come to me."

"It doesn't matter," she said quietly. She let her hand rest on his cheek, and they were quiet for a time, resting in each other's arms. Finally Daniel put his hand on her hair, letting it run behind her head. He kissed her again gently as if it were a seal of his love, and then he said, "We must talk to your father."

"Yes, and to your children. They'll be shocked."

"So will everybody. People will talk. Are you sure of this, Marian?"

"I'm as sure that I love you as I am that the sun rises in the east."

And then he kissed her again. He held her tightly, and she put her face against his chest. She could hear his heart beating loudly. His strong arms about her felt so protective, and she closed her eyes and whispered, "I wish the two of us were alone somewhere in a strange land with only each other. Then we wouldn't have to worry about what people thought. We could just love each other!"

"It can't be like that, Marian." Daniel pulled back and took her hands. "We have a country. There's a terrible war on, and we have a part to play in it. We can't hide from any of that."

"I know. I was just dreaming, I suppose."

"I like a woman who dreams," he said.

He smiled suddenly, and Marian thought how much younger he looked than he had in years. His eyes were clear, she saw, hazel eyes with just a touch of green. She studied his thin face, high cheekbones, a broad forehead, and then she smiled with him. "What a handsome bridegroom you're going to make, Daniel Bradford!" she whispered.

He laughed suddenly, picked her up easily, and spun her around the room, then sat her down after she was breathless. "Come along, woman, I'm going to take you home."

The two left the foundry. He held her hand in the carriage, and they were intensely aware of the love they had restrained for years. When they arrived at her house, he walked with her to the door, then said, "Good night, sweetheart. I'll see you in the morning."

She took his kiss, then whispered, "Good night."

He walked away and got into the carriage. Marian stood watching him until he was lost in the darkness. Still, she stood there, her heart full as she thought of the love she had for this man.

Finally she looked up at the stars where they twinkled and said aloud in a voice of wonder, "Mrs. Marian Bradford . . ."

Then she laughed like a young girl and threw her hands up in a wild gesture toward the stars. She spun around in a happy dance, then turned and walked up the steps and opened the door. Pausing for a moment, she took one look up at the spangled stars overhead. Then she smiled and closed the door, whispering softly, "Marian Bradford . . ."